"*The Lost Theory* is a creative mix of crime, science fiction, and delicate romance. Right from the introduction, the book takes you through a world of government conspiracies, absolute love and spirituality, quantum physics, and humor. It will tug at your heartstrings, steer you to an epiphany, and keep you in a constant state of suspense and anticipation. I recommend *The Lost Theory* to lovers of adventure stories that take one through the good, bad, and mysteries of life."

—OnlineBookClub.org

"Michael Kelley's *The Lost Theory* is a captivating account of an ancient realization—that love is the substance, the cosmic glue, around which everything coheres. In our age in which materialism is increasingly worshiped, this is a significant message with profound implications for our very survival. This novel transcends fiction; it deserves a category all its own."

—**Larry Dossey**, MD, author of *One Mind: How Our Individual Mind Is Part of a Greater Consciousness and Why It Matters*

THE
LOST
THEORY

THE
LOST
THEORY

MICHAEL KELLEY

GREENLEAF
BOOK GROUP PRESS

This book is a work of fiction. Names, characters, businesses, organizations, places, events, and incidents are either a product of the author's imagination or are used fictitiously. Any resemblance to actual persons, living or dead, events, or locales is entirely coincidental.

Published by Greenleaf Book Group Press
Austin, Texas
www.gbgpress.com

Distributed by Greenleaf Book Group

For ordering information or special discounts for bulk purchases, please contact Greenleaf Book Group at PO Box 91869, Austin, TX 78709, 512.891.6100.

Design and composition by Greenleaf Book Group and Brian Phillips
Cover design by Greenleaf Book Group and Brian Phillips
Cover image copyright Serg-DAV. Used under license from Shutterstock.com

Publisher's Cataloging-in-Publication data is available.

Print ISBN: 978-1-62634-884-4

eBook ISBN: 978-1-62634-885-1

Part of the Tree Neutral® program, which offsets the number of trees consumed in the production and printing of this book by taking proactive steps, such as planting trees in direct proportion to the number of trees used: www.treeneutral.com

Printed in the United States of America on acid-free paper

21 22 23 24 25 26   10 9 8 7 6 5 4 3 2 1

First Edition

Stephen Hawking, Albert Einstein, James Joyce, Bob Dylan, Lao Tzu, Jane Austen, Charles Dickens, T. S. Eliot, Buddha, William Somerset Maugham, the Stones, Samuel Coleridge, Dashiell Hammett, Humphrey Bogart, Tom Wolfe, Jesus Christ, Plato, Percy Shelley, William Shakespeare, John Milton, Thomas Huxley, Oscar Wilde, Carl Jung, Dante LaRocca, Miguel de Cervantes, Robert Towne, Peter O'Toole, Ralph Waldo Emerson, Brigitte Bardot, Stan Laurel and Oliver Hardy, the Clancy Brothers, Orson Welles, George Bernard Shaw, Cary Grant, Peter Sellers, the Pogues, Bob Marley, Edgar Allan Poe, Sir Arthur Conan Doyle, Jerry Lewis, Dean Martin, Tom Hanks, William Blake, Zeno, Mick Jagger, David Bowie, Lou Reed, Sophia Loren, Merry Edwards, Patti Smith, Beyoncé, Aimee Mann, Maud Gonne, Lord Byron, John Keats, William Powell, Myrna Loy, Natalie Wood, Katharine Ross, Elvis Costello, Nick Lowe, Bette Davis, Winona Ryder, Emily Dickson, B. Traven, Robert Louis Stevenson, Edward Stratemeyer, L. Frank Baum, Jennifer Lawrence, Ethan Hawke, Bono, Anton Chekhov, J. D. Salinger, F. Scott Fitzgerald, William Butler Yeats, Grace Kelly, Helen Schucman, Oprah Winfrey, Mother Goose, Bud Abbott and Lou Costello, Fanny Brawne, Dan Brown, Sheldon Harnick and Jerry Bock, Timothy Leary, Rhonda Byrne, James Redfield, D. H. Lawrence, Joe Strummer, the Clash, George R. R. Martin, Clark Gable, Sigmund Freud, Jack Kerouac, Alfred, Lord Tennyson, Victor Hugo, Harpo Marx, Robert Browning, Paul Simon and Art Garfunkel, Tom Petty, Roger Lancelyn Green, Jonathan Swift, Muhammad, Bahá'u'lláh, Dalai Lama, Quentin Tarantino, Charlie Chaplin, Steve McQueen, Samuel Beckett, Galileo, Neil Diamond,

Henrik Ibsen, Cicero, Rudyard Kipling, Bruce Springsteen, T. E. Lawrence, Mathew Arnold, Peter Tosh, the Beatles, Stephen King, Abraham Zapruder, Ray Gilbert, Jackie Kennedy, William Wordsworth, Gabriel García Márquez, Antoni Gaudí, Paul Gauguin, Henri Rousseau, Howard Pyle, Vincent van Gogh, Richard Feynman, Louisa Gilder, Eckhart Tolle, Paramahansa Yogananda, Herman Melville, Sir Isaac Newton, Peter Higgs, Truman Capote, Eric Ambler, Mary Shelley, Ian Fleming, Keith Richards, Gregory Peck, Spencer Tracy, Clarence Darrow, Fred Astaire, Jackson Browne, John le Carré, Charles Webb, William Goldman, Erwin Schrödinger, Margret and H. A. Rey, Gayle Lynds.

To all my readers, friends, and family who guide and support me on my path.

And to my father, William A. Kelley, who introduced me to my love of literature and old movies.

*The day science begins to study non-physical phenomena,
it will make more progress in one decade
than in all the previous centuries of its existence.*

—NIKOLA TESLA

ACKNOWLEDGMENTS

Beth Hill, who has been my writing coach and editor for over three years now. She taught me the craft, art, and magic of fiction.

Greenleaf Book Group team, for sharing the vision and bringing *The Lost Theory* to the light of each reader's eyes.

CHAPTER 1

AUSPICIOUS IS THE DAY!

I faced my mailbox, savoring the most significant event of the day—discovering letters containing messages just for me. Opening the small gilded door with my key, I pretended not to notice the neighbors as they passed behind me to exit the apartment building's front door into the light of the Manhattan afternoon. Instead, I focused on the dark portal that held my mail. As hands sifted, my gaze landed on the winning ticket—a real letter amid the junk!

The sender's name and the postmark, however, stirred up a wave of excited aggravation: Dylan Byrne, my distant but still best friend, writing from Kathmandu. With consternation, I realized that Dylan's catchphrase—a subconscious mantra—sang out in my head every day before I opened my mailbox.

I climbed the three flights to my apartment, aware of the agitation caused by the envelope in my hand. Once inside, I tossed the correspondence on the foyer table. There would be time for Dylan's incendiary nonsense later; it was nap time. This was my strict protocol; all letters were read after nap time, and I knew Dylan's letter would not bring peace of mind.

On my way to my bed at four o'clock, I picked up the day's *New York Times*—Thursday, March 15, 2018. The irony in a headline caught my eye. *Stephen Hawking Dies at 76 on Albert Einstein's Birthday.*

With the old gray lady in my hands, I ignored James Joyce as I slipped under the covers next to him. I shared my bed with one love at a time, and *Ulysses* was my current literary affair.

Hawking, a man severely riddled with disease and limited by his physical form, had a sharpness of mind that had kept his disabled body alive for decades beyond all prognoses. During this reprieve, he had led the scientific community back to the beginning of time and space. When sound could no longer escape the shriveled bellows of his body, he used his working thumb to speak and write by moving a joystick. And when his thumb would no longer move, he created a new voice by moving a cheek muscle—man and machine joined in an early miracle of brain-computer interface built specifically for his genius.

I shut my eyes, and the nap began with a wonderful image of a black hole appearing, a big bang in reverse, as my thoughts faded into hallowed emptiness.

I woke an hour later to a loudly haranguing voice inside my head: *An unread letter waits in the foyer!* I turned off the alarm and evaluated my afternoon nap with the same mix of emotions that followed each daily siesta, reconciling the pleasure of emerging from the black hole of sleep with the condemnation of a practice that had commenced years ago as a disciplined sitting meditation. From sitting, it had moved to a lying meditation and now, no longer with any pretense, was a nap. Evolution in reverse.

I spent most of my life in my castle keep, an academic's tower fortress nestled in a small one-bedroom apartment on 18th Street in Chelsea, NYC. A fortress of bricks and books with books *as* bricks— lining the walls, piled on any open surface, and scattered on the floor like stepping stones. Erect, seated, or prone, I reveled in the privacy of this disheveled library and its comforting scent of decaying forest—the sweet-smelling compost of the literary canon, not the pungent pulp. These books' authors had led me into universes of imagination and worlds lighter or darker than my own. Whenever I wasn't living in a book's mindscape, I was lost, alone in my gray mind.

The bricks on the wall made way only for a couple of framed posters of classical films I loved.

My final love was letters. Well-written letters were pages from a life meant for an audience of one, the intimacy of personal communi- cation that traveled over time and space. Electronic communications had reduced correspondence to a casual encounter, the trite message appearing in no time in a denial of space, often with multiple recipients. Exchanging the pleasure one receives from well-crafted prose for the endorphin release in the *ting* of a text.

On occasion, as a man of letters, I still received well-written and illuminating correspondence. Those letters were sent by colleagues, other professors, and writers from around the globe. I took pride in being part of the global intellectual elite, a position granted me by my tenured title, professor of literature.

Ah . . . esteemed academia, cowering in retreat in the face of men who would say and do anything, men of dark force, untethered by the Truth. Half the country considered me, a New York City liberal professor with an Irish Catholic father and an agnostic Jewish mother, a collaborator and an appeaser of alien rapists and jihadist killers.

My Irish agnostic tolerance and love of humanity were only limited by desire for comfort. Yes, I was alone most of the time, but only when *I* was dealing with *me and my* was I able to hold on to some semblance of control. The routine of classes, naps, letters, books, and the occasional movie served as a buffer from Churchill's "one damn thing after another."

After a bathroom break, I picked up the letter on the way to my reading chair and desk, knowing it would be full of hyperbole and New Age babble. Dylan claimed to have poetic license to bastardize the language. His letters were unsettling in other ways as well, as they inevitably proposed some unwelcome course of action on my part.

On the other hand, there was that intriguing postmark from Kathmandu. And Dylan was my oldest friend.

We were classmates from elementary school through college. At the University of Pennsylvania, Dylan focused on poetry, rock, reggae, and punk, while I was more serious and focused on achieving good grades in literature and philosophy. Dylan and I both dabbled in meditation and Buddhist philosophy, which endeared us to the girls we tended to like. We also shared tastes in poetry, music, and film. Though we often competed for the affection of the same lady during those days of beer and weed, our friendship always came first.

Dylan Byrne had been named after the poet, not the songwriter, though now the songwriter—Bob—was a Nobel laureate poet. Dylan was a fan of both these lyrical masters that shared his name.

Over the last decade our relationship had become limited to a few memorable meetings and much-hyped letters better forgotten. Dylan's letters forced me to labor over my response when I couldn't just let his newest call to action pass through inaction. Typical suggestions included that I read some great book recently unearthed in a desert and translated from the original Sandscript (his word) or that I start a yoga practice with his teacher in Timbuktu or go into a sensory deprivation tank on a microdose of acid.

Dylan had somehow enjoyed a successful career on Wall Street, a strange fit for the restless dreamer with a rebellious spirit. But after leaving the big-name investment bank, he became an increasingly odd and esoteric world traveler, which suited him. Despite the distance between us, we remained close over the years. Dylan now served mostly as a reminder of days gone by. His appearances in person and in writing rattled the cage of my comfortable life.

By way of example, the last time I heard from Dylan, he'd sent a postcard from Central America. He told me about joining a shaman troupe for a ceremony in worship of the "medicine" ayahuasca. Though Dylan acknowledged it wasn't for everyone, he said, "I found it to be a wonderful experience, and I was so fortunate to have met a true shaman—a beautiful incarnation—with a lovely singing voice, and she also practices in Upstate New York!"

Dylan had thought the spiritual ceremony—which extended over a week, in a large yurt in the jungle with strangers ("the family")—would make a good short story topic for me to write about. The details, peppered with frequent dashes, had been crammed onto a postcard. I wondered what the post office thought. The suggestion was dismissed out of hand. I wasn't going to perform any ritual that required me to digest a substance that would make me sick.

That was almost two years ago now, so I'd been due a message rattling in from Dylan's world. I studied the envelope with more than some apprehension—examining the letter, shaking the letter, thinking the letter might contain some white powder stimulant or "medicine." Like Prufrock inspecting a peach, I was filled with dreadful anticipation.

Setting fear aside, I sat at my desk and used my treasured letter opener to part the envelope's lips.

PO Box 6699
22 W 32nd
9-9-9

Dear Sean,

Auspicious is the day! I hope this letter finds you full of the joy of life. You know Hope would have wanted you to find new love and move forward. Have you, old buddy? You know that it's our choice to be born each instant or to be busy dying. Karma now turns faster in our lives since we have several incarnations within one life as we awaken.

Now to my miraculous and risky business: I have been blessed by a revelation of a theory of everything—the constant creation theory. The theory is the scientific grail, marrying the infinitely large of astrophysics with the infinitely small of quantum physics. Constant creation suggests there is no first cause of Michelangelo's God or the big bang but rather an infinite and eternal constant source of creation. It has the beauty of supersymmetry in the reconciliation of spirituality and science.

The ToE, to use the jargon of my brilliant friend and science collaborator, has been met with the great resistance of orthodoxy, oligarchy, and dogma by both the scientific and religious communities—with my friend being the one lovely exception. She led me to my all-encompassing theory by sharing a lost theory of Einstein's that posited that everything in our expanding universe is constantly traveling at the speed of light.

I'll introduce you to her while in the city. If I was not a married man . . .

Since you and I already had one best-selling—or at least sold-out—literary collaboration, I want to discuss a novel based on the theory. My intent is to promote the theory, while yours, I'm sure, will be making it a literary masterpiece. What better mystery to be solved than the theory of everything, the act of constant creation in life and art—the end of the zero-sum game. I'm hoping the irony of illuminating the illusion through fiction will intrigue you—the ineffable expressed in 150,000 words, more or less. A magical story of Big Love.

I see you shaking your head—we'll get it nodding over dinner. Saturday June 2 at Momofuku Ko at 8:00 p.m.? I've taken the liberty of making a reservation and will treat. There we'll discuss the ToE and my novel idea and all the wonders of life.

Warning: I no longer trust email and hope this letter hasn't been intercepted. I'll explain that over dinner too, but I—or the ToE—is now of interest to the government (CIA). I believe they're watching me (actually maced me when I caught them searching my desk here) in Kathmandu, and they've asked me to meet with them as soon as I return to the States.

I worry about Natalie and Grace but not you. You need to take some risks to wake up. I'm changing my phone number, so please just come to dinner, or you can reach me through my PO mailbox in Kathmandu. It has been too long without a letter from you, though I hope not to find a rejection of my invitation there. This is an important date. I'll see you at dinner soon.

Remember Lao Tzu: "New beginnings are often disguised as painful endings."

Peace and love, your oldest and always best friend,
Dylan

Whistling "Whew!" and uttering "Wow!" I put the letter down. I was speechless. Dylan had his quirks, but fear of Big Brother was not one of them. Most likely they were interested in his "medicine" rather than his theory.

He must have been serious, as the letter was relatively well written and his handwriting legible. Maybe he was suffering a midlife crisis, as it sounded as though he was reverting to the sixties' free love with his mention of big love.

I picked up the day's newspaper and marveled at the timing of Dylan's letter. To clear my perturbed mind of his drafting me to chase windmills as his Sancho, I continued to read the article about the death of the man who brought us the big bang and black holes.

I confess I became lost in the explanation of *imaginary time*, a concept Hawking lit upon in his final years. Unlike finite time that commenced with a big bang and moved along a horizontal axis in space, imaginary time consisted of infinite time on a vertical axis. As I finished the article, I laughed to think how science was always so sure until it wasn't. But now Dylan claimed to have figured it all out.

The joke in the letter, regarding a prior literary collaboration, referred to a very short story we had written together in the fifth grade and then distributed on the playground of our elementary school. We sold "The Little Stevie Story" for a quarter after xeroxing copies with the unwitting assistance of the librarian. We sold out of all fifty copies—*cha-ching*!

The controversial subject matter of that story almost got us expelled. In the end, however, we had to return the quarters and retrieve the copies of the story for destruction. The First Amendment didn't apply at Highland Elementary School.

It was a sufficiently remarkable event that as a young professor I'd written a short story based on that very short story and its aftermath and included it in my only collection of published short stories. That story received the most interest, and the collection won me a Story Prize, the literary summit of my career. I'd moved from writing short stories to letters while intending someday to write a novel.

Now I was faced with the aftermath that always followed Dylan's letters blowing through my life. How to respond? My eyes rolled as I shook my head, much as Dylan had anticipated. While Dylan's dinner date was over two months away, I had no intention of agreeing to his literary collaboration even if I had all the imaginary time in the world.

I was determined to write my own novel soon and didn't need Dylan's amateur poetic assistance for my prose. My head said *run and hide*. Collaboration would lead to trouble. That was why I always found a way to avoid being sucked into his grand plans for us. He would provide the big idea and after he lit the fuse, go flitting off to some new adventure, leaving me—as the *real* writer—to do all the work and take the risk of the project blowing up in my face.

And who writes a novel based on a theory? Typical Dylan, without concern for precedent and convention. My first novel would be a serious work. I knew my abilities weren't comparable to those of my beloved Austen, Dickens, or Joyce, but perhaps along the lines of Maugham.

To avoid awkwardness, I'd accept his invitation and play along by asking that he send me the theory in advance—if the risk was not too great, of course. Then over dinner, I could gently reject his proposal. Momofuku Ko had a two-Michelin-star tasting menu. I threw his letter into the basket that sat beside my desk.

CHAPTER 2

PLEASE ALLOW ME TO INTRODUCE MYSELF. I am Sean Byron McQueen. Dylan always said I should have been the romantic poet and not just teach transcendental poetry. I'm a forty-five-year-old widower in the dead center of life.

Time had started to accelerate, with each decade seemingly a year shorter. As a tenured professor in the literature department at NYU, I considered teaching my life, but my passion was literature, and my secret dream was to write a great novel. I'd always feared my dyslexia made great writing impossible for me, but I had spellcheck and F. Scott did not.

It was noon on June 1, the day before my looming dinner with Dylan, a date that had hung around my neck like an albatross and dredged up memories of my dead wife. The days since his letter arrived had percolated in a disturbing brew of past suffering and future dread.

I was grading student papers in my comfortable NYU office. On my schedule was a meeting for *anytime in the afternoon*. I regretted not specifying a time.

My office was another fortress of books, with a vintage Cure poster on the brick wall. The poster was there to let students know I was still young and hip, or at least once had been. I no longer danced. By way of balance and to not appear too much a poseur of youth, I had hung an even more vintage poster of Bogart from *The Maltese Falcon* on the opposite wall. Here I worked and met with students and faculty when they couldn't be avoided.

The student papers were all either overly naïve and grandiose or the minimum of safe regurgitation to get by. Years ago, as a young professor,

I'd looked for each student's authentic voice and attempted to bring out the genius in the gifted students whose essays exhibited extraordinary insight, sensitivity, and a new take on old literature. These days I graded based on objective measures and to fulfill my duty.

Still, I kept returning to one essay from an independent-study student, which addressed Coleridge's view of the reconciliation of opposites as allowing for the sublime to be reflected in the art of the Romantic poets. There was perhaps a spark in this student's writing, or at least in her enthusiasm.

I had turned my attention from the young lady's romantic epiphanies to the reproachful glare of an elf statuette that sat on my desk, when there came a knocking on my office door. It was another elf, jolly but tall—my literary agent. My anytime meeting arriving at four.

I had sent my agent the very beginnings of a novel idea, and he wanted to meet in person to provide his critique. Revealing my writing for the first time was always nerve-racking, but I was eager for positive feedback. I was sure I'd had a breakthrough and that my novel's course was set.

Now that I had started my own novel, I wouldn't have to lie to Dylan. I generally adhered strictly to the truth, even when it had to be manufactured. No one has complete integrity and holds to all promises and secrets, but truth is something to aspire to, especially with one's best friend.

My agent made an entrance like a star actor coming on stage. He'd actually had a brief career in the theater before becoming a literary agent. I didn't know if he had blue blood, but his name was Elliot Pennington. He was my own Elliott Templeton from *The Razor's Edge*, my small bon vivant window into Manhattan social life from my now very circumscribed world. I usually had to pretend not to enjoy his company immensely.

He entered my literary lair wearing his Tom Wolfe costume of immaculate white coat and pants but giving off the aura of a peacock in full plume. His long, slim hands were full, cane in one and my novel's introduction in the other. As the fop flopped into my chair, he slapped the pages of my manuscript on the desk with a bang. I stood, the student ready for his lesson.

He wasted no time in launching his attack. "So you're really going to do it this time, a novel about a dead wife who doesn't die? A bit of macabre fantasy? You need a therapist, not an agent."

"It's an adventure, not a fantasy. You don't like it?"

"It's fine. It's your past life with Hope, explaining in great detail how you met."

"Well, it's just the introduction."

"There will be other characters, then?" His tone blended hope with skepticism.

"Funny. But, yes, in the course of the adventure they'll meet many interesting characters."

"I'm afraid you'll lose your reader before your wonderful flight of fantasy takes off. You know, with *fifty* pages looking back, all in your head, at how you and Hope met. Couldn't you just say she was the most beautiful and passionate student in your Huxley Perennial Philosophy class your first year as a professor, an extremely talented evolutionary biologist having a dalliance with literature? You fell in love and married, she inspired your work, and then get on with it."

"Not a dalliance . . . They have to understand the depth of my love and loss."

"That's just it—there is no loss. She lives on in your fantasy."

"Adventure."

"Got it. I did like the challenge you posed to her and your Huxley students." He stood straight and tall—picking up his cane as if it were a prop—and read dramatically from the introduction pages.

"In the grand finale, the minister's final flourish, inspired by the Holy Spirit speaking through his native tongue: 'If you agree there is a perennial philosophy . . . if you agree that there is a way to transcend the suffering human condition and be of service to humanity . . . if you agree with Christ and Buddha . . . if you agree with Plato . . . if you agree with Einstein in this perennial philosophy—a state of self-realization and a possible connection with all-knowing inspiration—how can you live your lives without that being your primary focus? Mystical union is either the ultimate goal or a dangerous pathological delusion.'

"In Huxley's own words, 'Man's life on earth has only one end and purpose: to identify himself with his eternal Self and so to come to intuitive knowledge of the Divine Ground.'

"In writing your papers, I ask you to choose whether self-realization is the purpose of life or a grand illusion. This is a very big question and one you now must answer."

Elliot bowed before he reclaimed his seat, dropping my introduction back on the desk. "There's your challenge to the reader. So let the adventure take off with flights of fancy from that."

"It was more than that. There's the sublimity of our first kiss and the first time we made love and our metaphysical discussions where we connected with Shelley's intellectual beauty."

"Is that Percy or Mary?"

"Percy, you philistine." I could give as good as I got.

"Yes, as you said—'The inspiration Shakespeare tapped into with each dip of his pen.' All very poetic and quite long."

"So was *Paradise Lost*," I said, refining my defense. "Everything Hope did was inspired by truth and beauty, and while we were together, all of life became magical. We traveled the world each summer break, and events and people responded to her bright spirit and our love. I believe this is what happens with true love—the world opens up, and people and events become more vibrant and alive. Like I say here—" I looked down at my abandoned introduction. "The frequency was turned up as our days tuned in to the eternal spring of life's becoming."

At hearing the words spoken aloud, I shrank into the smaller seat across from my agent. "Okay, maybe it is a bit over-the-top. But that magic is what the adventure will be all about, once my imagination is sparked and the novel is written."

"Okay, you're the writer; I'm just the agent. And if anyone can use their writing to resurrect their love, it's you. Though you do tend to swing wildly from the flowery poesy to the dark abyss. I blame your Romantic poetry. Consider more pulp and less literary. That's what sells."

He patted the elf statue on the head. "I recognize this little fellow. You could mention Hope was a posthumously published evolutionary biologist. That book sold fairly well for us. Just get out of your head as soon as you can and send me your fantasy—*adventure*—outline or draft when you're ready. And don't look so downhearted. I'm just an actor making humble suggestions to an award-winning writer. Get some sleep. You look tired."

I'd missed my nap thanks to his arrival time.

He stood, holding himself perfectly erect in what appeared to be defiance of autumnal age, then picked up his cane and tapped it three times on the floor. I heard *done, done, done.*

"Great. Thanks for the criticism."

He left his script, my emotionally charged introduction, dying on the desk. I started after him but decided he had left it behind to be buried. The introduction had its opening and closing matinee in one act.

He was right, of course. I'd begin anew after my dinner with Dylan.

I collapsed into my chair. Was I able to write only from memory— did I lack the imagination for sustained fiction beyond a short story's scope? This was the most I had opened up and discussed Hope since she'd died, and my agent told me not to talk so much about her. Going forward, I'd keep my novel secret and not share the pages with anyone, even Elliot, until it was done. I'd find some other excuse for not writing Dylan's collaborative novel based on some pseudo-scientific theory.

From my desk, I picked up an old picture of Hope and Dylan at the dinner where I introduced my best man to my soon-to-be wife. My parents died a few years before the wedding. William and Sylvia McQueen had an old-school marriage where when one spouse died, the other soon followed. Because I was an only child, those bang-bang deaths left me without family, but I always had Dylan, who was my adopted blood brother. Still, every life is a Hamlet-like battlefield littered with an increasingly high body count as time moves us toward our inevitable end. Hope and Dylan had been kindred spirits, which had made him a painful reminder of my loss for the past nine years.

That dinner had followed a panel debate Hope participated in at

NYU. The debate topic was Evolution and/or Conscious Design, and she'd won even before it started when her adversary had fought to have it entitled more simply Evolution or Conscious Design. The debate ended with incredible magic that sprang from Hope's belief in a divine life source.

I put the picture down, trying to forget that image of the past.

Following her death, my classes were canceled, and I took a year off from teaching. I would never again teach Huxley Perennial Philosophy, the class where we had met. It too had run its course.

During the days before and after the funeral, death's denial of life consumed me. I would stare at the urn that held Hope's ashes, telling myself I had been deluded in my belief regarding life's meaning and purpose, a purpose I had derived from her certitude of belief. All I wanted was the comfort of sleep, not meaning. Meaning was dead to me.

Later, summoning the smoldering remnants of Hope's spirit, I managed to compile and publish her lectures. They were transcribed from YouTube videos that had been surreptitiously recorded by an "ELF," a member of the Education is Literally Free movement. Somehow that project had made her seem less dead. I wrote an introduction to the book of lectures, which Hope and I discussed extensively in my mind.

Elliot insisted that a picture of the ELF statue—sent to award recipients for the best online lecture series—be placed on the cover of Hope's book. Because so few were awarded, an ELF on a professor's desk was a coveted item, even though the practice of surreptitiously recording and posting the lectures online was outlawed by the thought police. Hope had kept her ELF bronze at home in a closet. That statue, bearing Hope's name, now sat proudly on my office desk.

I met Hope's ELF creator only once—at Hope's funeral. She had become notorious as a renegade internet sensation in hiding, so her appearance was at some risk to her, or at least to her reputation. One of the most moving tributes to Hope had been written by this founding ELF and posted on her popular and controversial blog.

I pushed the elf aside and turned to thoughts of Dylan, again looking at him in the picture. He'd been at the funeral too, had rushed back from Tibet to be there. It was a long way to come, but I was unable to spend time with him back then. I couldn't handle the memories and the pain.

Hope's legacy, to my dismay and satisfaction, was that even nearly a decade later, you couldn't pick up a New Age spiritual book without the emergent evolutionary leap of humanity being its topic.

Dylan would want to discuss Hope over dinner, and my agent had just reminded me why I didn't like talking about her.

I dreaded the all-too-soon dinner date with Dylan. Even his theory's title, the theory of constant creation, was a reminder of Hope's belief in an ongoing conscious design behind evolution. I turned their picture over, leaving it facedown on the corner of my desk.

I resumed reading the independent student's essay, but my enthusiasm for her and Coleridge's romantic view of the reconciliation of opposites had waned, and the essay no longer seemed so bright and new in the fading light of a day without a nap.

CHAPTER 3

TIME HAD PASSED QUICKLY after I received Dylan's letter, which left me shaking my head as to how engagements, only agreed to because they are distant in time, eventually arrive. I shouldn't have been surprised June 2 had come. I went about my day pretending it was like any other.

By midafternoon, when I returned home from my routines, I was more on edge than was normal for a dinner date. Elliot had shaken my literary confidence, and I hadn't slept well. There had been no further communication from Dylan, the man of mystery, following my letter saying I would join him for dinner.

At four o'clock it was nap time in my Chelsea book sanctuary. As I lay down next to 730 pages of Joyce's stream of consciousness, I was aware Joyce and I had grown apart and were now suffering artistic differences. I'd been on the same page of the book since receiving Dylan's letter.

Sleep brought on a most lucid and literary dream. I was sitting in my reading chair when Dylan appeared and handed me an exquisitely bound book before becoming invisible. While no longer physically present, he was still there, watching me.

The book in my hands was my favorite—a hardback, its spine unbroken. It had no title, but the cover was painted with a tropical mountain-jungle setting with a waterfall cascading down a crevasse and surrounding lush flora bursting into life. I imagined it was one of the many magical places Dylan had discovered on his journeys.

I knew the pages were blank, yet I also knew that if I opened the book, I would be transported into a stream of characters in action within the story, becoming part of the story itself. Summoning courage,

I determined to open the book to the first page. I felt Dylan's presence approve of my page selection as *a good place to start.*

Sadly, I woke before opening the book. The dream left me strangely awake, with the impression that the reader was the main character of any book and that each word and sentence appeared only as the reader observed the page and became lost in the illusion. Dylan's ghostly appearance made me suddenly curious about his theory of everything, with a feeling that this constant-creation thing of his might be a source of artistic inspiration. That might make a good dinner conversation topic and allow me to appear less dismissive of his novel-collaboration idea.

I checked my phone; still no confirmation email from him. Even if he didn't trust email or want to send his theory in advance by the old mail, he could still send a "Good to go, ole chum" by text—he had my phone number. Momofuku Ko was an either six- or eight-course prix fixe, so I'd be engaged with Dylan and his ToE for three or four hours. He was always jovial but an intense and emotionally challenging companion. In his new bohemian incarnation, he sometimes liked to hold lingering eye contact too long for me.

How radical would this theory be? My friend was brilliant in his way, but he was no Einstein. My strategy was to show interest and be supportive without agreeing to take on the suggested collaboration.

Arriving at the restaurant punctually at a quarter past eight, I was unfortunately still the first to arrive. Momofuku Ko was self-consciously, eccentrically hip, with a variety of chairs in multiple colors and tables of different shapes. Our table for two was an oval paired with one bright red chair and one dark blue one. I took the blue for myself, which provided a view of the door. From there, I could see my friend's arrival or devise my escape.

The space and the height of the ceiling allowed for privacy, as well as a means of checking out other diners as the room filled. I was a novelty sitting there solo, pretending to be comfortable in my solitude while defiantly not looking at my phone.

By eight thirty the restaurant tables were filled with well-heeled patrons who knew how to dress for a first-class seat. I sat in my tweed blazer impatiently nursing a twenty-dollar glass of simple village Chablis 2014—not grand or even premier cru—the cheapest on the list and a tad green but complemented by a very tasty amuse-bouche that the kind waitress, no doubt taking pity on me, brought to the table. I stretched the one bite into three.

Admitting defeat, I took out my phone to call Dylan, only to be reminded by a metallic voice that his number had been changed. My best friend, and yet we never spoke over the phone. I emailed him instead, despite his dire warning about that mode of communication and his paranoia of the CIA, asking simply, "WTF are you?" Emails and texts were not the places for literary flair.

By a quarter past nine, after a second glass of Chablis and checking my phone a half-dozen times, I was out of patience. Leaving a fifty-dollar bill on the table, I apologized on my way out. They didn't ask for more money, for renting the expensive table for over an hour, but my sorry exit cost me a knowing look from the maître d'. I imagined that he imagined I'd been stood up by a Tinder date I was looking to impress. The coat-check attendant was happy with a ten-dollar tip for my light jacket, as I didn't dare ask for change.

A deflated and poorer man, I slunk into the alleyway out front. They must have had Dylan's new phone number at the reservation desk, but I wasn't sure they would give it to me, and I didn't want to go back inside for more humiliation.

As I walked home, my mind was busy writing off Dylan as an inconsiderate flake who couldn't even take the time to call the restaurant or email me an explanation.

Safe in my library tower, I penned a self-controlled email to Dylan before bed, not wanting to display anger: *I imagine with your big love you were kidnapped by ISIS and lost in the throes of tantric sex in a vortex void of time and space, absolved of all social obligation and common courtesy.*

After numerous drafts, I decided saying nothing was the best revenge. Dylan came to represent an indictment of all things New Age—self-centered, hedonistic, and shallow, a *crystals, stars, and angels flowing into a potpourri of Kahilda Braun poetry* kind of guy. That Hallmark poet's name I always bastardized, as I'm hopeless with names. Real poetry required too much depth and sensibility for the addlebrained New Age. The whole New Age thing was an infantile regression that comforted and stroked the ego rather than transcending it, as claimed.

The next morning, Sunday, still no word from Dylan. I relaxed in my reading chair with *The Tempest*. I could recite the Shakespeare line by line, just the ticket to clear my mind. I took a deep breath, relieved at no longer having to reject Dylan's theory and novel ideas and by my decision not to write Dylan any more emotionally charged draft emails. I was embarrassed that my upset bordered on anger, but smiled at my clever mind saying *Dylan is Daedalus to me*. As good Irishmen, Dylan and I had shared a love of Joyce in college.

Years ago, Dylan had written a letter with a subject-line typo announcing "Creating Deadalus." He'd meant Daedalus, the mythical Greek father, artisan, and creator who built a labyrinth for a king and god-damned wings for his own son. Wings his son used to fly to his death, a cruel god's reward for artistic creation and scientific advance. Or maybe the price of hubris.

With his usual arrogance, Dylan had suggested a class for me to teach. I went to the basket that I kept by my desk, the wicker holder for all of Dylan's letters sent over the years—embarrassed to have maintained one—and pulled out that letter.

I read Dylan's brief course description for James Joyce's *Ulysses*:

The class should be built around how Joyce used stream of consciousness to show the creation and fluid nature of the ego of Stephen Dedalus. Each student will be challenged to write their class paper in stream-of-consciousness style, with the hero being their online avatar. It should come naturally from their tweeting and twittering image making and is intended to bring them to full consciousness of the avatar they are creating and the mirror impact social media has on their real lives. The goal is to become Joyce, the self-realized, witnessing presence balancing on the razor's edge of imagination and reality.

The letter had stood the test of time and was just as exasperating as I remembered. There I was—Shakespeare on my lap and Joyce in my bed—reading old letters from my ex–best friend. I tossed it back into the basket. I imagined lighting the whole lot of them on fire, but that image of revenge was all too Wicca and more suited to a jilted female lover. Though I really did love those letters.

Soon there would be another letter explaining why he didn't show up for dinner, or he'd really be dead to me and I'd truly be all alone in the world. There was something darkly seductive about the thought. Contemplating this last step into deep solitude and isolation set my mind to imagining a novel that fully embraced the macabre fantasy of a wife who dies, eyes wide open, in bed next to my dark hero. His top-floor apartment would have secret attic access, like where the portrait of Oscar Wilde's Dorian Gray was stored as it started to age. He'd move the body and bed there and open the skylight wide to the cold winter air. He'd then go about his days teaching, coming home each frigid night to imaginative conversations and trips of fancy, snuggling with his cold dead wife.

I had embraced the epicenter of my existence, where only a flickering candle remained, the only light in a black heart. Dylan's betrayal left me in a dark romantic state to write my macabre masterpiece, a dirge with just one setting—that chilly attic bed—and the sole dialogue the rattling, half-life voices in my unstable hero's head that refused to let love die.

CHAPTER 4

DESPITE THE ONGOING VISCERAL indictment of all things Dylan and New Age, I did allow for synchronicity, the course of collective and individual history turning on meaningful coincidences. This belief was based on Jung's synchronicity and not on the tenet of the New Age gospel. A few days after the dinner that was not meant to be, my life took one such turn.

I was already on summer break, enjoying my solitude among the multitude on a leisurely morning hike down the biking, jogging, and walking path adjacent to the Hudson River and the West Side Highway.

The sky was overcast and foreboding, but the clouds were sponges determined to hold their water. I wondered what my morbid novel's hero would do when it rained and warmer weather started decomposing the dead wife in front of him.

It was Wednesday, with still no letter of explanation from Dylan. I was determined to forget his unforgivable behavior. As I crossed into the financial district, to my right rose a gray Taj Mahal of money, the building that Dylan's investment bank had built for itself. No signage announced the Wall Street name of the business within the stone fortress. This discretion wasn't based on lack of pride but on fear of attack and shame over all the money hoarded there. This mecca for those anointed by wealth, this unnamed mausoleum for dead souls, wasn't the least bit humble.

I turned my back on all that building represented and crossed the broad highway overpass to go to my favorite Tribeca coffee house. Dylan had introduced me to the Meta Bean, a very conscious space. Despite my indictment of all things Dylan, I did allow for an excellent cup of coffee in a den filled with books and vintage movie posters. I could have been the Meta Bean's decorator.

Waiting ahead of me in line were two young female professionals from Dylan's investment bank. I recognized them from an annual margarita tour I attended every other year. The tour was hosted by Dante, another college friend and another managing partner, with Dylan, at the Wall Street firm that will not be named.

The ladies took their coffee to a table. Although one of them was a spitfire of lively conversation as I recalled—I had forgotten her name. Elena or Ella? It began with an *E*. She was just two inches short of being a Fox News host clone. The other woman's name I wasn't sure I ever knew.

My social skills had atrophied, and I tended to be shy before my first margarita, so I sought to avoid the two women. I was successful until the barista yelled, "Sean, double latte!"

Elena or Ella jumped up when she saw me. She greeted me with arms wide open for a hug. "Sean, I'm so sorry about Dylan."

How would she know? "Hello. What?"

"You don't know?" She looked down, as if she were about to tell me that Dylan had killed someone. "He's dead. I assumed you knew."

Dylan dead?

I didn't want to believe her, but I did. And I didn't know how it was possible, but my heart had always known. It was the most logical explanation of his behavior.

The other woman joined us, flanking me on my other side, while I remained speechless.

I mumbled a greeting with my right hand outstretched, but the second woman wanted a hug too. She splashed her hot latte onto the floor in letting go of me.

Elena said, "He didn't know about Dylan. The family notice says he died in his sleep. Sounds like drugs to me."

The other woman chimed in. "Joe thinks that a prostitute probably killed him in the hotel bed. Why else would he be at a downtown hotel when he had a wife in a townhouse in the Village?"

Ella, seeing me grimace, said, "Joe is the dog; Dylan was a gentleman. I should know . . . Well, it's a mystery to me and maybe suicide, though he was one of the happiest people I've known. But his sweet shining star would want to cover up drugs or suicide."

"Drugs or suicide, maybe both! Excuse me. I'm going to get some napkins to try to clean this up." The second woman skipped up to the Meta Bean counter.

I finally managed a reaction. "I wonder why Dante or Natalie didn't call me."

Elena said, "Dante is at sea on his sailboat."

"The *L'Allegro*." Strange that I remembered the name of Dante's sailboat, but it was thanks to Milton. I was finding it hard to breathe and wanted to be alone with my thoughts.

Ella said, "The wake is Saturday at a Quaker meeting house in Flushing. Noon. If you want, I can send you the details."

"No, that's all right. I'll find my way."

"You okay?" she asked.

"Yeah, just a little light-headed and catching my breath."

She gave me a flirty look, as if I'd just paid her a compliment.

Elena's friend returned with a handful of napkins.

I awkwardly hugged them both goodbye, wanting less contact than the moment of shared grief and their embrace demanded. I left in a fog, my double latte clutched in both hands as they danced about with napkins under their shoes drying the floor.

I returned to the pedestrian/bike path on the West Side Highway and found a bench beside the Taj Mahal to ponder Dylan's death. As the Hudson flowed languidly by, I noticed the second woman's splatter on my white tennis sneakers. Dylan's passing reminded me of Hope's death and . . . and both deaths had incomprehensibly come so young. People I loved died, and they died well before their time. In the end, people I love all die.

I closed my eyes. Tuned out the blare of cars and the bellow of a boat. I closed out the increasingly cloudy sky and the foghorns of life. I was alone in a world getting darker.

The dead are forgiven all sins. I was the one who needed to be forgiven for my small-minded condemnation of Dylan after his failure to show up for dinner. He was dead, for God's sake. Like everything in my small circle of life, I'd made it all about me, how I was inconvenienced and diminished. Even his death was him completing my isolation. *Dylan, I'm so sorry.*

I imagined him laughing at me. *Nothing to forgive, old buddy. You know what you must do. Remember Lao Tsu.*

We shared a laugh, and Dylan was resurrected in me. Over that cup of coffee on a bench on the side of a busy highway, Dylan was transformed from capricious betrayer back into my best and oldest friend—Dylan Byrne, troubadour of truth.

Now I wanted to see his theory, that theory of everything. I felt cheated of a masterpiece, deprived of artwork that had become invaluable with the artist's death. Dylan's theory became as precious to me as the final pages of Shelley's "The Triumph of Life," lost at sea with Shelley when his sailboat was scuttled by some nefarious force. Shelley's sublime voice had drowned with him. And while Dylan's voice had been silenced too, I would see that he, like Shelley, got his final triumph.

Cardenio? I suggested.

Cardenio! came his reply.

Since first discovering Shakespeare, we had joked about gambling our lives on finding Shakespeare's lost play, told by Cervantes's Don Quixote. We half joked about how we would sleuth as Holmes and Watson in the archives and pubs of London to find the lost manuscript. Though now, I assumed, we were speaking metaphorically.

I hoped someone at the Quaker wake would know more about Dylan's death and his theory of everything. The theory might be distributed to all in attendance as a fitting memorial. And then there was the "mystery" of his death, as Elena or Ella had called it. Dylan had said he was being watched.

Heat lightning flashed in the sky as the cloud sponges finally started to release their load. I sat in the rain, writing letters to Dylan's wife and daughter. One-way communication to avoid full engagement with their

grief. I expressed my love and sympathy while striving to provide truth-
ful comfort that he would always remain with us in our hearts, minds,
and souls. I omitted the part about speaking to him. When done, the
letters were wet, with the ink a bit streaked, but that added a romantic
touch of gravitas.

I hiked home without an umbrella. I felt Dylan urging me on and
demanding I celebrate his life and not dive into my deep reservoir
of self-pity. Grief had been wrung out of me, and something stirred
in my core, gestated in me, was ready to erupt straight out of Jung's
collective unconscious.

Inspiration for life had come in the form of death. I wondered if
Dylan's Quaker wake would answer my questions and if synchronicity
had found me again after all these years.

CHAPTER 5

EVEN ON A SATURDAY AND WITH A SEAT, it was a long ride on the 7 train to Flushing, Queens, and the Quaker wake. Emerging from the subway, I said to the Dylan in my mind, *Forget it, Jake. It's Chinatown.* It took another thirty minutes to find the Quaker meeting house, only a few short blocks from the station and secluded in its own wooded lot apart from all the asphalt and concrete. A cloistered anachronism, this outpost of brotherly love hid in the bazaar of Little Taipei.

A Quaker service was fitting, as Dylan and I were both Philly boys who had attended the University of Pennsylvania and therefore were Penn Quakers. We shared an appreciation of the Quakers and the Amish. No one ever heard of a Quaker or an Amish committing a hate crime.

Dylan's grandmother was ex-Amish. We would take her to breakfast many Sundays after a night of hard drinking of the high school, beer-guzzling kind. She was wise and caring, a great tonic for a hangover when paired with greasy eggs and bacon, rye toast and butter. She had only one complaint, which she made each breakfast: "The weather hasn't been the same since they landed on the moon." Dylan would later credit Nan with discovering climate change.

I entered the meeting house just before noon, glad I'd left extra time to get there. The timbered sacred space was over three hundred years old, a stubborn and creaky large wood-frame house—an Emerson of upright architecture composed of nature and soul—that stood its ground against time. I took my place in one of the rear pews—center row seat P-11, like in a theater.

About a hundred people filled the stern wooden pews, a mix of three major types. The first group was family, waiting for Dylan's wife, Natalie, and his daughter, Grace, to enter. Everyone knew Grace. She was a young Hollywood movie star who looked the part.

As Grace moved down the aisle to the front pew, arm in arm with her mother, the old meeting house came to life. Everyone pretended to be solemn and respectful, but many were clearly starstruck by Grace's presence; some sat up straight and glanced sideways, while others swiveled and stared wide-eyed as she passed by. Excited whispers followed her. The star-gazing idol worship embarrassed me.

Heads jerked around as mourners looked for Grace's celebrity friends. To register my displeasure, I stared straight ahead, though I did notice that Grace, for her part, was simple and unassuming in today's role as daughter of the deceased.

As she passed, Natalie managed a warm, sad smile for me, as if I were the guest of honor. She must have found solace in my maudlin rainy-day letter of condolence.

The second group consisted of businesspeople and lawyers from Dylan's investment-banking days. There, Elena/Ella and her friend mingled, whispering their conspiracy theories. Elena/Ella was dressed to kill, grabbing the attention of the businessmen, not allowing the limelight to fall all on Grace.

The third grouping was the New Age contingent: a middle-aged man with a ponytail and another with a monk cut; a woman with a stud in her nose sitting near an angel in a long flowing white dress, who seemed to have other young ladies as attendants; a loose affiliation of yoga teachers, meditation gurus, and nature lovers bowing to each other in greeting and repeating namastes and aums. Some sat in solemn mindfulness and others in communion. Despite my prior indictments, I had some affinity for those who took the road less traveled. Dylan had gone far off the beaten path on his way to his current dead man's pose at the front of the church, fortunately obscured by the closed casket.

My focus, however, was on five outcasts who didn't fit neatly into any of the aforementioned categories. This small group sat scattered but near me toward the back of the congregation.

Sitting to my right, perhaps only a yard away, was the first outcast who demanded my attention. I didn't want to conspicuously look, but she was a very attractive, very athletically built Brigitte Bardot look-alike in a flowing but tight-fitting dark blue dress. About thirty years old. From her fashionable book bag to her commanding presence, she looked to be from academia. I let my lonely imagination loose to enjoy the presence of my pewmate for the wake.

A tear in the corner of Brigitte's eye was poised to follow a path already moistened on her cheek. Why were women even more beautiful when they cried? I so wanted to look into those wet nut-brown eyes, but they were focused straight ahead at where Dylan lay at rest.

Closed casket is a good choice, my old Irish friend, but I can still see you smirking.

In juxtaposition, the gang of five also included two old men who sat together in front of me and to my left. This couple radiated self-importance and demanded respect merely for living so long—Laurel and Hardy in costumes but not at all funny. I was a good judge of types, and as a freshman novelist and longtime film buff, I was consciously building characters.

With his faux elbow patches on a snug blazer that stretched over his round abdomen, Hardy was obviously an academic from the old school. Angular Laurel, on the other hand, was clearly a Catholic priest, as he wore the cloth and collar and smelled of incense. Of course, the smell may have sprung from the old meeting hall. I could hear their muffled voices but not their words, just tones of disapproval or disdain.

The other two misfits sat behind me in the last pew by the doors. They weren't together but struck me as forty-something and fifty-something members of law enforcement or maybe private detectives—the Dicks. I felt their eyes were fixed on me.

From a small balcony at the back of the hall, a solitary Irish-sweater-wearing piper started playing a marching tune. He was accompanied on the small balcony by a man I assumed was the choir director, his laptop open as he followed the musical score. Red-haired like the piper, he was immaculately dressed like an English country gentleman with a remarkably white face. Or maybe he was the pastor, intent on fading into the woodwork as he revised his next sermon. The rousing fife song provided me an opportunity to swivel around and catch a sweet-sad smile crossing Brigitte's moist face. And to get a better look at the two Dicks.

The younger Dick looked like a sneering Bogart, the older like an actor in disguise. They did not pretend to project remorse.

As I turned back around, catching the now sad-joyful expression on Brigitte's face, I placed the piper's song: "The Rising of the Moon."

Of course, the Clancy Brothers, I said to Dylan. *Another excellent choice. For me?*

This misfit group—of which I considered myself a member—was loosely affiliated, in that each scanned the crowd in much the same way I did. Were they also looking for Dylan's theory? Did the movie cliché of the funeral being the location where detectives and murderers came together actually happen in real life?

I shook my head. These people might look as if they'd slid into roles, becoming characters, but that was merely a function of my outlook and current literary pursuits.

I tugged at the sleeve of my blue blazer, frowned at my Brooks Brothers powder-blue Oxford shirt and khaki pants. My mother must have dressed me to play a middle-aged professor. I shook my head again, but I couldn't erase the fact that I too dressed to suit my role.

Natalie walked to the small podium near the casket, standing strong like a figurehead on the prow of a ship, in the middle of tempest-turned seas. There to say goodbye before the casket slid off the rails and into the fires of cremation.

She spoke lovingly, blending humor with tenderness. She also spoke briefly. She finished by saying, "My heartfelt gratitude to each of you for coming to celebrate and say goodbye to our dearly beloved Dylan. Please let me introduce our daughter, Grace, who will say a few final words on behalf of our family."

Grace delivered a well-crafted and moving eulogy. She wasn't acting or playing a role; her words were authentic, raw, and real, and full of love for her father. She read Emerson's poem "Brahma," which set my mind reeling into the rafters, as I'd already felt the poet's presence in that place. He was one of Dylan's favorite poets. The authenticity that made Grace a great actress also made her a wonderful public speaker.

She concluded, with tears streaming, "It's fitting he died in his sleep. I'll give my dad the last word. He wrote to me shortly before his death, saying, 'There is no death but sleep, and there is no sleep without awakening.'"

She spoke those words in perfect imitation of Dylan's voice. I wanted to cheer her and throttle him. Instead, to my friend hidden in a wooden box about to experience the inferno, I said, *Well done! That's a perfect twist of irony. You know sleep is a serial killer in my life.*

Following Grace would be a hard act, but everyone was invited to speak if they were so moved. Quaker protocol. It was surprising, once it got going, how many people were so moved. There were some well-crafted, poignant words but mostly embarrassing sentiment and quaint Dylan stories. Some of the speakers, though trying to be respectful of the report that Dylan had died in his sleep, nevertheless questioned the mysterious death as incomprehensible, or as one lawyer-type put it, a "wrongful death."

None of the speakers mentioned Dylan's theory or big love, though the New Age contingent reported that he was now in divine oneness and that "Dylan will surely return a bodhisattva."

One speaker sang. She rose from among the group of New Agers and floated to the stage, angelic in white. Her mystical voice was heavenly too as she sang in some Latinate tongue. The words held no meaning for me but touched me with their deep feeling. Three young ladies stood, swaying to the skylark's song, and were joined by the rest of the swaying New Agers and then by the family and next by the business group, with Elena/Ella and her friend dancing as if the wake was a rock-and-roll show, their arms flailing in the release of their young and passionate remorse. From my gang of misfits, Brigitte stood to sway, so I stood and swayed too. My first dance in a decade.

So this is big love? I heard Dylan's laugh.

Except for Laurel and Hardy and the two Dicks, everyone was swayed by the mystical voice. The song served as the closing; no one had the bad taste to follow the high-note ending. The Quaker Holy Spirit was present and provided a fitting send-off for my best friend.

Afterward the two Dicks exchanged out-of-place and unpleasant words as they stood to leave, the younger one saying something harsh about photos. I didn't pay them much mind, as our dance had given me confidence, and I believed that perhaps the attractive young Brigitte might know something of Dylan's death and the theory.

I turned to approach her just as a beam of light entered the hall from one of the small windows, a spotlight landing on just the two of us in the relatively dimly lit congregation. A powerful presence pulsed behind her tear-soaked eyes and through the curves of her well-shaped body, now bathed in holy light.

The unexpected illumination increased my attention but shook my confidence. "Hello. I'm Sean."

She was taken aback and composed herself with a deep breath. I shuffled my feet to keep them from running away, while making my best harmless face of apology.

She turned tolerant and cordial, though still guarded. "I'm M, short for Emily." Or was it Em? I didn't want to get her name wrong or forget it.

My confidence continued to wane, but I pressed on. "I'm curious about the mysterious nature of Dylan's death. What do you think?"

Something—my question, I assumed—led her to pull back from me, and she looked over my shoulder and then behind her for the exit. "I know nothing about it."

"How well did you know Dylan? Did you know about a scientific theory he was working on?"

There was some recognition in her lovely wet eyes, but her focus fixed on something behind me. Before she could respond, the much older and much rounder academic from the gang of five landed at the periphery of our circle of light. He stood over my left shoulder. M waved hello—out of obligation, it seemed, more than in welcome—and he snorted in response.

"Emily."

Up close he seemed less Hardy and more an ominous, overweight, and old Orson Welles with high blood pressure.

She backed away, saying to both of us, "I have to go. Bye." She fled abruptly, swept away by emotion and by my foot faults, with me stepping over the baseline with each question volleyed. Her seat, number 9, was my lucky number, but she was gone.

I decided a funeral wasn't the time and the meeting house wasn't the place to conduct postmortem interviews. I should have offered condolences to Natalie, but she stood with Grace up front, and there was no getting near her. I was now distracted and light-headed. They had my drip-dried letters, and there would be a time to visit with them later.

I was completely starstruck and spellbound by M. How had that light shone on us so perfectly, as if by stage direction? Feelings were emerging—had been since our brief dance—that I hadn't allowed since rewriting my life as a confirmed bachelor and a widower nine years earlier. My head was spinning with distress at my shy and clumsy greeting in my clichéd blue blazer. I had to get out of that holy house and regain my composure.

As I stumbled out into Little Taipei, I was met by the sun and a gaggle of photographers taking my picture, in case I was famous, while they waited for Grace to emerge. Word of Grace's attendance had obviously escaped the Emersonian walls of the meeting house.

Elena/Ella, dramatically working the red carpet like a warm-up act, spotted me and ran over for an extended consolation hug as the cameras clicked. She slightly swayed and softly intoned, "Sean, Sean, oh, Sean." Her tears moistened my neck and chest. "Sean, Sean, how, Sean?"

Stiffening, I opened my eyes and pulled away when she didn't let go. Among the flock of paparazzi, the older Dick was taking our picture too. As his camera lowered, I caught his lifeless expression. Something was not right behind those Charlie Manson eyes.

CHAPTER 6

IN THE WAKE OF DICK'S EYES and M's lovely presence, I didn't sleep well. The next day I returned to my day-to-day life. I was working in my library sanctuary, grading the last of my final student essays, determined to forget all about ugly men and beautiful women. I would not see them again.

Forgetting M wasn't easy. How was it that a single awkward meeting had left her fingerprints on my mind and an *M* tattooed on my heart?

My attempts to divert my thoughts from M left me feeling impotent and pathetic. Elena/Ella deliberately stirring my eros under the flashing cameras and stiff sun had left me lonely and wanting. For a nine-year widower, teaching Romantic poetry to adoring young, impressionable students wasn't the answer but only more frustration. I was no longer a young professor, and times had changed.

My attraction to M was different and new and a bit out of my control. The spotlight shining on her and then on her seat—number 9—was auspicious, as Dylan would say. The short film clip of that moment played over and over in my mind. I imagined myself a Cary Grant but had played my part like Peter Sellers.

I banished the scene from my mind. I was torturing myself to no end.

I rushed through the last paper, a C-plus level that I gave a B minus because I was grateful to be finished, and it was a mercifully brief essay by a long-legged student who always sat in the front row in a short skirt.

Then I changed it back to a C plus to be fair. It was bad enough my teaching had become uninspired; I didn't want it also to become corrupt.

Then it was time to work on my novel, the macabre fantasy where the hero continues his life while his wife's dead body molts in their bed. The change of seasons would actually serve as a dramatic clock, accelerating the decomposition with the coming summer heat, increasing the horror page by page as the mad hero imagines a baby growing in the rotting womb.

Twenty minutes later, I put my pen down and rubbed my face. Contemplating dead eyes bulging out of their sockets reminded me of Dick's eyes. I needed to clear my mind. Dylan's death and his ToE business had set me far behind on my to-do list. The theory had been cremated yesterday with Dylan's lifeless body and inert mind, and I was morose. I felt that Dylan was watching me, like a play's narrator hovering just offstage.

Despite my best efforts to focus, a monkey mind cannot be tamed. Returning to the matters of Dylan's death, the theory, and M, I googled and found a brief blurb bemoaning that the good die young and declaring that the death of the revered Dylan remained a mystery. I was glad to hear that forty-five was still young. Apparently he was beloved, at least to a New Age blog dedicated to *Oneness*.

The entertainment press had also picked up on poor Grace's father's untimely death. One picture that caught her emerging from the meeting house was captioned "Grace in the face of her father's mysterious death."

No new information was provided other than significant innuendo, the implication being that only the old and feeble die in their sleep in a hotel bed. That conclusion was one I was uniquely qualified to refute.

I became lost in scenarios where Dylan had been murdered because of his discovery of the ToE. I'd been dismissive of the theory as something born in fiction, but that didn't mean the theory wasn't true. Maybe someone had killed him for it. I'd read somewhere that the hunt for the theory of everything had become the leading edge of a quiet new arms race between superpowers. It had sounded like science fiction at the time.

And if the theory was so life-altering and lethal, surely Dylan had written it down and stored it or shared it with someone. It must be recorded somewhere.

While obsessing over Dylan and the mystery, I recalled a strange feature of his last letter. I retrieved the envelope from the top of the basket.

In the letter, Dylan had included a PO box in NYC and not the one in Kathmandu. Beneath that address was what I'd assumed, at the time of the first reading, to be a date. I looked again—9-9-9. Not a date. It might be the combination to the mailbox or Dylan poking fun at my magic number.

My imagination went wild; I was sure the mailbox contained the theory and perhaps a clue to Dylan's death. Boldly deciding to skip my afternoon nap, I grabbed my small academic briefcase, my writer's bag with all the tools of the trade, and headed out the door.

Across the street stood a man who reminded me of the sick-eyed Dick who'd snapped my photo with Elena/Ella at the wake, though he was dressed very differently—a European tourist with a fedora dipped over the eyes.

The resemblance was my imagination, admittedly getting a vigorous workout the last few days. The man was soon gone down the street and around the corner. The sighting reminded me of how I still saw Hope routinely on New York City streets and sometimes followed an innocent lady for blocks. One woman noticed and hurried away, which made me an embarrassed stalker.

The Koreatown address from the letter was a long walk from my Chelsea home, and for each step I felt certain, the next I felt silly. This two-step turned into an urban hike in search of my old friend's final manifesto. I marched through a valley where, in the not-too-distant uptown and downtown, pencil-dick skyscrapers had been raised in testament to little men with nerves of brass and hearts of frozen steel. I pondered how Dylan had worked with those megalomaniacs.

To avoid glaring in disgust, I turned my attention to the street-sign trail markers pointing north to Koreatown. The chessboard street design made this Midtown jungle trek easy to navigate, and a half hour later, I was at the post office.

I was directed down a flight of stairs that opened into a cavernous mortuary with innumerable PO boxes lining the walls. Many—mostly older—people approached their boxes, only to turn away in mourning from the empty or junk-and-bill-filled crypts. I felt young in that crowd, ever hopeful that in the middle of the grim rectangular mall of mailboxes, 6699 held the elusive ToE.

I found Dylan's box, with its old-fashioned tumbler of a combination lock, between boxes 6698 and 6700. As with the hike to get there, I was sure the moment held a rare significance. Out loud I softly said, "Auspicious is the day!" An old lady opening a nearby box nodded her agreement.

Taking a deep breath, I turned the tumbler three times—right, left, right—to nine. No click. It didn't work. I tried again, slower. No click. And again, even more slowly. No click. The old lady shook her head with reproach, as if I were a thief trying to crack a safe. She took her junk and, muttering, shuffled away.

I shaded my eyes and peered into the little window of the box. It wasn't empty. This was torture, a mailbox with a letter I couldn't get to after fourteen short and three long blocks.

I joined the parade of sad patrons, watching my feet as I trudged up the flight of stairs and out of the post office. I headed to the subway to return home and resume work on my novel's grim deathbed tale. Halfway down the mouth of the subway entrance, I stopped like the murderous husband in *Dial M for Murder* when he figures out where the key is hidden to the apartment where he murdered his wife, before he then backtracks to find the key, disclosing his guilt and sealing his fate.

Running, I too returned to the scene of my attempted crime, half-convinced I had the key to crack that PO box wide open. I drew an even deeper breath to summon magical powers—or for dramatic effect—and without lowering my voice, so the entire congregation could hear, I said, "Auspicious is the day!" before entering 9-9-9 as it appeared on the letter, with a space between each digit, thus going fully around the tumbler twice before entering the next nine.

With a *click*, the door popped open!

I wished the old lady could see me about to retrieve my treasure. Some patrons did look on enviously as I, gloating, pulled out my real letter.

A letter to Dylan in New York from Dylan in Kathmandu. I weighed the ethics of opening the letter; surely legally and ethically it was for the family, for Natalie, to open. But if it was the theory of everything, and it had to be, Dylan had been coming to share the theory with me. And more practically, it was a standard envelope with a loose seal that could easily be resealed and delivered later to Natalie with no harm done. I couldn't *not* open that letter. I had found the precious ToE, and there was no leaving it sealed in its small crypt a moment longer.

The envelope seal broke cleanly with the letter opener Hope had gifted me. The small knife was always in my writer's bag of tricks. My weapon of choice.

A folded piece of paper slid from the envelope. I unfolded it.

I experienced both disappointment and excitement when the envelope didn't yield the ToE but a list of People To Be Trusted With The Theory Of Constant Creation.

Too many caps, old friend.

There were three—no, four—names with contact information. The first name I recognized—Sean Byron McQueen. He only used my middle name when he was serious.

The second name was Emily/Em. Last name Edens. Emily Edens—perfect. The only name I may never forget. Her address showed she was a professor in the quantum physics department at Columbia. I knew it; she was a teacher. I liked to be right. I was wrong about her name, but I'd stick with *M* for the sake of my already tattooed heart. She *must* have the ToE.

The third name was two names paired with one address—Juno and Yogi Mangku and the Deeksha in Kathmandu. No doubt that was an ashram. There was a second location for the yogi but no street address—Badhrahni, Nepal.

Why had Dylan compiled the list, sending it to his PO box? He couldn't have expected me to find it, though he had included the post office address and the box's combination at the top of the letter. *Why not include a copy of the elusive theory?*

I smiled when the answer came to me in Dylan's voice. *Couldn't be sure you'd get here first, old buddy. Anyway, where's the suspense in that?*

I had no problem answering in kind. *Nice. A beautiful quantum physicist and a theory of everything that illuminates the grand illusion. But what I really want to know is, what is big love?*

CHAPTER 7

NO THEORY OF EVERYTHING, but I was still excited by my discovery. I went directly from Dylan's mailbox to my favorite Korean barbecue and beer place in Koreatown to celebrate the people to be trusted. The PTBTs. The elevator to the second floor transported me to the heart of Seoul, where my Western face was a curiosity.

I was enjoying Tsingtao beers with a tasty steak, prepared on a hot stone in front of me, when Bob Marley's "No Woman, No Cry" started to play. That song had carried me for nine years. I raised my beer in tribute.

My cell phone kept me company as I googled the names on the PTBT list and found a significant amount of information on M and Juno. M's listings were mostly about her work as a professor, a quantum cosmologist, at Columbia. Along with the many scholarly articles she wrote, there was an article in the *New Yorker* that caught my eye. Its focus was the impact of quantum physics on the arts, and the accompanying picture of Professor Edens was captioned "Quantum Beauty."

Based on her scientific expertise and her reaction when I asked about the theory, she must have a copy of the theory and be Dylan's brilliant and beautiful scientist friend he referenced in his letter—the one that called it the ToE. The ToE it would be! Pleased with my powers of deduction, I ordered another beer and another cut of steak to celebrate sexy intellect.

Juno was a musician, artist, designer, and master chef. My search suggested she was a master of all things artistic and spiritual. She was also a reluctant celebrity in Kathmandu, her appeal only increased by her desire for anonymity. Her refusals to meet with famous and powerful people, take interviews, or allow herself to be photographed had the perverse effect of adding to her mystique. Juno, with just one name, was an almost mythical being. There was only one picture of her, and in it she emanated an ethereal beauty from a slender and small but shapely frame. But it was her eyes—like skylights open to the infinite consciousness of a saint—that drew me in.

Juno owned and managed a social hub/art gallery/spa/teahouse/resort called the Deeksha. Apparently the Deeksha served the most wonderful food, which Juno prepared, but it was not to be called a restaurant. As a Chinese expat, she seemed to lord it over Kathmandu like a Rick of Casablanca. Her poetic writings mused about spirit and nature fused in art and meditation practice.

The only reference to Yogi Mangku was on the Deeksha's site, a description of a monthlong yoga retreat that the yogi and two of his students provided each year. Those students, twins, apparently taught yoga at the Deeksha year-round. Beyond that one mention, Yogi Mangku didn't seem to exist. With such a slight internet footprint, he likely lived completely off the grid. The retreat materials referenced his "vow of complete Truth to the way," which perhaps made him unfit company for mere mortals.

Badhrahni was hard to find, but after some effort, I found it—a small ethnic village—in the wilderness outside of Kathmandu.

Dylan's PTBT list was an odd mix of scientific, artistic, and spiritual. I was one-dimensional and conventional compared to the accomplished and enigmatic group. *But I did make the list. And as the first name.*

At that moment, with steak in my belly and beer in my bloodstream, I was illuminated by an all-encompassing inspiration to write the novel Dylan had suggested I write and start it at the point Dylan's letter arrived. The story could end in Stockholm, with Dylan posthumously winning a Nobel Prize for his discovery. Of course, I would rediscover the ToE, fueling my bonfire of imagination.

I fell back in my chair.

This is it, the blank book you handed me in my dream the day you died.

I sipped my beer as ideas flew at me in a stream of constant creation.

I'd heighten the drama by having Dylan killed by a revered scientist looking to purloin his theory, while my character becomes the sleuth that solves the mystery and almost dies from the same untraceable poison that killed his best friend. But my hero is saved, at the last minute, by an antidote that can be transmitted only by sexual intercourse with a beautiful quantum biologist who has developed the antibody, at great risk, within her own body. My hero's lover almost dies from using her body as a test tube, but she lives when the hero . . . well, when he does something heroic.

I quickly emptied my writer's bag of notebook and pens to capture the sophomoric fantasy of an overripe freshman novelist, high on beer and discovery, who would have to do some medical research when sober. I argued with myself—if life could be created in the body through sex and disease could be transmitted that way, why couldn't a healing antibody to some fictional poison be transmitted via sex? Maybe it would make more sense if he injected her with the lifesaving seed. It also might be more metaphorical truth than medical science, as my hero was dying from abstinence.

I'd have to find the ToE, but that shouldn't be too hard. Dylan would have saved copies somewhere.

The novel's new direction was exciting, and shedding the macabre dead wife rotting in the funeral-parlor attic of my mind was liberating. A genre shift was like taking on a new identity. The hood of Poe was lifted, and I raised the beer of Hemingway and drained it dry. Maybe more Sir Arthur Conan Doyle . . .

A table of four young American Korean or Korean American ladies had taken notice of me and my onslaught of epiphanies and chugging of beer. They were open in their expressions of interest in the older man so excited by steak and beer, now madly writing his arousing fiction. Their coy way of acting impressed might have been mockery, but I chose to accept it as flattery.

I returned to the excitement of the novel's new direction, already a passionate calling. I called for another beer so they couldn't ask for their table back now that I was finished ordering steak.

While writing the novel—perhaps it would be more character driven—I would pursue fodder and inspiration by meeting with Dylan's three other people to be trusted. I determined to use the names of the people I met in my fiction. I'd have to change them eventually to protect their privacy—and protect myself against lawsuits. But if I used real names, I was bound to remember them and keep them straight. Emily Edens . . . My M would be the exception. She was already my fictional Brigitte. Changing her name would give me more liberty to do what a man must do.

The idea of traveling to Nepal to research the novel rather than spend the entire summer on the fourth floor in Chelsea was an enticing fantasy. I hadn't enjoyed the thrill of exotic travel for nine years now. Hope's death had left no desire for destinations reachable beyond subway rides and car trips of less than a few hours.

In reality I knew I'd end up staying put this summer too, but floating on beer and enthusiasm, I could fantasize for a few moments.

In my novel, Juno would be a goddess befitting her name, and the yogi would be a transcendent man of absolute Truth who might have the power to disappear at will, as I've read certain yogis can do. I could research them from the safety of my Chelsea apartment and use my imagination for their character development. I still held out hope that medical research would allow my hero to be saved in that singular fashion.

Even if I didn't venture to Nepal, the PTBT list provided me the perfect excuse to see M again, and she *could* be reached by subway. Professor Edens would be my first target after I read everything she'd written. Given that first feckless meeting, I'd have to finesse my approach. Less Jerry Lewis and more Dean Martin.

A femme fatale, the mysterious death of my best friend, a lost theory, and a work of fiction all arriving in the course of a few days meant a watershed week for me. And this was only the beginning. I would solve the mystery of Dylan's death, and of course I'd find his theory. I smiled to think that this was the collaboration we both would have wanted—a story about Dylan and his ToE but totally under my artistic control.

A theory of everything must be invaluable, and people had loved and died for less.

Still, I was determined to write a work of fiction. My view of fiction was the past remembered or the future imagined. Nonfiction is only and always now.

As I sat writing ideas in a beer-and-steak-fueled passion, one of the young Korean American ladies sauntered over to my table. Her friends giggled and blushed as they pretended not to watch. My attractive suitor said, "My name is Mi Na. Would you be so kind as to autograph my book?"

She handed me what appeared to be a diary. With the innocence of one with nothing to hide, she widened her eyes, letting me inside. She might have mistaken me for an actor—it's been said I look like Tom Hanks. Or she was mocking me or flirting. Didn't matter. I lowered my pen and wrote, "To the courageous, lovely, and wonderful Mi Na, who recognized a great novelist before he was discovered by the rest of the world." I didn't choose modesty but did exercise restraint by not adding my phone number to my sweeping signature.

When I handed back her diary, she gave me a look, which I returned with a shrug of *if only I were younger. . .* She gracefully bowed in taking her leave. I ached with each step until she sat and flashed me a smile.

I was reminded of the mental interpretation of reality and its impact on reality and imagination. Mi Na had come at just the right time as a booster shot of confidence before I saw M again. I believe Mi Na saw in me the promise of that moment, so that promise became my reality.

I saw everything through the glasses of my unconsciously engrained beliefs. Those included the belief that reality was a dreamlike mental projection. In a word, an illusion. A nonreligious Buddhist, I recoiled at dogma or man-made law but revered dharma or natural law. Though I believed one should not judge, I judged. And I tended to put the people I met into a good or a bad basket. Mi Na was good. I rationalized this practice by telling myself my decision merely reflected whether the person was egocentric or love-centric, to coin a term.

This predisposition to judge others was amplified by the reignition of my imagination and by the fantastic events I anticipated were coming to me. I could envision multiple universes of possible realities based on what was playing out in the real world. In *my* world. My life would impact my fiction, and my fiction would impact my life.

Half an hour later, my last beer gone, Mi Na was competing with my writing for my attention. She'd become more attractive with each beer.

I paid the check, and on the way out I looked hard into Mi Na's eyes and said, "Good night, Mi Na. And thank you."

She said, "Good night, Sean. And thank you. You're already a great novelist to me."

Her friends giggled. I'd swear she was sincere.

CHAPTER 8

THE NEXT MORNING THE C TRAIN crept north, with me on my way to watch M give her last lecture at Columbia before their summer break. Between each stop, I replayed the spotlight scene from the Quaker meeting house, complete with the recognition in M's eyes when I asked about Dylan's theory. As one of Dylan's people to be trusted and a scientist, she must have worked with Dylan on the ToE and therefore would likely have a draft, if not the final theory.

M was just old enough for her role as Brigitte, the novel's thirty-five-year-old leading lady. I was living inside my novel now, populating it with fictionalized versions of real people, and curious where imagination and reality would lead me. The real me was already more than a bit smitten, which added an element of nervous anticipation to the upcoming encounter.

The train stalled at the 72nd Street stop, underground from The Dakota, where John Lennon had lived and been shot dead. If the subway didn't start moving soon, a simple twist of fate might foil my entire plan and change the course of destiny.

It did, however, start up again and delivered me to 125th Street. I still had to find the lecture hall and gain admission to the building. Security on all campuses was tight for both proprietary and mass-shooter concerns. At NYU in Greenwich Village, I'd barely noticed the fuss, since I had the easy-pass provided to tenured professors, but here I was entering Columbia in West Harlem, a foreign country, without a visa.

The Columbia campus was more striking than I remembered. But all of life is vivacious on a sunny spring day. The student body was lit up and joyful too, transitioning into summer by removing as much clothing as society would allow. The beauty of birds and human nature resonates directly with the vibration of the day, perking up in the sun and drooping in the rain. It was a perky day.

Using the campus map on my phone, I easily found the science department's ivy-covered building on the main mall. At security in the lobby, I presented my NYU credentials with a feigned confidence that I'd be admitted without delay.

The security guard said, "These are passes for NYU. This is Columbia University."

"So it is," I said, sounding haughtier than I intended. "But I know the dean of literature here." We had met only once and at a party. I didn't recall his name.

"This is the science department, not literature," the guard observed.

"So it is." In for a penny . . . "People write literary works about science too, you know. There's a whole genre called science fiction. I'm sure the dean would expect me to be offered the professional courtesy of admission. Should we call him?"

The guard took note of the line forming behind me; looked me over once again, no doubt concluding that I appeared harmless; and honored my middle-aged white privilege and let me pass.

Following my fraud, I passed through the metal detector without detection, though I felt like an outlaw packing a gun. I located the room where the lecture would be held with five minutes to spare. Not wanting to be conspicuous and determined to properly reintroduce myself after class as a member of the exclusive PTBT club, I sat at the back as the large lecture room filled to capacity.

After all the years on the other side of the lectern, sitting in class among the students was exciting and intense. Memories rushed in, but today's perspective was heightened by what Blake called imaginative innocence, the transcendent state one might reach after innocence and experience. Here I was an innocent student again.

M came out to the lectern, and we noisy, excited students became mum as she commanded the classroom through the force of her presence and intellect. Columbia used excellent stage lighting that brought clarity to her features and expressions, and the acoustics of the lecture hall were also finely tuned. It was only the two of us, despite the hundred other students, and I could almost smell her sensual scent from over thirty feet away.

She lectured with grace and fluidity on the wave-particle duality challenge raised by quantum physics. Her lecture style recalled the way young professors who loved their field spoke, inspiring and commanding the attention of her rapt audience—lecture as a religious experience. Her clarity, voice, and word choices allowed me, a man with no scientific background, to follow the grand ideas found in the very small, "as the nature of the quantum dances in and out of view." She half danced herself, swaying as she had at the wake. Her beauty brought into focus the outer limits of the observable universe, luring me and the entire class to the precipice of the infinite mystery beyond.

She suggested that the wave-particle duality was mirrored by our inability to know momentum and location of a particle at the same time.

When she made the analogy to my favorite Zeno's paradox, I was embarrassed that—like a high school student who couldn't control himself even in a classroom—I became physically aroused. The erotic tension between mathematically not being able to get to a place ahead of us because we always have to go halfway there first and the experience that we do actually arrive had always stopped my mind and sent a rush of blood from my heart to the other organ of love.

Luckily, the horizontal desk obscured my vertical embarrassment. As I fidgeted in an attempt to straighten things out, M might have looked up from the stage and seen me squirming. I looked down, frozen like an ostrich statue, so as not to see if I was seen in my comical indignity.

M ended the lecture by saying, "We have to consider consciousness as the witness and cause, determining whether the photon appears as a wave or a particle. Perhaps pure consciousness, without thought, *chooses* to see it in motion or isolated in location, the result of which our thinking minds and instruments may then measure and record. Quantum physics suggests consciousness is the fundamental field in which all physical phenomena occur. The study of consciousness is the next great scientific frontier."

With that climax, the students spontaneously rose and gave her a standing ovation for the final class of the semester. I felt fortunate to join the celebration of a most wonderful teacher. My blood had returned to my heart and mind.

I didn't have much time to get to the head of the class before she would be gone, a trail of students with questions in tow. Because of my self-consciousness as I came down the stairs and the way she looked at me—she *was* looking at me—I felt like an assassin approaching his target. She clearly recognized her stalker from Dylan's wake.

When I reached her, what I had imagined to be a grimace of horror was actually a welcoming smile. Though students awaited her attention, that attention was turned entirely to me.

I apologized with my rehearsed lines of reintroduction. "I'm so sorry to intrude again. I'm a literature professor at NYU, as well as the abrupt man from the funeral service for Dylan." I added cryptically—and, I hoped, enticingly—the prescripted, "May we speak in private? In a way, I've heard from Dylan, and I really need to speak to you."

"Sean, right?" She beamed as bright as a spring bulb about to reveal its flower. "I was a bit distraught and put it together only after the service. Dylan told me all about Sean. I'm so sorry. Please come to my office."

I imagined what Dylan had said about me as we walked down the corridor and she quickly dealt with her students' questions and crushes. *My best friend, so much promise. A bit of a lost soul since his wife died.*

What exactly did you say?

Dylan's devilish silence tortured me.

At her office door, the students dispersed. Her office was full of her presence and the luscious scent of spring. She had an eye for the smallest detail but had created a relaxed décor. Paintings and photos of simple but dramatic quantum and cosmic art adorned the walls with color and vibrancy, giving the uncluttered room a sense of multiple dimensions. Light poured in from large open windows that overlooked the sunny quad below. Her office made mine feel like a dark dorm room. And every detail drew my focus to the center of that radiant awareness, to M herself.

She laughed. "You look more innocent and wide-eyed than my students. Dylan told me . . . Well, excuse me. I don't have much time, or I'd offer you a drink and a seat."

We stood face-to-face, eyes connecting. I had to say something to stave off a blush. "I'm still high from your magical lecture on the effervescent and ephemeral nature of our reality."

"You're a good student, I see, with an impressive vocabulary." I must have looked like a student who just got scolded, because she added, "Sorry. Dylan told me you were sensitive but with a good sense of humor."

Studying a solar-powered gyre spinning on the windowsill, I pretended to look uninterested in what Dylan had to say. *So that's what you told her. Damning me with faint praise?*

"And I'm sorry for so abruptly and rudely leaving Dylan's service," she said, drawing my eyes back to hers. "I thought you were there with the chairman of my department and that he'd sent you to question me."

"Don't be so sorry. But I don't know your chairman. And I'm the one who needs to apologize for my behavior and for startling you with insensitive questions and without a proper introduction. Sounds like you know that I've known Dylan since elementary school. We'd planned to meet for dinner on the evening of his death to discuss his theory of everything and then potentially collaborate on a book to help promote that theory."

"You have the theory?" she asked.

"No. I assumed you did."

Her face said no. I felt great disappointment, but she looked crushed.

"In his last letter to me," I said, "Dylan included a New York City PO box address and some numbers I guessed were its combination. In that box I found a letter, actually a list of people to be trusted with the theory of constant creation. We share the honor of being on the short list, and we're the first names Dylan included." I teased her by holding up the copy of the PTBT list I had brought. I would show how humble I was by not pointing out the very first name on the list was mine.

M's face lit up again, even more dazzling in her excitement. "Who else is on the list? I worked with Dylan on his research, and he was going to present me the final theory on this last trip to New York. He thought the theory solved entanglement, and I was very much looking forward to studying and working more with him on it. I wonder where the theory is and if others on the list have it."

I boldly declared, "I'm going to find it!" I felt myself blush, so I added, "I do sound like an excitable schoolboy. Excuse my enthusiasm."

"It is exciting, and I love your enthusiasm. Dylan was—" She checked her wall clock and shook her head. "I have a meeting in fifteen minutes, a fifteen-minute walk away. Perhaps we could arrange to meet again." She picked up papers from her desk and slid them into a stylish academic bag that married serious briefcase and Italian pocketbook without boasting a discernable brand name.

I was ahead of her as we headed to the office door. "How about an early dinner this evening?"

"Maybe, yes," she replied. "I'm free tonight. Let me give you my phone number."

"No need." I handed her the copy of Dylan's exclusive list and pointed at her number.

The list was the best calling card. She accepted it as though I was handing her a diploma and placed it carefully in her bag as we left the office.

Once back in the light of day, we shook hands goodbye—my first touch of her high-frequency radiance, held one beat longer than might be expected. It was a meaningful handshake for me and a touch more than a purely professional academic parting. I was already imagining a kiss.

I watched her until she disappeared across the lawn filled with buzzing pupils and sunbathers stretched out under flying Frisbees. I then called Momofuku Ko, wanting to impress M and feeling cheated out of a dinner there. She was splurgeworthy. They had an early reservation at six thanks to a cancelation. I hoped the maître d' wouldn't recognize me and that my date would show up this time. I texted M the time and place, adding, "My treat."

M's immediate response was "That's great!" accompanied by a thumbs-up emoji.

I didn't find the ToE, but I was going on a date with M!

I lay down on the great lawn and looked up at the blue sky, taking my full measure of sun. As if on cue, my blood started surging, and like a vampire, it wanted more. Old soundtracks started playing in my head, declaring that I'd be like Jagger or Bowie that night, *slipping her the convincer*, as those Brits would say. No professor's blue blazer or tweed this evening. I'd wear a black tailored jacket and white Nehru cotton shirt to project a New York, Lou Reed–type artistic sensibility.

The rock-and-roll voices of the dress rehearsal playing in my mind were more easily dismissed now than when I was young, though I'd always been more a romantic in my actions than in my thoughts. Thankfully, the voices struck me as comical and dated and nothing like the way real men would act. Yet it was strange how those old repetitive thoughts had returned. It occurred to me that those "real men" were all quite androgynous.

I'd thought my body and mind were no longer young enough for the torture of passion, particularly unfulfilled passion, and yet I was already more than a few steps outside my cherished comfort zone. The crazy chatter of lustful thoughts was not a welcome intrusion on my loftier aims for M and my promise to find her the ToE. Maybe I'd have to go to Kathmandu after all. Dylan must have left a written version of the theory somewhere to be found.

But your ToE can wait. I'm going on a date with M tonight!

CHAPTER 9

THE MOMOFUKU KO MAÎTRE D' offered a deadpan "Welcome back" as he led me to my oval table. M was already seated in my blue seat, a bucket of white wine chilling next to her.

I became self-conscious in my black jacket, white shirt, and skinny blue jeans. Just another cliché, more metrosexual than artist. Only a person who is not an artist thinks an artist dresses a certain way. Damn my lack of authenticity and insecurity.

To make matters worse, M wore a simple and elegant red dress perfectly suited for the mod décor. Something Brigitte Bardot would wear to a café on the Left Bank on a warm spring evening.

To avoid an awkward greeting as I took my red seat, I motioned— yes, awkwardly—for her to stay seated.

From that moment till the end of the evening, that oval table and its two chairs were all that existed. The rest of the lounge retreated like the night sky of our ever-expanding universe; I had done my homework in preparation for my date with a quantum cosmologist. We floated in a small pod, the oval and the chairs ensconced within a transparent egg. With our approval, the servers could penetrate the permeable force field for just the time needed to earn their Michelin stars.

M's vibrant red dress—draped artistically over her smooth, oil-softened skin—created a striking contrast to the gray world of the city and the black-and-white pages I had dwelled in for nine years. Her face, her elegant shape and beauty, were a work of art on an Yves Klein–blue easel less than three feet away.

M rescued me from my frozen gaze by breaking the ice. "Hello, fellow person to be trusted. I'll let you treat to dinner if you let me treat the wine."

"Thank you, my PTBT. That is, person to be trusted."

She was kind and offered me another lifeline, saying, "My father was a xenophile and Francophile and passed those traits and his extensive wine cellar to me. I've taken to bringing my father's mostly French and Italian wines to restaurants and paying the cork fee, drinking wines I couldn't possibly afford these days in restaurants. To celebrate tonight, I brought a bottle of white Burgundy and a red Burgundy. Only premier crus—I'm saving the grand crus for when we find the ToE. We don't have to, probably shouldn't, drink both."

I was relaxing, getting into the groove even before my first sip with this perfectly aged grand cru lady. "I hope we will drink both in celebration of Dylan. I enjoyed your lecture; you're a great teacher."

"Thank you," she said. "I wasn't sure what you were thinking. You looked agitated when I brought up Zeno's paradox."

My chest began to pound, and heat flashed over me as I started to squirm. "No, no, the inclusion of the paradox was great and perfectly placed. It just brought up strong memories. I loved that paradox when I was young—*ger*." I coughed to clear an imaginary tickle from my throat. "I also enjoyed your grand finale on how consciousness interacts with the physical world."

M gave me a smile, and my furnace glowed at the strike of the match. I removed my sport coat and draped it over my chair, since I didn't want my internal heat to show as beads of sweat.

As I was undressing, M said, "Next semester, based in large part on my work with Dylan, I plan to teach a course on consciousness itself and how it might direct the outcome of probabilities of our quantum reality and how one consciousness or universal mind might explain the mystery of entanglement. I'm struggling with keeping the course scientifically grounded and hoped Dylan and his theory would have helped me there. That's why I'm so glad you committed to finding the ToE."

Her eyes smiled as her lips focused their attention on me. Or something close to that. My rational mind was crashing in her presence. I cautioned myself to stay coherent and impress her with my words. Words were the tools of my trade and my way to connect with this Eve of Edens.

But no clever words came. I needed some wine first.

The server had come to pour the 2009 white Meursault premier cru that was now properly chilled. A tasting was provided to us both, even though we couldn't send the bottle back. The waitress was the same young woman who'd brought me two glasses of lowly Chablis and the amuse-bouche that I made a meal of ten days before. Her expression said she was glad my date had shown up this time. She laid the same tasty morsels on the table and listed the ten ingredients of the one bite.

M held out the plate for me to take my first taste. "Mmm—an amusing little bouche."

She raised her glass. "To Dylan and the constant creation theory. And speaking of Dylan . . . let's play a game he taught me, seeing who can follow the 'finish' of their first sip farther, before, as Dylan put it, 'all the tingle of taste remaining in your tongue's consciousness fades back into nothing. A game of heightened sensibility.'"

As the competition commenced, excitement radiated from my mouth and into my body, amplified by my first deep dive into M's lovely nut-brown eyes. Not just my tongue but my entire mouth tingled with the taste of tenderly aged fermented grape and the hint of crisp mineral and honeydew melon. Sharing this sensuality with M, so early in our relationship, was an erotic christening for my lips and tongue.

We sat in still silence, staring into each other's eyes in this sensational sport. *Following the finish* was like following a bell's ring to its final audible vibration. Like Zeno running naked halfway and then halfway again and again to the end of sensation. As the last taste of grape faded, I gestured, silently indicating my finish so as not to disturb her own finish with sound.

"Well, that was fun," she said to conclude the tasting.

"I'm glad you won."

She tilted her head, considering my words, before smiling with her eyes and lips again.

The server was good and had watched the long-sip finish from the wings of our spaceship-egg before filling our glasses and bringing over the lengthy tasting menu. Since there was no choice and neither of us had food allergies, it was more playbill than menu.

I said, "I suggest we opt for the eight-course menu." *Four hours with you, if you please.* In M's company, there would be no limit to time or money.

"Sounds wonderful." She swirled her wine like a sommelier. "I think I might have a fine palate. Or maybe I just really like wine. I want to be a winemaker someday, when I'm ready to leave Columbia. My father was a successful entrepreneur and died last year of brain cancer. He had led the dishonest life of a serial philanderer, and we had become estranged until his cancer came. My mother died young of a broken heart. My father's illness strangely made him more lucid and compassionate right up to his passing, a month after his diagnosis. He showed a love and particularly an honesty I hadn't seen in the healthy man. He had a peaceful death."

She paused only to find I was not good at giving or receiving condolences. It had taken me over two hours and ten drafts to write Natalie Byrne a two-line expression of sympathy.

"While he was dying, I worked on forgiveness, and we worked together to establish a large charitable trust—made possible from the proceeds of his estate and that I now administer—to be used to establish a nonprofit winery and college when I'm ready to manage it. Dad was a liberal enough thinker to provide allowance for the winery to grow marijuana. My thought is to make it a college for impoverished young adults, where they can live, work, and learn a craft. There would be once-a-week wine and weed tastings, and I've already reserved the trademark and domain name: Vine and Weed.

"Oh my, you are a good listener."

She leaned toward me in half-bowing embarrassment or gratitude, causing me to admire her lovely form, barely contained by the red dress.

"Thank you." I shook my head to loosen my tongue. "I've been told that, but I really am interested, and I'm so sorry to hear about your father."

"And now Dylan. The men in my life seem to die suddenly and unexpectedly, so you better watch out."

I could have said the same thing about the women in my life, but that truth seemed too significant to share so soon.

The first plate came, and I didn't follow the introduction, as I was thinking about what to say next. I took a bite. "That's effervescent and ephemeral, just like your quantum."

She seemed to appreciate my humor.

"I've read and have come to believe that female wine producers, like Merry Edwards, are now producing some of the best wines." Hers was the one name I could always remember. "It makes sense that women would have a finer palate."

"Why is that?" M asked.

"Darn it, did I just fall into a sexist pothole? They are so hard to navigate these days. Well, I generally find women more open and sensitive and in tune with beauty."

M laughed. "Women are ascending in all fields after being shut out for centuries. Music is a leading indicator; women's lyrics and music are blazing new trails, especially for the young. Muses stepping out with their songs and messages."

"Like Patti Smith?" As I dropped the name, I realized how it dated me.

"Yes, though I was thinking of more current artists. But I love Patti Smith too."

I bit my tongue to keep from blurting out Beyoncé or Aimee Mann in my defense, since I couldn't name a song by either artist and didn't want to be a complete poseur. Instead, I moved on to more solid ground. Riffing on the women-in-music theme, I turned the topic to the historical impediments to and prejudices toward female authors. I then took a great risk and inched close to the edge. "However, these days it seems the whole literary industry is populated with women, and most fiction readers are women. If any prejudice remains, women have themselves to blame."

I looked to see how this landed. She smiled slyly, sensing my fear. "Really? But yes, women do need to support women in all professional spheres."

We went on to discuss the books we liked, and though I had the home-field advantage within the library of my mind, M held her own and had a fine palate for authors.

The white Burgundy was very good, and we finished quickly, lubricating our lips and words. Waiting on course number two, I took pictures of the wine labels to show my appreciation of her fine vino. As the red 1999 Domaine de la Romanee-Conti's Vosne-Romanee premier cru Cuvee Duvault-Blochet was poured, I was again thinking about sharing a kiss with those exquisite full lips while diving into those soft brown eyes. Delaying that premature gratification, I suggested, "Round two on following to the finish?"

She smiled yes, yes, yes. We held the wine and each other's eyes for an eternity that passed in a minute, in which we seemed to share one consciousness between us. We came to completion at the same moment, finishing together.

She said, "Wow, a dead heat!" and laughed. I was speechless but laughed like a schoolboy, sharing her high vibrational frequency. The wine was starting to take effect. Our spacecraft-egg was taking off!

The red was a magical elixir that transported us into a cask built for two. Our space pod was now enclosed in oak, and we were two pickling fish happily fermenting while enjoying wonderful food as our intimacy grew. We swam around each other in the dance of charming, first-blush conversation.

I was studying the wine label as if I knew what I was looking for when it hit me.

M said, "You look like you want to yell *eureka*. What is it?"

I hesitated, trying to find an explanation that didn't sound as silly as my belief. "The synchronicity of nine keeps popping up in my life." I raised the bottle and read the year on the label. "Nineteen ninety-nine. Do you know what your seat number was at Dylan's wake?"

"Yes," she said. "Nine. Funny that the pews had seat numbers."

"I thought so too. And I don't think I told you, but you know what the combination was to Dylan's mailbox, where I found our list?"

"I'm guessing it's got a lot of nines?"

"Eureka! Nine, nine, nine!" I shouted like a drunk Nazi emphatically crying *no*, forgetting that our spaceship-egg was not a cone of silence floating there among the Michelin stars. I continued in a softer voice as the other patrons returned their attention to their tables. "I hope you don't think I'm strange, but I just remembered that for much of my life, although not for years now, I believed in a conscious design to the universe, one reflected in my literary mind as some omniscient communication with us through words and signs. Inspiring words from a letter or a book or a person or even from within your own mind that come at just the right time to guide you to your purpose and meaning in life."

I paused when a wave of fear and vulnerability splashed over me. M was an iridescent deep-sea mermaid, and I was a mere black-and-white mortal clumsily wading about in the shallow end of the pool.

Yet M appeared undaunted, her eyes and smile supplying the support I needed to continue.

"I know it doesn't sound at all scientific, but I've read that the subconscious tends to find patterns that support our beliefs and then orders our lives accordingly. Something akin to Jung's collective unconscious. Or maybe it's just self-fulfilling prophecy. That is, my belief in the significance of nines—and synchronicity, more generally—means that that is what I experience and see when I'm open to it."

I twisted my napkin under the table, fearing I might have put M off. "I haven't been open for some time. Don't get me wrong, I don't believe in numerology. And I don't really know what I am talking about. The wine—"

M gave me that smile. "I don't think your belief in intelligent design and synchronicity is far-fetched. It sounds like the observer effect of quantum mechanics. I'm studying the possibility that there is an omnipotent universal consciousness that may be able to communicate through our consciousness. One universal mind. Dylan and I discussed this at length in connection with his developing theory. He—*we*—believed entanglement and telepathy are related phenomena."

Still feeling a bit exposed and competitive with my dead friend, I said, "Once you have a theory of everything, it seems everything else would just fall into place. Perhaps he had nothing left to live for. Or in discovering the grail, got killed by those who wish to keep it secret?"

My overuse of offensive wit and irony—pushing beyond boundaries—was why Dylan had called me One Step in college. I often went one step over the line when I was excited.

Luckily, M didn't judge me, saying only, "We'll see. As far as Dylan's death is concerned, I've heard nothing to cause me to think it was murder." She shuffled in her seat. Time was moving in slow motion and long-held intriguing glances.

I was prepared to dial up my own suspicions to add to the excitement of the first date, but before I could titillate the conversation further, another of the eight courses arrived. Each course was delightful but immediately forgotten in the next moment because of our flowing conversation.

She said, "My relationship with Dylan was a philosophical affair; I knew, of course, he was married."

I sighed, perhaps too loudly, and she smiled at my childish rivalry.

"He reminded me of my first love in high school, a romantic poet. In Dylan's last letter to me, he expressed his total confidence in the truth of the theory that had only recently been fully revealed to him. He said he would share the fully realized theory when he returned to the city, and he invited me to stay at the Deeksha in Kathmandu when he went back in early July." She studied her wine after twisting the knife. "He told me such wonderful stories about the place and people there. Juno, one of the people to be trusted, runs the Deeksha. Dylan made it sound like nirvana, a peaceful haven, with Juno the wise teacher of love."

"Big Love?" I asked.

"Yes, he used those words."

"She sounds like a goddess." I was looking to make M jealous too, but she just laughed.

I could listen to M and look into those eyes all night, but I sneaked another glance at her red V-cut dress and sipped my wine. They went so well together. I was a good listener, so I continued to let her speak.

"When writing about the ToE, he conspicuously avoided saying *his* theory. The theory, he said, was a gift. Dylan thought creation was using him as its portal and messenger and that the ToE was probably being visited upon others around the world at the same time. He had the littlest ego and most brilliant mind of all the men I've known."

I felt jealous of my dead friend. Dylan's conviction and enthusiasm seemed to have been transmitted to M. As she spoke, her already animated features were lit from within. Her eyes and lips were intoxicating me with each rise and fall of her sweet breath.

"I hope you don't mind me speaking so much about him and the theory," she said. "I haven't had anyone I could speak to about him and our work together."

"Please. It's exciting. I'm not at all jealous. I'm truly interested and feel cheated not getting to see him and learn about the theory. He said you deserve a lot of the credit. In his letter he mentioned a lost theory of Einstein you provided him as inspiration for what became his theory of constant creation."

"Einstein's lost theory? Hmm, I did find an interesting—unknown—speculation of his, buried in Einstein's mountain of archives. That undeveloped theory of light did excite Dylan, but it may just have been one of Einstein's many thought bubbles that he later popped—" She paused, looking ravished and ravishing.

"What did Einstein say?"

"Simply that everything in our expanding universe is constantly traveling at the speed of light." She looked up at the heavens from our spaceship porthole, like the first astronaut looking down at earth. "And at the speed of light, time stops. Wow! The implications are mind blowing."

Time was suspended between our eyes and flushed cheeks. I felt like an overexcited stoned college student speaking about the infinite cosmos with the most radiant teacher of quantum cosmology, illuminating the light of consciousness in me.

"I heard Tesla said, 'Everything is light!' It sounds like he and Einstein may have agreed on that. But what about finding the ToE is important for science? I only vaguely understand that."

"Yes, but saying it is light is like saying it is love; do we really under-stand a thing after we give it a name? Dylan thought, and I hoped, the theory would answer the question of how entanglement works. To me, that's the key to unlocking the mystery of the universe. Are you famil-iar with entanglement? 'Spooky action at a distance,' Einstein called it." From her flashing eyes and waving hands, I could tell this was her Zeno's paradox. "A riddle even Einstein couldn't solve. Two particles separated by any distance are able to communicate instantaneously *if* they've first been connected. And they can communicate faster than the speed of light, yet according to Einstein, *nothing* with mass can travel faster than the speed of light."

I waxed poetic, saying, "Perhaps it's loving consciousness, which has no mass."

"Well, that is along the lines we were pursuing."

She took my musing seriously and seemed impressed. Score one for me!

Fearful of losing control of my words and excited by her talk of quan-tum physics, I returned to the prosaic. "Dylan suggested in his last letter to me that the scientific community's complete resistance to entertaining the theory was due to its challenge to existing laws of physics."

M shook her head. "Not so much a challenge to its laws but to its theories. Science always asks, *Where is that math?* or *Where is the proof?* and often forgets that most breakthroughs in scientific theory came from thought experiments and eureka moments. To Dylan, applying concepts or laws of astrophysics—that mostly worked in time and space for matter larger than quarks and strings—to the source of all time and space was like thinking that thought could be the source of thought."

"'I think, therefore I am' is one of the most laughable propositions of all of philosophy." I was showing off my dexterity with philosophy, my minor in college.

She smiled, so score two for me. I was on a roll.

"I believed Dylan was on to something, that it was futile to look for an all-encompassing theory of the physical world without including consciousness or the nonphysical as its source.

"He challenged me to think of the instant, each instant, of creation as a big bang, and so I've dusted off Zeno's paradox—which I now use in my lectures, as you know—to demonstrate how math fails as you move from one instant to the next, cutting time and space in half until they collapse into the instant from which they constantly emerge, or that in each instant the infinite light illuminates or projects the film that our senses and thoughts perceive as reality. Solving the question of how we get from one to zero and zero to one."

My heart was pounding out waves of blood to every cell of my body as the distance between us was constantly being cut in half.

Whether it was the wine or M herself, her introduction to Dylan's theory made sense in the excitement of the moment. My mind was a blank sheet she was writing upon, and my body was primed to a fine pitch.

A man familiar with words, I couldn't think of anything as fascinating as what she'd told me. Channeling Hope, I finally said, "It would be odd if a creator acted once and then abandoned creation."

After we drained the two bottles from Burgundy, I ordered a 2010 Margaux off the wine list, as I couldn't afford another Burgundy other than a much lesser class than we'd been drinking. We needed more wine for courses six through eight. Six was a medallion of Japanese Kobe steak, so we definitely needed more red.

I claimed to finish my first sip when she did, but I don't know that I did, as my mind was an empty ocean when I looked into her eyes. She approved of my choice of grapes with a silky smile.

As we took our first red bites of beer-fed and belly-massaged cow, M sang, "Yummy, yummy, yummy."

"I got love in my tummy." I didn't think she knew the song, even though she twisted her head and smiled. We ate in silence a few moments, the food delicious but not the star of the evening. At least not of my evening.

"A strange relationship developed between Dylan and the chairman of the science department at Columbia," M said, her empty fork waving freely. "He's the seventy-plus-year-old astrophysics professor who came over after you attempted to introduce yourself at the end of the wake. Dylan had been consulting the chairman on the big bang, black holes, dark energy, and the dark matter of astrophysics.

"What had begun as a cordial relationship apparently didn't end well, at least from the chairman's perspective. He was concerned that I was still meeting with Dylan after he had cut Dylan off. If within his power, I think he would have demanded I stop meeting with Dylan too. He went so far as to say Dylan was delusional and that he didn't think we should be encouraging his very misguided and overly simplistic views. In a very long email, he wrote something along the lines of 'The university certainly wouldn't want any association with this man or his fairy-dust concepts.'

"When I saw the chairman at the wake, I found it strange he would attend a service for Dylan. However, he was fixated on Dylan in a strange way and perhaps felt remorse for how their relationship ended. I can't conceive of the chairman murdering a man or even arranging a murder—not out of any sense of humanity but because he's a man in a bubble and very circumscribed in his actions and thoughts. Oh, that sounds judgmental."

She shook herself in mild self-reproach. Her use of *circumscribed* made me glad we'd just met and she didn't know me last week.

"But if you met him, you'd understand and see my description of him is somewhat objective." She gestured at the table. "Plus, I've had a lot of wine."

A pondering, perhaps disapproving, expression crossed her face.

I asked, "Are you okay?" I hoped she hadn't become disconcerted by the intensity of my focus upon her that increased with each glass of wine. I was in a constant state of Dylan's *heightened sensibility.*

"I'm fine but perplexed. I'm just remembering that about a month ago I was woken by a call from the Columbia security department. Someone had broken into my office and failed in an attempt to hack my computer."

My big sigh of relief was a strange reaction to what she had said.

"If you'd ever been hacked, even unsuccessfully, you'd realize it makes you feel violated. The third failed attempt to get in had alerted university security. The friggin' hacker had tried variations of my dead dog's name and my dead father's and mother's names. If they had known of my dead boyfriend, they may have gotten into the system."

I thought about all the deaths she mentioned and that I should rethink my own password soon. As a tech illiterate, I didn't even know how one would change a password.

"When I met security there, the office was a mess, and it wasn't until the next day that I determined some files had been removed from my desk. One of those files, my Dylan file, was full of notes, emails, and letters from Dylan. It makes me sad to think of the loss."

I'd have to check my letter basket when I got home.

"Security believed it was a drunk or a drug-crazed student or a prank, and I'm not sure they even reported the break-in to the police. Security footage of the building showed a man with folders under his arm leaving around the time of the break-in, but the guy was careful to conceal his face with a hoodie. It wasn't the round body of my chairman, I can assure you. My biggest concern was that I might have a stalker, but I changed my locks and nothing came of it, so I'd almost forgotten it."

"That is strange," I said, "and if they were after info from Dylan, they wouldn't just take his file and be so obvious about it, would they? Dylan said the CIA had expressed interest in him and his theory and was watching him, had even broken into his room and maced him in Nepal."

She smiled dubiously. "Wow. Now his death is a mystery."

We finished our third bottle over courses seven and eight. I took little notice of the food but consumed every bite. Then our attentive waitress, whom I had also all but ignored from inside our egg, poured sweet dessert wine, on the house.

"Just what we need," I said. "After this, we're finished." I called after the kind waitress, trying to make amends: "Thank you, for the wine on the house and the wonderful meal and service."

For my novel, the evidence of murder was mounting in conspiratorial twists. I told M, "I'm going to follow up meeting people in the city who might know more about Dylan's death or the ToE. And if needed,

I'll contact Juno and the yogi from the people-to-be-trusted list to see if they know where it is. Dylan must have left the theory somewhere, and I will find it."

My proclamation served its purpose, as M was clearly impressed by my determined pursuit of Dylan's masterpiece.

I half-heartedly—for fear a full heart would be too forward—suggested, "You should join me in this quest and meet here in New York with those who may have the ToE."

She surprised me by saying, "Well . . . maybe. Yes."

I loved her ability to be in the moment with total spontaneity.

"Was that a maybe yes or a yes yes? I'll find the ToE for you!" I heard myself exclaiming.

"Thank you. But let's find it together, for science's sake."

Time paused as we gazed on in silence until a glass was dropped in the kitchen. That sound brought us back, and we noticed, despite our early arrival, we were the last table in the restaurant. Never wearing a watch, I checked my phone for the first time and saw, to my surprise, it was almost midnight. The staff had been kind in not rushing us out and remained gracious as we paid.

M said to me, "Let's leave, but I won't let you go until we have a plan."

We stepped outside and into the secluded courtyard out front that I had seen as a dark alleyway the night Dylan died, demonstrating the impact of perception. We found a bench there that cradled us until our plan was fully hatched.

With our course of action set, we sat in a moment of silence. I imagined that my novel's Brigitte would go with her hero to Kathmandu in quest for the theory of everything.

M ended the silence by saying, "Dylan told me a lot about Juno and the Deeksha and the yogi, since they were spiritual sources for his theory. He and I discussed my going back with him to the Deeksha in late June for a couple weeks. I wanted to hike the mountains and meet Dylan's amazing friends." She lifted her head and smiled. "I think he also planned to introduce the two of us while he was here in New York."

"Yes, he mentioned in his last letter that I should meet the beautiful quantum cosmologist or something like that."

"*Beautiful.* Hmm . . . Even now a woman's accomplishments always seem to fall second to her looks. Dylan and I had a deep mutual respect, but I guess we're all more or less a product of our gender and conditioning."

She folded her hands—concluding that topic? I hoped so but noted her point, determined to monitor my own deep-seated habit of noting a woman's physical attributes first. M was well blessed by all three elements of being: spirit, mind, and body. I was determined to be equally balanced in my appreciation.

"Maybe his wife or the police have the ToE," she said. "We should meet them first." She shook her head. "It's irrational, but I can't help being upset with him for not sending me his final work before he died. I know he didn't know he would die, but still . . . In any event, since my early summer plans with him are not to be, I'm free for a while for our investigations in the city. I don't leave for a fellowship in Athens until early July. I moved the date up, since now I won't be going to Kathmandu."

To say I was excited would be an understatement. I was experiencing an ecstatic state that I attempted to mask, though my wine-soaked eyes must have betrayed my true elation as I thought about the amount of time I would spend with M as cohort and co-sleuth traipsing about the city.

As I got a taxi to send M uptown, I weighed a kiss good night but thought, *Not yet.* I didn't want to risk the miraculous evening of our epic first date; there would be time later for kisses. And there was something in the way she held the moment that wasn't uninviting but which also didn't ask to be kissed. I opted for a hug, saying, "I'll find it for you and science." I concluded that my embrace was the perfect middle way to seal a friendship with the potential for more.

As her cab pulled away, I told myself, *Prufrock, it's just a kiss, and you are light-years from slipping her the convincer.* I recalled my novel's lifesaving sex scene that now I'd call "making love."

But I was flying drunk and oh so happy, like a teenager with my first love, racing in a convertible with the top down on my way to the Jersey Shore on the first day of summer, shotgunning beers all the way.

I would delay the hard work of actually writing the novel while gaining more material for it. I'd held back from telling M I was writing a novel, but something in me wanted to tell her everything.

What had Dylan told her about me that made her willing to eagerly become my partner in the mystery?

On the walk home, my drunken state encouraged my imagination to run wild before reason could suppress an overeager heart. Love burst out of me. Her eyes—her lips—her agile intellect—her breasts—her smile—her wit—her spontaneity and joy. Her presence. Her essence. Mmmmm . . .

Real love had caught up to the fictional love my novel's protagonist had already declared for his Brigitte. I had taken the leap. I saw that I had loved M from that proverbial first sight, smell, and touch. But I'd yet to taste and follow the finish backward to the source.

My life worked in quantum leaps when I loved. My first leap in high school had propelled me all the way to grad school. She was a strong Maud Gonne beauty and muse that challenged me to liberate myself and grow intellectually and artistically. To be free of parental superego. She was the Queen of Spades, and I was the broken Jack of Hearts. She left me for Italy and an older successful Italian man. I was unworthy.

Nine years after meeting my first love, Hope arrived and with her, another quantum leap in my imagination, my self-discovery, and my literary career. That time it was life that was not worthy of love.

And now nine years after Hope disappeared, M materialized. I didn't dare imagine that she might already share my love, but she was now the beloved after just one date. *May I be worthy to win that love and die first.*

This bursting bud of love didn't so much cause fear as bring courage forward. My belief in quantum leaps had been reinforced by a particularly convincing fortune-teller I met between my first love and Hope. She said she saw *Hope* in my future and that love was never lost. Finally she prophesied, "You need a beloved for your mind's eye to see."

My life had been circling a black hole of ever-decreasing radius, a comfort zone, since Hope died. And only a love, a true love, could release me from that gravitational pull. Now I was horrified to see what my life had become. Committing to break free of the abyss of fear I'd been circling for nine years, I determined to be fearless in pursuing M and the quest we had begun. It took Dylan's death, a theory of everything, a novel inspiration, and now, most importantly, my fledgling love for M to start me pulling free. I would fulfill my promise and win her love.

Back in my apartment, at one o'clock, Dylan's letter basket remained unmolested by the chairman's henchman and the CIA. Lying down to sleep, I spoke to Dylan.

I'm drunk, my dead friend. Thank you for your parting gift—the introduction to M. I hope she stays alive and my heart isn't broken again. I love M!

There, I said it. There was something liberating in confessing my love to Dylan. I knew he approved. I sat up and started to text M to tell her too.

Stop, you drunk fool! Way too soon.

His laughter followed me into unconsciousness.

CHAPTER **10**

I HALF WOKE AROUND NINE, falling in a descending spiral toward a crash landing. Icarus returning to earth with a hangover. And I was still in my silly skinny jeans that constricted, like a Chinese finger trap.

My forehead dotted by beads of sweat and my stomach roiling, I began to attack myself. *Why did you drink the sweet wine after all that Burgundy and Bordeaux?*

In remembering that sweet taste, I was drinking it again like backwash. This was the opposite of following the first sip to its finish. An alien was seeking escape from my gut.

I pretended to go back to sleep despite the discomfort, but my condemnation was wide awake.

Are you crazy? Love after a first date? How could you be a suitable suitor? She was probably in a relationship with someone younger, handsomer, and more accomplished. Someone who'd made love in the past decade.

I flopped over violently, looking for escape from my polluted body and shackled mind, and knocked my current literary love out of bed; it landed with a big bang. We had lost the passion we shared in college. We were done. I was tired of hearing for a second time everything that came fresh into Joyce's mind when he'd stumbled around dreary, drunken Dublin.

I could no longer pretend to sleep. Still, with Dylan dead, possibly murdered, caution was the best course; better to stay in bed hungover.

That was when a very unwelcome habit returned full force after years of lying dormant—a vigorous-to-violent two-handed face rub that came on when conflicting thoughts churned inside me with strong emotion. The last time I did the face rub was after Hope's funeral when I was alone in my bed. I deviated my septum with that rub.

The pendulum was swinging wildly between the star-bound elation of love last night to this quicksand morning. Love had ruptured my comfort zone; there was no going back. The ill feeling was no match for the flood of joyful memories of the first night with my newly minted beloved. I had M to think about now. Flesh and blood and spirit.

I managed to check my phone, and as I'd hoped, there was a text from M. Maybe last night she'd been drunk and was lovesick too and wrote to confess her love.

Dream on, Lord Byron. You weren't such a romantic hero in your skinny jeans, unable to summon the courage for a good-night kiss.

But still, I'd reward myself with reading the text when I was able to get up.

M's presence, even in her absence, was still with me, like a first sip that I didn't want to lose. Each sound of the letter *M* was a sip of magic morphine, drops of peace dripping into my muddled state, settling the murk and mire of mind. I repeated *M, M, M* in a calming self-hypnotism as I took my first deep breath in, cherishing the memories of the night before. I exhaled *Mmmmm.*

My anticipation of our next meeting was interrupted by the fear that she'd had second thoughts about going with such a new acquaintance to meetings with Dylan's widow, the detective in charge of Dylan's case, and the chairman of her department. Maybe her text was her canceling those meetings.

No, she was clearheaded and not fickle. It was her plan I was following, the one she'd given birth to on the bench in the romantic courtyard at midnight.

I swung my legs off the side of the bed, eager to claim my reward. Her text was better than a letter. I could respond right away, and she could respond to that response, like two birds singing.

Using *Ulysses* as a footrest, I raised my head to see her words. *Auspicious is the day!* I reminded myself, rising to the exclamation.

"Good morning, buddy! I drank too much but am so excited about our hunt for the ToE and suggest the code name Operation Creation in case our texts aren't safe." (winking-face emoji) "I've sent you an email with more details. Your PTBT." (thumbs-up emoji)

Buddy. With one word I was thrust into the friend zone and the door slammed shut behind me. She used emojis. She was younger than me. But our quest was on, and I'd find that damn door's key!

With that inspiration from M, I kicked *Ulysses* under the bed. After a visit to the bathroom, I moved slowly to my coffee maker that made one cup at a time and then to my reading chair to rest from all my exertion.

My mornings after were usually spent following the hangover down a gyre-like rabbit hole, making myself even more miserable by attacking myself with feelings of remorse. But instead of circling down, I was moving up that same rabbit hole through a hazy, colorful glow of pleasant reveries from the night before and looking forward to the adventure ahead. Looking forward to being with M again. Her eyes, her lips, the swells beneath the neckline of her dress, and her sexy intellect all still smiled on me. The sweet smell of honeysuckle that I'd almost tasted on her neck when we hugged good night hadn't left me. My new mantra was *M, my love*, followed by a quiet refrain of *Let me be worthy*.

I forgave myself for the damage done; it was wine, not heroin. Equilibrium and well-being were fully restored. The first date with M brought a passing pang of sadness, bittersweet, as I let go of the grief of losing Hope that I'd held for almost a decade. It was a miraculous feeling, the infusion of M and the release of grief. The return of love.

Though I took no pride in bravery, I had no fear of running into the unknown concerning Dylan's possible murder. I felt what can only be described as great appreciation and gratitude for Dylan. *All because you died*.

You rebounded quickly. What a maudlin confession of love you made last night. Good thing I stopped you from playing the fool.

Maybe it's time you told me about this big love of yours.

No answer came. I wondered whether it was a problem, this Dylan in my head.

I was a crazy fool, determined despite all odds to prove myself worthy. Yet I believed in love and had no doubt M's love could cure me. The ToE would be my letters of transit to consummate my new love. I was traveling into the unknown and would go anywhere to be with my queen of the quantum.

I started to text M back. "Creation takes two, buddy." Then I erased that beginning and wrote "Re Operation Creation: Do you think we need an encryption device, my PTBT?" (winking-face emoji) "I drank enough for both of us. Let's start with Natalie—I'll arrange that meeting. Let the quest begin!"

I omitted the heart emoji I desperately wanted to send, but I refused to debase the moment with a thumbs-up ending, opting for an exclamation point. I was an excitable boy who had made the quantum leap.

CHAPTER 11

OVER THE NEXT COUPLE OF DAYS, the quest plans were drafted over texts and emails—like two dancing streams of consciousness meeting to plot and project reality, yet onto computer screens rather than onto the pages of a book, as Joyce's lonely torrential stream had been. M was only to be found on the computer and iPhone, so I plugged in, dedicated to my electronic windows until I could see her again. For love, I'd fully embrace the technology I'd always cursed as the end of the world as we know it, wooing my love through modern means.

I became my novel's hero—the dashing lover—full of daring and cunning. I was a writer, and my words would win my love. I was an online Romeo courting my virtual Brigitte.

Interesting how fast I became a tech addict, with my phone always charged and set to ring. I always kept my phone in my pocket or hand, ready for the *ting* announcing incoming love or the *tap* to send love.

As fortune would have it, I was taking a piss when my phone *tinged*. Excited to read the message, I wrestled the phone from my pocket and fumbled it into the toilet between my legs. Disaster and ignominy had struck in one swift swoosh. I watched, my wet hand holding the small dying screen, as a twirling multicolor beach ball disappeared into black. I heard the snickering of an invisible clown mocking me behind the dead screen.

While all lines of communication slept in a bed of rice with my SIM card and phone, I became a junky jonesing for my next fix of M's words. I prayed the microchip brain just needed time to dry and would awaken before M slipped away like a fish off the hook. And how would I explain not responding first thing? I couldn't call her without my phone, as I had canceled my landline years ago.

Character is based on one's level of honesty, but I didn't want to admit the nature of the calamity. After the rice trick worked and Eve's bitten apple returned to power up my screen, I used my literary skills to navigate the truth.

M's message had inquired about our upcoming meetings and mentioned again the mystery of entanglement. She loved it. I replied: "M, thanks for all the quantum beauty. Sorry for the delayed response. I dropped my phone in a basin of water. Natalie is available on the twentieth from 4 p.m. on, if that works for you. I'm worried I've offended her by my distance over the past years. She didn't notify me of Dylan's death, and I couldn't share my condolences at the wake, though she saw me there and managed a smile. Your quest partner misses you. Sean."

M responded immediately. "You shouldn't use your phone on the toilet." (smiley face) "That works for me—let me know what time to pick you up. Miss you too, buddy. M—only for you!"

I did not confess, elaborate, or further fabricate in response. My embarrassment was offset by the joy that she—for the first time—specifically accepted, just for me, my shortening her short name. Good thing, since a tattoo on the heart is death to remove.

Over the next days, each night before bed I looked for an inspired excuse to text some heart-captivating message—an article from the entertainment press about Grace's father's death, lines of poetry, a note on synchronicity, something sublime from Keats or Einstein. I was thrilled with each response, even if they just said, "Sounds good," "That's right," or "We shall see."

One night I wrote, "William Powell and Myrna Loy are on the case," unable to edit myself even though I doubted she knew the *Thin Man* movies. She passed the test in the morning, writing, "I love Asta!"

Her emails were more substantive than her texts.

Buddy,
Thanks for arranging for us to meet Natalie tomorrow as a first step in our private investigation. She must know more than we

do about his death and should have Dylan's cell with the theory saved there.

Natalie became a famous activist following the publication of her book, *Woman of Peace and Activism.* It's one of my favorite books of the last decade. You may know a movement grew out of the book using Natalie's chant of *WOPA*.

She's my hero! And see how attractive she is! (picture attached). As a film buff, don't you think she looks like the actress?

Natalie did look a lot like the dead actress, the one who had died so mysteriously at sea, lost to life like my hero, Shelley.

You asked me the other night why the ToE is important to me and the focus of the greatest minds of science. I described what it might solve, as if it was a key to a riddle. The unraveling of entanglement would lead to great scientific advances. And like $E=MC^2$, the beautiful supersymmetry of the ToE may be perverted for purposes of artificial intelligence and mind control. Perhaps that's why we haven't been handed this last apple of knowledge or enlightenment before now.

But it's more than a tool like fire or a wheel. My heart tells me it's a wonderful opening to the miraculous universe we see only in shadows projected on Plato's cave wall. Working with Dylan showed me my life's purpose—Truth. There's so much joy in the clarity of discovering our life's purpose. We saw the shadows, and in his last letter to me he was convinced he'd found the source of those shadows and its expression in scientific terms, which he thought would usher in a new era of humanity. So you can see why I'm so determined to find the ToE too.

She was pursuing the ToE as the holy grail of scientific truth and to culminate her metaphysical affair with Dylan by finding Plato's sun.

My determination to find the ToE was more a hope that the lost poetic truth of my dead, maybe murdered, best friend would provide inspiration for my novel's prose. But mostly the search for the ToE would bind me to M while I looked to win her love.

I also fantasized about taking Dylan's place and traveling with the lovely M to the exotic land of Kathmandu. My fictional hero, to whom I'd given the working name James, and Brigitte were already in Kathmandu. There, James and Brigitte enjoyed making love at every opportunity: discreetly in the back of a taxi, where they pretended to cuddle and sleep on the bumpy road into the wilderness; on top of a mountain; under a waterfall; and on a float at sea. They were just warming up and would become increasingly creative. I realized, even as I enjoyed writing them, that I would have to cut back on some of the Harlequin Romance scenes.

M's scientific views had me starting to believe as she did that Dylan may have discovered something earthshaking. He was, after all, my brilliant friend.

Her email concluded with "I look forward to meeting Natalie with you tomorrow. I'll pick up my PTBT brother at a little before four. Your M."

Brother! From buddy to brother was even further from being her lover. I was heading in the wrong direction. Dylan always won the girl by tossing out lines of romantic poetry; prose took longer. But my blood was already simmering. My mind kept positing the nagging fear that M's love would only ever be real in my fiction.

I could conjure a quest with the most amazing lady and quantum cosmologist, but I no longer knew how to pursue romance, when to kiss, and when to make love. I'm not sure I ever knew. I was a star-crossed romantic who wanted his love returned before opening his heart and declaring his love.

CHAPTER **12**

I SPENT THE ENTIRE MORNING and better part of the afternoon preparing
for our second date, even skipping my nap. I should have been mentally
and physically exhausted after a day full of anticipation; instead, my
spirit burned brighter each moment my M drew closer. The arrow of
time was in flight, aimed at my heart, and soon would arrive.

She picked me up in a taxi on her way south to the Village. We
exchanged a seated brother-sister hug. Patience, my Achilles' heel, was
in a tug of war with my shy romanticism. James was much bolder.

I was a bundle of nervous energy, traveling with my new love to
meet my best friend's freshly widowed wife.

"Natalie's inspired *WOPA*, an acronym of her book title," M said,
"is now often uttered by women when a man has acted in a misogy-
nistic way toward them or another woman, or girl, in their company.
Of course, hard-liners—true feminists—still use the old-school tack of
raising the middle finger."

"Well, I think the unsung hero in this #MeToo age is the man who
has always respected women," I half joked.

"I'd like to meet him," she counterpunched. Politely tee-heeing,
I turned my eyes from her piercing gaze to look innocently out her
window.

When our cab pulled up in front of Natalie's Village town house,
I insisted on paying the fare, and M sighed, "WOPA." Heading to the
door, she said, "We're still figuring out how to react to a gentleman who
follows old social conventions. I'm so excited—Dylan must have shared
the ToE with his wife!"

Lost in her enthusiasm and my lust for love, I had failed to tell

M that Dylan's letter indicated that for fear of their safety, he hadn't shared the ToE with Natalie or Grace. It was too late now; she had rung the bell. She would find out soon enough, and it remained a possibility that Natalie might know where we would be able to find it. She must have Dylan's phone, where a copy of the ToE was surely stored.

Natalie greeted us at the door, a glass of wine in her hand.

"Sean, hello. It's been such a long time, and I'm so sorry—just yesterday I received back the letter I wrote telling you about Dylan and his service. I didn't have an email or phone contact for you, and Dylan's phone is missing, so I couldn't reach you that way. But I apparently used an old or wrong address. I'm so glad you reached out to me. Here's the letter, in case you still want to read it later."

Natalie, full of nervous energy too, finally paused before adding, "I wanted to thank you for being such a wonderful friend to Dylan. And for your condolences. Glad you kept my address. Your words, along with Grace, have been my greatest comfort . . . since he—" She smiled sadly in place of the last word.

Maybe I was better at condolences than I thought. I thanked her and slid her letter into my coat pocket. "I'm so sorry for you and Grace. He loved you both so much. Excuse me, Natalie, this is M. I told you about her." Either out of subterfuge or jealousy, I had introduced M as my friend in my email correspondence with Natalie, not mentioning that it was Dylan who had introduced us. The women greeted each other in a foyer as big as my one-bedroom.

"His phone is missing?" I asked and turned to M. "That was where we'd hoped—"

"Yes, the missing phone bothers me—it's a bit of a mystery. Let's go into the living room."

"It's an honor to meet you," M said. "I'm sorry for your loss. He was such a wonderful man."

We were seated in the well-decorated living room in front of a large fireplace, an expensive space courtesy of Dylan's years on Wall Street. A large framed picture resting on the mantel showed Dylan and Grace on a mountaintop. They both looked ecstatically awake, full of the joy of life, as if they'd just summited Everest. Dylan's presence was strong here, and I could hear him say, "*Auspicious is the day!*"

"That's beautiful," I said.

"Grace had that made," Natalie said, "and it just arrived today. I haven't had a chance to hang it properly." She smiled, but she angled her body away from the fireplace, putting the picture behind her. "I was relieved to see you made it to the service and sorry I didn't have a chance to say hello. And I never got to express my condolences for Hope, even at her funeral. She was such a remarkable and lovely woman."

I'd forgotten I hadn't seen Natalie since that day over nine years ago. She had aged well, with only a few lines of mourning around puffy eyes shrouded in remorse.

"Please join me in a glass of white Rhone," she said, pouring the wine into two glasses already sitting on the table. M and I weren't difficult to convince.

"Dylan was such a great friend my entire life," I said. "I feel he's still with me and always will be—as I said in my letter. I'm sure you're feeling the same way."

"He loved you very much, Sean. I don't know what I feel, but I'm glad you're here." Turning to cast a fleeting, pained look at her dead husband on the mantel, Natalie leaned back into the couch. "I watched Hope's ELF lectures on YouTube and took to heart her view of women's roles in the next evolutionary advance. She was a great inspiration to me. Knowing she was your wife, I followed her work closely. I sent her book of ELF lectures with your wonderful introduction and commentary to Dylan. He was very impressed by the lectures and said her theories influenced his own work."

"Are you talking about Hope McQueen?" M asked. "Sean, I know your wife's work too; she's another hero of mine. You might have mentioned her. I've quoted Hope for my quantum physics students, something to the effect of 'If we could see the quantum reality, it would be like a fish seeing through our eyes. A quantum leap of vision and the mind of humanity.'"

I'd forgotten Hope's interest in quantum physics. I had also lost all ability to control the flow of the conversation, which I was hoping to move to Dylan's death and the ToE. I thought it ill-advised to bring up his mention of big love, though that was a burning question too.

Natalie said, "I just thought of something Dylan sent me years ago that you'll want to see. Hang on."

She hurried out and a minute later returned with her laptop. "It's a video Dylan recorded of Hope and another evolutionary biologist in a panel debate at NYU. I'll play just the end, which I found so incredible, but I'll forward you the entire video."

I joined the ladies, sitting between them on the couch. Natalie had concrete evidence of Hope's magic. I hadn't remembered that Dylan had recorded the event.

There was Hope sitting elegant and composed. I sat up straighter. After a few moments of watching Hope at her most vibrant, I realized I was rubbing my face, that habit I'd thought long behind me. I shifted in my seat, thrusting my hands under my legs.

"She looks like Katharine Ross. Such a strikingly intelligent lady." M apparently shared my practice of identifying a person by their resemblance to a famous film look-alike.

"Yes," I said. "In Annie Hall's clothes." There was something awkward and yet so natural about watching Hope with M.

Hope was saying, "I think it improbable that a random singularity would have produced the perfect fine-tuning of our universe—the earth's electromagnetic field, for example—to provide for life to exist and evolve. The earth's shifting plates allowed for heat to be ventilated from the inside to the outer crust and for water to be conserved from outside—protected within. Tectonics calibrated for continents and oceans to separate for species specification and competition to occur. Isn't the evidence of conscious design right before our eyes? And I'd go even further to suggest it would be illogical to assume that this conscious design operated only once at the big bang and didn't continue to operate through evolution."

Hope's obviously more senior male opponent, acting superior based solely on age and sex, laughed and said, "You are well named, but despite what you may *hope*, there is no proof of conscious design. Life-forms develop from evolution and mutation over the expanse of time. Though we may wish for a peaceful and loving hand steering Noah's ship of life, the truth is simply survival of the fittest without any divine intervention." He laughed again at the takedown of his weaker-sex rival.

Trying my best to restrain my emotion, I stammered, "WO-PA," to which the ladies gave rueful smiles.

Hope said, "Darwinism needs to evolve too. And what's so funny about peace, love, and understanding?"

At the sound of laughter and disruption from the audience, Dylan had swung the camera to pan the crowd. He stopped on a guy who looked like a humble and embarrassed Elvis Costello in big black glasses.

When M laughed, I paused the video and said, "Elvis was one of my and Dylan's favorites. We hadn't known he was in the audience, and Hope later swore she hadn't seen him."

I restarted the video where the moderator and audience insisted Elvis go to the stage. Not knowing what better to do with his stage call, he sang "What's So Funny 'Bout Peace, Love, and Understanding." Elvis then hugged Hope while her adversary, in the background, hung his swinging head, unsuccessfully trying to be a good sport in defeat.

The video ended. If I could cry, that would have been the time. Dylan had recorded evidence of the magic Hope created every day of our life together. I moved back to my seat facing Dylan and Grace.

Seeing the video filled me with the desire to find the ToE, not only for Dylan but as a continuation of Hope's enlightened beliefs and as a means of allowing the miraculous back into my life.

Hope, M, and Natalie. It was incredible to me that these three women had intersected and influenced each other with Hope—or was it me?—as the nexus, a triangulation in the emergence of a brave new woman's world.

Natalie said to M, "After Sean told me you were coming, I read the *New Yorker* article about you and quantum art."

My quantum beauty laughed. "It was based on an essay I wrote, and while I was well ahead of my time in that, I know quantum physics will ultimately dramatically impact every area of thought and human endeavor. I was just making that point and trying to use my love of quantum physics to inspire young artists. In response to the essay, I received some remarkable poems and paintings inspired by the discoveries and theories of quantum physics, astrophysics, and string theory. All by artists seeing with quantum eyes. But I believe that art through the ages is constant and adheres to Keats's 'beauty is truth, truth beauty.'"

"Hear! Hear!" I heard myself saying in parody of British academia, excited to discover a dormant romantic streak in my love. "You've done your research, Professor. 'Ode on a Grecian Urn' is one of the best poems in the English language."

M raised a brow, but she was fighting laughter. "I read your syllabus online."

She read my syllabus? That meant that *she checked up on me*! Dancing around Natalie's living room would have been in bad taste, so I stayed seated.

An hour later we still hadn't learned anything about Dylan's death or the ToE. Natalie was opening a fine red Bordeaux 2000 Saint-Emilion and serving stinky cheese, a baguette, and pâté to go with the wine.

"Bitching pâté!" One Step said after taking a bite. The ladies looked at each other, shaking their heads at the cute male dog in the room. "Well, it was funny when Winona Ryder said it in *Heathers*."

Natalie said, "A clear case of gender appropriation." The ladies laughed.

Fuck me gently with a chainsaw, I heard Dylan say in poetic and buddy-movie solidarity, quoting from the same film. I restrained One Step from the WOPA of following Dylan's prompting and repeating his wicked words.

In New York City, or at least in my circle of academia, everyone drank, making the practice impossible to avoid. I instructed myself to pace the wine and not drink more than my share, as I already found myself one-stepping. I really did like the pâté. I could tell M was happy with the Bordeaux by the way she swirled it, and she was content and patient, letting Natalie lead the conversation. I'd do my best to be patient too.

Following my mental cue, Natalie said, "I'm drinking too much wine since Dylan's death. These bags under my eyes remind me of this self-abusing punishment. We shared a love of wine, and each sip makes me feel close to him, as if he was still here . . . Dulls the hows and whys too. I really want to speak to him . . . so much left to say. Instead I drink."

I was lucky to still be able to speak to him. A secret too crazy to share, even with his wife and the woman I loved.

"I drink as much, I'm sure," M said, "and I also still smoke weed from time to time."

"The kids call it flower, which is more poetic than weed." I'd hoped to sound hip and literary, but I just sounded old.

Natalie looked like an excited schoolgirl as she jumped up and hurried over to the side table next to me. She opened a little wooden box and pulled out a neatly rolled modern-day joint with a built-in filter and a lighter. I couldn't remember the last time I smoked, but in the company of charming ladies, who was I to say no? In a self-medicating world of vodka and whiskey, powder and pills, a little wine and pot didn't seem so bad.

As we started smoking, I told Natalie, "This pairing of wine and pot reminds me that M has reserved the label Vine and Weed for a future school, a vineyard and a weedyard to teach the business. She's got the funding all lined up."

"Something like that, but maybe I should call it Vine and Flower?" M said. "It'll be a real college with liberal arts and sciences for those who can't afford for-profit education."

Natalie paused after taking a sip of her wine. "Hmm . . . just a hint of ganja in that."

It was a smoky old Bordeaux we mingled with the pungent pot.

I picked up the baton. "M might put some buds in the vats during fermentation."

"Maybe a few drops of distilled THC right into the bottle," Natalie suggested.

M, bemused and deliberating, said, "I won't sacrifice quality or taste."

We were all a bit buzzed already as the powerful new strains of marijuana flower pollinated very quickly inside the mind.

"I've just started my research for the right location for the vineyard and college, but I think that with global warming, Oregon's terroir might be optimal in a couple years as, unfortunately, other regions may suffer."

"I'd like to contribute to that venture in some way," Natalie said.

"I've been considering a focus on young, impoverished women, and your assistance would be a big help," M said.

They proceeded into a deep discussion that didn't include me. I was back in the wading pool, listening to highly educated women speaking an English I could only partially comprehend. I pretended to study a Buddha statue on the coffee table, feeling out of place as I listened to them converse about how some men were incapable of taking women seriously in a professional setting unless the women were completely devoid of sexual desirability. My God, did male academics really treat women like M as a "peer-plus-sex object," unable to separate her brain from her body?

"A look, a pat, and an offhand remark about liking *that* blouse . . . ," M said. "And have you heard the one about the three wise men and the blonde?"

They laughed, but I couldn't. I wondered if I'd fallen headfirst into the category of men they were talking about; I *was* obsessed with her body. I felt the weight of shame for my entire sex and was relieved when they transitioned into a discussion about Grace's next film—a modern adaptation of *Pride and Prejudice*—which allowed me back into the conversation to fawn over Austen's talents and poignantly quote from Dickinson. "Unable are the loved to die, for love is immortality." I looked up at the photo of Dylan on the wall.

Natalie and M shared a look of appreciation before a muffled chuckle, no doubt noting my overcompensation. I turned back to address my buddy above the mantel. *I'm partying with your wife and the love you bequeathed me, but they're taking the piss out of me. We've all moved on and are doing quite well without you. But tell me, please—how did you die, and where is the ToE?*

CHAPTER **13**

NATALIE, WHO HAD POSITIONED her seat to face us, noticed my stoned engagement with the picture of Dylan and Grace behind her.

"That photo is hard for me to look at, though it's so good of them both. With time." She shifted position, tucking one leg under her, and looked over her shoulder. "It was taken earlier this spring in Nepal. Grace had such a great time with her father and the people there. She returned from her trip with a clear sense of purpose to use the power and privilege of her fame to help educate, feed, and care for orphaned and underprivileged children. She encouraged me to go to Kathmandu, claiming it had transformed her. She was always driven to success, but that's now *graced* with a sense of direction and compassion."

"That's so nice that they had meaningful time together," M said. "Can you tell us something about Dylan's work there?"

Still focused on the picture over the mantel, Natalie said, "Dylan learned to love mountain climbing when he went to Tibet, the year he left Wall Street. It was the same year we became empty nesters, with Grace moving to LA to follow her dream. She's such a good daughter. A better daughter than I am a wife." She faced us again with a fearful look in her eyes.

"After leaving Wall Street work, Dylan focused on new developments in science and his spiritual studies. He came to love quantum physics because of you, Em, a new passion he added to his other loves of poetry, travel, yoga, meditation, and hiking. We both respected the other's work, though our projects often led to us being worlds apart, culminating in the last two years with Dylan almost exclusively abroad in Nepal. Oh no—" She started to cry, crying harder the more she fought it. She was determined to get the words out through the tears. "I feel so guilty. Almost cheated on him once. Last year. Couldn't do it, but . . . it went pretty far. A passionate kiss."

Thank God she didn't *do it,* or that would have really shackled my buzz. I wasn't good with women's emotional outbursts, and this was a Niagara Falls I did not want to go over. I nudged M with my eyes, encouraging her to comfort Natalie. M was already on the case, taking Natalie's hand. I took my cue to leave, saying, "No worries. Only natural and nothing happened. Where's the bathroom?"

I followed Natalie's bobbing finger down the hall to exit stage right. I took my time relieving myself and my stoned emotions, girding myself to reenter the estrogen-charged scene. Looking into the bathroom mirror, I addressed Dylan. *So you were almost Poldy Bloom, a Shakespearean cuckold. She didn't do it, and what did you expect with your big love? You were an absentee husband. While a best friend is happy with letters and occasional get-togethers, a wife needs more. Your presence, no less.*

A man's gotta do what a man's gotta do.

Hah. A bastardized Grapes of Wrath *defense.*

Just exercising my poetic license.

The ladies acknowledged my return with tolerant glances before the now-composed Natalie continued speaking. "I saw him only a couple weeks each year when he came to see me and to attend meetings with scientists at Columbia and with a priest. Dylan mentioned you very fondly, Em, and enjoyed so much his meetings with you and learning about his new passion. He said you were the only one who was steeped in the new science yet not lost in it, and who still had an open mind, like Einstein."

So much for the subterfuge of introducing M as *my* friend. I wondered if Natalie was jealous of M's relationship with Dylan and had confessed her near affair to catch the conscience of my queen. But M's reaction would have put any such suspicion to rest.

"I wish like Einstein," M said. "Thank you. We shared a love of quantum physics, and Dylan's insights into the fabric of the universe were profound. By the end, I was learning as much from him. And thank you for notifying the physics department of his death and the service. I was moved by Grace's eulogy and the last singer's song."

Natalie nodded. "Grace did a great job, didn't she? I was so proud of her. That composure she got from her dad. I had a hard time just *introducing* her. And I loved the end to the service too. I think everyone was moved. I didn't know the singer, but she introduced herself later as a shaman. Rachel. She befriended Dylan years ago."

Natalie relit the joint and took a couple puffs that became small fragrant clouds as she exhaled. "Rachel wants me to take some medicine—to *heal*—in a ceremony with her. Maybe. I'd love to listen to her sing all night." She passed the joint to me. "This pot is strong."

I took a polite puff and returned it to the ashtray when M waved off another toke.

Natalie continued, "To get back to what he'd been doing . . . the last few months his work continued along the same arc but with increased intensity and secrecy. He was always private in his affairs of spirit, but he'd been concerned and wary in our last few conversations. He'd been contacted by the CIA, who wanted to meet him. I don't know if he ever met with them or what interest they had in his work. Perhaps they have his phone, or he lost it like the detective suggested. I do suspect—and it haunts me—that there may be more to his death than just his falling asleep, but for Grace's sake, I don't want to go down that dark rabbit hole. I tell myself Dylan wouldn't have wanted me to."

I didn't want to impose on Natalie's grief, but I did want answers if she had them. "I understand, but please tell us, if you can, what happened leading up to his death."

"Well"—Natalie took a deep breath—"the wine and the smoke and being with his good friends make it easier to speak of now. Grace is having a harder time leaving it alone but so far is honoring my wishes. She's coming back to see me again in a couple days."

Hands in her lap, she fiddled with her wedding band, turning it around and around and around. I cursed Dylan for dying, for forcing me to comfort his grieving widow, something I was ill-equipped to do. She fought off additional tears.

"Dylan believed he'd had some big breakthrough in his work. He planned to work with the two of you on whatever it was, but he was concerned about secrecy and my safety and Grace's. I thought he was being dramatic. He had a wonderful and at times overactive imagination." She managed a laugh before saying, "Sean, you know that. I thought he was going to come home from this trip and explain he was now enlightened, but that wouldn't explain any danger to us, and besides, how would he work with you two on *his* enlightenment? That's when he told me about the CIA, asking if they had contacted me. They hadn't."

I said, "Did he give you any specifics about the CIA and their interest? A name perhaps?"

"No. Sorry. I was going to ask when I saw him. He was to join me at our country house upstate following his arrival back in the city, which would have been the day after his death. Alarmed when he wasn't on the train, I called his cell. But when he didn't answer and his message didn't pick up, I knew something was wrong."

"Has there been any activity on the phone since that day? Will the phone company say?" M asked.

"No calls, according to the detective, but other than that I'd need the NSA to tell me if anyone has been on the phone. But it's strange how I knew something bad had happened."

"I think when someone like Dylan—someone we love so much—dies, somehow our hearts just know," I said, winning the prize for most sensitive man in the room. "But what happened next?"

"I called the Beekman Hotel, since that's where he'd planned to stay. The front desk confirmed he'd checked in the day before, and they rang his room with no answer. When I pushed for more information, as my husband was *missing*, they noted that he'd had a seven p.m. wake-up call the prior evening and then around ten that morning the Do Not Disturb light was still lit, delaying housekeeping's first pass. Room notes indicated that when there was no response at noon, the maid had opened the door, only to see the guest still in bed. Since it was then one p.m. and past checkout time, I insisted they go to the room and tell him his wife needed to speak to him. That was when they found him dead in the bed. Though it's strange and sad and maddening, my heart wants to believe he had become enlightened and that his spirit left his body since it was no longer needed."

M said for us both, "We're so sorry. He was a very conscious man. I mean—"

"I know exactly what you mean. Awareness. Dylan was so full of life."

And then both women were crying and clasping each other's hands. The tender sisterly action by M aroused admiration in me, a man to whom compassionate physical action did not come easily and crying not at all. I wanted to hold M's hands and look into those comforting moist eyes and . . . I decided to impress her by pressing on with our investigation instead.

"What do the authorities think happened?" I asked.

"Sean, a moment maybe?" M said.

"No, I'm all right," Natalie said while relighting the final third of the joint and taking a puff. She then passed it to M, who took a social hit. "The next day the detective assigned to investigate Dylan's death came to see me. A Detective *Mulhearn*." She said his name with more nasal disgust than was already inherent in those two syllables.

"I think being a wife always makes one a suspect. I had dinner with friends in Rhinebeck the evening of his death and returned from the country immediately, which gave me a good alibi, I thought, though I imagine that in the detective's mind I wouldn't have done it myself. I was in shock, and Grace was on a plane home from LA. The detective, who trailed smoke around on his clothes and skin and left the room smelling of cigarettes for a couple days, seemed concerned about the fact that no cell phone was found. He asked if he could check Dylan's computer. I told him the missing phone was strange but that Dylan didn't use a computer."

It was my turn with the joint, so I took a shallow puff and didn't inhale, wanting to keep One Step from going one toke over the line on his second date. "So they still haven't found his phone? Would he have traveled home without it?"

"No, that would be odd, though he didn't use it often in his new life. Mulhearn thought he must have lost it. He mentioned that Dylan was found naked, which was also odd. It seemed an intimate detail at the time, and I didn't want to raise unnecessary suspicions, so I didn't mention the oddity to the detective. Plus, maybe it was a new habit developed in Kathmandu. Still, he had never slept naked before."

She took more than a sip of wine, and I stood to refill her glass, which seemed to comfort her.

We all were a little past buzzed. M was still seated next to Natalie, watchful of her delicate state, while I tried to lighten the mood. "Well, he never slept naked when we traveled together the year after college. I would have been traumatized if he had, and we'd have been kicked out of the hostels."

"Ha." Natalie acknowledged the humor and moved on. "I did tell the detective that Dylan seemed to think whatever he was working on may have put him in danger and that that made me suspicious. When I told him about the CIA's interest, those three letters got some attention from the relatively disengaged detective. He said the CIA had contacted him and offered to assist in any way they could, so there was nothing suspicious there—they had just wanted to discuss his academic work. I found that even more suspicious, the CIA contacting the detective. He asked if I had any of Dylan's academic work. I didn't."

M and I exchanged frowns. I had so many questions that I couldn't pick one.

"After that, the detective, who never seemed to have any real interest in me as a suspect, said Dylan had died in his sleep in a luxury hotel bed. He had to acknowledge Dylan's missing phone was, as he called it, a loose end. *Mulhearn* struggled to feign sympathy, which didn't come easy to him. By way of comfort, he said, 'I've seen worse ways to die.'

"Then, get this: In leaving, the so very unsmooth Don Juan suggested, 'If, after you get yourself together, you ever want to . . . *talk*, you have my card.'

"My impression—beyond that he was a nasty predator—was that if the detective determined he wasn't able to resolve the matter, he wasn't anxious to label it suspicious and would rather rush to close the case. He shared my concern, for different reasons, about the potential tabloid interest due to Grace."

I said, "You mentioned Dylan was seeing a priest, but I thought Dylan had lost his interest in the church when we were children. We weren't choirboys."

"I thought that odd too." She nodded. "But he'd been doing some research with a Catholic priest; he'd assembled an eclectic group of acquaintances and friends the last couple of years. The day following the detective's visit, that priest—I forgot his name—called to say he was an acquaintance of Dylan's and asked if he could come by to pay his respects. He introduced himself as Father something, though he made it clear he was really a bishop.

"When he arrived, he said he'd been providing Dylan spiritual guidance for his work. He didn't seem comfortable around me, a woman, and his handshake was like undercooked spaghetti. I had opened a good bottle of wine for him, and less than an hour later I'd had one glass and he'd finished the rest and was ready to leave. By the time he left, I didn't like him much at all. He asked if Dylan had left any writings with me. He thought they might be, in his words, 'misguided but of interest.'"

I leaned forward. "Like us, everyone seems interested in Dylan's work."

"It does seem that way. I told him I hadn't been fortunate enough to see Dylan before he died and that he had died his first night home in a hotel room. I still cringe when I remember how his bushy brows arched impossibly high in judgment of our marriage. He also implied in words and manner that Dylan may have committed suicide. I have to assume that he was one of the many interesting people Dylan attracted into his life. I saw him, as well as the detective, at the service."

M stood. "So that's the priest who sat with my chairman. That makes me stoned and paranoid. I'm going to the bathroom. Need to splash some cold water on my face. Please don't talk till I get back. I don't want to miss anything."

Natalie pointed again. "Down the hallway on the right." When she laughed, I joined in.

I called after M, "We'll just sit here giggling until you return." I stopped laughing when I realized I'd left the seat up. A man living alone for a decade . . .

I imagined I'd face reproach when M returned, but all she said was "Please continue."

Natalie said, "You didn't miss a thing other than Sean's bitching pâté."

I looked innocently at the empty plate as I swallowed the last bite of the smooth goose butter.

"Detective Mulhearn also asked why Dylan didn't stay here the night of his return. I told him that was due to Dylan's knowing the owners of the hotel for years, from his Wall Street days. The restoration of the old building and development of the hotel and condos was one of his last deals in his final year as a banker."

"Dylan told me about that deal," I said. "It sounded like an amazing space. He said his business partner called the building's reconstructed atrium 'real estate porn.'"

"Whatever the relationship, it enabled Dylan to stay in a 'luxury room'—the detective's words—for free at the Beekman, where the architecture is sublime, a description I prefer over *porn*."

I quickly interjected, "Me too."

M gave me one of her sensitivity-training looks; she wasn't a fan of big love.

"He'd been wanting to stay there, and with my being out of town . . . And he flattered me by saying he wanted me home for the true homecoming. I was going to tell him about the near affair. *I had to.* But now I'll never get the chance."

I didn't mention I had just told him about it.

"I had to be upstate for a talk I was giving, but he was going to see you for dinner in the city that evening before joining me upstate. I hope you don't mind my telling the detective of your dinner date."

"No, that's good to know," I said. "M and I want to meet him. Perhaps if I'm a suspect too, he'll be more likely to take our meeting."

Was I a suspect, and was the detective gathering evidence before meeting a person of interest, or was I just stoned?

I then told Natalie about the theory of everything Dylan was planning to present to me at dinner and of his interest in working on a novel as a promotional device for the theory. By the time I was done, Natalie was twisting her ring again.

"A theory of everything?"

"Yes. The ToE, as M and Dylan like to refer to it."

"That's a better explanation for his behavior than mere enlightenment."

With some guilt, I handed her the people-to-be-trusted list and the envelope with its broken seal. I was afraid it might upset her further, as she was not a PTBT. "I found this in a PO box in Midtown by using an address and a combination Dylan sent me in his last letter. I apologize. I should have given it to you to open."

"Not to worry," she said. "He was your best friend, and I failed to successfully notify you he had died. You must have been curious. I've been meaning to check that box. Dylan had his important mail sent there, but I find that post office so depressing. I'd collect it for him periodically. It was a strange habit, since he could have had everything mailed here, but perhaps, since he didn't use a computer, it served as his cloud. He used it as a mix of mailbox and safety deposit box when he traveled. He had the same setup in Kathmandu, where I sent his important correspondence and gifts."

She nodded toward the coffee table. "He sent that wonderful bronze Buddha to the box for me to find on my birthday while he was away. It's a treasure and comfort to me now."

I picked up the fat bottle-size Buddha. It appeared solid, but I could tell it was hollow by the weight. "This looks valuable, and such a lovely, serene face, but it's so hard to tell the authentic from the mass-produced."

"What matters is what it means to you," M said.

"True," I said. "I find it curious that the most beautiful Buddhas are so androgynous."

An image came to me of that Buddha sitting in the box in Kore-atown, looking out its window and waiting patiently for Natalie to free him. It now made sense why Natalie's name wasn't on the people-to-be-trusted list; she was meant to find the list. *Or was I?*

It would have been considerate if Dylan had included the ToE with the list in his box. And why had Dylan included the PO box's address and combination at the top of my letter? Maybe he really had feared for his life and had left bread crumbs behind in case he died before we could speak.

"I can't imagine a theory was that important or got him killed," Natalie said. "Or why the CIA would be interested in it. I'd rather have more of his poetry than this theory that consumed him at the end."

"M thinks the ToE is of great scientific value, so we're determined to find it," I said. "I hope you don't mind?" I prayed that she didn't. The quest had become vital for me.

Natalie stood and paced the length of the room before stopping in front of the fireplace and the photo of Dylan and Grace, studying it intently. I imagined she was consulting with Dylan on how to respond and perhaps making peace with him.

"It certainly is of scientific value," M said. "And if proven true, it's of value to all of humanity. But if he was my husband, I would have cherished his poetry too." M showed no sign of losing enthusiasm as she added, "I know you have reservations, but as Sean said, we are commit-ted, and I think Dylan would've wanted us to find it. Do you have any idea where to look?"

"Let me think," Natalie said, rallying to our cause. She steadily tapped one fingernail on the mantel, Betty Davis–style. "Dylan would, of course, approve of your search. You are, after all, people to be trusted. I'll ask Grace if she knows anything about Dylan's theory. She had a wonderful time with him in Kathmandu after filming *Kim* in India. I'll let you know if she knows."

"Thanks. I loved that movie," M said. "I went to see it the week it was released. She should win an Oscar for that."

"I have to see the movie now, but I read the book as a boy." I turned to Natalie. "Can you provide us the detective's and the father's or the bishop's contact information?"

She pulled two business cards out of a drawer, and I grabbed pictures of them with my phone.

"Chairman Chandler Litton and Bishop Stanley Horton," I read in a pompous tone, though the names did most of the work.

"That's my larger-than-life chairman. I'm surprised he has a friend, and a bishop no less."

"Oh, sorry. I forgot the bishop gave me two cards so I could contact either of them if any of Dylan's papers were found. Here's the detective's card."

I took a third picture, reading aloud, "Detective *Mulhearn*," and returned the cards to her.

"I don't think they'll have the ToE," M said, "but perhaps they might have a lead for us. And Sean is always looking for interesting characters for his short stories."

I was so thrilled she supported my writing that I almost blurted out "novel."

Natalie returned to the couch, but she perched on the edge rather than relaxing into the soft cushions. The social signal was clear; our glasses, the second bottle, and the joint were all finished. Still, she didn't rush to goodbye but said, "The detective might know something about the theory, and they both are characters."

"After we meet all of these New York characters," I half joked, "we may have to go to Kathmandu to meet the other people to be trusted."

"Sorry, Sean," M said. "I told you I've committed to a fellowship in Athens starting in early July."

I had gone my one step too far and was disheartened by the rebuke of my personal fantasy and novel plot.

Natalie looked sad too. "I regret never visiting Dylan in Kathmandu; I always had some work conflict or excuse. I think now I may have been jealous of his life there and of the Deeksha, which he spoke of as if it were a magical kingdom abounding with good and loving people. When he first mentioned the big love that found him there, I thought he might have meant he had one or many lovers. He laughed as he explained Big Love—in caps, mind you—as the unconditional love of God for everyone and everything."

One Step was inching over the line again, saying, "So big love is a New Age catchphrase of a magical kingdom?"

M looked at me sideways as Natalie started to tear up. Natalie said, "I could never go there now without him, but I hope you get to go someday."

As we moved through the foyer to the door, Natalie said, "Your search could be dangerous. I hope Dylan died in his sleep, but maybe he didn't. I would avoid the CIA. Good luck finding his theory, and please keep in touch. You brought some part of him back with you today. And, Sean, I hope I didn't burden you with too much information about . . . you know. But telling you was somehow like telling him and is a weight off my shoulders. Thank you."

"I knew him pretty, pretty well—still do—and know he understands and would forgive, if there was anything to forgive. You had a wonderful marriage, and you gave him freedom to be Dylan." I felt like a Catholic priest granting absolution by the powers vested in me as his best friend. The lightening of her eyes made me feel I had done some good.

M and I hugged her goodbye and thanked her for the fine bottles of wine, the flower, and the hospitality.

On the taxi ride back to Chelsea, still feeling like a padre to the women of the world, I said to M, "Are you worried about our quest? I wouldn't want to put you in danger."

"*You're* not putting me in danger. I understand the risks, and I'm excited, determined to not miss this opportunity to find the ToE, which, if true, is the pinnacle of scientific endeavor. Even if it's not a complete or a final theory of everything, I believe Dylan was on to something and not prone to exaggeration. He believed. And you?"

I shaded the truth, saying, "No worries. I'm with you and believe in our quest. They can't go around killing all of Dylan's friends, my brilliant and fearless partner."

She accepted my flattery and amends but was quiet the rest of the trip. The cab pulled over to the curb on 18th Street, and I went in for my hug.

"Good night, M. Perhaps the detective found Dylan's phone or a physical copy of the ToE in the hotel room. And I'll let you pay for the cab."

"Thanks for the encouragement," she said, "but why wouldn't Mulhearn have told Natalie if he'd found something? I'm thinking maybe we can host a dinner party and invite him and all the unusual suspects. Let me give it some more thought."

I paused before exiting the cab. So that was why she'd been so quiet. She'd been plotting our next step.

"That sounds like a scene from a Tarantino film dripping with tension but hopefully no blood. But you go to Athens in only a couple weeks, and that's short notice to arrange a dinner and have them all attend. We might fare better meeting them individually, even if we have to work around their schedules." I liked her plan and Tarantino films, but it meant less time together than my more drawn-out plans allowed.

"I'll send you an email. I think we can make it work, my *Thin Man*."

I smiled at her ability to play the game. "That's the perfect film, spot-on for your dinner-party scene, my dear Myrna."

I went in for a second hug, trying for more than a brother-sister vibe. She was warm and didn't pull back, and I felt her breasts on my chest, and then the scent of her hair and skin made me lose my mind. I kissed the top of her head, like an older brother at Thanksgiving. I think it took all her power to hold in a laugh as I left the taxi. This practice of patience was slow death by humiliation.

As I prepared for bed, this rusty lover remembered Natalie's letter to me, the one she had sent to the wrong address. It wasn't in my sport coat pocket and must have fallen out in the taxi. I texted M, and her reply bounced right back.

"I didn't see it, sorry. Do you think it was important? I paid cash and don't have a cab receipt."

"It's old news now, about Dylan's death and the Quaker service. Good night, buddy."

I really hated losing a letter, especially one unread. Also, it only now sank in that my *buddy* would be leaving for Athens before my dream could come true. I'd be all alone again and nursing a freshly broken heart.

I didn't sleep well, trapped in a nightmare where I peered through a small window at a Buddha locked inside the mailbox in Koreatown, the 9-9-9 combination no longer working as I tried it over and over again. It ended with the bent old lady returning to my side, smirking like a wicked witch.

"You can't find love there. She's already dead if you just flip ahead," she said, handing me Dylan's blank-page book from another dream. The painting of the exotic scene of nature on the cover was still mesmerizing, but I no longer wanted to look within.

CHAPTER 14

THE NEXT MORNING I WROTE DOWN the old woman's words. I rarely remembered dialogue from my dreams, but the hunched old lady's words haunted me. Maybe I was cursed and had failed to crack open the box because I forgot to intone the magic words, "Auspicious is the day!" I wished I could go back into the dream and do it again.

M put her plan for a dinner party into motion. I was to review her draft evite and then call Natalie before it was distributed to her, the chairman, Father Bishop, and the detective.

I waited in my NYU office, reading in the *New York Times* about the bad news erupting in the Middle East and our government's nativist reaction, trying not to give in to the fear that M's flight to Athens would be further proof that all love dies.

M's email soon landed in my inbox, with the evite attached.

Please join us at the Beekman for dinner on July 1 in honor of our friend Dylan to discuss his research and theories, and his life and death. We have arranged, as your hosts, a table in the bar lounge, under the amazing atrium, for drinks starting at six and dinner from Augustine's at seven. We regret the short notice, but look at the wines on the attached list that we will serve!

By way of a cover note to me, M added,

I know my chairman likes good wine and loves food, so I think his thirst and hunger will convince him to come. His mouth is a quasar for words and a black hole for food. It will never be shut. At department dinners I've seen him speak and eat enough for three. He gulps air at one end and emits it from the other. (blushing face emoji) Sorry, but I thought you should be forewarned. And Natalie told us the father likes his wine too. Who could resist a free meal from Augustine with this wine list?

I wrote back:

Well done! I'll leave it to you to make sure my place card isn't next to your chairman's. Detective Mulhearn will want to question me and meet our other suspects even if he doesn't love fine wine and food. I'm calling Natalie now to warn her about our book club dinner.

I was teasing the idea of my book—I had yet to tell M about it.

A few minutes later, I was speaking with Natalie.

"M is about to send out invitations to you and the people we want to meet to talk about Dylan and the theory of everything: the detective, the chairman of physics at Columbia, and the father or bishop. We wanted to include you on the invitation but understand you may not want to attend."

Natalie declined, with her regrets focused on the wines.

"Well, I hope you'll miss more than just the wines. I mean us too."

Natalie mentioned Grace, and I laughed. "She's certainly welcome to take your place. We'll leave a seat open for her. I'm glad she's coming into town to be with you. Let me know if you change your mind, and I'll let you know if we learn anything interesting and if—when—we find the theory."

I hung up wondering if I should have told her I lost the letter she'd given me. I told myself it wasn't that important, but I was embarrassed by my carelessness in losing such precious correspondence. As mail by post became a relic, each letter became increasingly valuable, and this letter was from my best friend's wife telling me he had died and I would no longer be receiving any more of his letters.

My Natalie-call summary was sent to M with the green light. She immediately sent out the evites, since there was only a week until the July 1 dinner date. Less than an hour later, I received a call from Detective Mulhearn, asking if we could meet before the gathering, as he had questions just for me. I negotiated, and he grudgingly agreed to allow M to attend the pregame meeting. I knew she wouldn't want to miss it. She had no fear that I could discern.

I didn't like the idea that Mulhearn wanted to question me. I wondered if I should take my lawyer along. I didn't have a lawyer, though I thought my agent could play the part. Mulhearn rudely ended our call by saying, "I may or may not be able to join the dinner after our interview."

His words sounded like a warning, and I always felt violated when a call ended without a goodbye.

That night before bed, M texted me that our two other targeted guests had agreed to attend in a very formal response from the chairman. The fine dining and wine list had worked.

By dropping Dylan's name with the Beekman's food and beverage manager, M had successfully arranged a table starting at five. The manager was an old friend of Dylan's from the hotel reconstruction days and eager to accommodate us. For the evening, he would hold us a prime table—in the lobby and under the atrium—that could seat four to six diners, with service from Augustine next door and a forty-dollar-per-bottle cork fee, the cost of bringing your own wine. Although we were both listed as hosts, M insisted she pay for the entire show or "book club"—as she came to call the affair for me—and I didn't want to be sexist and refuse her generosity.

I was curious and eager to meet the men who were already primed to be characters in my novel. Animated by the urgency that my love and muse would soon fly away, I was determined to muster the confidence to kiss M and profess my love at the end of the evening, patience be damned. I had my lines and location set. I'd insist on dropping her off uptown in a taxi and say, "And now I'll subway home. But first I must tell you . . ." followed by the rehearsed words that would open any heart. The kiss, the first kiss, would ensue. And then, perhaps, I'd be invited up the brownstone stairs.

CHAPTER 15

M AND I RETURNED TO THE SCENE of the crime. The Beekman Hotel and atrium fully lived up to their hype. We walked into a timeless building. No, it was more like a building where time stood still—in the Beekman's case, since 1899. Dylan was right; the building boasted the most amazing architecture, and the space had the gravitas of years of upright elegance, dissolute neglect, and upright elegance again. Peter O'Toole in architecture.

The atrium was a dreamlike hive of cast-iron railings rising above us. Two rabbit-ear turrets framed the large skylight, which shone down to a marble floor nine stories below. One sensed ghosts dressed in turn-of-the-twentieth-century grandeur dancing there between the floors. I imagined Dylan's ghost had joined that waltz in the funnel of swarming light.

The walls were adorned with exquisite bookcases and art that would do a museum proud. "It truly is an amazing space," I said to M. "Dylan's relationship with his partner here soured, but Dylan didn't judge and half defended him, saying, 'He's a New York City real estate player who lives in the world of the *Treasure of the Sierra Madre*, playing a sad zero-sum game of getting the most gold for himself.' Dylan liked Bogart movies almost as much as I do."

At the hostess desk, we were asked to wait. Soon a very solicitous man joined us.

"Emily Edens? I'm the manager—we spoke on the phone."

We shook hands and introduced ourselves to Randy. I didn't catch his last name after attempting to remember his first.

Randy said, "I was a friend of Dylan's from the time we started bringing this grand old space out of mothballs. What a good man he was. He was always a gentleman. I was so upset by his death that I couldn't get myself together to attend his funeral. I'm so sorry . . . Let me show you to your table now, and if you need anything during the course of the evening, just ask. We have the wines you sent down, two chilled whites and four reds. A very nice selection."

"Thank you," M said.

"Is there anything you can tell us about Dylan's death?" I asked. "There are so few details, and he was so full of life."

"Not really. He was found dead in his bed. And that's not as odd as you might think. Most hotels have more than one or two deaths per year, usually a heart attack, drugs, or suicide. He was younger than most, however. And his death got more law enforcement interest."

"We'll be meeting the detective on the case here shortly," I said.

Randy's intentionally jovial face turned unintentionally pale. "He's a nasty man, if his name's *Mulhearn*. Let me show you to your table before he gets here," he said with an outstretched arm.

A skittish Randy quickly led us to a circular table set for five and removed the Reserved sign. The table was right in the middle of the lounge. He asked, "Would you like a drink, or do you prefer to start with the white Burgundy?"

M looked at me. "White Burgundy?"

I smiled.

"I'll send your server. Nice to meet you," Randy said, backing and turning away.

M called after him, "Please open all the reds so they can breathe."

He nodded over his shoulder. "Will do."

"He was in no rush and then a big one," M said.

We sat directly under the high skylight and waited for the "nasty" detective to arrive. I held up my glass to toast the white Burgundy. Neither of us called the game on, but our eyes followed to the finish of our first sip.

"We'll soon find out if Detective *Mulhearn* suspects murder and if he has any leads." I said his last name using the nasal tone of those that had already met him. "I still hope he found Dylan's phone or the written theory pages. And I hope I'm not a real suspect."

"I like playing sleuths and hosting a dinner party of interesting suspects, especially you," M said, adjusting her seat and dress. "I like my cloak with dagger." She picked up a stiletto-like steak knife to make her point.

"My femme fatale, you're killing me." I looked her up and down, pausing briefly on her breasts before sliding down to her long crossed legs—the kind of look that used to pass as admiring chivalry but now might be deemed offensive. She didn't thrust her stiletto into my heart but accepted my lustful eye movements with the smile she reserved for me.

After this derring-do, I said, "Are you always so fearless, my brilliant friend? I'm a bit worried about being questioned as a suspect; even the innocent don't like that role. And thanks for making me a cliché by suggesting we return to the scene of my crime, though it is the perfect stage for you to play beautiful dinner-party host, my dear Myrna."

"I agree, my dashing Mr. Powell. We should be guzzling martinis, not sipping wine."

"Perfect." I sighed and shook my head in appreciation.

I imagined that the room's architecture, with those rabbit ears for reception, funneled energy like an antenna into the lounge. Or was M the magnet that attracted the vibrating frequency I felt?

As we waited, diners at other tables stole glances at M. She commanded attention with her lovely face, which bore little or no makeup, and luscious body veiled only by her elegant but casual black dress. On M it was more a timeless look than a current fashion, one that allowed her to shift from professorial chic during the day to sensual vogue in the evening. Due to her siren-like presence and our greeting by the fawning manager, who had dispatched us to the best table, the other patrons must have thought she owned the place.

As we sipped the wonderful Chassagne Montrachet 2009, I focused my attention on a simple bracelet M had worn each time we met, a thin leather band with silver inlaid with opals or lapis lazuli.

She held her arm out. "You noticed my treasure."

Her eyes and the bracelet sparkled as she spoke. And I wanted to kiss that hand or arm. Well, any and all parts of her other than the top of her head.

"This was made by a Navajo friend whom I met one summer in Santa Fe. Iya initially was my teacher in meditation and yoga. We shared a love of nature and hiking, and also wine and weed. Excuse me, I mean flower."

I raised my glass to her with two hands, as if presenting a chalice or fully opened white wine flower. She followed suit. *Ting*! The lips of the two white roses kissed before we drank.

The spell was broken when she continued. "Iya made this bracelet and gave it to me at the end of the summer. As I was about to board my plane home, he said, 'With this bracelet, my final blessing, we are bound.'

"He died that fall. He'd known he was dying and knew I would have stayed if he told me before I left. He was the strongest, most vital and spiritual man I had ever met, and two months later he was dead."

I listened with the rapt attention of someone hearing something heart-wrenching they really didn't want to hear.

"Iya's sister wrote me that autumn and enclosed a letter from him. He'd also left a note behind for the tribe, telling them where he was to be found on our favorite mountain peak. They found him lying peace-fully on a funeral bed—a pyre—he'd made for himself with his last bit of strength, and the tribe took care of the rest. It was a very conscious death, one he chose for me to miss."

"Everybody dies in bed these days."

Before I realized I'd one-stepped, a tear was rolling down M's cheek, taking the same path as the tear I'd seen when she sat in center row P, seat number 9. Her emotions were so raw and so beautiful. I instinc-tively touched her hand and bent forward to kiss her cheek, but she slowly pulled her hand away before my lips could make their move, acknowledging the awkward gesture with a tear-kissed half smile.

"While I say it was a conscious death, I felt betrayed by his not tell-ing me before I left Santa Fe or in the many long calls, emails, and texts we exchanged after I left. I did forgive him—or so I tell myself—but all that communication between us was tainted by his lie of omission."

She drew a ragged breath. "My strong reaction to his denying me the truth was—is—probably related to my father's history of lies to my mother. I no longer believe in romantic love, which requires total honesty. I fear my heart's grown cold."

I wanted to hold her chilled heart in my warm hands and kiss it tenderly until it awoke.

"I do love this bracelet, though, and the memories of every moment that preceded it," she concluded.

Before I had time to become fully crestfallen or allow One Step to further blunder, the detective arrived punctually for my five-thirty interrogation.

Detective Mulhearn was a ruffled and weathered man who looked as if he had just returned from a long sea trip. More likely, he'd just been too long on the dark streets of New York drinking black coffee and whiskey, with little to eat but a big appetite for vice. His fingers were yellow and his face gaunt, puckered and pockmarked, but still he managed rakish good looks. He was a Casablanca Bogart after all-night drinking with never enough cigarettes. *A man, only more so.* The sting of cigarette smoke drifted from him into my nostrils, making me wince. He eyed my M as he greeted her with a soft two-hand handshake after nearly crushing my hand. He took his seat across from me, looking about as though the fancy place and well-dressed people were a big joke.

While we were drinking the first fine white wine, he ordered a double Johnnie Walker Black, neat, with ice on the side. He smiled meanly at me as he ordered, no doubt assuming that the suspect who had asked for the meeting would be picking up the tab. Some detective. He didn't deduce that the little woman was his host and paying the bill. I returned his smile with a grimace meant to challenge his authority.

He announced, "I have to respond to this," and started typing angrily on his phone with one finger. His drumming morse code was loud enough to draw the glares of other patrons.

He clearly wanted to make me uneasy. He succeeded. When his drink arrived and he was ready to talk, he said, "So . . . suspect number one. It's nice to meet you, Professor."

He was only half joking, and I couldn't decide which half held sway in the detective's inscrutable mind. As he took a manly gulp of whiskey, he managed to keep his squinting eyes on me, sucking me in like one of the Marlboros from the box he'd laid on the table. I was thankful he'd left his horse tethered to the hitching post outside and hadn't ridden it right into the saloon.

"Explain your relationship with Dylan and your activities the day of his death."

M blithely asked, "And will you be staying for dinner, Detective Mulhearn? I hope so."

"No. I have a hard stop at six thirty for this meeting. But maybe if the professor here confesses, I'll ring the boys in blue and take his place with you."

"Lovely," M replied.

I wasn't amused, and M must have been disgusted by the innuendo.

He took out a notepad, adding to my discomfort, but like the ice he ordered, he didn't use it. I proceeded to tell him my long history with Dylan in detail, as if ample prior opportunity to murder my some-times-annoying friend was a good defense. He drummed his powerful fingers impatiently during my decade-by-decade account of Dylan and Sean. I could tell M enjoyed hearing the history more than the detective did. The saga led, at length, to Dylan's last letter. Prepared, I handed him exhibit 1 for the defense. The detective, who seemed not very interested in the copy of the letter, took it anyway.

I paused, waiting for a question that never came, then continued to explain the dinner plan at Momofuku Ko and Dylan's failure to show up. Suspect was a new role for me, and I thought my long patient wait at the restaurant with a tight green Chablis was an airtight alibi. I even mentioned the amuse-bouche as an interesting tidbit.

But after I played my get-out-of-jail-free card to close my case, he said, "But, Professor, if you were the killer, of course you would still show up for the reservation and be surprised by the dead man's failure to appear. Even the most amateur of murderers would think that many moves ahead."

But I hadn't.

He asked, "Did you call him from the restaurant?"

I thought this was a trick question. I knew from Natalie that no cell phone had been found. I went with the truth. "I didn't have his number."

"Such a good friend over the centuries, and you don't have his phone number? Hmm, maybe you knew he didn't have his phone."

"I only learned that from his wife a week or so ago."

While I was considering a further defense, the detective moved on and asked a few questions that demonstrated a disdain for Dylan as an elite ex-banker and esoteric world traveler and me as an effeminate, intellectual professor. Leering like a Mr. Hyde, he concluded this line of questioning with "His theory of everything . . . What is one of those worth? And do you have it?"

"It's priceless. And no, we don't. We were hoping you might," M said.

As he angled toward M, he transformed into Dr. Jekyll. "Priceless like you, lovely lady? I'm sorry not to be paying you more attention. It's just my questions are for McQueeny here."

I'd hated that nickname since grade school, particularly when properly used and followed by *the weenie*.

Mulhearn shook his head, checked his watch. "Another double Johnnie Walker Black, neat, ice on the side," he called to a passing waiter.

While One Step was desperate for a comeback line that didn't come, Mulhearn twisted his head to look at me with his inquisitive Larry David bug eyes. "The professor and I know everything has its price. Please continue with your alibi. Focus on that day and just the facts."

I remembered the day's activities. Still, the word *alibi* was a slap to the face.

"Just between us men, huh, Detective *Mulhearn*?" I said, not enjoying the look in his eyes. "You didn't answer her question."

"Which?"

"Do you have the theory?"

"No. Now continue, and I'll ask the questions." He rolled right over me. "Please don't try to impress Emily. We can continue this down at the station if you'd like to keep it just between us two men."

"That won't be necessary, and I'm not—"

But he was still rolling. He angled toward me and pulled on the left lapel of his worn gray sport coat, discreetly revealing, just for me, a big dark, hard, and I assumed loaded Glock strapped to his heart. And then as the smoky curtain closed and his creepy schoolyard grin faded, the moment of intimacy passed as if it had never happened.

"Continue, Professor."

"So I got out of bed around eight o'clock that Saturday, read the paper, and had coffee before going to the NYU gym and working out from around nine to eleven. After that, before noon, I went alone for brunch at a café called Claudette."

I paused as the detective finally picked up his rumpled little book to write for the first time. "*Claudette*," he said with an effeminate lilt and jaunty notation, "of course. Continue, Professor."

The waiter delivered the double scotch neat. Mulhearn ignored the waiter. He looked at his drink the same way he looked at M. The same way I had looked at M earlier. And now, in his company, I felt ashamed.

The fresh glass of ice sat next to its sibling, the ice cubes melting like sand in an hourglass.

"And then I went to my NYU office, where I graded essays until three, when I went home for a nap and to dress for dinner."

"Interesting . . . Since you're a widower"—he looked at M as if to say *What are you doing with this loser?*—"I assume there were no witnesses to that nap and the dressing? And it was actually closer to two forty-five when you left your office. The approximate time of death was shortly after seven, so you see, Professor, you could have done it, as you didn't get to the restaurant until after eight."

He paused dramatically and smiled like a serial killer about to enjoy a kill. "I dug around. Found out people close to you die mysteriously in their sleep. Like your ex."

It was a punch in the gut. I was reeling, disoriented, my mind spiraling and looking for escape. Was I really a suspect? Why bring Hope into it? This was all so harsh and only warranted for a real suspect. And why this kind of questioning in front of M, *and did M now think I may have killed my wife and Dylan?*

I rubbed my face vigorously with both hands.

A tense interval passed while the detective waited for me to confess. M leaned toward me and gently removed one hand from my face, helping me off the ropes. Mulhearn laughed and said, "What was your motive? Don't worry, Professor. You're not a suspect."

He was playing with me while enjoying his two double scotches, black and neat, and checking a box before his next cigarette.

He tapped the cigarette pack on the table, pulling my attention back to his face. "There are no suspects, and I will officially close the case tomorrow. Had to meet you first. There was no sign of forced entry or struggle. Though, come to think of it, he might have let you into the room, Professor."

Jekyll turned his grin and attention to M. "The cause of death was that he stopped breathing and his heart stopped, or the other way around. No heart attack, no drugs or alcohol in his system. And no suicide note.

"To die in his sleep at his age was strange, so I was called in to investigate. The only mildly suspicious finding was that no cell phone was found. But people lose their phones every day. We checked the phone log: no calls or texts other than to the restaurant confirming the dinner reservation. With no sign of a struggle, it was just the mysterious death of a relatively young man and not a bad way to go."

He eyed his second double, which was almost finished, and then checked his watch and the melting ice. I checked my phone. Six twenty-five.

"I found no real enemies. The coroner's autopsy will list the death as a case of SUDS—sudden death syndrome—which is more common than people realize."

It was as if by giving death a name, the mystery was solved. Dark energy and dark matter, and there you have it—case closed with a bang.

I was relieved not to be under arrest following Mulhearn's gut punch and wondered how I would explain Hope's death to M.

Undaunted, M said, "Dylan expressed concern that his theory had put him in danger, danger we don't fully understand. Maybe you can address that. And you didn't find any papers in his hotel room?"

He looked torn between M's looks and the allure of the cigarette pack. M won. He threw the cigarettes to the table and pushed back in his chair. "In all my years as a detective, my dear, I have never found a theory to be a motive for murder. Detective lesson 101: It's always sex, money, drugs, or the end of a marriage. So your theory goes nowhere. No papers or phone were left. His wife has his personal effects. Unless you can tell me that the professor here has his phone. And if you can, you'll have solved the case for me." He may as well have added *you silly girl*.

M sighed, "WOPA."

"Wopa? Sounds like fun. If you'd like to meet another time to discuss your theory or his theory—any theory—I'd be happy to, but unfortunately my time is up."

His manners offended me even more than they ticked off M. I decided to torture him with questions, delaying his next smoke. "The chairman of Professor Edens's department at Columbia University and a priest that Dylan was meeting with—you may have seen them at the wake—will be arriving soon. Don't you want to stay and question them?"

"Absolutely no interest or time."

I wasn't to be bullied anymore in front of M, so I asked, "How about the suspicious guy who sat near you at the wake—looked like a private detective? You exchanged words with him at the end. Do you think—"

"No, no, no." Mulhearn pushed his chair away from the table. "I was annoyed by how much time I wasted at the service and objected to that man taking pictures, like he was at a wedding. I caught him taking one of me. He was a photographer, not a PI. There because of your dead friend's star child. I found nothing suspicious about anyone at the service, and it's now time for me to go."

I hazarded a counterpunch. "But Dylan was worried about the

government. The CIA had become interested in him and the theory. He noted that concern in his letter to me. The one I gave you. Have you spoken to them?"

He picked up his cigarette packet as if it were his gun to menace me with. He rapped angrily on the table, firing words at me. "Yes, I did, Professor, and they had nothing to do with it. They didn't even know he had returned to the States and was dead. Why don't you go see them—I'm sure they'll confess all to you."

I was confused. "His wife said the CIA contacted you—"

"We were in contact, and how I run my investigation is not your concern." He pounded his chest like a one-handed Tarzan or an insurance salesman with indigestion, reminding me he was armed. I reminded myself that in my fiction Chekhov's Glock would have to take its shot. I didn't press my luck in reality.

For the detective, it was time for pencils down. We'd hit his hard stop of six thirty, and he really needed to smoke. He stood, saying, "I take my leave of the fetching Nancy Drew and her eager Hardy Boy. Good luck with that theory of every little thing."

M didn't stand to say goodbye, but I did. She said, without a hint of irony, "You're going to miss a good dinner."

"You have my number—perhaps another time when it's just the two of us?" *Mulhearn* gave M one last hungry look. Then, like a detective out of central casting, he drained the last of his whiskey, slammed the glass on the table, and went striding away.

No goodbye or handshake. Just left me standing there, calling after him, "I don't think Professor Edens is interested, but we'll let you know if we have any more questions."

M shook her body in a gyrating dance. She raised waving hands toward the skylight, then collected them as prayer hands to her chest, releasing the sarcastic and dark detective from our presence.

With her hands over her heart and peace in her eyes, she was poised to receive my confession.

CHAPTER 16

AFTER M'S ATTRACTIVE and surprising shimmy, the manager magically reappeared. "Are you okay?"

"Fine, thank you, Randy. It's just my shake-off dance."

"Please let me know if you need anything. I had some work in my office, but I'm finished now."

As the manager returned to the wings, I said, "Now we know why Randy ran away from us earlier."

M fluttered her lashes. "What a lovely man that Detective *Mulhearn* was. A charming dinner guest he would have been; I should have insisted he stay. Can I have his number?"

I ignored her teasing, as I was about to "stick a pen in my heart." I painfully offered, "Should I explain what he was alluding to, people dying in their sleep around me?"

"Please. Otherwise I'll have to stay awake all the time around you."

I had a passing thought that maybe she was considering sleeping with me, but first I needed to confess.

I dragged in a long breath, preparing to tell the whole heart-wrenching story as it had played over and over in my head for almost a decade. Other than the cleaned-up and dumbed-down version I'd told the police that day, I'd never shared it with anyone. I took another deep breath, and the fearful child that lived in me floated up into the atrium above, watching as the monologue was finally spoken out loud.

"On an extended Labor Day weekend, 2009, in Cape May, Hope and I stayed at Congress Hall as a celebratory end to a wonderful summer break; we had explored the amazing Amazon, and she wanted to see the ocean after living in the wilds of the jungle rainforest. We planned to drive back to start the new school year the next day. We had a most romantic dinner. I ordered her favorite red Bordeaux, a Brane-Cantenac Margaux 2005, though it cost almost two hundred dollars. Upon returning to our room overlooking the sea, we made love for the last time. Went to sleep. She never woke up. When I woke at first light, her dead eyes were open to me. The doctors said she'd died of an enlarged heart that she had her entire life and that she didn't die alone—she was pregnant. Neither of us knew of the heart problem or about the child inside her, a child conceived in the Amazon forest under a canopy of stars. We probably shouldn't have left our communal tent to venture naked with our sleeping bag into that Garden of Eden, but we did." I trailed off just as the story always did at that point, the biblical reference now taking on even greater significance.

M was tearing up. "I'm so sorry, Sean. Thank you for telling me."

"I blame myself." I looked up at the skylight to avoid eye contact. "I've never admitted that even to myself."

"Why?" She held my hand, and her tenderness drew my gaze back to her. I could say anything.

"I felt her heart so full of love that last night, but after, as we were falling asleep, its beat wasn't quite right, or so I now imagine. You know how you can feel your lover's heart beating?"

"Sean, your only crime was loving her. You can't blame yourself."

I floated slowly back into myself at M's sweet words of forgiveness, and my focus rested on her moist eyes and her hand's soft touch. We observed silence. I felt at peace and liberated after years of torment and guilt from that cold case.

I realized the story included a reference to the last time I made love. I wasn't just rusty; I was the Tin Man. I looked longingly at M, hoping the art of making love was like riding a bike, an activity with long muscle memory.

But would this woman love me? Could I be so fortunate a second time?

M let go of my hand to drink her wine. I lifted my own glass in gratitude for the forgiveness and sense of release.

I had another secret to tell M. Remembering the story of Iya, I wanted to tell her everything to avoid any hint of dishonesty. I took another leap into vulnerability and said, "I haven't told you for fear that if I did, it would have to be good, but I'm writing a novel about Dylan and his ToE, and you play a lead role as the heroine, Brigitte. It's fiction but based loosely on fact until my flight of fancy takes off." I wanted it to sound romantic. "I think the hero and his love will die in the end."

After listening to my somewhat dramatic delivery, she teased me by widening her eyes, looking up, and saying, "See, the atrium didn't come crashing down, did it? And I sort of suspected that you were writing a novel. Dylan told me you were writing one, or at least planning to, so I figured it out—that was why you wanted to meet the chairman and the priest. You know they're not killers, and I don't think they have the ToE. It wasn't the bishop in the bedroom with a candlestick."

"Maybe the professor in the study with a book?"

She folded her hands and leaned forward. "Didn't you wonder why I used your book club title for our dinner? In the novel's movie adaptation, can Jennifer Lawrence play me—or Brigitte, I mean? I hope the hero and Brigitte live and it doesn't end in tragedy."

"That would be well cast, since Bardot is dead."

She smiled at my flattery, which had the beauty of being true.

"And what's your protagonist's name?" she asked.

"I'm using James J. Holmes for now."

"Full and haughty literary name. Will Ethan Hawke play the part?"

"Ouch. It's just a placeholder." I looked down and folded my arms.

"You are sensitive, James," she teased.

"No, *he's* bold and full of daring." If she only knew of his passion and sexual prowess. I unfolded my arms, wanting not to be weak in her eyes. "I'll have to toughen up to be a novelist. I thought Tom Hanks would play James. He's taller and more congenial." I'd already planned to cut all or most of the sex scenes.

"They're both older than you and not as handsome and charming," she said, softening the blow to my ego and fictional name. "And it really is a book club we're hosting then!" she added with contagious enthusiasm.

We almost finished the first bottle of wine while we discussed the novel and plotted our next moves. She hoped to get the chairman and Father Bishop talking about their meetings and discussions with Dylan, to see what they might know about his work and perhaps where it might be hidden. We debated contacting the CIA but decided it wasn't safe and that *Mulhearn* was right; they weren't going to tell two professors anything different than they had already told the detective.

"Sean," M said, her tone serious, "I too have a confession to make."

My heart banged away, ever hopeful.

"I know it sounds grandiose, but I'm determined to find the theory of everything, with or without finding Dylan's work. So meeting the chairman and priest may provide me some guidance in that direction too. Dylan and I had already made a lot of progress on the path; it's now my life's work and purpose. I think we all are either looking for our truth or suffering in the despair of giving up that search."

It wasn't the confession my heart had hoped for, but I was grateful for the intimate confidence and grand nature of her dream.

"Imagine, Sean, if science discovers that which explains the infinitely large and the infinitely small. It wouldn't be a theory but the Truth that encompasses all laws and theories. Sure, there would be deniers, like there are of climate change, and those that can't accept the interconnection of all things at the quantum level. Regardless, the Truth will be a unifying force for good and for humanity's awakening. Dylan and I believed this with all our hearts. Imagine it—the double helix genius of a Buddha and an Einstein. I know I sound a bit crazy, but I know it's true."

I was dumbfounded by the passionate intensity of her words. That passion called for poetry, but I could only inarticulately gush. "I-I understand. You're . . . you're wonderful. Perfect. The ToE we'll together find!" I became lost in her eyes, imagining a kiss. I was thinking too much like a Hamlet or Prufrock.

"Sean, please don't put me on a pedestal. I am far from perfect." Her words punctured my dream of a kiss.

I hadn't put her on a pedestal. I just . . . No, she was right, so why deny it?

"I tend to judge people that way, all good or all bad. One critic of my short stories wrote, 'McQueen's characters are flat cardboard cutouts with no nuance, completely angelic or completely evil.'" I laughed. "Yeah, you tend to remember the bad reviews. Anyway, I know you have flaws, but I know you're good, so I don't see them that way. As flaws."

"Tell me of these flaws?"

"Well, for one, you don't trust men."

"Should I?"

"Maybe not, but present company ex—"

"Excuse me." The words were huffed as a greeting by the much larger and rounder of the two men Randy had led to our table.

I'd forgotten our other dinner guests. The night was still young.

CHAPTER 17

"HELLO, PROFESSOR EDENS," said the chairman. There was no mistaking him. He looked like a Macy's Thanksgiving Day float hovering over us.

M, who I'd imagined would be reserved around her imposing chairman, stood and beamed a welcoming smile. "Hello, sir, and Father . . . Bishop. Welcome! I'm so glad you could join us. Please meet our cohost and literature professor for the evening, Sean McQueen. Sean, this is Chairman Chandler Litton and"—she angled toward the other man—"Father *and* Bishop Stanley Horton, I presume?"

"Father, my child," Father Bishop replied.

M had them seated with a flourish of her arm, the same arm she used to pull the wine bottle from the ice bucket. With the other arm she waved off Randy, who was rushing over to relieve her of the pour. She showed our guests the label before half filling a glass for each.

Father Bishop said, "Ah, yes, the 2009 Chassagne Montrachet Grand Cru."

He nodded knowingly at the chairman, who attempted to puff up his chest. It was more an inflation of his belly upward. The clergyman grimaced disapprovingly as the first—empty—bottle was taken away by one waiter while another opened the second bottle of Chassagne Montrachet.

The chairman said, "My apologies we're a bit late; I got stuck on a call with visiting Cambridge professors who are soon to be lecturing at my university. Time is of the essence, and I had to set them straight on the black hole information paradox, and that's not something one can really rush through. I think they got it in the end. Father Stanley was kind enough to listen, as we had met in my office and I made his driver wait."

"It was fascinating to hear you school them. Information cannot be destroyed . . . but nothing can escape a black hole . . . all the sucked-in matter's information is recorded in a porous ring around the black hole's mouth . . . Something like that?" said Father Bishop.

"Good enough for a layman."

As chairman of science at Columbia and professor of astrophysics, Litton carried himself as a man of great importance who was accustomed to making people wait and having them listen to him. His chair was just able to accommodate his Humpty Dumpty butt, body, and head sitting atop one another. Up close, he smelled musty, like an old barnyard. I mock glared at M, who had failed me in the seating arrangements.

Father Bishop, sidekick, was a bookend to his friend. To the chairman's pomp and intellect, he was righteous and divine; to the chairman's self-importance, he boasted reserve that required respect; and he met the chairman's musty puffs with whiffs of incense.

Father Bishop was a crooked walking stick of a man, smaller and more a triangle, with no round edges. His pontiff's black hat, about a foot high, looked like a ship with its sail coming to a point. His arms were held akimbo to balance his buckling knees. He was all old translucent skin over bones. Even his sharp broken-blood-vessel nose celebrated the trinity. People were staring. I was glad he removed his attention-grabbing hat after being seated, placing it like an off-center-piece on his side of the table. Removing his hat exposed matted and sparse tufts of gray hair.

I was predisposed not to like either of them, based on M's and Natalie's descriptions. Father Bishop's bushy dyed black eyebrows—the brows he'd so offended Natalie with—seemed permanently arched and mangled. I was always uncomfortable around priests, as I hadn't been baptized, and therefore they knew I was going to hell for missing a sacrament whose time had passed me by.

"Father here insists on being called father, though he is ordained a bishop," the chairman said, telling us what we already understood. He then asked M, "Can we get some bread and butter?"

I called the waiter over and passed on the request.

Father Bishop said, "I'm a humble father when dealing with my flock and only a bishop to other bishops and the pope." Here was a man of the strictest hierarchy.

M, hostess and provocateur, said, "Thank you for joining our dinner-party discussion. Think of it as an intimate book club, with our friend Dylan and his research being the book."

The chairman grumbled, "Research? Hmm."

M nodded agreeably. "Yes, research and open-minded investigation into the unknown horizons of scientific discovery. Speaking of investigations, the detective who was assigned Dylan's case was here earlier, although he seemed more interested in whiskey and cigarettes while grilling Sean as a murder suspect than in science, religion, or food and wine. Don't worry, Sean is in the clear—less due to his weak alibi than his not being right for the part. I don't imagine the detective would have added much to our book club in any event. So . . . please tell us about your work with Dylan."

Father Bishop seemed content to sit back and drink. He gulped each glass as though it were his savior.

The chairman spoke for them both when he said, "We're not the smartest men in the universe."

"Just the smartest men in the room," One Step said. I hoped the words sounded more self-effacing than wiseass. M's chuckle didn't help my case. Luckily, the bread and butter arrived.

The chairman paused before choosing to accept my words as sincere, grabbing the bread and dousing a large chunk with an equal measure of butter. "Well, as you know, *Stephen* and I pioneered work into black holes and the singularity of the big bang."

"Hawking," M clarified.

To the chairman, saying Stephen was like saying Mick or Bono, or like my saying J. D., F. Scott, W. B., or T. S.

Butter greased his lips as he regaled us with the obviously well-worn story. The way he told it left the impression he and Stephen had come to the big bang and black hole theories in lockstep collaboration during

Stephen's life, and ". . . now, following his death, well, the burden has all fallen on me."

The chairman presented his and Stephen's theories as fact. I wondered what he thought about imaginary time, but we had only finite time, so I didn't dare ask. It struck me as odd that scientific *theory* was assumed to be fact by those outside the scientific community and even by some of those within it.

"I've taken it on myself to continue the work and defend the honor of his memory," Chairman Litton said. "With his death, the detractors and challengers have become emboldened, even those from his own Cambridge, going around and around on the ring of a porous event horizon. All the discipline and years of painstaking work are now being threatened by scientific mystics pushing strings."

I smiled as an image came to mind—the chairman pushing a wheelchair with his dead hero in it. I was going to enjoy book club. I sat back to observe and take mental notes for the novel.

We let the big chair do almost all the talking, as that seemed to be his expectation and preferential mode of interaction. He spoke in circles, with one repetitive loop after another, each successive loop only slightly advancing the same thought.

"Dylan asked me why the universe exists, and when presented with the accepted wisdom of the science of the big bang, he thought he knew better. *Why the big bang? Why the first cause? Why a universe at all?* And like a child fool ignoring an answer, he was going to teach the wise men."

I felt M bristle at *child fool*, but playing the admiring student, she innocently asked, "But what was before the big bang?"

The chairman gasped before he reassumed his role of smartest *man* in the room and let out a breath. He took infrequent shallow and hard breaths, which were whistles on the inhales and snorts on the exhales. His round head was like a ready-to-pop balloon, and when he got excited, it seemed the incoming air was difficult to take in, and the outgoing breath pressed through his pursed lips like an emission of a bottom burp. He was a very oral and anal man.

"That'sss the question everyone asksss." The red-faced Saturn finally let out his gas. "And though I'm not omniscient, I do know the answer to what came before the first cause of the big bang." After a dramatic pause with arms outstretched, he said, "*No thing*, of course!" He laughed at what he must have considered a clever turn of phrase, as though he'd dunked a basketball over M's head. We laughed politely, or nervously, as we were called to do.

Father Bishop giggled at his clever friend's oratory skills and reveled in being poured a new glass, yet he frowned at the level of the pour. Here was a man not used to an abundance of good wine.

With his rhetorical flourish, the chairman dismissed any concern that the big bang was preceded by no time and no space and no laws of physics. Nothing and a bang, that was it; no more questions, please. It was the accepted wisdom of the current astrophysics game that required all to play by the same rules.

He added, "It's a singularity and by definition happens only once and requires no cause."

"A tautology," I mumbled. I was ignored, except by M, who appreciated my humor and literary take on science.

M turned to me so as not to insult her chairman by telling *him* anything. "It's now believed that the universe is expanding in all directions from every point, so the earth and everything—including you and me—are once again at the center. Dylan agreed everything came from *no* thing, yet he believed everything arose not only one time with a big bang but constantly. And we were considering not only that information and knowledge might be stored in the event horizons of black holes, but that all of it—omnipotence—may be found in the constant source of all creation. An infinite eternity where all past and future and space meet."

The chairman snorted and shifted, looking uncomfortable in his quite comfortable-looking chair that generously accommodated his girth. "He took a partial understanding of the black hole information paradox and was applying it erroneously to everything. You should stick to very small things, Emily."

He and Father Bishop laughed at his astrophysical put-down of a quantum physicist.

There was a reason I had never joined a book club. They were mean.

Our unflapped host took the put-down good-naturedly and said, "Yes, but I'm a quantum *cosmologist*, and didn't the universe emerge from an infinitely small, infinitely dense speck of infinite energy in the big bang—in theory? But please tell us about your meetings and discussions with Dylan and his work."

The chairman acted surprised at the question, though discussing Dylan's theory had been the purpose stated on the dinner invitation.

"Oh, that's another matter." He refueled with more lavishly buttered bread. "I liked the boy very much, with so much enthusiasm for physics despite no education or publishing record in that or any field, as far as I could tell. We were introduced by the dean. Dylan was a friend of a big alumni donor from Wall Street, Dante Laroccafella or something like that. So it was clear I had to tutor Dylan for free, for the sake of the department and university. Dylan's daughter attended our school of drama and, I understand, is quite the starlet now."

I sighed, "Woo," and M sighed, "Pa." I did appreciate his comical take on the seafaring Dante LaRocca's last name.

The chairman took no notice of the sighs, no doubt used to the letting out of wind; whiffs of barnyard continued to bubble up and lingered in my nose. I tried unsuccessfully not to breathe. I blamed M again for my seat assignment. She had taken the seat a safer distance away.

Bringing the chairman to mind would be the perfect antidote if M brought up Zeno's paradox again, and I didn't want to fidget.

The chairman hadn't stopped speaking as I'd taken my mental detour, and I tuned back in to hear him say, "I took Dylan under my wing to teach him the fundamentals of astrophysics, stuff one might get from going to a planetarium and really a waste of my time, but all Dylan was interested in was challenging the big bang—a concept and proof he could not possibly understand—and asking about the possibility that somehow each moment was some sort of big bang. Imagine that! I'm blown to smithereens each instant and reconfigured on the spot!"

It pained me to restrain One Step from reciting the nursery rhyme out loud, so I did for Dylan instead: *All the king's horses and all the king's men couldn't put Humpty together again.* I heard him laugh.

"The best I could glean was that his theory boiled down to one moment leads to the next moment, and one can touch God in the moment. It was all New Age power-of-now silliness and ultimately infuriating. Despite all proofs and reason and my attempts to educate him, he insisted on his challenges to the big bang and other established tenets of physics, telling the chair of astrophysics at Columbia, 'I was looking for laws and math to prove the source of all mathematical laws of time and space.' What rubbish!" He burped again and then, with effort, caught his breath.

For the chairman, speaking was like running a short distance between breaths. As he'd been speaking of Dylan and his theory, his face had become even redder—I thought he might have a heart attack. He looked like a beached whale, out of water, gulping air with a mouth full of bread and butter.

I waited and weighed the medical ethics before entering my first question of book club. "What happened at your last meeting with Dylan?"

Chairman Litton drew some big breaths and said, "Well, after his expression of disregard for math and all scientific proof, I ended our meetings and wrote Emily here—as you no doubt recall—since he mentioned he was meeting with you too on a regular basis regarding quantum physics. And I asked you to consider discontinuing meeting with him, as his arrogance and interests were more in astrophysics and he had insulted the school and my department. You didn't heed my suggestion, did you?"

He glared at M in the bloated and contorted manner of a blow-fish, an expression tamed, with effort, into a grimace and then into a forced smile.

M smiled back at the chairman, though I could see she was taken aback at being chastised for continuing to meet Dylan. I wondered how he knew.

Never the victim, M regained her composure. "Dylan wasn't a university-trained scientist, but he studied more diligently than my students and had a more brilliant mind than all my professors. He was committed to discovering the theory of everything, and many of his insights illuminated areas of quantum physics in new ways. So, yes, I was honored to collaborate with him."

"Yes," the chairman said, "he fancied himself a visionary and genius but was more a Jim Jones than an Albert Einstein. Father Stanley, help me here; what did you think? You were meeting with him too."

Father Bishop, without any loss of focus on M's fine wine, seemed pleased to take a turn pontificating. Nodding, he said, "First, may we have a moment of prayer for Dylan?"

He bowed his head, and I followed suit reflexively.

"We pray Dylan had no hand in his own death and that you called your child home, dear Lord. May God have mercy on his soul. Amen."

One Step begged for release, and M's lips were tightly pressed together, but we both held our tongues.

During a moment of silent reflection, M started to blink at me, and I wondered if the blinking was code for *Okay, let One Step go!* Before I could decide, Father Bishop resumed.

"At the request of my good friend here, I met several times with Dylan on his quasi-religious and quasi-scientific theory research. Dylan was a child who asked why there was something rather than nothing. And then when presented with biblical wisdom, the Word of God accepted for centuries, he knew better. He had some clever charisma, I'll grant him that, but so does the devil."

Is he referring to Milton's sympathetic devil in Paradise Lost *or Blake's angelic devil in* Songs of Innocence and Experience? *You were that kind of devil, so One Step will let that insult pass too.*

"I tried to correct the young man's thinking and his misguided belief in direct experience of the divine, as well as other misplaced views that removed God as creator from the equation."

He paused to gulp from his glass. The chairman seemed lost in his own thoughts. He slapped his menu closed as a sign he was ready to order.

Father Bishop, missing the point of his friend's gesture, talked on.

"Both science and religion have settled that there was a first cause. Science finally came to agree with the church, though our time frames are different, that the universe emerged from a point before which there was no earth and sky, for which God must be the cause, the creator. With the big bang and the questions raised by quantum physics and strings, scientists are now falling back on the mystery and concepts of Catholicism. You see, I'm a bit of a lay scientist." He turned to his partner for approval. Chairman Litton raised his empty fork in salute and protest.

When the priest paused to refresh himself, M said, "That's true. Science more and more is confronting the mysteries of the observable universe as we ambitiously struggle to find that elusive theory of everything that will marry the infinitely large cosmos with the infinitely small quark."

"May I get another glass, please?" our priestly bishop asked, eyes wide and looking shocked that M had interjected her opinion in the middle of his homily.

The chairman added, "And isn't it time to order dinner?"

M signaled to Randy, who seemed distracted by a commotion occurring in the lobby, a disturbance that had drawn the attention of the entire staff. There was currently no one available to take our order. Seeing this, the chairman released a long sigh. Father Bishop carefully adjusted his sailboat hat, as if it needed to be at the exact right angle to the wind while M poured him another glass.

After a long lustful French kiss of his wine, Father Bishop said, "Dylan's ideas were naïve to the point of being hippie-like and perhaps drug-induced; on this point, my friend the chairman and I are in complete agreement. Dylan was only interested in points of great depth regarding creation, atonement, revelation, rapture, and other esoteric church matters and the banned gnostic texts. He had no interest in confession or redemption. It was as if he wanted an advanced theological class without understanding or accepting the basic tenets of faith."

Father Bishop was all church dogma and hierarchy without any of its grace.

"There's a reason the book of Thomas isn't included in the bible. I have prayed that Dylan's godforsaken theories didn't lead him to take his own life. Perhaps he was on drugs. It really is so sad . . . I took the time to attend the young man's strange funeral service at the Quaker Meeting Hall. Quaker was fitting for him. I don't know much about it other than it seems a godless religion of self-reliance."

He paused to watch M fill the chairman's glass and then mine. That was the second time he suggested Dylan might have killed himself. It was also the second time I had to force my shoulders away from my ears. Okay, he didn't know Dylan well, and his death was mysterious. But the possibility of suicide more suited this man's own twisted notion of the just end to Dylan's sacrilegious life. Not setting him straight was difficult, but I was keeping One Step on a short leash. I wanted a kiss more than sarcastic satisfaction tonight.

M topped off the priest's glass. "Do you like the wine, Father Bishop? It must be better than the wine they serve in church." She gave me a secret smile.

He drew in a deep breath and said, "Just Father, please. And your wine is very fine, but the wine of the Eucharist isn't wine when we drink it. You have, of course, heard of the Last Supper?"

"Yes, what a dinner party that was, and what a great man and host was the historical Jesus Christ," M said.

When we married, they'd call us Two Step. And I was definitely going to keep calling the needle-dick Father Bishop, if only in my head.

He arched his brows to an impossible angle in defense of the son of God, cryptically adding, "I asked Dylan if he would take confession each time we met, and he was such an arrogant man he said he had nothing to confess. Nothing offends God more than a sinner ignorant of his own sin. I thought his old friend, who came to me following the Quaker service after he saw me there, was coming for confession, but he wasn't. But that's a private affair, and I digress."

"Dylan's *old* friend?" I asked.

"In age," Father Bishop replied. "I'm not sure how long they'd been friends. He was older than Dylan by maybe a decade." He sighed. "A confession is a sacred matter, and all my consultations are held in the strictest confidence—as you can rest assured ours is today."

The wine had started to take its effect on Father Bishop's thin frame, and either his dry old mind was muddled or he was now hiding something. As I weighed another question about this old friend of Dylan's who went to confession but not to confess, a buzz of fresh air entered the atrium.

A woman flanked by an eager Randy and two other staff members approached our table, the procession weaving through the other gawking patrons with the smoothness of experience. The whole Beekman lounge was stirring, and the energy twisted up and through the room as if a ghost had arrived, dancing in the atrium air. The commotion continued even when the group stopped next to us.

Grace Byrne, Dylan's only child and an award-winning actress who looked like Grace Kelly, grinned cheerfully as she laid a hand on the back of M's chair.

With that dramatic entrance, the stage was set.

CHAPTER **18**

"HELLO," GRACE SAID. "I hope I'm not a totally unexpected guest and not too late?"

I was shocked, but M wasn't at all flustered. "I'm Emily Edens—Em, please—one of your hosts this evening as we honor your father. You are most welcome, Grace; I hoped you might make it."

I belatedly stood as Randy pulled out Grace's chair and ceremoniously poured her a glass of the Chassagne Montrachet, as if she were the Princess of Monaco. Saturn and the crucifix were nailed to their chairs—starstruck.

"My father told me so many good things about you"—she looked pointedly at M and me—"and so much about all the people he had been working with that I couldn't miss this dinner." She smiled at our other guests.

After we adjusted our chairs, with mine still next to the chairman's, Grace turned to me from her seat between M and Father Bishop. "Sean, I hope you remember me. I've heard stories about you since I could first remember. My dad taught me about bullies and karma with your Little Stevie story. He had a copy of the original and said the writing was all yours. I loved your later story too, based on the schoolyard masterpiece, though you made my father a brilliant villain in it."

I was meeting a ghost. She was Dylan in her eyes, speech, and manner but a young, attractive lady. She even let her eyes linger the way he did, but her being female, that was okay. Our table was now the center of the universe. Some of the patrons at the bar and lounge may have recognized the bishop and his pontiff's hat, but all recognized Grace and Grace and M's collective beauty under the atrium sky.

"It's so nice to finally meet you. Or actually *again*. You probably don't remember our last meeting; you were maybe only ten."

"Oh, yes I do," she said. "I remember you and Dad were so silly together. I had so much fun at the merry-go-round and Central Park Zoo that day."

Dylan and I may have been high, as her lingering and quizzical gaze suggested.

"Your words were so well chosen at the wake," I said. "You have your father's poetic talent in your use of words. We both loved Emerson."

M nodded. "It was a wonderful eulogy. But, Sean, we haven't yet introduced our other guests, who've been telling us about matters of physics and religion that they discussed with Grace's father. Grace, it's like a book club getting together to discuss your father's life and work."

Introductions were made. Grace, the most successful, was the only one without a title. As with M, her outward beauty was merely the wrapping paper for the extraordinary gifts of spirit and mind.

Grace was delighted with the white Burgundy. Father Bishop pursed his lips at seeing the last drop go to someone else. But he recovered when new glasses and the two bottles of red arrived.

"The 1999 Giacomo Conterno Barolo Monfortino Riserva." Randy read the labels, auditioning for Grace as the waiter in a Fellini film. He then poured the padre's lifeblood into the fresh—and larger—glasses.

Despite their self-importance, the chairman and Father Bishop seemed to realize they were trumped at book club by the movie star daughter of our honored dead. And they were subdued for the moment, perhaps feeling guilt after the one had been talking trash about Grace's father's academic delusions and the other suggesting he committed suicide.

Grace's presence would change the topic and cause our rude guests to be better behaved and, I feared, less forthcoming.

After we placed our dinner order, I was content to sit back and enjoy the fantastic food and wine while watching the lovely ladies dance between the twin pillars of ugly oligarchy.

Grace was pleasantly disarming in her choice of topic. "Dr. Litton, my father told me that you and Bishop Horton were involved at the time *A Course in Miracles* was being written. I've read it and am fascinated by your disapproval of the book. Can you tell me about that?"

"We feared the supposed revelation by two professors in the College of Physicians and Surgeons at our university would negatively impact the school's good name. The university asked me, a young but well-regarded professor, to discreetly investigate the work of the professors. It was the mid-seventies, when hippie thought was coalescing into New Age occultism. And the two claimed to be 'channeling' Jesus into a New Age bible."

The chairman was again content to do all the talking, at least before his food arrived. Bread with butter wasn't substantial enough to slow him down.

"We shouldn't use *bible* in association with that book," Father Bishop added.

"Okay, Father," the chairman said. "After some research, I found that the church was also interested in the crazy project. It was then I started consulting with a humble, brilliant priest who was looking into the matter from the church's perspective—my good friend here." He looked across the table at Father Bishop, who seemed pleased to have been admitted into the chairman's high orbit of important friends.

"The father's initial gracious view was that the two professors were having collective hallucinations—perhaps LSD-induced—and were totally deluded but not frauds. In any event, the church considered the book they were looking to publish to be misguided and more. *Dangerous*." He raised his fork like Poseidon's trident and pointed it toward his holy friend. "Father?"

"*A Course in Miracles*. That title is a misnomer," Father Bishop said. "Very unfortunate false revelation by a blasphemer claiming to speak in the name of Christ and distorting all Christian theology. It has deceived many earnestly seeking God. It's based on the forbidden practice of transposition mediumship."

The chairman said, "At the time—and I still believe this—that was a charitable explanation, and I thought they were a conman and a woman academic who may have been an unwitting accomplice in the collaboration. Let me explain," he added, leaning forward.

I leaned back and angled my chair even closer to M's.

"I discovered that the male professor working on the book was at the same time working with the CIA on mind-control experiments, and I came to believe he was controlling his poor colleague, a female Jewish professor who was supposedly receiving messages from Jesus."

I mused out loud, "That makes sense."

"How's that?" Father Bishop asked.

"Well, Jesus had a Jewish mother." I almost said *and father* but chose not to one-step.

"I'll take it you're joking," Father Bishop said, unamused.

I wished I hadn't been so restrained.

"*A Course in Miracles.*" The chairman choked on the words. "Even the name should have set off alarm bells for any sane person, but we were too late. The book was published and Oprah later endorsed it, and now she may be president! So millions were brought under the spell of this cult and mind-control system."

Grace said, "What a good story!"

She shared her father's enthusiasm. Even when they didn't agree with others, they both had a way of being engaging and keeping the conversation lively.

Though the chairman didn't need the encouragement, he had the floor and a head of steam. "While seeing what could be done to prevent its publication, I contacted the CIA, and they were convinced the male professor was using their mind-control techniques but didn't believe it to be within their jurisdiction—or concern—to intervene, despite the use of their techniques by one of their own operatives. I think they were actually proud of the effectiveness of their brainwashing methods.

"Despite refusing to help me, they were only too willing to recruit me as the price of making contact. Since then, I have been operating as a free expert consultant to the Agency on matters of astrophysics. I am a humble patriot at heart."

Father Bishop, sloshing his wine in a failed attempt to swirl it before swigging, said, "An important service to our country. We all must do our duty."

The chairman again saluted his friend with his empty fork, which he was keeping at the ready. "You might be amused to know that they, the CIA, took a passing interest in Dylan's theory of an unlimited source of energy coming into being each instant. Such silliness . . . Sorry, Grace."

"What? You must tell us about the CIA's interest in Dylan," M said.

"I want to hear too," Grace said.

So did I. The CIA *had* been interested in Dylan. *Sorry that I doubted you, buddy. It sounded like you might have been smoking too much of the new high-powered* flower *and become paranoid.*

The chairman tapped at the table with his fork, hesitant and calculating how to cross a minefield.

"I can't disclose any confidences or government secrets"—he tapped again—"only the science. So . . . while discussing the second law of thermodynamics with my scientific supervisor at the CIA, I made a lighthearted entropy joke regarding Dylan's view that more energy was entering the universe every instant, somehow increasing the collective consciousness and leading to the expanding universe. Next thing I knew, I was meeting with—*again*—the *Guru*." He trailed off the name quite softly and waited, as if he expected a big bang to follow.

"A lighthearted entropy joke," I said. "Please tell it."

"I just did," he replied. "He's the same man I met many years before about *that* book."

Grace expertly swirled her wine, as M did when she became excited. "A guru in the CIA! This may make a great movie script. What can you tell us about this guru?"

The chairman peered around as the Guru's name was spoken aloud, and still speaking softly, he said, "Please forget I mentioned him and that . . . that *code* name. He's a legend in the small circle I operate within in the CIA. And let me be clear—I am not CIA but an unpaid expert consultant, a patriot, working with the full knowledge and support of the university. This man is the head of a CIA division and my supervisor's manager. His epithet . . . He was named for his mandate being all things otherworldly: mind control, telepathy, remote viewing, space travel, and more recently, artificial intelligence, internet warfare, quantum computing, and neuro-computer interface. Despite being a master of fantasy, he's an intimidating man even for me and not a man to cross."

"For you, Chairman?" Grace said. "I find that difficult to believe, a man of your stature and position."

She was definitely good at playing a part and drawing out our other characters' lines.

"He has Putin-red eyes, lasers that draw one in. Though his words and manner put one at ease, it's the ease one feels swinging on a trapeze or sitting on a wall high above the ground."

One Step could not resist an aside to M. "All the king's horses." She smiled but remained focused on the guru story.

The chairman never paused. "This man, a scientist by training, lectured me on the importance of his new single-minded mission—to discover and control the theory of everything for our country. We were in some race with Russia, he said, rambling off some knowledge-as-power reasoning. He went on about how $E=MC^2$ led to nuclear power, and quantum physics is leading to quantum computers that will be able to predict the outcome of any event. The discovery of a theory of everything would give an individual or company or country the ability to rule financially and militarily and to control the minds of the vox populi. He was certain that the key to his power and glory lay in the ability to reconcile the infinitely large with the infinitely small, to be found in some nonphysical primary constant state."

"Well, that's where they would meet," I blurted out to amuse myself, and in that alone succeeded.

"What?" The chairman looked at me as if I were an annoying third grader.

"In the instant of constant creation," I said to complete my amusement and trying to impress M and channel Dylan.

"Moving on . . . His charge at the CIA led to great advances in artificial intelligence, including an AI that can read minds, which he called Veritas, and an AI computer program that can alter any written treatise, essay, or article with a few keystrokes to suit his ends. He called that Apate."

"A-pa-te." I corrected his pronunciation. "The goddess of deception."

"Thank you, Professor. Well, suffice it to say he's convinced the theory of everything will be the last great leap forward in AI and will animate his crazy quantum-computer dream. And how that relates to brain-computer interface—well, he lost me there." He shook his oversize head in disbelief, a wobbling bobblehead with jaws and chins that jiggled like JellO.

"So one by one I had to explain Dylan's concepts the best I could. He kept me over two hours, asking about everything I'd discussed with Dylan and at times seeming sympathetic to Dylan's views. He finally let me go, asking me to forward my notes and communications with Dylan. He would have gotten them in any event, so I sent him the paperwork. He said to let him know if I heard from Dylan again, which I did when Dylan wrote me about his coming home."

Grace, swirling her wine again, said, "I want to meet this Guru!"

The chairman's large flabby frame visibly shuddered. "You don't. And please don't use that name. I shouldn't have." The chairman waved his arms like a baseball umpire signaling safe, and the topic was closed. "I've talked too much, and *ahhh* . . . here comes the food."

Seeing he felt anything but safe, One Step pondered how to use *guru* in a sentence.

The appetizers had arrived, a cause of distraction to the chairman. If talking was his strenuous exercise, eating was rough sex with bread and butter foreplay.

With fork and knife poised to strike, he turned to Father Bishop, who was still more interested in the wine than the food. "Father Stanley, tell them how you saved the woman author of that book."

"Only Christ can save a person's soul. I was merely his instrument."

"You are too humble." The chairman's fork was full of delicately balanced warm and wet foie gras, and his attention was on that and not the discussion. He was eager to pass the torch. "Years after it was published and the damage done, the good father was able to change the mind of the duped woman author, the alleged 'channeler' of Jesus. Now, do tell."

Without further delay, he set to inhaling his hot goose liver, sucking up fat with an inward whistle.

His glass having been empty for almost a full minute, the priest gazed longingly at it and asked M, "May I have another glass of wine?"

Refreshed with Barolo, Father Bishop could begin.

"Years later there was some redemption as I worked with the lady professor who had been convinced by the devil—or through mind control—that she was receiving messages from Jesus. On her deathbed she recanted and cursed the book, made confession, and although a Jew by birth, was baptized and took communion and received God's forgiveness through me. May she too rest in peace."

He looked at his audience, expecting us to marvel at his humble ability to forgive a woman who had done so much damage to the Word of God. I was more impressed by her ability to take all the sacraments in one final sitting before heading to heaven with all the credentials necessary to enter the pearly gates.

I tried to paste an expression of appreciation on my face, but I probably just looked baffled by how God's forgiveness flowed only through anointed ones known by their collars and black dress. I had to avert my eyes for fear Father Bishop might see my unbaptized heart. His eye contact was aggressive. He was a male lingerer, and as inebriated as he was, one with no inhibitions.

M asked the two oligarchs, "Did either of you receive Dylan's final theory or even a draft?"

Father Bishop shook his head, while the chairman, eyes on the last bite of his still-warm foie gras, must have forgotten Grace was there, because he replied, "No. And I'm not interested in juvenile science fiction."

"All science is fiction or theory until proved as fact," M declared.

Grace, more sweetly than the context warranted, said, "And you saw my father's work as a threat similar to *A Course in Miracles?*" There was a method to her acting.

The chairman, who should have been embarrassed that the nexus had been made, replied, "Let me finish." He took in his last gasp and swallowed the loose goose without chewing. "Not a threat exactly, but not something based on science and scientific research and discipline or proof. More New Age poetic fantasy. He should have stuck to poetry. His theory had some simplistic lay appeal, but it might have become a diversion to serious scientific inquiry. I really liked your father, and he was special in his way. That's why I introduced him to Father Stanley here. You would think Dylan, a Catholic by birth, would have heeded the guidance of a bishop."

"God rest his soul," Father Bishop said. "He spoke in quasi-scientific terms, but in denying God as the first cause, he was no religious man. God rest his soul."

Grace said, "I'm not sure that's what he wanted. He believed in reincarnation until enlightenment is obtained—perhaps then the soul may rest with God. Though he did show me where he wanted his body to rest in peace. He—"

"Well, as long as he accepted Christ, even at the very end," Father Bishop said. "There are many paths to salvation, but only if we accept the Lord Jesus Christ."

The conversation was taking a dark turn, and I feared more insensitivity to come, but then M said to Grace, "Dylan and I agreed that there was a source of creation—perhaps one universal consciousness—and his insights into matters and questions of quantum physics were very profound."

Grace smiled. "Thank you, Em. I know he didn't believe in a patriarchal God who acted just once in a single act of creation but in one that was a constant infinite and eternal presence each moment of creation." She sounded like a student of Hope's.

"Your father was brilliant, and he loved you so much," M said.

The main course arrived on that note of harmony between the actress and the quantum cosmologist. It was presented along with M's two 2007 Brunellos. Old Father Bishop was lapping me in glasses—two to my one—determined to match my every sip with a gulp. It was clear the six bottles would be finished, though Grace was on only her second glass.

While the clergyman was a prolific drinker, the scientist was a pro-found eater. The steak and *pommes frites*, with a side of creamed spinach, looked small in front of him. As the chairman shuddered and ogled his rare steak, I made the mistake of looking into his mouth, poised in an O. It felt as if I was peering into a black hole ringed by inflamed red lips. I considered allowing my plate of roast chicken to be sucked in. I'd lost all appetite.

Humpty Dumpty's ecstatic feeding was interrupted only by the heated breaths he took while carving the next big bite. If it wasn't for my negative judgment of the man, there may have been something endearing in his sheer primal enjoyment of meat.

M, who was outside the pull of the event horizon and who didn't share my fear of priests, engaged in banter with Father Bishop while the chairman focused on his snack and I worked on settling my stomach. Grace sat back to eat her mushroom-asparagus risotto and enjoy her costar's lines of inquiry.

M's questioning began. "What was there before God created the world?"

Father Bishop replied, "God." He drank.

"Why did God create the world?" M asked.

"Only God knows." He drank.

"Once creation was created, what was God's role?"

"He sent his only son to provide us the New Testament and now speaks through the pope—who ministers through his bishops and priests—and the Holy See." He drank.

"Who created God?" M asked.

Father Bishop arched his already arched eyebrows and said, "God needs no creation."

For M's amusement, I said, "He's just like a singularity!"

Father Bishop was not amused and held up his hand, silently demanding that M cease her questioning so he might drink his wine in peace. After finishing the glass, he called for more wine with the same raised hand. But for my negative judgment, he might not have been a glutton of fine wine but a grand master Chevalier du Tastevin.

M said, "Here you go," and poured him a college pour of Brunello for suffering through the ordeal. "Thank you, Father. Please excuse my questions. I find it all so fascinating."

"We are all seekers until we find Christ. Are you a Catholic, my child?"

"No, but I like Christ's teachings and the Buddha's."

There was another awkward pause and an arching of the eyebrows following M's kindly heresy and her One Step. So many things to love about her.

As Father Bishop sought how best to regain his authority and convert M, we all set to eating, engaging in small talk and catching up to the chairman, who had almost finished his slab of beef.

As the main course was coming to an end, Grace posed a question to the old men.

"Do either of you know anyone who may have my father's theory? Dad's friend here"—she smiled at me—"may go all the way to Kathmandu looking. Perhaps you could save him the trouble."

"No trouble," I said. "I want to go and meet Dylan's guru there!" One Step was ecstatic. The chairman grunted and let out some gas revenge.

"No," Father Bishop said. "And in the end, I'm not convinced he even had a theory. I think it was merely an aspiration that he had proclaimed to Chandler before coming back to New York to die or take his own—" He bit down hard on his wine-soaked words before changing direction to say, "Before leaving us all wondering where it was."

Then, out of context, tipsy Father Bishop started into an invocation. "Dear Lord, may Dylan find peace in the sacrifice of Jesus, our Lord, who said, 'Suffer the little children to come unto me.' May God have mercy on his soul."

With those ironic words and his insistence in front of Grace that Dylan had committed suicide, I was done with him. My mind was torn between an Irish Catholic boy's duty to honor a bishop, regardless of how debased, and the ornery One Step. One Step won.

"Regardless of what you thought of his theory, Dylan had more integrity than anyone I've known and wasn't one to take his own life.

Of this, I have no more doubt than that Jesus didn't hang himself upon the cross."

I mentally deconstructed my use of negatives, but I'd clearly gotten my point across, as an awkward pregnant moment passed with everyone looking down at their plates or up at the skylight.

Finally, M turned the page. "Dessert or after-dinner drinks, anyone?"

With the chairman finishing his last bit of steak fat and Father Bishop succeeding in obtaining the last glass of Brunello, both were satisfied, even if my words left a bad taste in their mouths. They declined with shakes of the head.

Grace said, "Not for me, but thank you for a wonderful meal. We must get together when you and Sean get back from your trip so I can hear all about it."

Something I'd said to her mother must have led to Grace's thinking we were going to Kathmandu.

Before I could correct her, Grace Byrne demonstrated her Academy Award–worthy skills without uttering a single word. In one take, she turned fluidly from M and me to Father Bishop, her hand gracefully sweeping the tablecloth, her middle finger catching the very tip of Father Bishop's wine glass. He had let go of the glass for just an instant to straighten his pontiff's hat, which had floated on the table the entire evening.

Such a lovely *ting* as her nail caught the lip and set the crystal gently spinning. In desperation to save his savior, Father Bishop reached out too quickly, knocking the glass from its axis. The bloodred stain splashed over the white tablecloth as the glass shattered. Book club was over.

CHAPTER 19

GRACE GASPED AT THE comical communion. "Oh my God, I am so sorry, Father! I mean Bishop!"

As everyone stood to avoid the spill, I couldn't hold back a grin, but I managed to restrain One Step from clapping.

"I'll have a bottle of Brunello sent to you tomorrow first thing" was M's quick peace offering.

Father Bishop weighed the loss and gain and then, with some difficulty, said to Grace, "Don't worry, my child, accidents happen." Without any pretense of sincerity to M, he added, "And that won't be necessary."

As goodbyes were said, even their handshakes offended me. The chairman's shake was too strong and long, with the alpha male tug of hands toward his gut. And while the bishop held out his hand—for a kiss, perhaps—I chose to shake the cold skin and bones. After that, he tried to avoid shaking the women's hands, but when confronted with their outstretched hands in turn, he shook them as if they were made of jagged glass or the women were suffering from a menstruating stigmata.

Randy, who had rushed to the scene of Father Bishop's wine tragedy, suggested to Grace that she might want to slip out through a delivery door to an alleyway to meet her driver, as photographers had gathered at the exits of the Beekman and Augustine. M and I joined Grace and left with the manager, while the chairman and Father Bishop waited at the table for their driver to arrive.

Out of their sight in the lobby, M started her punklike shaking dance, similar to the one she'd performed when the detective had left. She looked goofy and sexy and endearing at the same time—a good look for her. She made me want to dance with her, fast or slow, any way she chose.

"My shake-off dance," she told Grace.

Grace and I joined in the silly pogo-twisting shakedown that concluded with prayer hands lifted high and then brought down to the heart. We all laughed, relieved of the negative energy of stale dogma and insults.

Randy was eyeing a group of patrons who had followed us out from the bar. Judging from their loud exclamations of disappointment, they'd apparently failed in their attempt to get their cell phones in position to record our dance, thereby missing a bonanza of hits and likes on their social media pages for catching a dancing star. They now were rudely snapping pictures and video of our escape.

We escorted Grace to her secret exit and away from the gathering gawkers. The manager led the way through the hotel lobby, behind the front desk, and to the side, where an Asian silk screen of Shangri-La hid a door to a corridor that held a small back office and storage rooms.

As we stood in the corridor by the exit door to her alley getaway, I asked Grace, "Do you have your father's original copy of 'The Little Stevie Story'? I'd love a copy of that."

"I actually do—I found it recently. Dad kept all his memorabilia in a chest in the basement. I'll send you a copy; I assume my mom has your contact info?"

"Now she does, yes. Do you think he kept his work notes or the theory there too?"

Grace, voice shifting from LA actress to innocent child, said, "No. Sorry. I've been rummaging through Dad's time capsule of memories since his death, and there is nothing about a theory or any papers regarding his scientific work. I hope you don't mind—I've read the letters you sent him over the years."

"Now that's embarrassing," I said, secretly pleased he'd kept them and sad I'd stopped writing him years ago.

"Not at all. You had such a great relationship all those years. Thank you for being a friend to my dad. The condolences you sent to my mom brought her comfort in her darkest hour, and your visit brought her around as well. Will you keep in touch?"

"Of course. You remind me so much of him. It's strange, he still feels very much with me. Almost more than before. I hope you don't mind me saying that?"

Grace smiled and gazed at me the way Dylan did. "Not at all. It's very sweet of you."

She turned to M and held out her hand. The women did the four-hand female version of a handshake, more than a man-shake but less than an embrace.

"Thank you for hosting. It was great to meet the two of you and I was curious to meet the two of them." And then she turned to me. "And I won't spoil the surprise, but you're going to love the Deeksha and the people there in Kathmandu."

"That's just a fantasy of mine. I don't think we—I—will actually go." I felt obliged to correct her this time.

"But do tell us something about Juno and the Deeksha," M said.

Grace laughed. "That's a tall order. Hmm . . . It's like a great film that can only be spoiled by my description of it, but I came away believing that anyone with an open heart who is admitted into the ambit of Juno's Big Love will come away with that heart illuminated. What an experience it was." Her eyes became angelic with the memory, and she clutched her chest, taking a deep cleansing breath.

"Well, Sean wears his heart on his sleeve," M teased. "So that's pretty open-hearted."

"When I went there, I was being pulled down into a whirlpool of celebrity ego, the snort of cocaine and the bubbling of champagne. I see it so clearly now—how beauty becomes divorced from truth, lost in mirrors of diamonds and glass. I was saved by . . . Well, I hope you'll see someday."

M asked, "Do you think the theory is there?"

"I would think so. That's where Dad was working on it. But he didn't share it with me while I was there or after. Either way, it's worth the trip to meet Juno and the entire family."

She pulled a scarf from her bag and draped it over her hair for her exit. "I do have some doubts. My mother's trying to keep me away from the negative conspiracy-theory press, but I don't share her concern about that, and I'm not so sure my father died in his sleep. After meeting Abbott and Costello in there, I don't think they had anything to do with it, but the CIA . . . That Guru! We aren't in Russia, but maybe they . . . I just don't know. Be safe. And let me know if you decide to go to Kathmandu. I can write the Deeksha, telling them to expect you. Please let me know if you find Dad's theory."

I nodded, and M said, "Of course. Good night."

Grace asked, "Can I give you a lift?"

"No, thanks; we have a car coming," M said. They hugged.

I had to ask. "Was that really an accident, your tipping of Father Bishop's wine glass?"

"Professional secret. Thank you for defending my father." She smiled.

I laughed while hugging her goodbye. Grace opened the door, and flashbulbs went off as she got into the waiting car. She had won the award but lost her game of cat and mouse.

As we backtracked, Randy, who had stayed in the corridor during the goodbyes, excused himself to go to his office. M and I proceeded through the hidden door, but we both stopped when we saw, through the slats of the Asian screen, the chairman and Father Bishop standing in the lobby.

I grabbed M's arm and pointed to the floor, a signal to stay right where we were. I didn't want to say good night to them again and perhaps resuffer their awkward handshakes. M nodded.

"My driver will drop you uptown if he ever gets here." Father Bishop was on his phone. "Where are you? Nassau Street hotel entrance. That's right, the hotel entrance, not the Augustine side." He ended the call. "These downtown streets are a labyrinth. He'll be here soon."

M and I had to suppress giggles, holding our breath as we hid less than three feet away. She squeezed my hand to prevent me—or was it her—from laughing. Her gesture calmed my funny bone, as my attention was now flowing into our hands. Those two hands were one, shared fingers and palms making love. Time to improvise and go for a kiss.

Before my lips could follow my inspiration, the chairman spoiled the moment by opening his mouth.

"I didn't expect to see his daughter here tonight; that was a bit awkward. Emily had told me the wife couldn't make it but said nothing about his starlet taking her place."

He leaned into Father Bishop and started to whisper, but we were near enough to hear.

"I'll have to tell the Guru they're looking and that he may plan on going to Kathmandu. That Guru bedevils me. He operates his mandate with almost complete autonomy within the Agency. I think it's because no one truly understands what he's doing, but they see results. He believes he's destined to be the father of the ultimate theory of everything, and he's convinced from Professor Edens's work with Byrne that they made a breakthrough and may have discovered this knowledge. He said something about the two of them finding some lost theory of Einstein's regarding the speed of light. It's all rubbish, I say. But he may have had Byrne killed. It scares me. He scares me. I've known you both since the seventies, and I've become convinced he's a soulless psychopath."

"We all have souls. But some have been sold to the devil."

"Okay, Father. Even so, the Guru's interest in Dylan's work is obsessive and pigheaded. No matter, I hope his theory never sees the light of day, and the Guru will see to that. He'll guard it like the nuclear codes if he gets his hands on it, and will try to make alienlike machines and weapons from the pseudo-science. He wants to go down in history as an Einstein, a Hawking—"

"Or a Litton." Father Bishop finished the chairman's thought.

"Well, that's kind of you to say . . . I felt obliged to tell him about this dinner. And he went on like a Baptist minister about how everything is energy, energy is power, and the true theory of everything would disclose the source of this energy and had to be kept from our enemies—and even the common man—for the good of the country and mankind. He's a bit delusional and got abusive when I tried to tell him string theory was close to the grand unified theory if you just assume nine dimensions of space and time."

"Abusive how?" I was glad Father Bishop asked.

"He accused me of pushing strings and said that was the problem with physics—people like me look up to the big sky, while string theorists and quantum scientists only look at the very small, and no one is looking at the nonphysical universe."

The chairman paused for his punch line: "Not much to see there."

Father Bishop found this hysterical, and his drunken giggling almost made me laugh.

"Well, we did our job to dissuade the two of them from their search; that was his directive. The Guru also said he found something of Dylan's that suggests where his man will find the theory in Kathmandu. Well, you heard me—I tried to warn the two of them about him. He's a madman in his pursuits. We performed our roles tonight. You did a good job suggesting suicide; he believes that will dampen further inquiries."

Now crushing my hand, M stared at me with wide eyes.

My blood surged. This was my first experience of the illicit joy of eavesdropping. We were naughty hand-holding schoolchildren hiding from the authorities and learning adult secrets. I was afraid they might hear my heart beating.

Father Bishop said, "It's your duty to inform *him*. And you did make it clear the CIA and Guru were interested. They can put two and two together—danger and stay away. We don't want Dylan's nonsense confusing my flock or your science. I found your Emily more than a bit sacrilegious, just like Dylan. And Professor McQueen seemed content to drink all the wine and let his women do all the talking until the end, when he committed blasphemy."

"But, Father, you don't know the true godless until you've spent time with the Guru. I don't know if it was to scare or impress me, but he lectured me today on his artificial intelligence for the future. Thank God it was over the phone. His withering presence always reminds me that he knows my secrets—and everyone else's—or could effortlessly fabricate a few damnable details. His view of the future is pure science fiction where brain and computer merge."

"Do tell, or dare you not say?"

Father Bishop sounded ambivalent about receiving the chairman's knowledge, though I could tell from M's big eyes that she wanted to hear it all.

"Well, beyond the benign toys of Veritas and Apate that I mentioned to our dinner companions, the Guru has turned all his focus and resources to AI and insisted he be charged with the country's pursuit of the theory of everything. He's convinced the theory will lead to omnipotent artificial intelligence. Putin and Russia have amassed a team of scientists, backed by all the powers of the state enterprise, to develop quantum computing. They believe the computer will arrive at the theory of everything first and somehow the theory and supercomputer will together lead to some evolutionary leap. The Guru is determined to take that leap first."

Through a peephole in the screen, I watched as the chairman shook his head, hands, and belly, as if in some grotesque parody of M's shake-off dance.

"His experience with the transpersonal, through something called the gateway project, has led him to believe in an omnipotent cosmic intelligence. Not a god but a platonic mathematical world that controls the physical world, a mathematical world that AI will someday soon access or replicate. His tech staff is working with quantum physicists on his universal quantum computer—"

"Sounds like that demonic movie, *Doma Matrix* or something like that."

It took all of my self-restraint not to correct Father Bishop. Instead I squeezed M's hand again and almost moaned when she squeezed mine back even harder.

"Well, Father, I think he's mad, imagining himself lost in a cloud of omnipotent artificial intelligence, realizing some ultimate culmination of self in brain-computer interface. It does sound like a science fiction movie."

"God protect us. And I think I see my car now." He left the chairman to check.

The chairman wasted no time in letting go a loud eruption of gas in our direction. A moment later he left, leaving only his stink behind.

M grimaced. "I can't hold my breath any longer."

We peeked around the screen to ensure they were gone. The front desk clerk, who might have heard the fart or at least smelled it, frowned at us disapprovingly as we passed, saying, "Good night."

M said, "Wow. Now we know what it's like to be a fly on the wall or somewhere worse. Our car's here; may I have my hand back now?"

"Sorry. I thought you'd given it to me to keep."

We left the Beekman in M's Uber. The radio was announcing a major volcanic eruption in Bali. "Eruptions large and small, distant and proximate," I mused for M.

During the silence and as the chairman's words sank in, I found myself in a two-handed face rub, which M laughed at. "You're going to hurt yourself."

My thoughts settled sufficiently for me to say, "A bad habit that's started up again when I get over-agitated and confused." I fisted my hands on my lap. "Dylan killed by the CIA. Alien machines and weapons . . . I couldn't write this. My agent would laugh at me."

"I'm thinking that the chairman led the Guru to have my office searched," M said. "Even if he's only half as determined to find the ToE as the chairman thinks he is, it can't be for effective killing machines— we already could kill everybody in a minute. A more likely application is artificial intelligence and mind control."

"M, this all may be putting you—us—into too great a danger. What if Dylan *was* killed by the CIA or even a guru gone rogue?"

"Sean McQueen, what choice do we have? To meet a challenge and an opportunity like this and then slink away in fear? We have to get to Kathmandu and find the theory before they hide it from scientific view and pervert it for their own use!"

After a moment of reflection, I said, "Onward. I will not limp away 'like a frog in frost!'" My fear was more than overcome by the excitement of going to Kathmandu with M and the chance to quote an obscure line from Keats's letters to Fanny.

"I wonder what they think they've found in Kathmandu," M said. "Maybe they have Dylan's phone. But we have the list of PTBTs. The chairman was just speculating and being dramatic. Like you said, they can't go around killing all his friends too."

I rubbed my hands together, itching for pen and paper. "What great material for my murder mystery. Your chairman knew Dylan was coming to New York and was ready to publish his theory, and he told his Guru . . . a Guru hell bent on finding Dylan's theory. What a character he'll be." I inched toward M and put my arm behind her on the seat. When she didn't cringe, I dropped the arm to her shoulders. "I wonder who went to Father Bishop for confession as Dylan's old friend. It will definitely be Dick in the novel, the man from the wake who sat near us and had a spat with the detective."

"Hmm, Dick?" M played along but inched away. "Maybe another name would do? In a Dan Brown novel, it would be time . . ."

She frowned at my blank face and pretended to push me away. I pulled my daring arm back to my side.

"Dan Brown, author?"

I shrugged. I knew he was a popular author of commercial fiction, but I didn't know much more than that.

"You literary snob," she said. But she was laughing. "He writes gripping religious and scientific thrillers. Anyway, now would be the time for us to go to the CIA and match wits with their Svengali."

"Maybe you should write the novel. I never respect an author until they're dead." I joked in a bid to appear less haughty. "You don't really want to go to the CIA, do you?"

"No. Not yet. I don't think we would learn anything; the detective was right in that regard. Though the chairman seems to think they may have had Dylan murdered. But that would be big, wouldn't it? Really big. Can that be real?"

I was overwhelmed and muttered, "Yes, so much we may never know. It's daunting."

"That's a good word for it. First, before anything else, let's go to Kathmandu and find the ToE before they do. My friend in Athens who heads the program there will understand my delayed start at the university. I can contact my travel agent and book the first flight we can get. Okay?"

Okay? Was she really asking that? "I'm so excited." So excited that not only my heart but my whole body might spontaneously combust. "Of course okay. I could go with you tomorrow. Wow, we'll be in Kathmandu soon—if the government allows us to go. You going to send that Brunello to the boozy bishop?"

M smiled. "Yes, a 1969. He'll salivate at the year and convince himself it's good, but it's aged as poorly as he has—thin and barren of all fruit, with a nose of old barnyard stink like his friend the chairman. He should like that."

I postponed my planned kiss and expression of love that would have made Romeo blush and Juliet gush. M wouldn't be dying to me in Athens but coming alive with me in Kathmandu! I was catching up with James.

She dropped me in Chelsea with an extra-long hug that bound us together in our dangerous conspiracy.

CHAPTER 20

A MONTH HAD PASSED SINCE Dylan died. But his death—along with the mystery and danger of our quest—continued to drive my imagination. I found myself speaking to Dylan about his homicidal guru and what we could expect in Kathmandu. He was as frustrating in death as in life, responding like a ghost each time I demanded he just tell me where the damn theory was. The same word would echo in his mocking spectral voice—*The Tao . . . Tao . . . Taooo.* I vowed not to ask again just to have him point me back, like a smartass yogi, to my path, to my way, to the Truth.

Thanks to Father Bishop, I didn't drink too much at book club the night before. By late morning, our flights were booked for Independence Day. That meant two days apart from M, dreaming of exploring with her in that exotic land of magic and mystery, gurus and goddesses.

I spent most of my time at my local bookstore and at my desk working on my novel while exchanging emails and texts with M. My thoughts alternated between those twittering with love of M and excitement for the adventure to come and those twitching with fear because of the Guru and what he might do to stop us.

My books looked sad, like yesterday's newspapers. The small apartment felt like a prison cell of my past circumscribed life. And I was glued to the news of the world.

A simmering Middle East had become a bonfire of ancient hatred sparked by global warming and a want of global humanity. Several Western journalists had been detained, and bombs were going off. My escape—our flight to Kathmandu with a long layover in Dubai—was now in doubt.

We watched to see if our flight would be canceled as the State Department considered moving from a level three advisory to a level four, a very stark do-not-travel warning for US citizens traveling to or through Dubai. The volcano erupting in Bali had shut down all alternative routes to Kathmandu. I also considered that the Guru might take action to prevent us from embarking on our quest, but bombings and volcanoes were doing his work for him.

My work on a surprise gift for M and the novel were welcome distractions from the heart-wrenching uncertainty confronting our travels. My writing allowed me to process the chairman's ominous words, overheard from the other side of Shangri-La.

The novel's first drafts would be dashed out as inspired pulp fiction, to be revised as great literature later. The detective wouldn't be much more helpful than the real detective and would also push to close the case, but the fictional detective would conceal an inconvenient fact that Dylan had answered his 7 p.m. wake-up call the evening of our dinner date. The fictional CIA had gotten to the detective, prompting him to rule the death another SUD.

Not only was there no cell phone found, but a folder of papers was also missing—I didn't yet know what they'd contain—and Dylan would ask for two card keys upon check-in, but only one would be found in the room.

No, not two card keys. Something more sinister.

Dick, the older man from the Quaker service who looked like a private eye, would entice a poor immigrant maid with a hundred-dollar bill into letting him into Dylan's hotel room at the Beekman "to surprise my old friend." All she had to do was stand in the hallway for fifteen minutes and let him know, by knocking on the door, if anyone approached. If Dylan happened to be inside, Dick would claim he had the wrong room. I finished writing the scene of Dick's brutal killing of Dylan by lethal injection. I had most definitely drafted a murderer. Should I change my mind, I could reconsider the nature of the death in a later draft. I found it surprisingly easy to kill off my old friend in the story, since he was already dead. The plot would lead to Brigitte and James identifying the murderer and his accomplices and finding the ToE. I might have to revisit the name of the murderer, as M had suggested, but for now Dick seemed a fitting double entendre.

I next turned my literary imagination to the Guru, whose name alone made me shudder. Based on the chairman's description, and as the potential mastermind of Dylan's death, he'd be my Dr. No. Writing about his demonic pursuit of all-knowing artificial intelligence, to be animated by Dylan's lost theory, allowed the international thriller to take shape. I moved from multiple third-person narrators to an omniscient one while not yet settling on the point of view for the novel. Speaking to Dylan helped my imagination put flesh on the bones. Perhaps he would be narrator.

I researched all relevant materials about the CIA. I was shocked to learn, from a difficult-to-find ex-CIA tech expert's report, about the CIA's keen interest in testing the boundaries of artificial intelligence and the Frankenstein-monster future of brain-computer interface. He'd also written that just before he left the Agency, a new priority mandate had been established to uncover the theory of everything. That mandate effectively became a race against state-sponsored Russian scientists. He made it sound ominous but knew no more. I attempted to reach him for an interview, but he had died. Not surprisingly, his report made no reference to a guru.

My writing imagined the Guru sending his crazy-eyed Dick off to Kathmandu to find the ToE and to take whatever measures necessary to prevent James and Brigitte from obtaining it first.

I put my computer to sleep at midnight. My fiction scared me with its over-the-top bad guys, but the chairman knew the real Guru and called him a soulless psychopath. A psychopath alone seemed a horrifying enough adversary, but one armed with governmental authority, state-of-the-art AI technology, and a killer named Dick seemed almost all-powerful and more than a match for me. Love is fearless and foolish.

I assumed they had Dylan's phone and wondered if it told them where to find his theory and if they knew of Dylan's empty mailbox in Koreatown and the one in Kathmandu.

I woke my computer and started to write again, imagining my adventure into the unknown of mystical Nepal, with M by my side, as flags waving, bugles blaring, and guns set to go off.

CHAPTER **21**

MY CELL PHONE WAS RINGING as I woke from my nap on Independence Day. It was M calling, and I was back in sixth grade before pimples and peach fuzz and my voice changed. It was my first phone call with my new girlfriend.

"Hello, buddy!" she said. "I'm so excited! You all set? They haven't shut down our flight to Dubai."

"Hel-lo, M." Damn, my voice actually cracked. I tried again. "The troubles in the Middle East, as the Irish would call them, won't stop us. I'm ready! We'll probably run into increased security even for a midnight flight, so should I pick you up at seven thirty to be safe?" Thank God, my voice was back.

"I'm only forty-five minutes to JFK. Eight will leave us plenty of time even if we hit a two-hour security line. You know where I live."

"Okay, I'm just the copilot," I said. "See you at eight on the Upper West Side! Bring your hiking shoes."

"Already packed. Goodbye, buddy."

"See you soon, my PTBT." It was the best closing line I could muster for our first phone call, but I'd made it through okay. Funny neither of us mentioned the three-initial agency and the psychopathic scientist racing to find this grand theory before his Russian foes did, though both were constantly on my mind.

The Mideast's troubles fueled my imagination. I was embarking on a crusade in search of the Holy Grail with my Guinevere. Hailing the yellow cab in Chelsea was my first test, one I met with no problem.

At her door we shared a long embrace to start our twelve-hour journey to Dubai. After that we'd have a three-hour layover and then five hours more to Kathmandu. I felt less like a Lancelot when I opened the door to my beat-up and stinky old chariot with its cold, impatient driver. But M's hugs were getting warmer.

Before we could become used to the odor of the taxi, the car was stopped in a traffic jam on the FDR while we were still in Manhattan. After ten minutes there was no progress toward the RFK Bridge, which would take us to JFK.

The driver snarled and seemed to blame his passengers for the traffic jam. He looked like a man who had known great suffering, which couldn't help but boil over into anger at further adversity. He stewed as we sat there with nothing to do and then bitched, "My shift is over in ten minutes."

"It promises to be a very good fare," M said, "and my friend here is a very generous tipper. Thank you for your patience."

I should have splurged on an Uber XL. I was descending into a limbo where my two biggest challenges converged—a delay that triggered my impatience and an angry man who triggered my judgment.

Bang bang. "How can you not have GPS?"

"You can get another cab."

M gave me a look of compassionate but stern reproach that made me sit up straight and tell myself to be a better man. It was the look a young and beautiful teacher might give to a silly and gifted student caught daydreaming or passing notes in class. I felt the distance between us growing as my schoolboy unworthiness was laid bare.

Being a teacher provided a consistent educational framework to life. I had always been in school and never really grown up. The only difference was I now stood at the front of the class. But I wanted M as a lover, not a teacher, though I'd accept her as both.

M checked her phone's Waze app, which claimed the forty-five-minute ride was now a two-hour trip to the airport, and the meter ticked ever higher.

I hoped Waze was wrong, or we'd miss our flight. M was talking to the driver, telling him there was no alternative but to creep toward the bridge's gate. She had won him over with her charm, patience, and good looks. Or was it my promised generosity that tipped the scales?

I searched my phone, but there was no explanation for the traffic jam. My impatience clicked higher. Like Woody Allen, I couldn't take my eyes off the meter—$99.60 already.

The city announced it would delay the fireworks display until it sorted out some possibly terrorist-related matter, but not to panic. Absent details, such cryptic news rose quickly to international attention based entirely on speculation.

Finally, the radio reported that all ports of exit from the city were subject to heightened security.

"Well, that's a first," I said. "Usually they worry about people coming into the city. The Guru must have cooked this up to stop us from going."

"He could have pulled us aside at the airport or had our flight canceled and not troubled the entire city."

"I was joking. Damn traffic jam. And we'll miss our flight."

M was calm and patient and gave me *that* second look. I was moving in reverse, revealing my negative character traits. I could face a Dick and a Guru for my love, but not a traffic jam. I decided to zoom out and show a broad-minded perspective, seeking redemption with her and the driver.

"It seems to me that the farther an incident happens from New York City and the less white it is, the less important the coverage. This will be page one even if no one is hurt. *Twelve dead in a Canadian bus crash* is page four news, and *a hundred migrants drowned off the coast of Myanmar* would land on page twelve. Even the liberal *New York Times* subscribes to this white- and Western-centric narcissistic view. One whiff of terrorism that snarls us up in traffic, and the world sits in rapt attention."

M gave me her nice smile and a mock pat on the back, a *that-a-boy*, indicating that my ploy had partially worked.

The meter read $189.20. I wondered if we were wasting a lot of money on a taxi and a tip for a flight we would miss. I checked the Emirates Airline site for boarding status and announced, "Good news. Our flight is delayed two hours, so we might make it."

The driver, still navigating traffic at a crawl, turned around with a genuine smile and gave us a thumbs-up. M had worked her magic, and he was a different man now and part of the team. I gave him credit for having a full tank of gas at the end of his shift, which helped me forgive him for not having GPS that wouldn't have helped anyway, and I no longer detected the cab's odor unless I thought about it.

I'd planned on giving M a gift at the airport, some airplane reading, but decided now was the time to further redeem myself and show I was at peace with the delay. We would be rushing through the airport, with no time for sharing gifts. I handed her a thin bound book I had put together. I got quick and good work from my local book seller with a small printing press, who sold me lots of books.

"It's the two versions of 'The Little Stevie Story,' the original that Grace copied for me from the one her father kept all these years— despite it being banned literature—and a short story I wrote about that story. This is the first time they've appeared in print together. And it's a very limited edition."

It was an attractive print copy, with a picture of Dylan and me from fifth grade on the cover. It was one of the few photos where I looked better than Dylan.

I'd always believed an unexpected and thoughtful gift was a wormhole into a woman's heart.

"How lovely. Thank you. I take it that there's some history behind the stories."

I looked to the front seat, where the radio blared the loop of news that nobody knew what the threat was, even as it kept repeating the fearful mantra *ter-ror-ism*!

M leaned forward. "Can you keep the radio on in case there's breaking news but turn it down a bit for us, please? Thank you." She was fearless.

I checked the meter—$266.30—before starting my story of stories.

"It's funny how small events can stick with a person the rest of their life. It was a very short story Dylan and I wrote in the fifth grade. We sold out of all fifty copies. Nine pages, with about fifty words per page, was quite a literary feat. We had the unwitting assistance of the librarian, since Xerox was the only way to copy and publish at that time in our little school.

"We presented a mean-spirited profile of a genius classmate. The story portrayed Little Stevie's prodigy-like accomplishments of being a proficient violin player and an academic wizard in the fifth grade. 'He was already doing college math,' the story proclaimed."

M was looking at the primitive artwork—a boy with inflamed eyes of great intellect and horror gazing out from beneath wild and tangled red Albert Einstein hair. I'd seen Munch's *The Scream* and added the flaming hair.

"Our story then took a dark turn," I went on, "laying out some equally negative aspects of Little Stevie's borderline personality. He was a hypersensitive misfit who could be triggered by words or a look to become hysterical, crying and 'screaming through the halls with his red hair on fire.' I've always remembered that line, which at the time I was immensely proud of."

I put my hands up to my face to partially conceal my shame. "Masked in an objective journalistic tone, the content was predominantly a how-to book. The applauding of his talents was more than offset by the recipe of how poor Little Stevie could be made a hysterical running demon of pain. This powerful unauthorized bio was the wicked creation of egos in gestation, kids newly realizing the power of words. Bullying with words. Perhaps that's why I've never been blessed by a novel and am cursed to write this story over and over."

Since M seemed to be enjoying the story and not judging its ten-year-old authors, I continued.

"This literary albatross haunted both Dylan and me, so I later wrote a short story based on this episode, which you have there as well."

"I've read everything you've written, and I didn't like that story"—she paused for dramatic effect—"but I loved it! Having the two versions together is something I'll treasure." She kissed my book and in that simple gesture, absolved me.

I gushed like a fifth grader getting a good grade and a smiley face from a teacher on whom he had a die-hard crush. "Thank you!" I felt blessed.

After dismissing the childish thought of giving her a peck on her lovely cheek, I said, "You know the later story then. Dylan told me the original story was one of his biggest regrets and the meanest thing he ever did. Dylan saw it clearly as a case of literary bullying. I had to apologize to Dylan for my depiction of him as the evil mastermind while I was just the wordsmith and editor. I reminded Dylan it was a work of fiction based only loosely on the actual incident. By way of pushback, he said, 'Perhaps you might have changed the names, then.'"

"Did you ever hear from Little Stevie again?" M asked.

"Ironically, yes. But it was more that Dylan did. Stevie left school before the start of the next year and wasn't seen again until high school, when we had all moved on. Dylan took a long-range interest in Stevie and wrote me later that 'Little ole Stevie had the last laugh. He's the billionaire founder of Goldstone Capital.'

"But that wasn't the end. Dylan later wrote: 'Stevie is rubbing it in with a twenty-five-million-dollar donation to our high school in exchange for it being renamed after him. Through wealth's ability to rewrite history, we now have to say that we went to Little Stevie High.'

"And there was still more retribution to come. While we were traveling in Barcelona one summer, Dylan told me about Little Stevie's final act of revenge and 'closure of the karmic circle,' as he put it. Stevie used his clout as founding partner of GC to install his top manager in Dylan's Wall Street firm as Dylan's new boss. Tom—a patrician introducing GC's ruthless capitalism to Dylan's entrepreneurial global business and team—brought an end to Dylan's Wall Street career and cost him dearly in bonuses."

I took a bow with my hands. "Thus answering the oft-asked question: Did Little Stevie remember us? I'm still waiting for him to take his revenge on me.

"Dylan told me then, and it echoes now, that the only good he found in that story was as a model of collaboration and an example of how karma works." I relaxed against the door, turning my attention from my narrative and back to M. "The end. Enjoy your book. It's a one-of-a-kind publication, and I wrote an inscription for your eyes only."

She held her gift to her breast and smiled appreciatively. "Stories by and about the two men I admire most as they stood at a crossroads. You are forgiven. You both chose the right road."

She sneaked a peek at my words of dedication and looked up in appreciation with her eyes seeing into my heart. She namasted me, so I namasted her. I felt as though the true gift was given from her to me.

The driver had kept the news down so he too could listen to my story. We'd reached $289.50. He said, "We have all done things we regret and can only use them to become better men."

M leaned forward and said, "That is so true, Bassam."

I followed her gaze. She'd been studying the picture of the taxi driver's wife and infant on the dashboard and had picked up his name from the cab registration.

"If you want to phone your girlfriend or wife to tell her you're all right, please do. We know you're working overtime for us."

The driver took M's suggestion and made the call. He spoke in some Middle Eastern tongue in sweet, endearing tones that I hadn't judged him capable of. When he hung up, he was all smiles.

M told Bassam about our trip, Dylan's death, and our search for his lost theory to pass the time as traffic crept forward. He was clearly interested to hear the story and asked many questions. M's enthusiasm was impossible to resist. But I was more than a bit paranoid, living within my novel of international intrigue, and thought she should be more discreet. The driver might be a CIA mole.

We finally arrived at the bridge's toll gate, the source of the long line of congestion, where police were questioning drivers and moving every third or so car to the side for an inspection.

The officer studying Bassam's license and registration was about to wave us over for a search, which would have been the end of our chances of making the flight, when M leaned forward.

"Hello, officer! I'm Professor Emily Edens from Columbia University on the way to the airport. I can vouch for this car and my friend Bassam. Would you like to see my credentials?"

"That won't be necessary, lady, but thanks. I can see them from here." He leered and waved us through.

I joyfully yelled, "WOPA!" as we pulled away.

We arrived at JFK around midnight to a frantic scene of delayed and panicked passengers. With the additional mayhem, it remained unclear whether we would make our flight even with the two-hour delay. The meter clicked its last cut at $399.00.

I was calculating my generous tip and the bite out of my discretionary spending allowance for the trip even as M was reaching into her purse, but the initially surly Bassam cleared the meter of all those dollar signs, declaring, "No charge. This ride is free."

M immediately shook her head. "But, Bassam, that's—"

He held up his hand. "As a good Muslim, please allow me this gift. It is done."

The way he said it made further insistence risk becoming insulting, so we accepted his remarkable generosity with abundant gratitude.

As we were moving through the large revolving door into Terminal C, M backtracked to the driver, leaving me alone in the vestibule. I watched from the other side of the glass as she hugged Bassam and handed him something. He looked like Zorba the Greek about to dance, delighted by his instant karma. I was witnessing simple grace from within a beehive of frenetic energy ready to explode inside Terminal C.

CHAPTER 22

M DIDN'T OFFER AN EXPLANATION of what she had given Bassam, and I didn't ask as we rushed to economy-class check-in. JFK airport was a mass of people, tension, and confusion. The heavily armed police wearing bulletproof vests and cradling automatic weapons did not make me feel safe.

The city is a body, and JFK its international heart, and with all the outgoing blood valves squeezed tight, the organ was not working well. The airport itself pulsated with anxious energy, as if bracing for an attack. I braced myself as we entered the extremely long check-in line, suffering deep envy over the shorter lines for the elite classes of travelers.

Brimming with impatience, I groused, "I'd hoped for an empty flight with the troubles in the Middle East and this being July Fourth; so much for an upgrade in our seats. We'll be in this line for at least an hour, and then we have security." I answered myself before M could give me that look. "I know, be patient."

M smiled. She probably could have flown first class with her father's money, but she was with me and without complaint.

My racial-profiling scan of the holiday line suggested it was packed with many individuals and families from the Middle East wanting to return home, despite the turmoil, before their ability to do so was cut off.

The attendant was as confused as everyone else and could only tell us, "All departure times are uncertain. Your flight is currently scheduled to leave at two a.m. Just get to the gate as soon as you can."

M had the presence of mind to say, "Thank you," while I raced toward the security line and checked the time—five minutes after one.

We'd be at least another hour in the security line. As we inched toward the checkpoint, my impatience was itching. Once triggered, it took a bottle of wine or a ten-mile run to defuse.

M said, "Good, now we can relax. Our bags are being loaded, so they won't take off without us."

"Yeah, but something is happening to cause this elevated security." I waved one arm. "This *in*security and the threat of terror in travelers and airport staff alike."

Terrorism was the ticking time bomb of neglect; it devolved the mind into a lizard brain and eroded the heart of a man until he lost touch with his soul. To the terrorist, terrorism made perfect sense as the only way out of his oppression.

I had just witnessed a cab driver's darkness vanquished by the bright light of M's kindness. She didn't prevent terrorism; he was no terrorist. She didn't prevent a wife beating; he was no wife beater. But I was sure M's kindness had made a profound difference in that man's life. The ripples of true kindness become waves unwitnessed but not unfelt after the stone is thrown.

We arrived at our gate just before two. Final boarding had already been announced as we entered another line. My mind, racing with disjointed thoughts, was a mixture of overtired and overexcited, wanting just to board the plane to Kathmandu and disappear into a book.

I tightened my grip on my carry-on, shocked to realize I'd forgotten to pack a single book. My transition to questing was marked by poor planning and obstacles at every turn.

Books were always with me, part of my arsenal, and now I was unarmed on my way overseas. I started shuffling through the library in my head for books that were apropos, and recalled two as the line to present our tickets inched forward. The first was about travel to Tibet and suggested all great journeys are met by the most challenging of circumstances, impediments that must be overcome before one can reach destinations ripe with portent, magic, and secrets.

Even without much planning we were guaranteed an adventure. Check.

The second was *The Secret*, a book Dylan had me read in high school and which, as a literature professor, I'd banned from my library. So it was a strange selection to have falling from a dusty shelf of my restless mind. The secret—spoiler alert—boiled down to this: Given time, if you believe something with your entire heart and imagination, the universe will manifest that desire. Now the secret is out. Cross-check.

I was ready to go. Yet there was another security checkpoint right at the boarding gate, after they scanned our tickets and before we stepped onto the ramp to the plane. My carry-on was selected for a search, which was quite thorough and likely to show they were checking white Americans too.

While the inspection of my writer's bag continued, I imagined there was some connection between the disjointed memories of those two books. If the level of the impediment to one's journey was correlated to the significance of the destination, we were in for a big adventure. And if our thoughts and desires determined our reality, Kathmandu would be a bonfire of discovery and passion.

I looked up to see a very animated inspector confiscating my letter opener. I hadn't flown since Hope had died and hadn't thought of it being there. My bag was being turned inside out as another inspector, older, was called over. The younger inspector, sounding as gleeful as if he'd found the most ornate easter egg, whispered that missing the letter opener might cost the bleary-eyed X-ray inspector his job.

"It's my mistake, not his fault," I said without conviction.

This was too much, after all the hellish delay, to doom our quest with my poor packing and inability to hold my tongue. The stern men ushered me and my terrorist bag and knife aside to determine my fate, to which they seemed negatively predisposed. Without wanting to draw attention to her, I nodded to M to keep moving and board, as I didn't want her to see me cry or do what men who can no longer cry—but want to—do.

CHAPTER 23

WHILE I WAS BLATHERING EXCUSES and apologies to the diligent inspectors, M disregarded my nod and hurried to my side, saying, "Professor, that was so absentminded of you. I should have packed the bag with your writing materials." Turning to the inspectors, she shook her head. "Literature professor and writer—doesn't get out much."

The more senior inspector, who was testing the dullness of the blade, seemed to soften at the absentminded-professor defense from my quick-witted assistant. I handed them my NYU credentials to bolster my defense. The inspector shook his head in final judgment and disgust, handed back my bag and ID, and turned away, tossing Hope's gift and my literary sword into a bin with disposable razors and a pair of sewing scissors, his way of saying *board before we change our minds*.

I threw my papers, pens, and pencils back into the bag, and we headed down the ramp to finally board. I hung my head in apology, my tail between my legs. But that tail started to wag when M put her arm around my shoulder.

She said, "Sabotage, no doubt."

Yeah, a bad case of self-sabotage, I thought. But what I said was "Must be the CIA. You can't think I'm that stupid?"

"Of course not. Definitely the handiwork of the Guru."

We both laughed at my expense and then became silent. I think we both had forgotten that name for an hour or two.

I didn't dare complain that our three-hour layover in Dubai had been cut to less than an hour and our connecting flight was no longer abundantly secure.

The flight itself was fodder for a novella, and all because of M. She was a magic magnet for magnificent vignettes.

Upon takeoff, outside our small window and over the Hudson burst the rockets' red glare of the bombs bursting in air—the delayed fireworks celebration of the city that never sleeps.

M befriended a harried Arab woman with children who sat behind us. She cradled the woman's baby for much of the flight while the mother tended to her young and impish toddler. The young mother read us Rumi in gratitude.

"O Beloved, where is the Beloved?"

Watching M, I knew.

Then there was the unexpected dreamless sleep next to my love in our economy-class seats until I awoke to pleasantly recline next to her for the last couple hours of flight. I counted it as our first night together, though only legs, shoulders, hands, and heads occasionally touched. She was an excellent and exotic travel companion. *How could I be so blessed by life after all the years of solitude?*

Deplaning into the Dubai airport concourse, we had thirty minutes to make our connection. With airport map in hand, we set off running through fields of malls and corridors from Gate C20 to Gate A9 a mile away.

Breathless, we made it to A9 in time; we were in group five, and they were boarding group two. A troupe of whirling dervishes entertained the passengers waiting to board their flights, and M and I settled in to watch. The head dervish immediately spied the beautiful M in her light blue V-neck cashmere sweater and soft blue jeans. He'd stepped right out of *The Arabian Nights*, approaching M in his high white turban and flowing white gown, asking for her hand. She bowed her head and allowed him to lead her into the center of the spinning tops.

He held up her arms to place bracelets with bells on her bare wrists. But her right wrist shouldn't have been so naked; her precious bracelet was gone. *That* was the gift she'd given to the taxi driver, Ba-something. I'd already forgotten his name. The ripples of her kindness became tidal waves crashing over my heart.

My mind stopped, overpowered by love as she started to dance as though she had dervish blood. The quickening bells spun the dervishes faster, and the flowing white-cotton dresses of the dervishes—symbols of conception, gestation, and creation—twisted around their spinning bodies and around M, a blue whirlpool in the center of the twirling white flow. Even as I caught my breath, she took it away again. I stood amazed by her authentic spontaneity. Something was being liberated in her and in me, and with each turn she spiraled deeper into my heart and soul.

I became anxious as the scene played out because it drew the attention of the male travelers, many of them Arabs, who appeared too attentive or too disapproving or both. The female travelers did not permit themselves to watch.

If it hadn't been time to board, M might have become the only female member of the troupe. Or been arrested for the crime of buxom beauty and siren sensuality.

M bowed goodbye to the dervish, who insisted she keep the jangling bracelets. She then ran over to me, with bells still ringing, exclaiming, "All aboard!" Throwing her chest into mine with an adrenaline-fueled hug, she whispered into my ear, "Next stop, Kathmandu."

Tickets, please!

CHAPTER 24

WE LANDED IN KATHMANDU on time after all.

"Johnny Appleseed" was playing over the loudspeakers in the airport arrival hall. We passed under a sign of greeting: "Welcome to Kathmandu—Where Spirits Are High—Population 999,999." The statistic seemed to declare that each next person to arrive would make it an even million.

I pointed to the sign, and M said, "Auspicious is the day!"

"Dylan's always with us—my lucky day," I replied, more happy than jealous. "You hear that song? Joe Strummer from the Clash, one of Dylan and my favorites."

Underneath the words of welcome, the sign also depicted three pairs of namaste hands and a set of noseless faces—happy eyes and Cheshire cat smiles with angel wings—in front of a mountain backdrop. Perhaps the Nepali didn't like their noses. I'd read that all cultures preferred and emphasized eyes, lips, and ears and sight, taste, and sound over the nose and smell—although that second-tier sense was front and center in Kathmandu, given the potpourri of odors that met us there.

Smiling Nepali served up a true welcome to the birthplace of Buddha, their eyes and lips flashing sincere greetings, their outstretched hands holding out blessings. Their welcome opened my heart.

Two more ambassadors of goodwill in the form of stray dogs showed us from our gate to the baggage claim. They looked to be mutts with some Labrador blood, sniffing us from behind, raising their long snouts in celebration of the fragrant air, and wagging their tails. They chose to follow M. When we arrived at the luggage carousel, they celebrated by demonstrating how to smell each other's butts in an artful doggie-dervish dance.

M laughed. "To a dog, all smells are good."

The sacred scent of M was with me all the time now, as she was never far from me. It wasn't rose, it wasn't lavender, even though she wore those scents. It wasn't any perfume but the holy fragrance of love itself that wafted from her skin. The imagined taste of her hovered just above the tip of my tongue. Ever since we met, I lived in a state of heightened sensibility.

When we wheeled the luggage to the exit, our canine chaperones took their leave for a peddler of aromatic food. Behind the food cart about twenty yards away, a furtive-looking character eyed me before quickly averting his gaze. He reminded me of Dick—from the funeral— mostly in the eyes. However, this man had a beard with more than a couple of weeks' growth, and Dick did not. As I avoided eye contact and discreetly tried to get M's attention, the man disappeared.

There were two explanations: One, it was Dick, and two, it was not Dick. Probably my imagination would now conjure Dick everywhere because of his key role in my novel. It not being Dick was the far more likely explanation, as the chances and beard were too long. He was just a Western man who looked like an old undercover cop, or maybe a trekker from the twentieth century who had retired his knapsack and long ago forgotten to go home.

Either way, I decided to let Dick's name stick for the novel; M would come to like it.

We stepped out of the airport into the thin and full air of Kathmandu, into an amphitheater of mountains and a foreign bazaar of people. Here was a true melting pot—tourists and locals, vendors and beggars, and dozens of sounds, sights, and smells. I felt liberated in this colorful, living mandala. The brittle shell of the austere academic was shed, left behind at baggage claim with a couple of dancing dogs. We'd flown through the looking glass and emerged on the other end of the world.

I was changing, becoming something new, becoming . . . becoming more myself. All due to meeting M and going outside my comfort-zone cocoon to find my beloved a lost theory of everything.

My love made everything seem more vivid and colorful. Brighter. I was fully determined to embrace the *illusion*, as Dylan had called it. I was prepared for anything in this potent vortex of the miraculous.

I eagerly followed M out onto the buzzing, dusty, noisy, and smelly street. The glare and cacophony snapped me out of my pleasant reverie. I stood with the two faces of Janus, seeing dreams and nightmares of both past and future. And if past is prologue, I imagined there might also be serpents in this paradise I had entered with my Lady M.

But we were going to meet Dylan's goddess in her ashram, which sounded like the most peaceful and safest place in the world.

CHAPTER 25

IT WAS A MAGNIFICENT DAY as we entered our gypsy cab, vintage Chevy circa 1977. The driver was jolly and playing jingle-jangle sitar music. He spoke English.

"Oh yes, I know the Deeksha. Everyone knows the Deeksha and sweet Mother Juno."

An elephant passed in the other direction, kicking up dust like ashes and snow. M grabbed my hand to share the mammoth mammal sighting.

"What a mystical beast!" our driver exclaimed. "She don't belong here but—" He shouted out his window, "Welcome, Lord Ganesha!" He shook his head. "First time ever I see that. First time for everything."

"Auspicious is the day!" I said.

"Sure is," he said.

The cab odor was strong but not necessarily bad compared to the smells coming in the open windows. However, when I relaxed into the fumes, they became more intoxicating than foul.

"Hmm . . . Smells like they haven't swept behind the elephant," I said.

M crinkled her nose and let go of my hand.

With the slow-moving traffic, we could have wheeled our luggage along the road and traveled as far just as fast. But the extra time gave us opportunity to stew in all the sights, sounds, and smells of Kathmandu.

"Luckily the temperature is so cool compared to Manhattan's— mid-seventies?" I said. "In New York's July heat, this stew would really stink, and rats—not elephants—would roam the streets."

M was enjoying the ride, paying little attention to me and my nose as she stared out her window. I bent over her to see what she was smiling at. It appeared to be the telephone wires or clotheslines above the row of two-story buildings. The lines were adorned with an endless procession of prayer flags—letters to God—waving hello.

M said, "Even the power lines are draped in spirituality."

I leaned over her again to take another look. "I thought they were telephone wires, but here the power grid still hangs from poles."

She pulled one of the two dervish bracelets from her fashionable yet Nepal-appropriate travel bag and presented it to me. "If you ever need me, just ring."

I bowed and bobbed to the taxi's music, giving my bracelet a jingling shake. M shimmied and jangled her bracelet in response. My heart bloomed with our ringing entanglement. "Spooky action?"

"At a distance," she added, smiling at her student's learning.

I put the treasure into my bag, like a precious memory to be stored away, and pulled out Juno's reply email to read again to M. I'd been glad to receive a swift response in light of Juno's apparent reserve and enigmatic personality.

Dylan was a dear friend and family, so you must stay at the Deeksha as our guests. Dylan would have wanted you to. We heard from dear sweet Grace, and the entire Deeksha family awaits your arrival. When it is time, I will drive you to Yogi Mangku's, as I plan to go to my sanctuary, which is near the yogi's compound, for blessed solitude. From there you can have my jeep to explore. Our yogi would love for you to stay with him too, though there is no way to contact him by phone. Peace, love, and light, Juno and the Deeksha family.

M said, "If we don't find the theory at the Deeksha, let's go to the yogi's as soon as we can. Once we find the ToE, we can hike every day through the jungles and up every mountain."

"I'll be there every step of the way," I said, though I feared I might not be able to keep up with her long, strong, sexy—and young—legs.

Finally we arrived. The Deeksha was set apart from the other buildings and the human bustle that lined the streets, and its *stately pleasure
dome* blended seamlessly into its mountain backdrop. As we turned
into the tree-lined entrance, we left Kathmandu yard by yard for a
hundred yards, arriving at a haven of peace nestled in a garden forest.
We had entered the calm eye of a twister. The building itself was white
and circular, with a reddish dome paired with a slightly darker nipple
on top.

"Xanadu! Where we'll meet Coleridge's damsel with a dulcimer," I
said to christen our arrival.

M and I approached the large carved wooden doors in silence.
Before we knocked, a tall and handsome young man with gentle features opened the doors. "Hello, I'm Ram. But everyone calls me Boy."

He seemed to embrace a nickname that others would find demeaning.

Because I was gawking like a tourist and paying no attention to
common Eastern customs, M had to prompt me to remove my shoes
upon entering the Deeksha. I checked, and my socks, fortunately, had
no holes, though I worried about their smell after the long flights.

Boy led us through a large central room with a cathedral-high ceiling that reached to the tip of the stupa. Round windows ringed the
spire like a bracelet of light, which then blended with the light from
the many ornate sliding glass doors that circled the floor. The flooding
streams of light painted the floor in many colors and highlighted the
craftsmanship of the fine furnishings.

Boy gestured at the windows, the doors, and the interior décor.
"Designed by Juno."

A series of long wooden communal tables had been paired with
high-backed and ornate black chairs. Modern Ming chairs, Boy called
them. Juno had created both a grand *Game of Thrones*–style dining hall
and a delicate spiritual gathering place.

We weren't in Kansas anymore. I would have been happy to stay
forever with M in that wonderfully magical space conceived by an
uncluttered mind.

Boy watched us with keen attention, registering his guests' first impressions of the Deeksha, confident no one could remain unimpressed. He was dressed in all white except for the colorful burgundy scarf wrapped around his head, and had arresting and glistening doe eyes and beautiful lips.

He was genuinely warm and made it abundantly clear, through his actions and only a few words, that M and I were eagerly anticipated. It was a good rule of service, too often not followed, to make the guest feel not only welcome but enthusiastically expected.

Moving with a grace and flow, in harmony with the space, Boy led us to a smaller room suited for greeting, meditation, and tea. Marvelous art bursting with scenes of nature, both modern Chinese and French Impressionism, adorned the walls. I determined to inquire about the artist, since they were unsigned.

I wondered about the cost of this artistic and spiritual resort; there'd been no mention of payment. M had suggested, "Let's just see. Sounds like she's offering her hospitality for free." M had more money than I had and obviously worried less about costs.

Boy said he would let Juno know we had arrived and would take our luggage to our rooms.

"Rooms" tolled like a loud bell in my heart, with me dismayed by its plural nature and cost. I'd wondered if we'd be offered a room to share, and while that was an exciting prospect, it also may have been too soon. So *rooms* was probably for the best. To share a bedroom before a kiss did seem premature, but it may have moved things along as it did for Clark Gable in *It Happened One Night*.

The Deeksha was ripe with oxygen, an anomaly in the thin air of Kathmandu. Perhaps they piped it in, as my body and mind were without hint of jet lag despite the long trip and high elevation. We were invited to sit on the comfortable yoga cushions circling the floor.

As Boy was leaving, he paused to look into M's eyes and then mine, an activity so ordinary but in that moment uncommon in both beauty and depth. The rule since the playground had been boys don't truly look at boys. Outside a staring contest, length of eye contact was strictly enforced: two beats, no more, *maybe* extended to three if you won the big game. Later, weddings and funerals were added to the three-beat exception. It was an unspoken heterosexual-man rule one had to follow regardless of the bond and situation; there was to be no true intimacy between men. Dylan often tried to let his eyes linger, but I had never let him.

That all flashed through my mind as Boy and I finished our extended gaze. I was grateful for the liberation from decades of heterosexually imposed restraint.

"Such a lovely boy," M said.

"Yeah, but too beautiful. I fear I'll pale in comparison in your eyes."

"No worries; I think he may be asexual, and I judge a man on his mind, on his spirit, and on his deeds," she replied.

"I thought androgynous."

"They're not the same thing, though they could coincide. Just a woman's instinct."

A woman like M who taught young men would immediately pick up on male attraction, so often inappropriately displayed even in a first meeting or hiding beneath a desk in her lecture hall. She would also recognize the lack of sexual interest.

"I feel so much energy here," she said, sitting with a straight spine in lotus position on her cushion. She moved her prayer hands to her heart. "Aummmm."

The Deeksha buzzed, and a wonderful soft music or lovely audible vibrations played almost imperceptibly in the background. M and I looked at each other, our eyes wide open and saying, *I'm so awake too* and *This is so cool.* I wondered if she was happy at hearing *rooms* plural and whether she might have been ambivalent on the matter too. It probably hadn't crossed her carefree mind.

Then she walked in. Juno. Her mystical reputation had been inadequate to prepare me for her presence.

Rising from my lowly seat to greet her, I thought I might pass out. It wasn't the elevation, as the air was now pure oxygen. Colors and light danced about the room. I felt weightless, as if floating. M was radiant, silhouetted by golden light.

Juno's presence was an energetic but peaceful poppy field that spread over me, while her turquoise eyes shone straight into my heart. Those eyes seemed to change color with the light—turquoise, emerald, green, and turquoise again, a captivating kaleidoscope. Her presence filled the room with waves of energy and a divine scent.

Juno enveloped us in warm and welcoming hugs, which we returned in equal measure. A good hug was even more important than a good handshake; Juno gave really good hugs. Her elegant, lithe frame was rounded by her fruits, peaches in front and melon behind. She wore a simple burgundy robe or dress that somehow looked both monk-like and fashionable. It clung loosely and modestly, half concealing her angelic shape. The spiritual and sensual combined in her without conflict, in perfect celestial harmony.

M was smiling her familiar joyous smile but even more brightly, sharing my appreciation of our goddess hostess. Standing there in that transcendent atmosphere, although impossible, I loved M even more.

"I am so glad you made the trip and are here, safe now. Please let us know all you will need."

The internet's lady of mystery was all grace and beauty in person. She moved like the wind over water, extraordinarily ordinary and simple in her way. A fairy queen of nature with a lyrical voice accentuated by British-accented English spoken in slow, soft, and yet crisp tones. Even the string of single-syllable words in her introduction sounded poetic.

She was obviously a frequent host and immediately made us feel completely at home.

We were seated at a low table for tea that was already prepared; Boy must have set it up while we greeted Juno. Juno proceeded to perform the art of tea service.

"This is the best tea I've ever tasted," I said after my first sip, blushing at what anywhere else would have been hyperbole but which here merely sounded banal.

"Thank you, but it is your loving focus that allows you to experience the love of tea," Juno said. "Would you like to go to your rooms, to rest, perhaps, before we share time and presence together?"

M looked as wide awake and *present* as I was and no doubt shared my desire to talk with this ethereal being who offered us instant intimacy. I didn't want to stare, but I couldn't take my eyes off of Juno's.

"We're not at all tired," M said. "You, this tea, and this beautiful place have fully rejuvenated me, and I can tell by Sean's face"—she nodded at me, and I smiled in boyish agreement—"that he too is excited to get to know you and see more of the Deeksha. May I ask the meaning of the name?"

"Our friend Dylan suggested the name. It means an energy transfer between two people sharing a vibration, where love is transferred and increased between the two. One can also receive it from nature or directly from the grace of God, our true nature. Or even from a sip of tea." Her smile tingled over me. "It's a space where all is focused on wakening to Big Love . . . in the illumination of love that animates us . . . in which we all appear and disappear."

She spoke in a deliberate and mindful manner—like Dylan's poetry—with rhythms and imagery that the rational mind would dismiss as nonsense. She had no trace of fear in speaking of subjects most people would find too esoteric or revealing to speak of. But absent their source, it is impossible to grasp how her words settled in the mind like flowers blooming, strung along in lines of posy, and when gone, never to be re-created with the same sense and feeling again. This made me come to attention when she spoke.

"Please share your experiences of Dylan with me," Juno said. "He spoke so fondly of the two of you."

I found Dylan's front-running me with his words disconcerting. *So what did you say? Something like I was in desperate need of big love?*

As I imagined all the good and the less favorable ways Dylan may have described me, M calmly explained both our relationships. She spoke more poetically too, saying, "Dylan and Sean were two trees that grew up side by side, always connected by their roots."

When she finished speaking, I became uncomfortable with the silence, and my impatience erupted. I abruptly said, "What was your relationship with Dylan and what do you know about his theory of everything and do you have a copy of it?" One Step added, "Once we have found that, then maybe we can learn all about big love." I meant it humorously, but I sounded like a jerk. The frenetic energy of my tone and the barbed words landed flat-footed over that invisible line of decorum, unsettling the spiritual space.

Juno and M had been speaking in measured and sweet tones, with synchronized speech that rose and fell in the proper place and order. My first words shot into the room like a blast of business testosterone. I had blurted out my question and snide comment to purposely shake the peaceful spell cast by Juno and the Deeksha, asserting that the man in the room would now be taking charge—*so move things along, little ladies*. I immediately recognized my severe tone problem.

One Step and his foot faults became dead to me in that moment's realization, and I vowed to use a more reflective speech and tone for the rest of my stay after such a rude start.

M wasn't impressed, giving me that second look of hers. Juno must have seen the apology written all over my face; I hope she had. She gave me a calm Mona Lisa smile, moving on, as if I'd belched, before I could beg her forgiveness.

"We shared a spiritual flowering. I was the yin of loving silence, and he was the yang of expression as we shared tea and chi and wonderful moments of silence and bliss. He could have been anybody. It was not a special relationship."

And then, after a silence I was happy to abide in, absolved of my tone-deaf one step, she said, "You want to know about Dylan's life here and about his revelation?"

CHAPTER 26

THAT WAS WHY WE'D COME. But before I could say anything, M leaned forward—probably concerned I'd insert foot in mouth again—and said, "Yes, please. Dylan told me life was magical here."

Juno, her smile wide, waved her hand in the air as though spinning a wand to cast a spell. "Dylan and I met in Beijing around the turn of the century. It was an auspicious day, as he would say. We both were starting to explore the spirit and commit fully to the discovery of self."

"I read you were a musical child prodigy," I said.

Juno pushed her teacup aside before folding her hands on the table, composing herself. I could sense—feel—a high vibrational current of her energy as she repeated, with another wave of her wand to strike up the band, "Mu-si-cal child pro-di-gy. At that time, I was still playing a couple of instruments but was no longer a child in years, only at heart." She had a musical and youthful laugh and must have been ten years older than she looked. "My focus was shifting to meditations on nature and spirit and the connection between the two."

M and I settled our seat bones deeper into our meditation cushions as we sat up straight, like children preparing for a reading from their favorite storybook.

"Dylan was a young international banker, but he saw his ego clearly. In his mind he had already left the world of finance, and his energy was directed inward. The day we met he was reading the Upanishads, and he gave me his copy. There was an immediate bond, as if we were destined to meet, an unspoken sharing of energy and a *knowing* we both recognized. It was not personal or *ours*. We always seemed connected, perhaps never more than in long intervals of silence while we were apart. Our sharing of spirit and oneness led into silence, through which we communicated at a distance. Dylan was writing a lot of poetry, which he would send or recite to me."

Juno paused. I realized she didn't fear serene silence. She had mastered communicating through silence and was providing us lessons in her well-practiced art.

We sat gazing at each other, the practice utterly pleasurable in that company. M's nut-brown eyes grounded me in love, while Juno's kaleidoscope eyes raised me up in love. Wow. There . . . there was something in that tea. Love or ecstasy or something. I tried again to confirm Juno's eye color. I was a bit color-blind, so maybe the changing color was just a trick of my eyes and the light, though when Juno was at rest, they became a vibrant though still-soothing turquoise.

She let go of the silence to flow back into her tale.

"My path led me to leave the big city of Beijing and come to Kathmandu to be closer to nature and the simple honesty of the people of Nepal. When I moved to open my space here, Dylan suggested the name, which seemed fitting, in that it was also the mission of the place—to share love, which is source energy, the source we are never separated from."

I raised my hand like an eager student wanting to impress his beautiful teacher. Juno waved her invisible wand again and aimed the point at my forehead, calling on me.

"Dylan, his theory, constant creation . . . Is *source energy* somehow related to that?"

M's smile awarded me an A, and Juno added the pleasing plus of her own smile.

"I believe it is. Dylan stayed at the Deeksha off and on for the last two years. During one of our trips to my sanctuary, he was given the theory that so animated him and became his passion. We all have a diamond of infinite facets in our hearts, and from that point of revelation in the sanctuary, Dylan was shining through many facets and maybe all facets. Full wakening is the shining through of all facets at once. It is abiding in Big Love."

Abiding in big love. I laughed at and chastised myself for my adolescent mind's ability, in that lovely company, to make sexual the most innocent of spiritual declarations.

Juno smiled at me as if she was reading her student's mind. "In Big Love we learn to control our thoughts as well as our actions."

Another long pause followed my internal tee-heeing, each silence more comfortable than the last, and each a crucial part of her story.

"I introduced Dylan to Yogi Mangku," Juno continued, "with whom he studied and practiced in solitude for much of the last year. I knew he would share what he felt he had to about his theory, but he told me I already knew. He said something like 'It's oneness and the power of now expressed in scientific terms and otherwise nothing dramatically new, other than showing it is scientific truth too.' He believed that through science—more than religion—there was the greatest potential for human wakening. Science or spirituality, truth is truth."

I turned my attention to Dylan. *You said that there's no sleep without awakening. But I feel I'm dreaming here, imagining you floating between a goddess and a yogi who gave you the key to the universe.* I felt his presence and heard his silence.

M asked, "Did Dylan leave the theory with you?"

"I know you're seeking it, but no. So sorry. He left nothing other than poetry and his loving spirit."

You left me the spaceship but not the key?

I returned my focus to the ladies. "Not even his notes or notebooks, drafts, anything? We . . . I was sure you'd have a copy." I was just able to catch my disappointment and impatience before I got the look from M. Unearthing M's love was my top priority, so I turned to her with a brave face. "We'll still find that elusive ToE."

I had averted the look and got half of her smile. This major setback to our quest was received in the peaceful aura of Xanadu without any loss of enthusiasm by M. That probably had more to do with the Deeksha's calm, joyful atmosphere than the depth of the catastrophe. Even my disappointment was tempered by the Deeksha's peaceful character and its singular host.

I was equally focused on my unspoken agenda and had formed the belief that even with our quest as yet unfulfilled, this would be the place M would fall in love with me.

"We're also excited to meet Yogi Mangku," M said. "Do you think we might find the theory with him?"

"It is most likely there, but either way you'll want to meet my yogi. He's a man of incredible enlightened insight and a teacher of Big Love. He's also a man who entirely honors his vow of complete truth in word, action, and thought. The Tao—his wonder-full way."

In measured words and tone, I explained the lingering suspicions surrounding Dylan's death, how he was to meet me the evening he died, and how I'd gone to the restaurant to review the theory for a book collaboration. I also explained that M was prepared to address the scientific challenges posed by the final theory she and Dylan had worked on together.

Juno nodded and poured more tea for all of us. "Dylan told me the theory had been committed to memory and that he was inspired to make changes each time he rewrote it, so it wouldn't be odd for him to travel without a written version."

That revelation distressed me, since my brilliant friend had a photographic memory, which allowed him to recite poetry in volumes. The theory might have been lost for good when that incredible mind was erased like a drawing on an Etch A Sketch, shaken by death.

Juno continued. "He also had become wary of Western men in Kathmandu and believed he was being watched by his own government. Sean, you will be staying in Dylan's room. Perhaps his spirit will guide you, as he is ever present here." She smiled as she added, "You've met Boy. Dylan also was a mentor, father, and student of my twin adopted daughters, YaLan and Astri."

On cue, two young women lit up the room, entering dressed like Indian princesses decked out for a royal dance. They were twentysomething identical twins with symmetrical smiles—two striking physical bodies celebrating youth well lived. They smelled of lavender and oils. Unconsciously following the Deeksha protocol, I stood to greet the twins with hugs. Based on the warm response, I had correctly embraced the atmosphere of the place.

Identical twins, yes, though YaLan's head was shaved like a monk's, while Astri's long black hair flowed almost to her waist. YaLan was no less beautiful for the want of hair. They might have been of Asian or Indian descent, or most logically, Nepali. And like their mother, they offered instant intimacy without restraint through the direct gaze of their turquoise eyes. Thank God their eyes stayed that color, or I would have thought I was going insane.

Juno poured them each a cup of tea as they joined us among the cushions on the floor. We floated on our pillows while Juno floated slightly higher on the tea service dais.

"I met these two when they were twelve years old, on the streets of Kathmandu, shortly after I arrived from Beijing and established the Deeksha. They agreed to live with me here, and I was honored to become their mother. A month before we met, YaLan and Astri's parents had left for a day trip from their village and were never heard from again. Their village offered young girls on their own no prospect of survival other than to marry while still children."

Astri said, "Which didn't sound so pleasant a prospect."

"Our parents' disappearance remains a mystery a decade later," YaLan said. "Mother made every effort to locate them or determine their fate, but to no avail. It must have cost a fortune to hire a Chinese investigative team that had ties with Nepali officials. That team searched for several months but found nothing, not even their car." She turned toward Juno. "I never thought before about the great expense of that."

Juno brought her hands together to her chest. "We are blessed. And one advantage of coming from a Communist country and having a high-ranking uncle in the Party is that it cost us nothing. The investigation made clear that based on their parents' character and love for the girls, Astri and YaLan had not been abandoned."

"We never thought, not for one instant, that our parents would leave us," Astri said. "It's an old mystery now, but the pain returns with the fresh loss of our dear Dylan."

The twins' grief over Dylan's death was palpable in their words and even more in their expressive eyes. Perhaps the grief was deeper since it was their first experience of the death of a loved one, and they were now burying three parents in their hearts.

My experience of Dylan's death was less a loss and more the physical absence of a person I would never see again. In a way, it was similar to my experience of losing Hope but without all the grief I had clung to for so long. Dylan was more alive than ever in my life and my imagination. I now spoke with him more often than before.

Juno changed the direction of our conversation, telling us about the twins' lives at the Deeksha. YaLan and Astri punctuated the tale with colorful commentaries.

Juno had been the girls' teacher as well as their mother, and they worked beside her and Boy. Homeschooling was woven into the life of the Deeksha, but their studies had included more than academic pursuits.

The twins had been students of Yogi Mangku since they were twelve years old and now taught yoga and meditation at the Deeksha. From their description, it was clear the yogi was family too. He would come to the Deeksha, or the twins would go to him, spending long periods of time training in his compound outside of town.

The Deeksha had become a true home, with Boy calling the twins *meimei*—little sister. They all called Dylan father. I'd always associated the overuse of the word *family* with cults, like the Manson family, but here *family* was a poetic truth. The Deeksha's was a family I was already eager to join with my cohort and co-sleuth. I felt completely at ease, and M looked the same, naturally comfortable in our new home after just one hour. Maybe we could be the aunt and uncle. Juno, despite being younger than me, was everyone's mother.

It was the ideal environment for creation and love. There in that magical place, M would soon fall in love with me. Like sunlight dissipating fog, the higher vibrational frequency playing within me was lifting me out of the past and rooting me firmly in the present.

The twins had an endearing way of knowing the other's thoughts and finishing the other's sentences in perfect British accents. Rather than share a private language, they seemed to share an empathetic telepathy, a contrast of twin interdependence and fierce independence. Their relationship seemed to be one of joyful competition and mutual encouragement.

"These young ladies were raised as spiritual warriors, and they have become that and more," Juno said.

Boy brought in a tray of tasty morsels and sat on the cushion next to mine. Juno said, "The twins learned from their big brother the joys of service, as well as inner strength and integrity."

"We are so grateful for all we learned from you and Boy and our yogi too," Astri said.

YaLan nodded. "Our yogi's vows require him to never speak a lie. His complete honesty can be funny or maddening, but he made us strong in meditation and yoga."

"It makes it impossible to speak anything but complete truth in his presence, but he is funny too." Astri added, "Mother was initiated by him in the way of Big Love."

Juno smiled as if remembering the day. "I was so blessed. His teaching reflects his reverence for the Truth. His liberated spirit moves in silence and through infinite space."

"He sounds wise," M said. "We can't wait to meet him." She gestured to YaLan and Astri, to their colorful dress. "You remind me of beautiful warrior princesses from *Game of Thrones*." M paused before editing herself, "But compassionate and colorfully dressed."

Astri and YaLan both said, "Thank you." Boy smiled.

"Sorry," M said. "You probably don't know the TV show, but your wonderful dresses—"

"We don't have a TV. We dressed like this to welcome our honored guests; this isn't how we normally dress." Astri stood and spun around, a fairy princess from old Siam. "Did you find father's—dear Dylan's—constant creation theory that you mentioned in your letter?"

"No, but we hope to find it here," I said. "With your permission, we'll search a bit, as he may have hidden it. And Dylan's wife reminded me he has a PO box in town that he used like a safety deposit box. Since your mother doesn't have a copy of the theory, we'll ask Natalie, his wife, for authorization to check there."

M patted my knee and grinned. "Color me impressed. I hadn't thought of that."

"It came to me while I was plotting the novel's mystery, and since mailboxes are my specialty . . . While I believed it would be here at the Deeksha, I hadn't given other options a second thought."

"Maybe you'll find it in Dylan's room, but we've looked and found nothing," YaLan said. "Let us help you in your search."

"Yes! We must," Astri added. "We've looked everywhere but believe we'll find it with you here now!"

They brought prayer hands to their hearts as Juno beamed a silent blessing on the solidarity of our quest.

The twins would become Miranda and Ariel in my novel. Both were resplendent and accomplished princesses and fairy spirits. Still, Astri was more Puck- and Ariel-like in her diction, and YaLan came across as more erudite, like Miranda. Juno would remain Juno in my story, though she was truly Prospero here on her Deeksha island. After less than an hour, I had no doubt she could conjure a tempest, commanding the fairies of earth and air.

Juno rose from her seat. "May I suggest you rest or meditate and then enjoy the garden and the spa? And you must please be my guests for dinner this evening."

It was my nap time, but first I'd search Dylan's room, where I hoped to find the ToE and win M's love, all on my first day in Xanadu.

CHAPTER 27

I WAS EXCITED TO SEARCH Dylan's room. I was escorted by the mostly silent Boy, while the yogi twins led M to her room. In drafting fiction in my head, I found words inadequate to describe the Deeksha's spaces. While *room* and *bedroom* are utilitarian descriptions of a chamber in which one reads, eats, or sleeps, the familiar connotations failed to convey the elegant grace and attention to detail of the spaces within the Deeksha. They were simple conceptions, reconciling the opposites of minimalist clarity with fullness of art in holistic, beautiful design. Dylan's room emitted a peaceful hum from its rich and textured wood and stone.

The Deeksha buzzed with a pleasant ambient *aum*. M's love would bloom for me here if it would bloom anywhere. My determination and confidence vibrated in anticipation. I hoped my words, those imprecise symbols and tools, wouldn't fail me.

Since Dylan was concerned about the CIA watching and macing him, it would make sense for him to hide the ToE. His simple, uncluttered room could be easily searched, and I was determined to leave no potential hiding place undisturbed. I sat in a comfortable yet firm wooden chair where I imagined Dylan sat to write, and I looked through his Asian-style desk with its dreamlike images of dragons, both etched and painted, and billowing opium clouds of smoke on which beautiful naked maidens floated by.

The center drawer did hold something of Dylan's: the Clash's first album. So Dylan, the incongruity of peace and punk. An album cover was a perfect hiding spot for papers, but the theory wasn't inside with the vinyl. I returned to the desk search, testing for a secret compartment or fake bottom to one of the drawers. They were all solid or empty. No nook or cranny of the room yielded the ToE or anything else of Dylan's.

Perhaps he hadn't left the theory behind but had taken it away with him in his photographic mind. It was nap time in this magical Xanadu, then to awaken to rejoin my love, but if the ToE was lost, would M's love be stillborn? Would the lost theory, remaining lost, bury my love at the failed end of our quest?

With me in need of a nap, my thoughts were muddled, mired in contradictions. The bed too was impossible to describe, as it seemed so ordinary but brought such extraordinary peace to my wired body and unreconciled mind.

I lay there musing on my writing, imagining how to fit Grace's visit to the Deeksha into the narrative. I closed my eyes to write in my head. To keep her safe, Dylan hadn't shown her the theory after being attacked by the CIA, but perhaps Dylan did show her the theory's hiding place, saying simply, "This is where I want to rest in peace—or at least my body, since my spirit will continue on and always be with you." Even though she shook her head at his talk of death, Dylan knew she had heard. And while not expecting to find anything, she would find the ToE in that resting place if anything happened to him.

I snapped open my drowsy drafting and drifting eyes, adjusting their focus. My subconscious or creative mind had lit upon the theory's hiding place. I jumped out of that beautiful berth, sure it concealed the theory somewhere in its folds.

After a twenty-minute search of bedding, mattress, and wooden frame, it remained just a beautiful bed, but one now in need of making. I made it and climbed back in.

Sometime later, as I lay between sleep and waking, a dark, heavy cloud gathered around me. It was an overbearing presence that filled me with a vivid sense of Dylan hovering above me. I felt as if I were waking in a sensory deprivation tank, unable to move, with an invisible apparition descending in the pitch-dark infinite and soundless space around me. There, but unseen. Known, but not identified.

Then, like Jacob's angel, Dylan was violently wrestling with me in that vast expanse of silence and darkness. We were evenly matched and rolled over and over, arms and legs twisting. Though there should have been grunting and shouts of pain, there was no sound. At first I attempted only to defend myself, but then I fought back until—exhausted and near death—I awoke. His invisible specter rose up and away.

Though he didn't identify himself, I knew it had been him. No words had been spoken. I rolled off the bed of our wrestling match—though *fight* might better have described the ghostly encounter—entirely spent but strangely buoyant and alive, as if a daemon had been excised from my body and mind. Though it may sound like a nightmare, I was liberated and oddly grateful for Dylan's violent wake-up call. Its full meaning eluded me or was just out of reach—another ineffable experience on day one at the Deeksha.

Juno had suggested that upon completing our rest, we should visit the spa and garden. Before joining M in that dreamlike setting, I needed to shower off my nightmare sweat.

After enjoying the waterfall, I put on a comfortable monk-like robe made of the finest linen, and soft hemp sandals provided by the Deeksha. I was disappointed that I'd failed to pack a bathing suit, as I wanted to use the spring pools with M.

Then I remembered from my search that the room provided a unisex Speedo swimsuit. I hadn't dared to wear a Speedo since I was twelve and on the swim team. But when in Kathmandu . . . I'd wear the red silk one. I put it on, pretending to be an overconfident European tourist with nothing to hide.

I wondered if M had packed her bathing suit. I hoped to see more of her soon.

CHAPTER 28

WALKING TO THE SPA AND GARDEN in my Speedo and robe, I was in a state of perpetual enthusiasm, my heart pumping waves of blood to every vessel. It was time to win M's love in this stately pleasure dome.

The Deeksha truly was a Xanadu, with hot and cold springs and a botanical garden that flowed seamlessly from inside the spa to the outside majestic gardens and further on to the forest, with the mountains and dipping sun beyond. I stopped and looked at M in awe, seeing her for the first time again. We were not our bodies. We were not our minds, not even that amazing mind of hers. We were spirits, pure and eternal. Something about this place made me see her in that light even at a distance.

M, in her robe, was standing in contemplation in the outer garden. I shook off my lofty thoughts and imagined the bikini beneath the robe. I was still a man, not a monk, despite how I was dressed for the ashram.

I moved slowly so as not to disrupt her meditative walk. Her smile said she was glad I had come. My sad smile said I hadn't found the ToE in Dylan's room. I went in for a consolation hug and got a good one. We shared the communal peace of the garden, where we walked in mostly serene silence. My mind was still, my keen attention focused entirely on the woman beside me.

I broke our silence, saying, "M, at the risk of you thinking I'm even stranger than you already do . . . I just had the wildest lucid dream. I couldn't see him, and we didn't speak, but Dylan and I fought a near-death wrestling match not thirty minutes ago. Yet strangely, despite the deadly struggle, I felt no anger, only love and a desire to live. The fight was so real I woke in a pool of sweat. But I feel oddly liberated by it."

"Did you ask him where the theory is?" she said. "Of course, you know what Freud would say?"

"No, and I'm hesitant to ask Freud's opinion."

"It's just an expression, but since you asked, maybe you competed with Dylan in the past and have some unfinished business, or you have unacknowledged homosexual tendencies and want to kill your father."

Her stare augmented a pregnant pause, which she followed with loud and inelegant laughter. I'd never have expected such a bellow of joy to come from the classy professor, but each new facet she revealed just added to her allure.

"I'm kidding. I have no idea what Freud would say." She enjoyed playing my therapist.

"You're probably right about Freud, and I am prone to Freudian trips." I took a mock stumble that opened my robe.

She chuckled again, this time at my revealing slapstick.

"That's why I always preferred Jung," I said, retying the robe's belt to hide my European-beachcomber state of undress.

We stopped in front of a circular rock garden, where a stone Buddha sat on a large marble pedestal surrounded by a little spring and a lotus pond. On the pedestal was a poem in English and Chinese, the Chinese calligraphy expressed with breathtaking artistry. We sat on a perfectly placed love seat, and I read the poem to M.

SPRING BLESSING

What humble blessing may I bestow?
Upon your fancy's arbor,
Passion child of your sweet labor.
When you shed ruby tears,
And red satin each step appears
—As you pass by—
Comets stream on up ahead,
A white swan on a burning bed
Bursts above the scene

—of your new beginning—
"As accomplished fingers begin to play,"
The warm wind whispers in each guest's ear
Exactly that which it needs to hear.
An old monk smiles and opens the way
—into your garden treasure—
Where a sacred stream meanders through,
To a timber teahouse from Xanadu.
Here Kubla Khan could finally rest,
Posting his sentries all around,
To keep out hungry ghosts and hounds,
Then lays his head upon your blossom breasts.
Your blessings—Spring—from those you bless.

M looked flush. "Oh my, this spot, that poem. I feel like we are standing in a vortex. I love that. I feel I've heard it before." Dylan's poetic words always hit their mark with the ladies.

"Good poetry always sounds like déjà vu; Dylan's poem, I bet," I said, sure that Dylan had written it, though there was no name on the marble. Channeling Tennyson, I added, "It would be easy to be a lotus-eater and spend forever here."

"All the more reason to focus on finding the ToE before you lose your will. How are we going to gain access to Dylan's mailbox?" She pushed soft strands of auburn hair off her tawny silk cheek. "That's our next step, right?"

"I wrote Natalie, asking for her to send some official-looking authorization, but I'm not sure they'll accept an email."

"Okay, let's run down that lead tomorrow, and if it's not there, let's go to Yogi Mangku's as soon as possible. Then you can get lost in the lotus here, if you like. While I hike."

"Not without me," I said.

"I hope you can keep up with me." She waved one hand, erasing her words. "I'm sorry. Teasing again."

"No," I said, "I'm not upset about that." I put my hand to my scratchy face. "I forgot to shave, and I wanted to look good for you."

"You look good. Like a beat poet or a kid from Brooklyn."

"Call me Kerouac!"

"Okay, Jack. And I think you're right that it's in his mailbox here—the PTBT list in the New York box and the ToE hidden in the box here. It has the beauty of symmetry."

"Dylan knew I loved mail, and he loved the symmetry, the poetry of life." I stood. "Let's enjoy the rest of the day and night and speak to Juno in the morning about how to get to the post office and about seeing the yogi. I want to meet him in any event, for the symmetry."

We went back inside to the botanical garden and springs. "A dip in the hot and cold pools?" I asked.

M hesitated before saying, "I didn't bring a swimsuit."

"I didn't remember one either, but I found a sexy Speedo in the room."

She said, "Me too," and without further hesitation she removed her robe, and I followed suit.

There we stood in matching red silk Speedo fig leaves—sans tops—prepared to step into spring pools in a world as far from New York as I could imagine. I didn't stare but politely noted the goddess in front of me. What a wonderland I was in, awed by M's innocence and beautiful nature. She just seemed to flow with the ever-changing environment.

The surge of blood in my Speedo shook me loose from her spell. I jumped into the icy cold spring, making a splash. She slid more easily into the hot one. Soon I was able to join her there.

Like joyful children in their first water park, we hopped back and forth from hot to cold for about an hour, chatting about matters great and small with meaningful silences in between. There was still no hint of jet lag, only the euphoria found in an unexpected paradise.

We'd been invited to dine with Juno, a renowned master chef, that evening as her honored guests. Therefore, we reluctantly dried off and re-robed and went to our respective rooms to change, agreeing that I'd stop at M's room in about an hour. We parted with a hug as if nothing out of the ordinary had happened; I wouldn't have been able to stop at an unshaven kiss, so I again banished the thought.

After the near-naked bathing, my heartstrings and other balls of muscle had reached maximum taut fullness, where they would likely remain until M's body and heart enveloped mine.

M had bared her perfect breasts to me. That surely was a sign, inviting more, that even I could see. The sighting had exceeded even my wild imagination, and now they were even more spectacular in memory. Yet looking back, I understood that it wasn't only her face or even those breasts I loved but the mind behind those eyes and the heart beating within that chest. *Mea culpa, M,* I said to WOPA myself.

Tonight we would kiss in this neverland of Big Love. I would see the love ignite in her eyes and know it was time. I needed only one more clear sign to take the fateful leap out of my mind and into the physical realm.

The mind argued that there was no love without passion and that passion acts without regard to consequences. But to what end, if M didn't share that love and passion, or worse, rejected it? I was a lover frozen on a Grecian urn. I told myself my greatest strength—or was it weakness—was my ability to balance passion's push and pull and to wait. The quest—love—demands sacrifice and the courage to act.

CHAPTER 29

I PICKED M UP IN HER ROOM around seven on what was still our first day. Though nothing life shattering had happened, the Deeksha had changed everything and compelled a new perspective, and I was primed to act.

M showed me into her room. She illuminated the space, wearing a simple, loosely clinging forest-green dress that revealed just the crescent of her chest. My Maid Marian dressed for a feast.

"You look amazing, and I shaved!" I announced as a prerequisite to the meeting of our lips. And then I almost fainted as M's cool-soft confirming fingers passed slowly across my smooth left cheek. I turned the other cheek, and she playfully complied, evening out the feel.

M's room was worth the visit, as it was the yin mirror image to my yang room, with a corresponding subtle shift of energy. It had the same ambience but more delicate detail, with less wood and more stone. Behind the bed a sheer waterfall flowed over the rock wall, where a Chinese character was etched in red, looking like a fairy twirling *en pointe*.

"YaLan told me it's the symbol for peace," M said.

The sound and visual effects were soothing and hypnotic. I wanted to share M's room, and the light that shone through her, at any expense.

I was weighing the pros and cons of a pre-dinner kiss when M turned off the waterfall and said, "Let's go."

We headed to dinner. Post-dinner would be best for a kiss.

Boy greeted us and showed us to the head table, recognizable by its placement at a large comfortable semicircle banquette that looked over the two rows of communal tables like the helm of a ship. All the chairs along the communal tables were the black Ming with six-foot-high straight backs. At the end of each long row was a similar Ming chair but with an even taller back, which curled rather like a question mark. Those two chairs had no place setting, and no one would be seated there. Our chairs, on the helm, were of normal height and a transparent bloodred, with comfortable cushions. Modern Quan chairs, Boy explained as he seated us.

Boy returned to his task of seating arriving patrons, an internationally eclectic, artistic, and curious crowd, each sitting up straight and ready for magic—as was suggested by their elegant seat and ethereal environment.

I said to M, "There's a lot of attention paid to the chairs and beds here."

"Well . . . that is where our bodies spend a lot of time. But it's really every detail. Look around." She mimicked Juno's wave of an invisible wand.

She was right; the space itself was a presence. The dining hall had been transformed by the night. The vaulted ceiling, clean lines, design, art, and furnishings—lit solely by abundant candlelight—struck me as being a setting from either a delicate Asian temple of two hundred years ago or a visionary new world a hundred years in our future.

Juno stepped up behind M. "May I join you?"

There were no menus. The meal—the best I'd ever eaten—materialized bite by bite like notes in a symphony or the words of a favorite poem.

First were exotically spiced mushrooms in a simmering seasoning, served on small boats of shaved wood with tea leaves as a bed. The delicious bites of earthy fruit were served with a red pinot noir from a vineyard in China that used imported French vines. M took her first sip and followed it to the finish. I could tell the xenophile in M agreed it was very good, but the Francophile no doubt wondered if the vines had been smuggled out of Burgundy. But like education, shouldn't fine wine flow freely?

M was gracious, saying, "This is an excellent pinot noir, mixing the best of California and France like the finest Oregon pinot."

Wanting to be profound and to please my audience, I held high my glass. "To the century of women and China's awakening!" It was a bit of a dud as a toast, but the ladies smiled graciously before we touched glasses and sipped.

YaLan and Astri had joined us on the helm, no longer dressed for *The King and I* but wearing what young female yogis do—forest green pantaloons and an oversized white shirt falling off one shoulder for YaLan, and for Astri, a sleeveless teal top revealing a taut belly and a cute belly button.

They raised their glasses for a toast more spot-on than mine. "To all the people to be trusted!" The twins sipped in unison and giggled, enjoying the fermented grape sensation on their young tongues.

Their words reminded me that I had copied the PTBT list for Juno and attached it to my introductory email. That made M and me knights at the round table and Dylan's PTBT list our letter of transit to this new world of wonders.

I always became more poetic with wine in hand.

Magic was the night. The attention lavished on us as fellow PTBTs in constant creation was a high honor. I felt odd feeling worthy of this loving focus, since worthiness was another issue for me. However, at this Deeksha dinner with the family, emboldened by my love for M and confident in our quest, I was letting go of self-doubt. There at the helm, I realized that unworthiness was putting a limit on the kindness and love we were prepared to accept and receive. It was a form of ingratitude. Perhaps that was the limitation Dylan had come to wrestle out of me. In any event, some self-imposed limitation had been lifted, and a vibrancy grew in and around me. Tectonic plates shifted within my brain as fine food and wine loosened my lips and warmed my soul.

Each guest was made to feel expected and eagerly anticipated, except the last, who arrived well beyond late. We watched as Boy confronted a bearded man who looked like the man from the airport, who looked like Dick. I had only seen them both once, for a short period of time and from a distance. And the place where my fiction started and reality ended was becoming increasingly unclear. I was in unfamiliar territory. The illusion was sifting the sand dunes of my mind as all my senses worked to settle into this Xanadu, which seemed to insist on a more authentic self while at the same time stoking the imagination.

Boy looked to Juno, and like Rick in *Casablanca*, she smiled sadly and shook her head. Boy was well over six feet, and strong and imposing in his role as bouncer. He stood sentry like a eunuch from an old movie supposedly shot in the exotic Orient.

His doe eyes turned to the smaller but still-imposing Western man, whose eyes were filled with swirling anger that could be seen even from a distance. The bearded man was attempting to bully his way in. We could hear his anger and see his stance, but his words were unintelligible to us. He finally left reluctantly and in a huff as Boy patiently held his position without hostility. On his way out, the angry man held the door open, pausing to watch the breeze blow out several candles on the near end of the communal table.

M murmured, "What an angry and petty man," under her breath.

I was thinking, *What a dick.*

Something the chairman had said about the Guru's man in Kathmandu convinced me that Dick was real and not just a character of my imagination.

"I thought I saw that man at the airport," I said. "And he looks suspiciously like a character who attended Dylan's funeral service."

"I agree," M said. "Quite a character for your novel. I saw the guy you're talking about after leaving you behind at the wake. He tried to snap a picture of me. The guy that just left bears a similarity to that man in New York, but it couldn't possibly be him with that beard. In any event, we're just as glad to see him go."

Juno sighed. "I don't know the man but have seen him around. He always looks so angry, and he has been ungodly to a beggar at the market and then rude to YaLan and Astri there just yesterday."

The twins were both dying to tell the story of the confrontation with the bearded man. YaLan was awarded the honor as Astri sat back with a smile, playfully yielding the floor.

YaLan stood with dramatic flair, but Astri set the stage from her seat, saying, "Remember Dylan told us Sean is going to write a novel, so make it a good story, and make me look good for Sean's book."

With Dylan's disclosure and Astri's humor, my novel was taking on an unwelcome reality-TV component.

YaLan gathered her audience with her eyes before saying, "This is a short story of beauty"—she bowed—"her sister"—she flourished her arm at Astri—"and the beast"—she glared at the door where Dick had just stood.

"We were in our local outdoor market yesterday when that bearded man started a scene by cursing a crippled beggar who asked for alms. We left our provisions on the counter of a merchant we know to make sure no harm came to the helpless man. As we approached, the bearded man spat into the beggar's face. It seemed a kick might follow, so Astri and I stepped between the face of anger and its unfortunate target. We could smell alcohol on his breath and heavy cologne . . . I think he soaked his beard in both, which glistened with stray spittle as he spewed out his words.

"His cold dead eyes—those dark beads spinning and sucking in the light—switched from violence to angry lust when the man was confronted by the two of us."

Astri jumped up, and playing the part of the bearded man, she got into YaLan's face, letting a little wine drip out of the corner of her mouth. Holding her body rigid, as a man of anger would, Astri took her turn with the story.

"As a crowd gathered, this dick—"

She blushed at her use of slang, and I may have laughed too loudly while looking at M to say *See?*

"He said to us, 'I'd like to have you both at once—how much?' Then as he moved eye to eye with YaLan to further intimidate her"—she pressed closer to her sister and glared—"he added, 'I think we'll go with the bald one first.' I was a little insulted, but under the circumstances, I let it go."

Astri broke off, or up, in laughter. It took her a full minute to compose herself, but she had us all laughing too, though except for her delivery, the story was markedly unfunny so far.

"Then YaLan—with his beard and his sick dog eyes an inch from her face—without blinking an eye, calmly replied, 'Angry man, you are a very rude guest in our marketplace. The way you treat people less fortunate will surely bring you no good. And the way you treat women must mask an extreme shortness of manhood. I am so sorry for all your insecurity, self-loathing, and lack of humanity. Please leave now, and know you are forgiven and blessed.'"

YaLan wiped her sister's lips and chin clean of dramatic slobber and sat down, yielding the floor to Astri.

"With that, I broke into laughter," Astri said. She went into another laughing fit before regaining her composure. "And the marketplace crowd that had gathered to watch followed in laughter at the unexpected civility and takedown by my sassy sister. The man seemed particularly disturbed that even the poor spat-upon beggar was laughing—though I doubt he understood English. The laughter was contagious and spread out in ripples that echoed back even louder on their return."

Astri took a sip of wine to replace the liquid that had foamed from her mouth. "The angry man had no retort. His eyes became homicidal, and he clenched his fists. He looked ready to strike my fearless sister. It would have been my fault for starting the crowd laughing. He managed with difficulty, after shutting his eyes, to control his ugly reflexes. Spewing and muttering curses, he slunk away, hostility chased off by the market's collective glee."

Astri moved around the table, doing an imitation of the man's fit of confusion and embarrassment, both exaggerated by her portrayal of him as a Quasimodo creature in retreat. We all laughed and enjoyed the joyful pantomime and the snorting end of her story.

I imagined that in the novel Dick would pull a gun at the Deeksha door and be subdued only after a shot was fired, mortally wounding Boy. Hmm . . . Maybe I'd seen *Casablanca* too many times. Perhaps *I'd* be the hero. I meant James, of course. But how could I kill Boy even in my imagination? Maybe I lacked the *Game of Thrones* guts to kill off admirable characters, although James's first wife and best friend were already dead. But killing those already dead was just a form of historical fiction. I might have trouble cold-bloodedly killing off fictional characters based on still-breathing good people full of warm blood.

M and I enjoyed immensely the rest of a wonderful meal. And although Juno was hosting us and managing the preparation of the food, each of the other guests also wanted time with her, requests which she accommodated with grace and ease. The pilgrims were all equally welcome after traveling to this far-flung mecca for the senses.

Still, Juno focused her attention on M and me as her fellow PTBTs. She personally introduced each dish, and her poetic descriptions made the small plates taste even better. The power of suggestion and the focused attention brought out the delicate and sensual flavors. It was a meal "on the house" and better than the one at Momofuku Ko that ended with a hug and my falling in love; this dinner would be capped with a kiss and a return of my love.

As the end of the meal approached, the crowd's pleasant hum was hushed, and waves of angelic music rolled over the still air. Much like Juno's words, the notes were amplified and enriched by the silence from which they arose. An unassuming minstrel was secluded in the corner, playing the most wonderful music on some flat organ-like harp that I'd never heard played before. Juno was a mystical Harpo, her hands and arms and body swaying as she played in a most otherworldly way. The music vibrated in me, magnifying my love, stirring my being. If consciousness is a light bulb that animates us, my dimmer switch was being turned way up.

After the first ethereal song's last note, YaLan leaned over and whispered to M and me, "She composed three songs for the guzheng just for this special evening."

"Beautiful," M whispered.

After her serenade, Juno rejoined our table for another interlude of communion over soothing tea.

I heard Boy explaining to one guest looking for his bill, "Oh, please don't worry about that. There is no bill. This is not a restaurant. Everyone leaves what they want to and can afford." He showed the man a little wooden box on the table.

I imagined each guest competing to leave the most money in the wooden box, as all were so very grateful. There was no box on our table.

As the crowd left, each guest wanted and received a warm goodbye hug from Juno.

I got a good-night hug from the entire Deeksha family before walking M to her room. I was ready, yet not for just any kiss. A first kiss from M.

I confided as we walked, "This place is magical. And our hosts, I've never felt such instant intimacy."

"I feel the same way, as though they're family I've known forever."

It was time. We arrived at her door, which she opened before turning to say good night. Our eyes met for an instant that seemed an eternity, where all was said and immediately forgotten. I started to add the soft murmur of enticing words. "I feel it all started with yo—"

She put her index finger to her lips in the sign of *hush, not yet.* I let out a long breath, then I namasted peace. Those gestures barred any further expression of love or a kiss, so I hugged her good night instead. Her door shut. My heart flopped with the sound of its closing. I stared intently at the wood portal I knew had no lock—stood there for at least a minute, willing that door to reopen and an angel's hand to emerge and pull me into the nirvana that was so near on the other side. The door did not bend to my will. I instead suffered the fool's walk to my door in the company of an old dead friend.

I hear you laughing, but please stay out of my bed tonight. I don't want to fight. I just wanted to taste her lips and share her bed under the peaceful waterfall.

CHAPTER 30

AS I LAY IN BED BEING MOCKED for my inability to kiss M, I attempted to take solace, telling myself this was just a short delay and no harm was done. Even the words that slipped out at the end of the evening hadn't betrayed my bleeding heart. And my love for M was so ripe with age and maturity, I'd be able to wait another day. I had not yet earned her love.

I turned my focus to our arrival in Kathmandu, the Deeksha, and Juno. I'd flown into a parallel universe where all was new. Bands around my heart and around my well-guarded and carefully cultivated sense of identity were snapping open. What it meant to be Sean was slowly but surely evaporating. My small circle of life as a professor in New York City was now more than nine thousand miles and twenty-four hours away.

That was a prior life. Priorities had changed. Tomorrow was another day in paradise. And tomorrow we'd get from Natalie the authorization for Dylan's mailbox, the treasure chest that would reveal to us the ToE.

Beseeching Dylan again, I said, *I know you have nothing left to lose, but if you kill me tonight, I'll never get that kiss*. Feeling somewhat reassured by being ignored, I dove into a deep sleep.

When the sun hit my face the next morning, I realized the Deeksha had no curtains or locks. I opened my eyes, wondering if it was too late to join M on her dawn run. YaLan had given her a jogging map at dinner, telling her to run early before the traffic blocked the streets and fouled the air. I hadn't set my phone alarm, and it was only six thirty, but M had been planning to be off to the races at six. I dropped my head back on the pillow, sad to have missed a run with M, and vowed not to miss any more opportunities on this trip.

Something was wrong. I opened my eyes. A foreboding and eerie stillness moved over the room. Dylan returning for round two? As I lay unmoving and expectant, a tremendous shaking exploded through the room, punctuated by repeated crashing sounds.

Living in NYC and having been downtown on 9/11, my first thought was of a terrorist bomb. Several seconds into the shaking and crashing, it came to me. *Earthquake*!

Goddamn . . . get up . . . bounce around . . . *ouch*! . . . leg in . . . *damn, damn* . . . won't go . . . fall down . . . shaking ground . . . shaking Xan-a-du . . . *Damn*!

Hitting the floor, I bit my tongue. Eventually the crash and bang slowed to a rumble and then a hum before the earth became perfectly still. Dead silence followed the violent shake, rattle, and hum.

Dressing wasn't the suggested first response to an earthquake, but I jumped up and finished pulling on my pants as I raced into the hallway. For such a peaceful place, I was getting the strangest wake-up calls. The silence had been replaced by wailing sirens.

Actus Dei. In medias res. Useless though apropos, Latin bubbled up from some deep recess to the surface of my mind.

Juno, Boy, YaLan, and Astri were all fine and already out in the hall. So far the only damage they'd found was fallen art and a broken urn. When my mind shouted *M*, I ran to her room, hoping she had slept in too. No, she was out on her run. I was shell-shocked and distraught, imagining that the earth had swallowed her.

Juno took command, looking like a Tibetan dakini in her intensity. She issued orders without pause.

"Boy, get Sean a jogging map and two face masks for all the dust that will be kicked up. Sean, find Em. Then, Boy, use your mobile and call the hospital and see what provisions we may supply. I'll start gathering what I know they will need. YaLan and Astri, ready the Deeksha for those who will need safety and refuge."

Three minutes after the earth's violent seizure stopped rocking the Deeksha, I was out in a war zone armed with a jogging map, a mask, and prayers.

CHAPTER **31**

KATHMANDU IMMEDIATELY post-earthquake looked like New York City on 9/11, but it was also totally different. Another surrealistically beautiful day, but instead of the rubble of two vertical skyscrapers whose destruction had covered the downtown in toxic dust, Kathmandu suffered destruction across a horizontal landscape, more like images of Hiroshima and Nagasaki.

On 9/11, I'd searched for a good friend by the still-burning towers, with people jumping to their death mere yards away, but I found him only later on a list of the fallen dead. Was I cursed with M now lost, sacrificed to the angry shattered earth?

An image of Hope dead in our hotel bed flashed through my mind, merging with the image of a battered M. I howled into the chorus of a thousand other howls screaming into the dawn of the post-apocalyptic napalmed Nepal.

It was hard to see through the swirling dust storm. How would I find M in this labyrinth of mayhem? I didn't even have her picture— my beloved and no picture. I considered going back for M's passport, but the compulsion to move forward was too great, so I pushed into the crowd streaming into the dusty and badly damaged roads.

Though I lacked a picture, I willed an image of M, bathed in light, into my mind's eye and then held it there—a vibrant still life lifted aloft to ward off images of death. I wished I had M's dervish bracelet to ring like a tolling bell to bring her back from the ruins of the abyss.

Although I never really prayed, I did speak to the dead. I heard myself repeating, "Give me M—you can have the theory." Was I bartering with Dylan—or God—with something I didn't even possess? I didn't know what else to offer.

God does not play dice.

I didn't know who answered.

My best bet was to stay at the Deeksha. But my heart said run and find her. If she made it back to the Deeksha, she wouldn't need my help.

The map showed three concentric loops for different runs: The outer one was nine kilometers, then six kilometers, and then three kilometers. They all started at the same point—on the mark where I stood. Knowing M, I guessed she'd take the longest loop and run maybe an eight-minute-mile pace. She was in good shape and a runner. But which direction should I go? After an earthquake, would she finish the loop or return along the route she'd already passed? It was a game of craps, and the odds were against me rolling the double sixes I needed.

Determining to run clockwise, I took only three strides before a burly man jumped into my path to block my desperate rescue. Dick from the airport *and* Dick from the wake, a foot from my face. Damn Dick with his beard and Charlie Manson eyes. I'd never seen him up so close, but it was definitely Dick, a devil rising from the smoke, dust, and blood. He was dressed in his clothes from last night and bleeding from a gash on his forehead. And he was smiling—as though he enjoyed the carnage and our chance meeting—as blood oozed down his brow and through his beard.

My body turned to stone, stuck between flight and fight, as he stared and smiled. On every side, strangers called frantically for loved ones in Nepali.

He licked at the blood that slid past the corner of his lips as though it were red gravy. One hand in his pocket might have been holding a gun—a gangster pose against a backdrop of dazed post-earthquake zombies stumbling among the debris.

"I saw your girlfriend run off . . . Maybe dead. Run ringing round red . . ." He spoke loudly but incoherently. "The universe is telling you"— something unintelligible—"you shouldn't have come . . . Now it's . . ."

Now it's Zimbabwe?

I couldn't follow his words but couldn't step away either, and all the while he enjoyed drinking his own blood. He was relishing the crazed moments of disaster and whatever he had planned for me.

"You don't want to fuck"—inaudible—"crush you." The joy of his demeanor and the anger of his clenched fists were reconciled in the pleased violence of his crazy eyes.

"What are you saying? Which way did she go?" I struggled to express anger, managing only resolute fear.

"I know you're looking . . . and we have it . . . they . . . the key soon me. They know now will step aside. You should too. Go home . . . fuck your beauty . . . if alive . . . Can I be any more clear, Professor? And, dude, zip your pants. Get set!"

I wasn't going to look down. "Which way did she go?"

Licking, licking, licking, he looked deep into my eyes and said, "I know. You ready?" And then he held my gaze as if playing some horrifying game, demonstrating the weapon of those mad eyes. The small irises emitted no light and permitted no light to pass, but they sucked at my energy. The blood streaming from his head branched off into a tributary that dripped into his right eye. He blinked, and I broke free.

I ran to find my love as behind me Dick shouted, "Go!" I felt Dick's bloody eye following me like a laser aimed at the back of my heart. I sprinted and zigzagged in case he sent a bullet to follow. I managed to zip my pants on the fly.

Running where I could, I focused on finding M. It seemed that every fourth building was damaged and entire streets were decimated while others had been spared—the randomness of tragedy. The uninjured but shell-shocked survivors had become rescue workers, finding the injured and pulling them out of damaged building after damaged building. There were very few official responders on the street.

I tried not to register whether the bodies on carts or being passed from rescuer to rescuer were dead or just injured. Traffic was at a standstill while the carted bodies lay bloody, groaning and contorted, or bloody, quiet and unmoving.

The noises of human pain and desperation were almost unbearable, a soundtrack from hell boom-boxing in my ears.

As I ran the gauntlet of blood, dust, and gravel, the image of M smiling and in perfect health streamed like a spotlight onto my mind and kept me in motion. I was galloping through a surreal film of death, destruction, and horror, incongruously detached as I maneuvered through the destruction and suffering with relative grace and clarity of mind.

The power lines with all their prayer flags were down, deadly hurdles snapping sparks.

After racing flat-out for over thirty minutes, I passed the halfway point on the map and pulled down my mask to draw in more dusty air. I must have missed M in the mayhem, but decided to keep going, as there was nothing else to do. My body had a mind of its own and knew what to do, running hard away from the thought of another person I loved dying.

An announcement from a loudspeaker seemed to precede me down the roads and alleyways: "Make way for the big love-crazed Western man barreling through!"

My body was numb, and I saw it from slightly above myself, like watching the path of a running back. I was no longer looking for M but rather looking only at her image in my mind. I didn't want to see the broken reality surrounding me.

The image began yelling, "Sean! Sean! Sean!" Only when it said, "Stop, Sean!" did I realize it wasn't a voice in my head but my name being shouted among the cacophony. Stopping and peering back about fifty yards, I saw M standing upright and strong, a young girl clutching her knees, her face buried in M's legs.

She wasn't dead!

Heart pounding, I ran back faster than my teenage track-star self had ever run and into the warmest sweat-drenched embrace, a little girl squished between our legs. Love among the ruins.

I returned to my body as if I'd come up for air into time and space, as they too returned to their near normal pace and place within the catastrophe. The background decibel level was turned down too, and the dust started to settle around our feet.

"God, M!"

"Sean!"

I searched for what to say and realized words would only get in the way. There were no words. We hugged again.

Eventually we released the hug to see if the girl was all right. Following her beseeching look and the small tugging hands, we hugged again with her in the middle. I didn't blame her for preferring the warm, safe place that shut out the sights and sounds of death and turmoil.

We slowly uncoupled, liberating the child from between M's legs. I gave M the mask I had in my pocket, and she put it on the girl, who finally felt safe enough to cry. I was glad M declined my mask so we could be together again face-to-face. As M comforted the whimpering girl, she explained that she'd found her immediately after the earthquake stopped rattling, but in all the confusion, she couldn't find anyone who knew her. Nessa was maybe two years old, and M carried her as we searched for a relative, friend, or anyone who might know her. I offered to help, but Nessa wanted only M to hold her.

We eventually found a man in a uniform. He had an air of authority but only due to his dress; he knew no more what to do than anyone else. Fortunately, he spoke English. M explained finding the girl, and I told him we were taking her back to the Deeksha. We asked that anyone looking for Nessa be sent there.

The official said yes, he understood, but he kept shaking his head no.

CHAPTER 32

WE RETURNED TO THE DEEKSHA shortly after eight thirty, with me watching for Dick's bloody visage the whole way back. I didn't want M to see him drunk on his own blood. She didn't.

We weren't the only ones walking the tree-lined lane to the Deeksha. Adults and children walked unerringly toward Xanadu, where what amounted to a refugee camp was being established.

While I'd been running the gauntlet and M helped Nessa, Juno and the family had converted the Deeksha's great room into a welcome center and cafeteria. Over a hundred refugees had already been welcomed. More were arriving on our heels.

The family paused to greet us with unbridled gratitude for our safe return. M was met with the enthusiasm usually reserved for someone who had risen from the dead. Nessa was embraced and fussed over. M and YaLan immediately took her to a family that had been assigned to M's former room.

I was astounded by what the Deeksha family had accomplished in so short a time. M and I didn't have more than a moment to catch our breath—and share one more hug and a gallon of water and a cup of tea—before we joined the work.

Juno led the triage, and no one questioned her instructions. Families with infant children, the elderly, and the infirm received the best spots inside, while Boy and the twins assisted the rest in setting up tents around the central garden just outside the indoor spa. The rooms M and I had been occupying were given to two families with very old and very young members. Similar families were also assigned to Boy's, YaLan's, and Astri's rooms. As more arrived, tents were peppered throughout the spa and garden, forming rows of rainbows with their prayer flags of white, yellow, orange, and red blowing in the wind.

Following the banging and rumbling of a large aftershock—shaking me and the already shell-shocked refugees more than a little bit—Nessa was back at M's heels, where she and M insisted she stay.

Boy took a picture of Nessa with his phone and had it printed and copied in the Deeksha office with a caption telling where Nessa could be found. The printer and copier were powered by a generator, as the electricity as well as the water had been cut off.

Boy and I took the picture to distribute at the hospital and around town in the area where we found Nessa. The chaos and stench at the hospital were overwhelming as we hung pictures of the cute little girl.

I *was* half hoping to see Dick again on the street to confront him with strong Boy by my side. I wasn't sure what I was going to say to, or learn from, him. *Did you kill my friend Dylan? Are you threatening M and me?* Most likely yes and definitely yes. But there was no Dick sighting, though the memory of his eyes lingered like a malignancy.

Boy and I hurried back to the Deeksha, where Boy passed on reports from hospital personnel and others we'd run into on the street. None of the news was good.

I literally and figuratively rolled up my sleeves, requesting and receiving from Juno my next assignment.

Juno and her team of YaLan, Astri, and Boy worked more efficiently than any military unit. Their undaunted enthusiasm and energy kept spirits relatively high among the new community. Everyone cooperated in the collective effort of transforming Xanadu into a fully operational refugee camp over the course of several hours. M and I worked hard as apprentices to our adopted family to ease the suffering of the newly homeless.

We were already part of the Deeksha family and therefore camp management. A refugee camp was a complete bar to romantic love and a major obstacle to our quest to find the ToE. Pursuing romance, and even a quest, felt selfish in light of the tragedy. I put my personal desires at the back of the line behind healing, food, and shelter.

By the evening's unofficial count, the Deeksha refugees numbered

333. Reports continued to come of death and destruction throughout the city, though when I'd been racing through it, it felt more like a large town or very large village that had been carpet bombed. The earth's destruction laid bare civilization's thin veneer of security.

To the Deeksha family, death, and loss were part of life, and we moved forward in silent atonement for the act of God.

Astri told us that Boy's parents had been heroes and died in a prior earthquake, which led me to marvel at Boy's calm, vitality, and endurance in establishing the refugee camp. There were more orphans today.

M and I took a short break from clearing and raking spaces for tents in order to sit on our bench by the Buddha pond. Nessa rested on M's lap.

I said, "Hope told me the shifting plates of earth that cause earthquakes and volcanoes are necessary for life's survival and the advance of evolution. At Natalie's, you heard her speak about that on Dylan's debate video. But it's impossible to reconcile that big picture of conscious design with this suffering. And . . ." I wanted to tell M about Dick but wasn't sure how, and I didn't want to upset her in front of Nessa.

M shook her head. "Especially today. There's no understanding it." She stood with Nessa, handing me a bottle of water and saying, "Back to work."

A woman maybe twenty years old—with a head wound and her arm in a sling—entered the garden with Juno. Nessa, with a happy shriek, finally left M's side. I translated the running girl's shriek, without an app, as Nepali for *mommy*. Mommy ran to Nessa and lifted her with her one good arm and twirled her around. A Simon and Garfunkel song replaced a Tom Petty tune that had been playing over and over in my head. M was in tears. Nessa and her mother, after thanking Juno and M, were gone fifteen minutes later.

Juno patted M's shoulder and said, "No worries, Em. The Deeksha is now mother to many children. The earth's violent wakening, and the suffering it causes, let it waken in us our full compassion and love."

Juno was called away to manage another crisis.

"Juno's right," M said. "There are plenty of children to care for, but still, I felt like Nessa's mother, and now like a woman who lost a child.

Strange how the earthquake created such a strong bond so quickly." She managed a smile. "Juno's now our mother too."

"The destiny of Roman mythology," I said.

M shook her head. I think a lot of what I said to her she wrote off as literary gobbledygook. Like Hope, M was a talented scientist. Both explored the world in a way different from the way I did, and I found the nature of their true scientific explorations enlightening and, in essence, not that different from my endeavors of artistic creation. But now, in the aftermath of an earthquake, we were all manual laborers, and it wasn't the time to ponder my own profession's reaction to the cataclysmic events. Hurting people had come to the Deeksha for help. We returned to the great room to perform our menial duties.

The Deeksha looked different with so many people milling around, yet it was still the same. I stood, hands on hips, watching as people came in looking shocked or lost or grief-stricken. That shock and grief eased back when YaLan or Astri squeezed their hand or offered water. I saw hope—or maybe it was simple relief—fill their eyes when Boy assured them they had a place to stay. The Deeksha had been a center for joy and peace before the earthquake; it was the same after. The only difference was that the walls seemed to have expanded, making room for those who needed safety and peace.

Knowing I was tired and searching for the mystical where I shouldn't expect to find it, I started gathering trash while I continued to watch and listen and marvel as selfless generosity was used as an antidote to grief and fear and uncertainty.

Suffering had entered Xanadu. Juno comforted the injured and distraught, some only now learning that loved ones had been killed. She lifted each petitioner's spirit by her steady presence and her compassionate words. Sometimes she laid her hands on their heads. It was unclear what prompted a blessing, but the people were appreciative. She had seemingly inexhaustible energy, and I felt honored to be a part of her team.

As dusk descended on the broken earth, I replayed my Dick sighting again and wondered what to tell M and what we should do about it.

The earthquake and Dick's incoherent threats were coequal chasms for me on that most inauspicious day.

At our next break, I led M by the hand back to our relatively secluded bench by the Buddha pond, telling her along the way of the demonic encounter exactly as it had occurred. After we sat, she said, "My hero ran away?"

Sometimes gallows humor was the best response.

"No, *you* had, and I had to rescue you and didn't have time for him just then in the middle of an earthquake with you running around or trapped under the rubble."

"Well, we have to tell Juno. We don't want to put the Deeksha in danger."

"Yes, but his presence makes finding the ToE now, before he does— if he doesn't have it already—even more important."

"Time is of the essence. And thank you, Sir Galahad, for coming after me." She clutched her hands to her chest to dramatize her gratitude and concern. "He and his Guru may have it already?" She did a short shake-off dance, raising her waving hands to the darkening sky before bringing them together above her head and slowly back down to her heart. "Let's pray they don't."

"Maybe. I don't know. It was so hard to hear him, or he intentionally made it so. But he made no sense, saying something about having the key." I still couldn't figure out what he'd been saying. "And why threaten us if he has it? Why not just send it back to the CIA and leave us looking?"

"The chairman suggested they not only wanted it but wanted to suppress it too. What key was he talking about?"

"Maybe Dylan's mailbox is opened by a key. Natalie's lawyer said he was able to research the post office regulations and is working to get the paperwork we need. He told Natalie her email to me wouldn't suffice. He says no one else will be allowed in while our claim is pending; he'll see to that."

"Does he know we may be racing the CIA?"

I shook my head. "I'm not sure how much Natalie told him."

"Okay, let's hope the post office is still standing, with the ToE hidden there and not buried under the rubble, and that Dick doesn't beat us to it. We really have nowhere to go following the earthquake; no flights are getting out."

"We could camp out by the river under the stars." I half wished we could share a tent for two, but the other half worried a wolf named Dick would find us there.

"Let's see what Juno says."

"We know what she'll say: 'Oh my, but you must please stay.'" I spoke in an effeminate English lilt, a poor imitation of Juno's lovely speech.

"Something like that," M said. She stood and pulled my hand. "You think something's wrong with this bench? Such a beautiful spot, it's funny that it seems reserved for us."

I read from the marble poem. "'What humble blessing may I bestow upon your fancy's arbor?'" *Dylan, Xanadu could use all the blessings we can get right about now.*

Over the course of a twenty-second upheaval, our experience in Xanadu had been transformed from our being exclusive, pampered guests into our being eager volunteers in the most humbling public service, and from a serene place where M's love seemed a sure thing to a busy beehive with no privacy. Romantic love was put temporarily in perspective by the tragedy and suffering so fully embraced by the Deeksha family.

I had the feeling I was watching Big Love in action.

After we quickly filled Juno in—while helping with food prep in the kitchen/mess hall—Juno insisted we stay. "To help host our guests and to be secure among the family."

I was relieved. The tent by the stream was just a dream and was too dangerous. I started looking for avenues Dick might use to attack us at the Deeksha. We were only a hundred yards from the street in a resort with no gate and no locks. But I believed that there, under Juno's command, among all the grateful refugees, was the safest place in the world.

CHAPTER 33

THE CAMP SETTLED IN, becoming quiet sometime after midnight. M and I stretched out to rest, still in our dusty clothes, on yoga mats on the floor of the great room. I didn't so much sleep as lie there, exhausted but full of life and love, a shipwrecked Gulliver lying alongside his long-legged mermaid after both had been washed ashore.

I watched the mermaid's breath rise and fall, imagining her dreams steeped in esoteric knowledge of the deepest seas. Not able to sleep, I began mentally drafting an email to Natalie, then got up before first light to write it. I asked if her lawyer might confirm the post office was still standing and when it would reopen. I also asked that he insist no one else be permitted access while her claim was pending, reminding her that we believed the CIA was working to get access too.

As soon as I pushed Send, I was immediately engaged with the rest of the family in setting up for a sunrise yoga ritual. Juno said it would be followed each day the refugees remained at the Deeksha, as "Meditation and yoga are the best practices for a healing start to a new day."

Boy had already printed a daily and weekly schedule of camp activities, which he posted around the camp.

THE DEEKSHA SCHEDULE

All day: Focus on love—let healing come

Yoga at dawn followed by breakfast in the great hall

Oneness blessings offered by Juno, Astri, and YaLan throughout the day

Dinner at sundown in the garden (weather permitting)

Nighttime campfire with pre-bed tea

Questions—please ask any of your hosts

The answer is always love

Blessings, the Deeksha family,

Juno, Boy, YaLan, Astri, Emily, and Sean

Reading the simple list made my chest swell with pride and a sense of mission, even as the last name on the list. It also brought M's smile to me and her hand to mine. We both felt it. We were full members of the family.

On the way to the first yoga class, Juno explained to M and me, "The mind in meditation is like a radio receiver with only one true channel in the center that connects us to God, and the rest of the spectrum are static streams of thought; the noisier it is, the farther you are to the left or to the right of center. As you dial in toward the center, you find illuminating and increasingly quiet thoughts until finally you tune in to God's channel, where there is only silence and love. God does not hear our words, only prayers from our hearts."

If anyone else said this, it would sound strange and perhaps silly, but out of Juno's lips, it sounded only beautiful and true.

We started class surrounded by the spa's springs. The large sliding glass doors of the spa were opened to seamlessly extend the space into the outdoor garden, where yoga mats or blankets had been laid. A small platform raised Juno about three feet off the ground so all could see her instructions and movements.

Class started with fifteen minutes of breathing and meditation. Peace of mind seemed amplified by the communal silence and stillness. Though I had only dabbled in meditation years ago, before it became a nap, and had never done yoga, I liked this way of greeting the day. It was clear M had more experience with both and was much more relaxed and flexible.

My meditation focused on M and the love I imagined radiating from her the moment I found her protecting Nessa. I prayed with all my heart for her love. My prayer was juxtaposed with my head's claim that it would be impossible for her to fall in love with me in a crowded refugee camp. I was left of center on the dial.

As she had been when playing the guzheng two nights ago, Juno was all grace as she led the stretches and poses, a yogi too. Astri and YaLan floated up and down the rows of mats and blankets, encouraging, instructing, and demonstrating. The three synchronized their elegant movements, choreographing a dance of yogic motion where it was hard to tell the yogis from the dance—a fairy queen with warrior princesses leading a ballet of refugees. It was yoga as a dance of the heart and not gymnastics of the mind.

At the end of class, Juno instructed us to lie in shavasana as she played the singing bowls. I'd found my favorite pose so far—corpse pose. Time to relax and let go. The bowls' vibrations echoed through the garden, and my body and mind felt like the prongs of a spiritual tuning fork. I imagined that a flowing current of vibrational energy ran through the collective corpses lying there.

As she played, the morning light came up, pairing with the sound of the tinkling springs and singing birds as the garden came alive to the hum of the beehive bowls. As the last harmonic tone faded away, a soothing tremble rolled beneath my body, another vibrational force. It was the small ripple of a shimmering aftershock, the earth relaxing and healing itself too.

Everyone sat up, laughing through tears, and namasted one another and our teachers. Joy and harmony arose, post the soothing aftershock, where fear and panic would have reigned in a shopping mall or office building. The day started, as I suspected it would end, with great communion and fellowship.

Juno's extraordinary abilities and a life that combined art and nature were simply part of her. There should be another word for work done in such perfect alignment with—and in acceptance of—what one was called to do. When I spoke with M about it at breakfast, we agreed that our work on behalf of the refugee guests didn't seem to be work at all. M said, "We are overpaid with abundant smiles and gratitude."

I felt that same way about the writing of my novel. Action taken and effort exerted in alignment with a higher calling wasn't work. More and more my writing—when I could squeeze it in—was just a witness to the amazing world of the Deeksha. That morning I wrote with some surprising literary flair for my first draft: *It was miraculous how the peaceful energy and calm of Xanadu was not darkened by the entrance of the refugees and the suffering of Kathmandu, but all were embraced and nurtured by the energy unaltered and amplified there. The space and its peace simply expanded to take in the crippled multitude. Darkness cannot exist in the light.*

I was increasingly faced with the limits and inadequacy of language and found myself wishing to know more than one. How could I not when exposed to the beauty of unfamiliar tongues spoken all around me? Other tongues might express what English could not. Still, I was glad English was the international language of the Deeksha, as that was all I had to play with.

That first full day following the earth's tremor—which sounded like a euphemism but was the only other English word for *earthquake*—I had little time to bemoan the quest's hiatus as we waited for our power of attorney to enter Dylan's safety deposit mailbox. We were too busy in service to Juno's guests.

Our role as assistants was never stated and didn't matter, as everyone did what they had to do. There was no hierarchy in Xanadu. Despite the printed schedule's suggestion to ask questions of any of us, all questions went to Juno. When M saw what was happening, she set up her own administrative desk to take the guests' questions, requests, and complaints. That service was a great help to Juno and relieved her of near-constant demands. I noticed that some guests seemed to want to just spend time with my love at her desk. I enjoyed calling her *concierge*.

When I wasn't needed for hauling supplies or as a second—or tenth—pair of hands, I focused on my novel. My only complaint, kept solely to myself, was that this wasn't the trip I'd imagined with M as my constant companion and lover-to-be. A kiss once measured in inches and seconds was now suspended in space and time over a light-year away, and only James and Brigitte were enjoying my sensual and sex-filled Shangri-La, in a tent they shared each night.

So much for *The Secret*'s power of manifestation. That book would lay the blame on me—my intention was not sufficiently clear, or the earthquake was the universe's way of bringing M's love to me but required patience and time. Either way, it hadn't worked.

Juno, Boy, Astri, YaLan, M, and me all shared Juno's room for sleeping. Juno's décor was minimalist, which allowed for four futons to be spread out on the floor, with small tables to hold each camper's personal effects. Against one wall was a small shrine alcove for meditation. M was given the place of honor and shared Juno's queen bed and its rich linens right out of *One Thousand and One Nights*. After another exhausting day, I set up my futon on the floor, by M's side of the bed, wishing I could climb aboard Juno's magic carpet. I chastised my imagination and its perversion of the real Big Love.

As the final candle light was blown out, Boy asked me to tell a short story as everyone drifted to sleep. Put on the spot, the author rose to the occasion, telling the story of how Dylan and I became blood brothers in sixth grade using the needle of a compass. At the appropriate point, I said softly, "The end," thinking the family was asleep—only to hear Astri giggle and say, "I can't wait to hear tomorrow night's story. Good night." Then, like the Walton's bedtime, down on the farm, everyone said *good night*.

In that ideal hostel room, there was room only for peaceful sleep and wakening to the real Big Love. Aftershocks, Dick, and AI contraptions of the Guru's wicked imagination could not reach us there.

CHAPTER **34**

THE NEXT MORNING A CHINESE aid delegation entered the Deeksha in a military coup—international aid arriving to take credit for assisting those injured and displaced by the earth. The invasion was led by a general in the People's Army, a square man with a square face, square jaw, and square body. He carried himself like a brick fortress. There was nothing soft about the general.

He marched into the great room of the Deeksha, where the not-to-be-called-restaurant had been, with his entourage of army men and one young female assistant who held a movie camera that strained her strength. The general, bearing a sidearm, commanded her to start filming. The other men appeared unarmed.

One of his men stepped forward, barking, "The honorable and esteemed General Liu Feng."

I was never sure with the Chinese which was the first name and which was the family name; they often seemed inverted. This added international degrees of difficulty to my trouble with names. Thank God Juno had just one name.

The general stepped forward to his spot, both standing at and waiting for attention in his uniform of dark green trimmed in red, with medals of many colors. His cap was emblazoned with a red star. His impressive dress allowed him to puff up his chest, and his gun made him deadly serious.

The family, still dressed for yoga, instinctively flanked Juno for a confrontation that she treated like the arrival of unexpected guests for tea. I was on her left flank with the twins, and Boy was on her right with M. We had moved abruptly from shavasana to armed conflict.

The general and his gun spoke in harsh tones in Mandarin while Juno responded in lyrical English, sometimes gracefully flourishing her hand for emphasis. Protecting us with her invisible wand.

The general demanded something in Mandarin.

Juno replied, "General Liu—welcome! How kind of you to personally offer assistance. There is no private place to speak, as we are now a refugee home with over three hundred guests."

The general, displeased with Juno's response, angrily told the camera girl to *cunt*. He meant *cut*. I almost laughed, but he might have shot me, or M might have kicked me in the balls.

Juno was the only one to break ranks, giving him a wry smile.

The general demanded in Mandarin.

Juno did the hand-waving thing. "I am so sorry again, but there is no room here for you to stay with your men and lady. But I'm sure one of the local hotels still standing will be able to accommodate you, or you can buy tents if you did not bring them."

The general demanded in Mandarin.

Juno replied, "That is another kind offer that I must humbly refuse. I wish I could be more accommodating of your requests."

The general, for our benefit, then spoke English and right out of the little red book. "You are still Chinese, and we all serve the Party and the People. I must insist that I take charge here."

Juno responded, "Yes, we are all Party people, but the Deeksha is a private establishment, and the Nepali, in this time of need, would feel less comfortable being in a Chinese government-run camp. I must think of my guests."

I thought the general might become more enraged than he already was at this response or even take Juno into custody. He clearly was weighing his options, but something held him back, and the jutting of his tight square jaw declared he was not happy at being restrained.

He then went into several minutes of berating Juno in Mandarin while she stood calmly listening, holding her unclenched fist at the ready for a flick of the wand.

When Juno finally had the opportunity to respond, she said, "You are welcome to film now and provide relief supplies daily, but I cannot have you filming daily and turning the suffering of the refugees and the Deeksha's healing into a reality-TV show. And I must insist on free rein of the Deeksha and its efforts on behalf of our guests."

I felt pride in being in proximity to this fearless woman. Now there were two fearless women in my life.

The ever-on-the-ball and practical Juno added, "It would be most helpful if you could arrange bottled water deliveries and maintain a fleet of temporary toilets in the vacant lot next door, beginning as soon as possible."

The general expressed extreme displeasure in Mandarin and then, seizing upon Juno's one concession, turned to the female assistant, demanding that she prepare to resume filming.

That ended the confrontation. Behind us a semicircle of about fifty refugees had formed to watch the cockfight in the center ring, where the single cock had banged its beak against an unyielding mirror. That beak was now bent out of shape.

The general directed his camera girl as if she were a child that deserved a beating. While she applied makeup to lighten the general's complexion, Juno spoke quietly to the family.

"This is why I came to Kathmandu. Men like him. It's the nature of egos engaged in power struggles to react to Big Love by denying it, seeking to control or corrupt it, and finally attempting to destroy it."

Even someone far less judgmental than I, like Juno, had to recognize the general as a singularly egocentric misogynist who wielded his power over others to create a cruel reality around himself, regardless of the consequences.

The general appeared to have aspirations to be a film director. He constantly berated his poor camera girl as he directed scenes throughout the camp, shouting, "Roll" and "Cunt." As the crew filmed the humanitarian efforts "led" by the Chinese at the Deeksha, Juno swept herself into the background. The general was only too happy to be in front of the camera taking full credit for the Deeksha's response, as well as to assume command of the Chinese response to the tragedy epitomized by this Xanadu amid the rubble.

He insisted on one final shot with the beautiful Juno thanking him for his assistance in the People's rescue efforts. She accommodated that final request. As he draped his arm around her, I thought she might disappear or wish that she could. She managed not to recoil, but with a graceful twist and bow, she gained her release.

"Cunt!" the general bellowed, liking the final take with Juno's charming and ironic bowing tribute. I was laughing, despite myself, at a safe distance. M thought it less funny than I did, and she gave me that disapproving look she usually reserved for my childish impatience.

She was actually angry with me and hurried over to say, "Sean McQueen, you're such an adolescent boy sometimes. Do you see the way he's treating his assistant? Nothing funny about it."

She was right, of course, and I shook my head in a hangdog apology. I was glad she couldn't read my mind to know the full extent of its arrested adolescence.

The general left behind one of his cadre to set up a tent for the purpose of coordinating relief supplies and the porta potties coming courtesy of the PRC.

After the general left, his man stepped forward and spoke in gruff Mandarin. Juno held up her wand hand. "English, please, so we all may understand."

He stood at attention, brushing off his infantry uniform and adjusting his cap before angrily continuing in the equivalent of a toddler's English to explain he was Comrade An, given this charge because his mother was Nepali. He spoke the native language, so he could tell *them* what to do, but otherwise he was pure Han Chinese like his father. His belligerent tone betrayed battle lines drawn within him from birth.

Juno said, "Welcome, Comrade An. What a lovely aspiration for a family name; may *peace* find you here. It is wonderful you learned Nepali from your mother."

Comrade An looked anything but peaceful. I decided to call him only Comrade. The general and Comrade would make great characters for my novel as foils for the so far barely fictionalized Juno. From his pride in his uniform and his military stance, with chest thrust out and chin lifted, I could tell that Comrade thought his charge of distributing supplies would give him power and importance at the Deeksha.

Juno seemed not the least bit concerned about the general's attempted takeover, his rude intrusion, and the surly spy he left behind. She merely set Comrade to work, a blot of darkness in the otherwise bright energy field of the refugee camp.

A few hours later, while taking care of personal business, I passed Comrade's tent. It was military issue and dark, which stood in stark contrast to the spectrum of colorful tents used by the refugees. A Chinese flag hung outside and stood apart from the concentric rainbow arcs of the refugee tents and their prayer flags. No one told him that he'd set up perhaps too close to the secluded rail at the edge of the garden, where the men peed into a ravine.

In my novel, which was weaving in and out of reality, Comrade became a dark predator. He may have been a danger to the children of the camp, as well as a real-life spy for his general. This character flaw came to me after Juno told the family, over evening tea, how she saw a young boy playing hide-and-seek dart into Comrade's tent. The Nepali had very little sense of privacy and would routinely pop in and out of one another's tents.

Comrade, seeing this intrusion into his lair, entered the tent not far behind the boy, seeking God only knows what—punishment, revenge, depravity, a friendly chitchat?

Juno started to run to the dark tent as a high shriek rang out, and the boy emerged from the flapping jaws of the canvas door. Juno comforted the boy, who said nothing had really happened. The boy had immediately wanted to make his exit due to the stink of the tent but was blocked as Comrade entered. When the army man started fumbling at his belt as if he was going to use it for a beating, the boy shouted and flew out.

Juno gave the boy the oneness blessing, and he returned to his play. Juno then confronted Comrade, letting him know she'd seen the scene and the camp children were under her protection. She concluded her story by asking YaLan, Astri, and Boy to please take turns keeping one eye on Comrade An.

When M and I asked if we might help, Juno said, "Yes, of course, you may be the other eye."

CHAPTER 35

THE GENERAL HAD SECURED ROOMS and commandeered the common room as his command center at the Hotel Yak and Yeti. Rumors soon reached the Deeksha that his army doctor was selling black-market opioids to the suffering Nepali, extorting profit from the tragedy.

Each day stinky Comrade, who commanded a fleet of porta potties, would go for an hour around lunchtime to report to the general.

Juno must have had spies of her own in the Yak and Yeti and/or back in Beijing. She told us the general's anger had not abated, and he was still looking for ways to take over the Deeksha and manage the refugee camp. He had planned to make a documentary of his heroic work saving the natives with the mystical Juno by his side. He was urgently petitioning Beijing for permission to seize control and was awaiting an answer. Juno assured us it would be denied.

I imagined even more nefarious events were unfolding in that dark universe less than a mile away. My original novel draft reflected the general's point of view. Although I met the general only once in person, from reading Shakespeare and witnessing his actions, I felt I knew the man. The general was a master of jiggery-pokery and would not be outplayed by a little woman.

I wrote a horrible scene, destined for the trash bin, where the general plotted with Comrade. He directed Comrade to lure Juno into his tent, claiming he had a top-secret message from her uncle. Then, following orders, Comrade was to rape her. The general then would have to take charge of the Deeksha to avoid scandal for China and its People's Army by burying the "he said, she said" accounts of the affair. Nuance and moral relativism be damned. The general and his comrade were bad men, and their evil had no limits in my imagination.

CHAPTER 36

WHILE THE FICTIONAL GENERAL and his Caliban plotted, in stark contrast was the innocent harmony at the Deeksha and within our family as we served our guests.

M and I had skipped romantic love on our way to becoming part of Juno's family and refugee camp management. While we waited for our authorization to get the contents of Dylan's mailbox, time moved slowly in the days following the earthquake. My mind was impatient and doubting. My heart remained eager and confident. Our quest for the ToE would continue, and I'd find a way back into the hunt for my love. Time would quicken again, yet until it did, I would suffer patience.

The evenings at the Deeksha refugee camp were as special as the dawn yoga ceremony. The family would sit at tea and let go of the day. I never fancied myself a tea drinker, so I was surprised how much I loved the end-of-day ceremony after the long days of work and the beer with dinner. The uplifting yoga and peaceful tea ceremonies were the ceremonial bookends to each miraculous day. Rituals repeated, but always new.

Dawn and twilight transformed Juno and the Deeksha. As day and night exchanged roles, Juno's spirit moved like shifting tides in the yokes of yin and yang. As dark came on, she kept the love of light. As the sun rose, she kept the peace of night.

I bashfully admitted to M that I was enamored of Juno, "albeit in a fully spiritual way." When M said that she was as well, I repeated my claim, less bashfully suggesting, "We are her children learning Big Love."

Each twilight Juno and her team prepared and served a feast in the garden to the hungry that gathered there. There was never any leftover food, though everyone received their fill. The Nepali curtailed their appetites and had a different definition of what it meant to be satiated, one defined by what was available to be consumed and shared.

Everyone gave thanks except Comrade, who ate more than his share by himself in his stinky tent. The refugees were gracious to let him serve himself first and grateful that he would then depart.

As dinner was cleared, a large bonfire was lit in a big circular firepit in the center of the garden, by the spring pool with the Buddha and Dylan's poem. The Buddha pond was our love seat and private nook, where M and I would plot in the few moments we had alone, hidden away in the peaceful center of the hive of refugees. Each night the Buddha was illuminated and floated on the water of the babbling spring pool that reflected fire and moonlight.

There was plenty of wood from the toppled buildings nearby that couldn't be recycled. People loved the fire for its light and warmth, especially while we still questioned the firmness of the earth beneath our feet. You could really feel the night coming on when all you had was a fire. No lights, cell phones, or internet wires. Just the night sky and the fire.

Primitive man must have felt much more in tune with nature and the universe. And what they lacked in wider knowledge of the world was well compensated for by a rich spiritual life engendered by the fire-light. Lots of time to breathe in and breathe out and tell stories while watching the flickering light.

Even after the third day, when electricity was restored, the nightly fire ritual continued. No lamps or cell phones were used around the fire, an unstated rule that everyone followed. There were other unstated guidelines at the Deeksha that everyone somehow knew and followed that made camp life more harmonious for all. Culturally, decorum and civility of community came naturally to the Nepali.

On the third evening after the earthquake, as we sat enjoying family tea, a boy became my shadow in the firelight. He eventually approached me and sat by my side. The twins played interpreters, and a friendship was struck.

The boy's name may have been Jai, but I mispronounced it as Chi.

Chi liked his nickname. He pointed at himself and smiled, full of loving energy and joy, saying, "Chi, Chi, Chi."

As the family sat sipping their bedtime tea, Boy poured Chi a cup. And though he understood not a single word, Chi listened to everyone intensely as M and I told the family what we knew about the ToE and our quest. YaLan and Astri had to bite their tongues to hold back their questions. Boy listened as keenly as Chi, and Juno smiled.

M started in with her parable of Zeno's paradox, blinking innocently at me, knowing that I perked up each time the conundrum was mentioned but likely unaware of its full effect. I shifted my position and thought of the chairman.

She said, "I never got to discuss the final theory with Dylan—the theory of everything, or ToE for short—and that's what Sean and I are so determined to find. We both believe it will be found either here in Kathmandu, in Dylan's mailbox, or at Yogi Mangku's place."

With her students paying attention, she said, "Dylan and I believed that consciousness, or pure awareness as distinguished from thought, is the key to the source of all things, as thought is already a thing. Or perhaps full consciousness is the thought of all things in the mind of God." She laughed at herself. "This is why sages speak in riddles of the ineffable. I have a class on consciousness and quantum physics scheduled for next semester, and it's already overenrolled. I have to learn how to better present this stuff. I'm counting on the ToE to assist me."

YaLan waved her hand in the air—a magician's apprentice. "Let us be your students, and you can practice your lessons with us each day."

"Well, there is one practice that I'm contemplating for my consciousness class that might get me a leave of absence from the science department. It's based on discussions Dylan and I had about the mutability and omnipresence of consciousness."

"What is it?" Astri had to know.

"Well, if everyone's willing to try?"

We were all eager, and Juno smiled as though she already knew.

"Astri or YaLan, please explain to Chi we are going to sit in a meditation on expanding consciousness for ten minutes and that this is a college course he is attending."

Chi, being told, was first to full lotus. I was the only one in half lotus a moment later.

After a couple minutes of following our breath, M started to guide us: "Now focus on that primary state, pure awareness, consciousness before thought or into which thoughts appear. Be the witnessing presence." She paused, we breathed.

"Now realize that awareness is not personal to you but everywhere and with everyone." She paused, we breathed.

"Now firmly rooted in that pure consciousness, imagine it in another member of the family here." I picked M, and my consciousness became so bright and aware. When I imagined M was imagining my consciousness, my head spun like a tornado, and when it stopped, I was the eye.

Fortunately, she had paused a bit longer before continuing. "Now imagine that consciousness expanding to the entire family seated here, and see how it is shared."

The practice was so very intimate and cool. It was working. My awareness became even brighter as I imagined it within each member of the family and Chi.

"Now, seeing the omnipresent nature of awareness, project it light-years out into the cosmos." I felt like a child in a planetarium enjoying the most pleasant astral projection to the most sonorous voice of the universe.

"Now become aware that consciousness has not moved but was always there and everywhere, at every point from here to there. And awaken here and now!" She paused. "You may open your eyes."

"Wow! What a trip that was," I said as Chi got up and did the most inspired dance, channeling the energy from that vortex M had opened. I realized M could take me to a place that had become a distant memory. Everyone was laughing and namasteing while Chi continued to dance around us, the essence of joy.

"That is a very powerful practice. It will be the most inspired of classes, by a gifted teacher," Juno said, as the most experienced cosmic traveler there, though M was not far behind her.

"We must practice that course with you!" Astri said. Chi finally sat by my side and took my hand.

M turned to Juno, and they held each other's eyes. The love was palpable, sister to sister—or was it daughter to mother, despite their similar ages?

"Can you spare us for a half hour after morning yoga and breakfast cleanup? It would be invaluable to me to have these brilliant yogi teachers as my practice students."

"Of course, Em. What a kind offer. It's an important course you have promised to teach. May I attend too when I'm able?"

"I would be honored, but I'm not sure what I can teach you."

"We are all one another's teachers and students," Juno said. "The best teacher is a student and always learning."

Feeling left out, I jumped feetfirst into the lovefest, standing in protest. Chi followed me up. "I assume it's a coed class and Boy and my new friend here"—I put my arm around Chi, whose grin stretched across his face as he wrapped his arm around me—"and I are invited too?"

Boy stood and stretched his long arm around us both. The ladies laughed at the display of male unity.

"Of course they can come," M said, "and you can come too if you behave and sit still and don't squirm. Why don't you explain about the people we met in New York City before we left, Professor?"

She gave me *that* smile. Hmm. Maybe she did know about Zeno and me.

The twins turned their eager-pupil attention to Professor McQueen, so I used my literary talents to embellish the quest for the ToE. "We met with small men and larger-than-life characters in New York City not long before we came here—a pompous and flatulent chairman of astrophysics, a pious priest who was a proud bishop in disguise, and a petulant detective turning a blind eye to clues."

"So literary, Professor," M said. "Let me get out my dictionary."

The twins "ouched" for me and raised prayer hands, nodding eagerly for me to continue. I transformed M's book club dinner into an intense scene from a Tarantino film, with sinister old fascists—playing cards pasted on their foreheads exposing who they were—verbally jousting with beautiful ladies of the silver screen and science while the guns of subtext were drawn beneath the table.

Silent Boy was so enthralled by the scene I set that I thought he might speak, but instead he drummed an excited knee. Seeing me notice, he stilled the quivering leg and looked longingly into the firepit, as if he had little interest in what I had to say.

"After meeting all the usual suspects there, we came here to meet the wonderful people to be trusted in search of Dylan's theory, which he thought would change the world."

Then, to heighten the dramatic impact of my story, I stumbled into a telling of the danger we faced too. "The American government and a CIA operative called the Guru have developed a burning interest in the ToE, a do-or-die maniacal pursuit . . . and we believe they . . . I mean we don't believe . . . We have no evidence . . . no evidence that they had any role in Dylan's mysterious death. The authorities concluded that he died in his sleep, but—"

Juno smiled at my faltering tightrope speaking and said, "No need to spare us your suspicions. We know there are ignorant, unscrupulous men who do bad things and that Dylan is dead; any connection between the two doesn't concern us. We all share the light, but some have lost all sight and live trapped within, constructing, *protecting*, their ego identities. We know the bearded man you call Dick is here searching too, but we should focus on our light and not the dark in others."

Boy started to clear the tea service. YaLan and Astri were disappointed that Juno had shut down the potentially salacious line of inquiry, but still wanted every detail about our plans to find the elusive ToE. To the twins, their beloved father's lost theory was the Dead Sea Scrolls rolled up in the Holy Grail.

M patted YaLan's back. "We're determined to find the ToE; we have no intent of giving up the search."

My gaze on M—admittedly longing and warm—must have exposed

my heart, as YaLan and Astri shared a glance, and then both smiled at me knowingly.

The silent Boy, Juno, and the twins, with Chi in hand, excused themselves for bed. When we were alone, M said, "You're a wonderful big brother. Chi looked so happy going off to bed."

"You'd be happy too if you were a twelve-year-old boy being escorted to bed holding hands with those two beauties as all the other boys watched. That's something he'll still remember when he's as old as me."

"That long?" M replied, reminding me my summer was marching steadily into fall.

Before I went to sleep, I read with mixed emotions Natalie's latest email regarding her lawyer's progress on gaining us access to Dylan's box. Contact had been made, and they would soon receive the necessary paperwork. While this was a good step forward, my patience, like my summer, was running out. I was done waiting. We had the legal claim and had sought to freeze the box shut, but Dick had the CIA. I feared we'd be too late. The Guru wouldn't let paperwork stand in his way. I had a plan to act.

CHAPTER **37**

THE NEXT MORNING AFTER YOGA, I told M, "I'm going to the post office this morning with Natalie's email. Patience may be a virtue, but I don't suppose Dick is a virtuous man. The time is now. I'm putting on a bold Western face and will use my clever words to gain access to the box. Cracking mailboxes is my superpower."

"The time is now? Well, I guess it always is. Who would want to fly when you can open mailboxes? I'm coming with you. I'll tell the twins our scientific courses on consciousness will start tomorrow. I don't want to miss your honey tongue in action."

We got a pass from Juno after breakfast cleanup. She also gave us a note of introduction and a recommendation written in Nepali for the postmaster. "I tell him you're people to be trusted."

The post office was a good thirty-minute walk. We left out the back garden and doubled back to the road in case Dick was watching. The earthquake's scars had left the roads clogged with motorbikes and trucks. Moving cars were actually few and far between due to strict gas rationing. On the way, we met a cow going our direction on the jammed street. He may have been a sacred cow that, though unattended, seemed to know where we were going and led our way. He kept the path relatively clear for us but had two drawbacks. First, he passed gas from time to time, and second, he made us somewhat conspicuous. If Dick was looking for us, he wouldn't be able to miss us in our single-cow cattle drive.

I said, "M, ask me what I'll do if we meet Dick on the way to the post office with our escort here."

"Okay, what will you do?"

"I'll show him I'm no cow-ward."

M laughed despite herself. She loved a good pun, and that was a double score.

The post office was an old British colonial block building. It seemed to have survived the earthquake intact. We thanked our holy escort, and I asked him to wait for us outside.

Inside, the post office was decorated with playful Nepali art, their frames still off-center from the earthquake. There was a long line—mostly made up of young tourists stranded by the earthquake, looking for parental care packages that had yet to arrive. Forty-five minutes later it was our turn. I couldn't imagine Dick waiting patiently in line.

I stepped forward with a hearty and confident hello and a hand outstretched, which the clerk shook loosely out of bemused obligation. "Do you speak English?"

"Yes."

"That's good. We've come on behalf of a grieving American widow for the contents of her recently deceased husband's box here."

"May I have the box number?"

I gave her Natalie's email and showed her where the number was on the page, reading along. "Five nine six six six."

She smiled broadly, as if it were a winning lottery number, and said, "Please follow me to see our postmaster. Five nine six six six." She and the other clerk laughed.

Beneath her breath, M said, "You're a very funny man."

We followed the lady to a grand old office—decorated with swords and horns—fit for an old-world British officer of high rank.

The clerk introduced us by repeating the mailbox number.

The man slouching behind the desk laughed loudly at the joke I didn't get.

He stood briefly to exchange handshakes and introductions and sat back down. "Just call me Bibek" was dressed in a civil service uniform representing the rank of postmaster general. He didn't take himself too seriously, as his shirt was half untucked. The general would have dressed him down and made him sit up straight.

"Please have a seat and tell me why I should give you access to box five nine six six six." He chuckled again.

We sat across the desk from him. "Yes, good old five nine six six six," I repeated, since the digits seemed to bring him joy. Perhaps I didn't tell the joke correctly, as he only smiled politely. "The box belonged to our best friend who died, and his wife has asked that we retrieve its contents. We believe it contains a very important family record."

He peered at me over his spectacles, still jovial but shaking his head.

I said, "Here's the wife's email authorizing me access on her behalf."

He said, "Yours might be the best story yet. And the least angry in delivery. And presented in such charming company."

"Others have tried to open Dylan's box? Did they get in?"

"Yes and no. That box attracts angry men and lovely Emily here." He gave M a smile, which even in 2018 would pass for quaint chivalry and not a WOPA offense.

It seemed a good time to play my ace in the hole, so I handed him Juno's note. "Here's a letter of introduction. I hope it says I'm not an angry man." I namasted him to show there was no hostility in me.

He read the short note. "Ah, this makes me happy. It is from sweet Mother Juno. I hear the Deeksha is now home to many in need. She says you are good and people to be trusted. She asks I do all I can within my power to assist. And you bring me her blessings." He namasted us. "Thank you, thank you, thank you." The joyful postmaster had become even more blissful with Juno's blessings. "May I please keep this?"

"Yes, of course; it was meant for you," I said, wishing I had such magical powers in my writing.

"Juno, YaLan, and Astri teach me and all my staff yoga. All government servants here are so trained. It makes us joyful in our service. So let me joyfully explain why I am so amused." He leaned back. "I have had a very impatient and rough American man here two times, each time with paperwork on all manner of US government stationery. All having nothing to do with rightful ownership. He threatened me on his last visit and made me laugh. 'You going to kill the postman over some mail?' I asked. His answer, his non-joking answer, was 'Maybe.'

"He had no sense of humor, and just this morning I received a call from the mayor asking me to please allow him into the box. The mayor is a politician, and I am a civil servant. I told the mayor, my brother-in-law, no, but it does not matter."

"Did this man have crazy eyes and a beard?" I asked.

"Ah, yes, you know him. I assume as friends of Juno, he is no friend of yours?"

We shook our heads, and he continued.

"And I've been in contact with another man in the States claiming to be a lawyer for the owner's wife—I provided him the necessary paperwork just now. He demanded no one else be given access but the widow's representatives. You?"

We nodded.

"The lawyer was more insistent than angry. And my clerks tell me they suspect a Chinese man watches the box all day. I told them to let him stay—we are open to the public—if he's got nothing better to do. It does not matter."

"I can't help but notice you keep saying, 'It does not matter.' Why is that?" I asked.

"That's the beauty of the joke, and I really want to tell someone other than the clerks, so I will share it now with Juno's friends." He smiled at M broadly and dramatically, like a magician about to perform a trick.

M gave him back the smile he wanted and then put prayer hands to her heart. "Thank you, good postmaster Bibek."

He stood up, comically banging his round gut on the desk, and slapped his hands on his sides. "Come. I'll show you."

We followed Bibek, who walked like Charlie Chaplin with a big beer belly, into a room behind the mailboxes. He used his master key to open a box from the back.

"Five nine six six six. I won't forget that number till the day I die." He stepped aside.

There I confronted my biggest fear—a small dark tunnel void of matter. Mailbox 59666 was empty.

It may have been the look on our faces, but his jolly self transformed into a man of great warmth and empathy. "I should have said how sorry I am for your loss. And I hope you find what you are looking for. Please don't say I was disrespectful. I just like a good joke."

I considered asking him to keep stonewalling the angry American, but M said, "No, of course not. We all need a sense of humor. Thank you. It's a great story of doing the right thing in the face of what I imagine was very powerful intimidation. Do me a favor, Bibek. Next time, for your safety, please show the angry man the empty box too."

"Ah, good advice from a very lovely lady. I will take it. Though I don't think he will find it funny, it will be fun to see his reaction. I'll have to restrain a laugh, or I think there would be a dead postman."

Bibek insisted on a long goodbye hug from M first and last, giving me a short one in between.

I threw the number over my shoulder as we were leaving, and the jolly postmaster laughed uproariously.

In the lobby I noted several men who looked Chinese, though I couldn't be sure. Once outside, I exclaimed, "Shit! I really thought it would b—"

"You cussed!" M, despite the further disappointment, seemed to be the postmaster's sister in mirth. "Patience, my buddy."

I hung my head at my failure and my moniker. "And our cow has gone."

Once we'd started walking back to the Deeksha, M said, "Do you think the Chinese man may be another agent of the Guru's?"

"Or the general's? There's so much we may never know. Let's ask the family if there's any other place it could be hidden in Kathmandu or the Deeksha. Juno can't leave now to search at the yogi's place, but perhaps you and I can borrow her car and get directions. We could be back and forth the same day so we don't leave her shorthanded too long."

"Sounds like a plan. I've been wondering if Dick knows about the yogi and if, when he learns the mailbox is empty, he'll head there."

"Me too," I said. "Since the yogi has no contact information or phone,

I've been assuming he's off Dick's radar. Bibek's lucky to be so jolly and alive. And I'm Jokerman, whose superpowers failed us." I was doubly downhearted at not finding the treasure or the key to my love.

"You got us into the box, but the joke was on us. Dick still isn't in on it yet, and we're going to find the ToE first. There's no giving up hope. I mean—" She blushed. "You know what I mean. We're bound together and can't give up the quest."

My eyes were on M. As her words lifted my spirits, I marched lightly, with a cushioned footfall that felt like stepping on moist sponge cake.

"Fuck me!"

"Excuse me?"

"I stepped in cow dung, damn it. Shit. *Shit*." My good humor and patience had run out.

CHAPTER **38**

M JOKED THAT THE STEAMING PILE, because of its size, smell, and shape, might have been from the holy elephant that greeted us upon our arrival. She laughed, adding, "But cows are holy here too," while I continued to curse. On the way back to the Deeksha, we stopped at a stream so I could clean my shoe. M cautioned that it might be a holy stream, so I used a cup and paper from trash we found instead of sinking my stinking foot into the water and poisoning the environment.

M's holy and jovial response to my soiled failure was both annoying and endearing. She dipped her foot into the stream in solidarity. "Just in case it is a holy stream." She got me to smile as she took my arm, and we two-stepped home, each wearing one wet shoe.

At the Deeksha, we took our shoes off at the door.

I'd let the entire family down. And I still felt like shit, despite M's wet-shoe solidarity.

M, Juno, and the others saw only the effort and didn't judge me on the result, but I was focused on outcome. Before I could ask for other ideas, Juno said, "I believe it is meant to be. The theory will be found by increasing our awareness intuitively. You cannot demand the way but only follow the signs to your heart's desire."

Big Love could be infuriating to those not yet anointed by it, but one could never be annoyed with Juno, as she always spoke so beautifully from a place of pure presence.

Astri clapped her hands and said, "Let's have a family competition for ideas of where the ToE may be found."

Was this a mind-reading family? M gave me a look that said she agreed.

Still, by the next day no one had any new ideas, though we all had tuned in to our intuition for possibilities. M's morning courses began with her short meditation invoking the universal consciousness. She was unsure if she would continue that practice at Columbia in the fall, but what a novel way to start class at a major old-school university.

While counseling peace and patience, Juno welcomed us to use her car to visit the yogi. However, there was now the matter of gas rationing following the earthquake. I sighed with irritation when Boy announced, "The jeep is running on empty." Of course the gauge registered no gas. Juno's patience and peace would be welcome, but frustration kept getting in the way. My kingdom for a tank of gas.

We believed Dick was watching the Deeksha, so it was agreed that Boy would use the secluded garden exit to obtain one gallon of gas per day, the maximum permitted per car. We were relieved to learn from Juno that Dylan had been concerned about maintaining Yogi Mangku's privacy, and I was confident that his location wouldn't have been on Dylan's phone.

But I was in a rush, racing those three letters that seemed to hold all the power—CIA—and its four-letter master of artificial intelligence.

That evening I pulled M away from clearing the dinner and took her to our Buddha love seat and pond. I was eager and scared to tell her my new plan, as it wasn't foolproof and put me at some risk.

"M, I've ridden a motorcycle—once in the desert in Utah and, of course, with Dylan. A motorbike will have enough gas with just a couple gallons. I'll rent one tomorrow and go to the yogi's. How hard can it be?"

"That would be suicide on the jungle's dirt and rock roads."

She was more right than wrong. I'd almost died in the desert, flying over the handlebars when the bike's front wheel planted down in the sand after being launched by some slick rock. But I was determined and would risk almost anything to be her hero and win her love. I put on a brave face. At least I hoped that was what she saw. "These roads are the Autobahn compared to the sand and rocks of Utah's Moab desert. I'd suggest you come with me on my bike—my biker chick—but that would make it more dangerous."

She said, "WOPA, Steve McQueen. Let's go to tea and then sleep on it."

That night, during tea, a spontaneous entertainment arose around the firepit while aftershocks continued to rumble. YaLan and Astri stepped onto a small stage Boy had set up using Juno's yoga perch. The firelight made for a dramatic effect. They proceeded to impress and mystify the crowd, in equal measure, performing a Beckett-like skit.

By way of prologue, YaLan said, "I am playing Mind," and Astri said, "I am playing Spirit." They namasted the crowd, who returned the courtesy.

Mind: "Why am I here?"

Spirit: Looks at Mind and smiles.

Mind: "Why do you stand so still and smile?"

Spirit: Looks at Mind and smiles.

Mind: "You are nothing if not listening to me."

Spirit: Looks at Mind and smiles.

Mind: "Your constant presence cannot last."

Spirit: Looks at Mind and smiles.

Mind [agitated]: "I have no time for you. I have better places to go. I have better things to do."

Spirit: Looks at Mind and smiles.

Mind [resolved]: "Please . . . Who are you that watches me?"

Spirit: "I am and was and always will be."

Mind: Is silent

Spirit: Hugs Mind

Mind: Smiles

Mind and Spirit bow.

They left the stage as the bemused audience cheered the short one-act play appearing a great distance off-Broadway. Their performance was wildly successful, with others clamoring to perform.

We watched as we drank our bedtime tea. Campfire stories are now only a small subgenre of art, because we've become too comfortable to camp. At one time, the campfire was the world stage and the cradle of storytelling. I took note of the stories as they weaved their way into my imagination, fodder for my fiction.

While not all of the refugees had lost a friend or relative to the earthquake, their beloved town had suffered, and this was a collective healing by ceremonial storytelling. Young and old spoke. Some spoke in prose, some in rhyme, and some in free verse. Some spoke in Nepali and some in English. Some sang and some danced.

A group of university-age German trekkers stranded by the earthquake sang a raucous beer-and-hash-inspired version of "Sweet Caroline" and soon had the entire camp singing the chorus. That song always caused me to think of *beautiful girls*. I looked at M singing along, and my heart joined her heart in song.

The communal event was so successful that the twins proposed we make a practice of it. Juno agreed, suggesting that we open the stage every other night. Since it was under the stars, I suggested we call it Globe Theater. The event was added to the Deeksha schedule under my nom-de-theatre.

On the second night of Globe Theater, after "Sweet Caroline" was again sung and the performances were drawing to a close, Chi stood, innocently took M by the hand, and led her to the small stage. M complied with a smile and without any outward reservation. I would have awkwardly held back or pulled away. My storytelling was reserved for the family each night in Juno's room before bed, at Astri's insistence. Luckily, Dylan and I had lots of stories to tell. Clearly M had nothing prepared, but she was so radiant standing there with her little man gazing at her so lovingly in the expectant silence, silence that Juno taught us not to fear. Her not-so-little man gazed lovingly too. What a brave woman.

M recited a short lyric poem. Chi continued beaming at her side while not understanding a word of what she said.

"Quantum touch, once correlated by heart / So the spin of one, is the spin of two / Forever, no distance can tear apart / So cease the incessant thinking for now / With correspondence, without question—Mu / For your beloved is awake in the Tao / This moment now, is all that's ever true."

Juno knew, as I did, the rousing and poignant words had been composed for Dylan. Even before M finished, Juno had set down her teacup and started moving through the attentive and appreciative audience. She hugged M as joy flowed between them, happy together in memory of Dylan. I had known for some time that M loved Dylan. I tried to convince myself I was no longer jealous. But it was a sight to see, those two goddesses so completely open in their celebration of Dylan in the firelight of Xanadu.

When M returned to sit beside me, I said, "Mu? A bit of whimsical nonsense?"

"It's used in physics—the twelfth letter of the Greek alphabet. It's Japanese for nothing, and it's a Buddhist koan."

"Mmm . . . I should have known it would be a multidimensional Mu. When did you become a poet too?"

"Funny," she said. "You were next to me when those words first came to me at Dylan's wake. They were private there, but sharing them here seemed right."

"Will you write me a poem someday?" I sounded like a needy younger brother pleading for his turn to receive the girl-next-door's attention, but M knew me well enough to shake her head and smile.

"Well . . . maybe. Yes."

"I'll take that as a yes?"

Yes, she smiled again. Yes, yes, yes!

As the curtain fell upon Globe Theater, Juno allowed the fire to go out early, leaving burning red coals. The garden was full of warmth and the darkness of a moonless, starry night. Everyone was still held in the quantum touch of M's short verse.

I could never have imagined being in such a place, experiencing so much that was new and unexpected—a constant spring of inspiration revealing layer by layer M's brilliance to me.

Without Dylan, I wouldn't know this Xanadu. I wouldn't know Juno and her family. I wouldn't know M.

Thank you, my friend.

I wiped at eyes that burned from the waning fire. I wasn't able to cry.

M sat next to me with the loving Chi on her other side in the garden planetarium, the stars of Indra's net above, an image Dylan loved to use.

Each stargazer in the garden sat inside a diamond and reflected all the other diamonds there and everywhere. We were one infinite diamond of infinite facets, a mirror of multiple universes all becoming one in our light of consciousness. A light that seemed to reach out to all hearts from the very center of my chest.

Then the symphony began, a meteor shower raining down on the garden, a silent fireworks display greeted by *oohs* and *aahs*. Juno, like Prospero, seemed to control the cosmos. I wondered if the spell would be broken if I kissed M.

In that moment I felt our hearts linked, so closely linked, within Indra's net that was now ablaze with shooting stars.

The earthquake had quelled any practical thought of romance. But as we headed to our bedroom for six, my desire for M was fully reignited by our meteor shower and the anticipation of my daring motorcycle ride in the morning.

CHAPTER 39

MY NAME WAS WRITTEN ON the envelope, my first letter since the border agents confiscated my terrorist knife. It had to be from M—a love note hidden under my pillow. It was a modern version of the school note being slipped to me in class, an event that always brought me to full excited attention. And it was an ingenious way to start a romance in the middle of the crowded sleeping quarters of a refugee camp. I would put my poetic reply under her pillow as soon as I could—M and I would share pillow talk. The meteor shower got her thinking of romance too—I knew it! I'd felt it. And she knew I loved letters. I held in my hand my love's first love letter.

My heart was beating like hummingbird wings as an overture to the big bass drumming I knew would accompany my reading of her sweet words. M slipped into Juno's bed in her soft white-cotton muscle tee and blue silk running shorts. As she slid between the sheets, she raised her brows—pretending to wonder about the magical letter in my hand? She blew out her candle so mine was the only one still lit.

Thinking about those lips and tongue, still unkissed, that had sealed the envelope, I wouldn't have used my letter opener in any event. I cleanly broke the envelope open and removed the thin slip of paper from it. I held my breath and read.

LEAVE THE DEEKSHA AND RETURN HOME—OR YOU AND
YOUR GIRLFRIEND WILL BE DEAD. DO NOT CONTACT THE
AUTHORITIES—WE WILL KNOW AND YOU WILL DIE. WHEN
YOU LEAVE THE DEEKSHA, GO ONLY TO THE AIRPORT AND
HOME OR YOU WILL DIE.

My chest was heavy, my heart constricted, my lungs unable to breathe. My brain, expecting love but finding terror, wouldn't function.

The family, all five of them, were staring at me, waiting for me to blow out my candle. Passing fear on the way to desolation, I blew it out to experience the full brunt of my emotions alone in the darkness. One hand rubbed at my face. The other crushed the thin slip of paper.

The writing was odd, with its capital letter punishment repeating the stark death threat. I assumed the style was used to mask the writer's identity. Dick. It was Dick's composition. English may not have been his first language, I now thought, recalling I'd heard a slight accent behind his incoherent and blood-soaked words punching piecemeal through all the noise on earthquake day. This was, no doubt, his bloody kiss of death.

Juno and M sat up, relighting their candles. I squeezed my eyes tight.

"Aren't you going to tell us what your letter said?" M asked as three more candles were lit and all eyes turned on me. I squeezed my eyelids tight.

There was no way to pretend I was asleep. I opened my eyes to M's unblinking gaze and immediately turned away, not wanting her to see into my fear-filled heart. Eventually, taking a breath, I handed the ransom letter to M, who read it and handed it to Juno, who then showed it to the twins and Boy.

I say ransom letter because that was what it felt like. They were holding M and me hostage and demanding we give up our quest in exchange for our lives.

I was the first to speak. "There is no choice now; M and I must go."

"But where will we go?" M said. "I agree, but flights out of Kathmandu are still impossible to get, with a backlog of flights and only one working runway."

Boy said, "You must stay until you can get a flight home."

Juno smiled. "Of course Boy is right; nothing has changed. We know your Dick is out there, and he knows you cannot leave and is trying to scare us. Love is the absence of fear."

I was hesitant to argue with Juno in her own bedroom—and because she was right, of course. Though I didn't have an alternative plan, I said, "I really must insist we leave, for M's safety and the safety of everyone here. Dick, who must have discovered that Dylan's mailbox is empty, is a real danger."

M laughed. "My knight in shining armor, where will you and your *girlfriend* go?"

Astri jumped in before YaLan could. "It's settled, then. You stay!"

YaLan added, "The people to be trusted must look after one another."

"We'll stay until we can get out of town." I was proud of my ability to assert myself in that room of women and Boy. "And, Astri, please excuse me, I don't feel up to telling a story tonight."

The next morning after yoga, the family huddled around the rock-seat area used for our nightly tea. Juno sat there carefree, drawing pictures. M checked with the Columbia University travel agent; no flights for ten days. We booked seats. Everyone wanting to leave the ravaged town professed exigent circumstances and felt the threat of death, so our claim of risk to life merely put us in the queue of those looking for an earlier flight. Not knowing we were threatened by the CIA, they suggested we contact our embassy.

Juno added a flourish to her drawing with a graphite pencil and said, "If it is Dick and he does not want you to find the ToE, you're safer here than anywhere else, as he must realize you already have it if it was to be found here. And everyone knows flights out take time to get. Just in case, I sketched these pictures. Boy can make copies and hand them out to our guests so all eyes will be on watch for him." She handed one of the two drawings to Boy, who showed it to the family.

It was a very good likeness of Dick with his beard and crazy-angry eyes. So good it scared me.

She passed around the second picture. "This is what he would look like without the beard."

It was Dick from the wake with his Manson eyes.

He wouldn't be able to get into the Deeksha undetected.

I thanked Juno. "You're a talented sketch artist."

YaLan, Astri, and Boy laughed at my faint praise.

The family huddle broke up, and the day's duties began. M and I moved to our secluded seat by the Buddha so I could share my grim assessment.

"I hate to say it, but I think our quest is over. We can't lead Dick—and that's definitely Dick—to Yogi Mangku's and endanger him."

"You're right. To protect ourselves—but more importantly the people here, the family, and Yogi Mangku too—we should leave as soon as possible and follow the demands of the death threat to go right to the airport. Perhaps afterward, with us gone, Juno can talk to the yogi for us, though she may be watched now." M fisted her hands but had nothing to hit other than me. She started shaking, with no shake-off dance or gentle prayer hands to follow. She was in no mood to dance. "I hate being intimidated and manipulated like this."

She couldn't shake Dick off as she had the other bad characters we'd met. "I'm going to lose myself in work," she said, taking her leave.

"Our guests do love their concierge." My levity didn't lighten the mood.

I hated the manipulation too, but I didn't want anyone to die. And I'd never really believed that someone had deliberately killed Dylan. I would now have to make decisions based on that probable reality. Dylan had been killed for his theory, and someone, probably the Guru at the CIA, wasn't above killing again to find the theory and keep it from us.

I was unsure what was just speculation and what was true. I *did* understand that there was much in life we might never know but often assumed we did.

Dylan wouldn't have wanted us to continue, even to discover and promote the ToE. For all I knew, we were putting Natalie and Grace at risk too. Any road to the ToE would have to be put to rest by Dick, who likely had the long and powerful reach of the CIA. To make an actual death threat on American citizens abroad, people who were simply looking for their dead friend's work, that threat must have been blessed by the Guru.

I felt lost within my story that was no longer mine but now a thriller being written by the Guru, a master of artificial intelligence traveling in cyberspace to find me from a penthouse in New York. I covered the peephole on my laptop with tape.

I couldn't believe this new harrowing reality. I hadn't expected to put our lives on the line. Sam Spade heroics were supposed to be reserved for my fictional James.

The only thing I was less able to tolerate than patience was patience rewarded with failure, an infinite waiting experienced as a slow, painful contraction of the heart.

The aftershocks might have abated, yet the danger of Dick and his death threat doomed our quest. Although nothing had changed between M and me, the loss of our quest would sabotage all chance of M's love. That love in gestation was bounded by the quest, and now the gyre would simply unravel.

CHAPTER 40

AS SUBJECTS OF A DEATH THREAT, M and I became prisoners within the walls and grounds of Xanadu. I was learning the difference between the chronic stress of one damn thing after another and crisis stress. The first was gray and dulled the light of spirit, and the second was black and white and forced a choice between darkness and illumination.

Following the earthquake, the Big Love reaction of the Deeksha family—their work in the service of those harmed by the impersonal act of nature—inspired me to act. The death threat was an act of man targeted at M and me, and it demanded that we take no action or suffer death. With such evil confronting us, I had to choose between the dark of fear and the light of love. As this binary choice battled in my heart and mind, I wasn't sleeping well. Darkness was choosing me.

The restlessness continued for a couple of nights after I received Dick's love letter; then one night I had another strange and lucid dream. In M's lecture room at Columbia, I sat in my same seat at the back of the theater, but all other seats were empty. M was at the podium, with Stephen Hawking listening to her lecture from his wheelchair. When M was done, Stephen stood from his chair and offered his hand. They danced a slow dance. They were laughing and dancing, and Stephen was changing, becoming a young and able-bodied man but somehow still Stephen Hawking. They paused, poised to kiss, and I woke.

While wondering about the dream's meaning, I remembered another dream and an old lady's grim words by Dylan's mailbox back in New York. Most of my dreams had little, if any, dialogue, and often communication in them was telepathic. Since dreams were all in one's head, that had some internal logic. Even M's dream lecture was a silent film, but I understood the lesson, even though I couldn't remember any of it upon awakening. However, I did recall what M was thinking at the end of the dream as she twirled—that the young, able-bodied Stephen offered her the truth of everything, or at least the brave, unwavering determination to find it despite all odds. And his infirmity and appearance could not hide his genius and beauty from M.

Earlier that day M had said, "Einstein's and Hawking's greatness was not their success but their willingness to be wrong, as they often were, without any loss of enthusiasm in their search for the elusive and beautiful symmetry of the theory of everything."

On the night of and the morning following my disturbing dream, we had a downpour for the first time since the earthquake. It was a miracle in the rainy season that this was the first heavy rain. The weather and dream reflected the dark clouds in my head and the choking of my drowning heart—the foreboding weather of death.

How could I maintain enthusiasm without the prospect of winning M's love? Without some kind of hope that we might succeed in our quest?

My small shadow was missing on that overcast day. YaLan told me that Chi had suffered a bad dream too and had slept in. I didn't believe in coincidence. Our minds were connected, even though we didn't speak the same language. Or the coincidence's cause may have just been the gloom of the weather.

After yoga, I enlisted YaLan's and Astri's help to translate Chi's dream, as he still refused to come out of his tent for breakfast. The twins translated Chi's grim nightmare as he lay facedown on his sleeping bag.

"Comrade An was burning down the Deeksha, and Juno and you were beaten and taken away."

YaLan and Astri assured Chi they would watch An and never let him burn down the Deeksha.

Through my interpreters I asked if Comrade spoke in Chi's dream. When Chi said no, I gave him the *there you have it, nothing to worry about* shrug of the shoulders with hands upturned look.

I told Chi, "I will personally be your bodyguard, and Comrade will never harm anyone while I'm around." I leaned close and wrapped one hand around his neck as he slightly lifted and turned his head to me. "And no one will be taking me or Juno away."

His familiar grin returned when Astri translated, and he offered me his hand to pull him to his feet.

I was pretty tall compared to Chi, and as part of Juno's family, I probably appeared powerful as well. With those assurances—and because Chi was a natural ladies' man and didn't want to disappoint the twin beauties or his old American friend—he agreed to leave his tent. He parlayed his agreement into hugs from YaLan and Astri that allowed him, standing tippy-toe, to bury his head in their breasts.

"That's my boy, Chi," I said, glad that M wasn't around to WOPA me.

Later that day I lost my shadow again. In Indian mystical lore that was a symbol of death, which added to my foreboding. But Chi and his family were leaving the Deeksha, their home now restored. I wanted to cry but long ago had lost the ability to do so. Saying goodbye, I gave the tearful Chi a hug, my phone number, and my email address.

That evening before tea, M took me, a moping sad sack, to our Buddha love seat. "Now you know how I felt when Nessa left. Do you know why Chi meant so much to you?"

"I do." I actually did but was embarrassed to say. But M knew I was sensitive; therefore, I didn't hide the silly-sounding truth.

"He brought back a flood of childhood memories and imagination and innocence. Being with him was like a chest of drawers long closed being opened and unpacked. I experienced it all—my childhood belief in magic and miracles, a nurturing and loving earth, darkness that reared from the mind of monsters, and the awe of life and beautiful girls that I shared with Dylan at his age. That was my childhood, my innocent world of imagination for many years, and I'm grateful for its reemergence here at the Deeksha."

I picked up a stone and threw it into the small pond and mocked myself. "It sounds like I found my inner child."

M laughed. "So you're marching backward from middle-age through adolescence all the way to childhood? You know what Juno would say. 'Nothing real is ever lost.'"

"Ouch, ouch, and ouch. So, do you want chi . . . to go get some tea? It's teatime." I caught myself, barely avoiding the third rail of inquiry with over-thirty-year-old ladies. M would be a wonderful mother if she chose to be.

Nothing seemed to have changed in our relationship since I received Dick's death threat, though I knew finding the ToE meant even more to her than to me. She met all calamity and danger with amazing equanimity that shone a glaring spotlight on my lack thereof. She was a faster learner of Juno's teachings than I was. That morning at yoga when Juno spoke of accepting each challenge as a perfect lesson, I was wrestling with clouds of impatience and a forecast of death.

M and I were two circling dogs—her chasing a grand theory while I chased her, desperate to win her love. She seemed to believe we would still find the ToE despite our departure date being less than a week away. But I was a child in a dark place, threatened and oppressed, as we went to bed that night. Reality shuttled between my dreams and my fiction and between a world of creators and takers—the Guru and his Dick and the general and his comrade trying to take what others had created.

CHAPTER 41

DURING THOSE DREARY DAYS of the death threat, unable to act or sleep, I continued to write feverishly each night about the villainous Dick. My novel, strewn with bodies, took on an international thriller bent with the Russians and Chinese competing with the Guru and the CIA to find Dylan's theory.

M was adamant that it was too risky for me to go into town and rent a motorbike. She went so far as to remind me it would put her and the family at risk too. I became consumed with a plan that would allow me to fulfill my promise to M and find her the ToE.

It seemed so simple. I'd lie. In lieu of telling stories—and as a form of therapy—I'd started late-night typing frenzies that had to be keeping the family awake each night. So it would be better if I slept alone in a tent. My first night of writer's solitude, I'd sneak out to hire a cab and make the round trip to Yogi Mangku's. But first I'd test-drive my plan by bringing it to fictional life. I wasn't thinking straight and needed to suss out flaws in the scheme's conception.

In my fiction, James found the ToE in Hope's book on conscious design with the ELF statue on the cover, in Dylan's room at the yogi's compound. Then something dark possessed me, and I was automatically writing what happened next in someone else's voice, using M's and my real names. The Chinese seized the theory. M was shot dead by Dick. And Sean was branded a traitor.

After rereading the pages that had just poured out of me, I asked, *Dylan, is that your way of warning me?*

Damn. I couldn't even write a way out of my black box. Lying wasn't the way to win M's love, and it wasn't consistent with Big Love, however worthy the ends might be. I would lie only to protect my love and the truth but not to win my love or find the truth. My vow was not as all-encompassing as the yogi's vow of absolute truth but a practical vow of mostly honesty.

Beyond the risk to M and the Deeksha from my ill-conceived plan—the real one, not the fictional one—there was also the practical matter of gas and the expense a driver might extort, even if he had enough gas. I didn't have two hundred dollars cash and doubted a driver would take plastic. Boy continued his daily trek for one gallon a day, even though now we couldn't use it to go see the yogi.

And who were we but un-American traitors to our country, defying its authority to share the theory with our enemies? Maybe the Guru was right that the theory of everything was a magic lamp containing a genie far too powerful to be entrusted to everyman—and one that certainly should not be shared with Russians and Chinese.

CHAPTER 42

ONLY FIVE DAYS REMAINED until we'd leave Xanadu at Dick's command. It was maddening that one man could end my dream and steal my love through the power of a gun and the willingness to use it. Or by simply saying that he would.

My dreams of Dick, my sleepless nights, and my disturbing fiction had given me a low-grade fever. I estimated 99.9 degrees—not life-threatening, but it further muddled my mind and weakened my body and spirit. My near-boiling frame of mind had me questioning myself and the quest itself.

The family was once again gathered around the fire for nighttime tea. I pretended nothing was wrong, as that seemed to be what M wanted. But my energy was on empty, and confused thoughts had mushroomed in me, with negative thoughts taking deep root. My reaction to Chi's departure and the fever were just symptoms. I was a dead man drinking tea, crushed by the end of our quest and the fading hope that M would ever return my love.

Even this nightly scene of harmony didn't bring relief. As usual, we all sat waiting for the best-tasting tea on our comfortable cushions in front of a glowing fire—which tonight burned with too much heat.

I sat quietly, sinking into a question that had been preying on me: What is love if it's determined by happenstance and can be derailed so swiftly by calamity?

My work on the novel brought only more darkness. I became convinced that my writing sucked and should be thrown into the fire, but since my story was on a computer, the laptop might explode in the flames. I wished I held the only copy in paper pages so I could burn away, leaf by leaf, the past that had led James and Brigitte here. For the first time, I realized my fiction was incendiary and would put M and the family in danger even if we escaped the present threat of death.

The image of Dick entering the Deeksha with a gun in hand kept stirring in my mind and dreams. My first reaction was always determining how to best protect M. I watched her now, laughing as Astri braided her hair. I think she noticed that I was even more in her company after the death threat. She neither sought nor rejected this further attention. *Tolerant* might be the best characterization of her response to my cloying closeness.

After noticing Comrade moving in and out of shadows in the firelight that evening, I moved even closer to M so that our legs were flush. She patted my knee. The Chinese private's presence added to my fevered unrest. He was usually in his tent lair by teatime, flaps shut tight, but had changed his routine.

M crooked a finger and had me leaning close to her mouth. "I know how much you want to find the ToE for me."

I couldn't meet her eyes.

"Promise you won't do anything stupid or without me, okay?"

"I promise. You're not reading my novel drafts, are you?" I joked, knowing that she wasn't. She either knew me well or was a bit of a psychic.

As Boy poured the tea, I was looking for solace and asked YaLan and Astri to tell the story of their loves. They had mentioned two American track stars from Oregon who had stayed nearly a full year as love had bloomed. I had an ulterior motive—I hoped that their stories might spark romantic feelings in M and take me out of my heated self-absorption.

YaLan elected to tell the story, with color commentary from Astri—storytelling in stereo. YaLan stood with the fire rising behind her, a dramatic image. She had flames for hair.

As the story unfolded—yoga and track training had been used to maintain an ever-deepening virginal love—my own celibate fire became inflamed. The young track stars had called on strenuous mountain runs to release their passion and cravings; I had a laptop and James and Brigitte in sensual setting after sensual setting discovering the myriad ways passion could be fulfilled.

Maybe I needed to start running after the fever subsided.

YaLan's story continued. "A competition was set between the boys and between the couples: Each boy would be trained by his yogi, and before they left Kathmandu, they would compete in a mile race. Each day we trained with them in the mountains and then in yoga on our return to the Deeksha."

Astri giggled. "At times we thought we saw Yogi Mangku on the path or in the trees ahead of us at a great distance, but when we got there, he was gone. He's a very old man but very spry of spirit. It is said our yogi can take any human form and play all types of musical instruments."

YaLan said, "We haven't seen that, though. But back to our love story . . . The boys had a bunk bed at a local hostel and—"

"We insisted on celibacy for race training and as a spiritual practice but mostly in the pursuit of true love," Astri said, unable to restrain herself.

I let out a loud, long sigh that stopped the story, drawing all attention to me. It had been an entirely spontaneous utterance. I blamed the fever for my lack of self-control. My face was heated as I said, "Forgive me. Must be something I ate." Or my love stagnating in the time of cholera.

I couldn't even dredge up a smile to make amends for my indigestion.

I hoped the source of my sigh wasn't as evident as its sound. The combination of my dammed-up desire for M and sleeping in a communal setting meant this forty-five-year-old reconstituted virgin knew exactly how those young boys had felt. However, they'd had more time. I was hot and overripe with a fast-approaching expiration date.

Astri took advantage of my grunt to giggle and add, "The boys accepted the challenge and the kisses and cuddling, and they trained extra hard. They spent a lot of time in the cold spring and river, saying it eased their aching legs."

As Astri said this, YaLan stole a glance at me and smiled compassionately. Like their mother, the twins were able to treat with all topics without reservation or self-consciousness. They had the innocence of the self-actualized. Or the very young.

While they noted my reaction to passion unfulfilled, I was watching M. She seemed uncomfortable with the story too. Juno picked up on the dark cloud descending over M and took M's hand between both of hers.

YaLan moved on to the auspicious race day, describing "the mile-long track fully draped with prayer flags that blew in the gentle breeze." The race became an event that would be joined by the best local runners.

YaLan said, "Mother, I saw you and Dylan meditating in the middle of the field that morning at daybreak. I imagined I saw prayers shining out from your hearts in all directions."

Juno smiled. "We each hung prayer flags with prayers we had written together for your love. That was a magical and mysterious day."

"So strange that Dylan left so suddenly that day in your jeep," Astri said. "With just a note saying he had to go. He didn't even stay for the race. Why do you think that was, Mother? You never told us exactly what his note said."

"The note said something like 'On this otherwise auspicious day, I was attacked within the sacred Deeksha. For the family's safety, I'm going to stay with the yogi. Please tell no one.' He said to tell the two of you that he knew you both had won already. And he added I should let him know if I needed the jeep back."

That must have been the day he was maced by the CIA, and I was looking for a delicate way to inquire further. But YaLan was already back on track, describing the festival grounds, the starting bell, and each stride of the race like a sportscaster.

"The pack continued to fly around the track, our young Americans looking like boys among the mountain men. Despite appearances, our training and coaching paid off, and the boys broke away from the pack with a quarter mile to the finish line."

Astri added, "YaLan and I held hands and our breath—only then did we realize and dread that one of our boys must lose and our team would be split in two. Whichever boy won, both our hearts would break for the other."

YaLan nodded. "The Americans were running with no thought— like dancers or yogis in the zone—with source energy flowing through them as though they were wild stallions. With two hundred yards to go, they broke into an all-out fierce sprint, neither leaving the side of the other. At the tape, they simultaneously reached out their arms and arched their chests to finish, flying, in a dead heat. Two winners and no loser. The clock read 3:59:59. Our young Americans were heroes, if just for one day."

I didn't think she realized the Bowie of her words.

YaLan turned to look at the children dancing around the fire before adding, "The date of the race had been timed to be the culmination of their gap-year visit to Kathmandu and the last day of summer. Focus on the race left no time—for them or us—to dwell on their imminent departure to Portland for graduate school and to continue running."

Astri picked up the pace of her sister's story. "The boys made their final impassioned plea and argument for physical love by proposing marriage. We told them not no but not yes yet."

I muffled a sigh that hurt.

"We made a commitment to write each other daily emails telling everything that was happening within our hearts and lives," Astri said. "That constant connection will bridge the time until we go to Portland. We have plans to go next spring. Mother says we get a gap year—or gap summer, at least—too!"

"Astri and I decided that if they hold out almost two years while we're apart, they will be rewarded. So far they have stayed the course without being told yes or given their reward."

I hoped M was putting me through a test of weeks and not years. That would be more than enough practice and patience for me. I nearly forgot the heat of my despair in their cool and certain belief in true love.

Tears were flowing down M's cheeks. Maybe she thought the love story wouldn't end well or was remembering an American Indian who built his own funeral pyre.

Juno mused, "Passion will pass in time, but we have to believe in the truth of God's love within us and all around us. The light of Big Love. We are like rays of the sun, ever moving forward into the dark, forgetting where we came from and forgetting that wherever we are and whenever we get to where we're going, it will also be light."

M managed a half smile at the cryptic but beautiful words of comfort. Juno turned to M and asked, "May I?"

"Yes, please."

Juno laid her hands on M's head. I felt warm peace enter me from the top of my head, as if Juno's hands lay on me instead. A moment later, as Juno removed her hands, a truly unfettered smile passed across M's serene face.

"Juno, I love you," M said.

Juno beamed and said, "I know, and I love you."

Love was that simple. I don't mean that it wasn't profound. But its expression . . . simple.

But for Juno, even the simple was too complex as she zeroed-in on the heart's core. "Now let us drop the duality of *I* and *you* and realize love loves love. We are love."

"Big Love," M said as she and Juno smiled at each other in some understanding I could sense but not conceptualize.

I looked around at the faces glowing from the sharing of love. What amazing men and women in Dylan's life. Though I hadn't met the yogi, I knew him, as he held a presence at the Deeksha. Dylan maintained a presence there too. They were all teachers and students of one another. During this musing, a wellspring of gratitude arose in my chest for my being a part of that company. From despair to hope over a cup of tea. Only at the Deeksha.

My hopeful reaction to the love story was entirely different from M's. The story rekindled my belief in and pursuit of love. But how would I win M's love, since we would return home empty-handed in just a few days, and M still saw only pain in romantic love?

Another day had ended, and we were one day closer to our departure, with me no closer to and perhaps further from love. As the family stood, Juno, in her soft-spoken and enigmatic style, said, "Excuse us, please. I think Sean has a question for me."

The rest of the family thought nothing of my having a heart-to-heart with Juno and went to bed, leaving me alone with Juno for the first time. To me this was a dramatic event, while Juno's calm presence made it clear that to her it was merely time to read my tea leaves.

We sat in the glow of the embers of the dying fire, waiting for me to speak. I didn't know what I had to ask. I placed my left hand to my right chest to cover my dyslexic heart, though I'd read that enlightened teachers believe the right side is where one finds the spiritual heart.

"Juno, what is love and how do we find it?"

"That is the big question and goes right to the heart of the matter." She mimicked my left hand–right chest gesture. "A description of love is always wanting, as it is really an experience of God in us, the end of our dual relationship with our self, the self before the *I am*. But let me try."

She smiled slightly and looked like a lovely sprite as she waited for the words. Then she waved her wand hand and started to speak. "There is only one love, Big Love, the unlimited, unconditional love of God and from God. It defies the laws of physics and is received in its giving and is increased thereby."

She captivated me with the radiant awareness flowing out of her colorful eyes.

"We often either mistake it as romantic love or as practical love. Romantic love seeks a person or soulmate to reflect our love, and it is limited to a person. Pragmatic love seeks to overcome the challenges of an insecure world by setting a goal of a stable home or a life's work, and although perhaps more productive than romantic love, it too is also limited to the object of its desire. Once obtained, all limited love will pass. In meeting, the two types of love will appear star-crossed."

Those turquoise diamond eyes focused on me before she added, "Big Love is the realization of God's love in us and all around us—unlimited and infinitely abundant. Not limited to one person or goal. Creation and being. It just is, and then from there, relationships become harmonious and flow from that love, with the only goal being more love."

With an innocent smile, she said, "You're thinking about Em, I know."

Another man might have been embarrassed to realize his secret love was so transparent. Instead, I threw myself at Juno's mercy, sounding like a child. "Tell me what to do."

"I can only tell you what I would do. Find Big Love. First, trust you will find it with full certitude of belief, and it will come. Big Love is always there for us to realize."

Following another pause, she smiled and added, "Love love." A verb followed by a noun. An action followed by a thing pointing to the ineffable source of creation one could glimpse in her eyes.

She stood. I stood. I looked again into those eyes. All had been said. We hugged. I felt loved. But as we walked silently to bed, I said to the Dylan in my head, *Big Love is for monks and nuns, not monkeys like me.*

CHAPTER 43

THE CLOCKED TICKED FORWARD without reprieve, and I continued to see Dick in every fissure of my fevered mind. And Comrade, lurking always just out of range in the dark, made his teatime presence felt. M, however, displayed no fear or even discomfort while the sharp sword of Damocles swung above us.

Our flight of failure was four days away, and my fever was rising, with incoherent thoughts blurring my reality. To make matters worse, the ladies of the Deeksha for the first time looked gray and remote to me, as if they were withholding a secret or had been abducted and replaced by aliens. Boy was in on it too—all of them looking and acting strange. Maybe they had cholera. Maybe I did. Maybe I was projecting my common ordinary illness and lack of light on them. I was sick of myself. I was the alien.

I rubbed one cool hand on my aching hot forehead and attempted to focus on my new plan. I wouldn't reduce this scheme to writing for fear of finding another fatal flaw in its conception. While M was safe in Athens teaching, I would confront the CIA upon my return to NYC and demand assurances to allow me to return safely to Nepal to find the ToE. There would be letters released to various news outlets if anything happened to me or anyone associated with the matter. I wouldn't mention M, the family, or Yogi Mangku to the CIA. I wouldn't endanger M or raise her hopes by telling her of my new plan, but there would be no need to outright lie. If the plan worked, I would meet her in Athens with the ToE in my hand or die trying.

I asked Dylan, *But what if it isn't found at the yogi's compound after all of that risk, intrigue, subterfuge, and expense?* There was no reply.

It was Groundhog Day, or Groundhog Night. As tea was served and the fire burned again, I asked Juno and the rest of the family about Grace.

"Grace was here not that long ago, right? Dylan must have shared something with her about where the ToE was, and she didn't realize. In my mind—" I lost my train of thought, so I improvised. "In my novel, in cryptic Dylan-like fashion he shows her where he hid the theory. Can anyone remember . . . He must have told . . . shown . . . her." I was distracted by Comrade's hovering around the Buddha pond. I don't know what I would have done if he'd dared to sit down in our private place. I couldn't stand that.

M sighed. "Sean, where are you tonight? This isn't your novel. I'm sure we'd know if he told Grace where to find it. You look pale."

She looked wan.

Realizing I was on the verge of betraying my illness, I tried to recover and focus. "Well, that's not a good look, is it? Thank you, no worries. You know I love stories. And I'm all right. This wouldn't be the first time my novel came true. And it's story time. YaLan? Astri? Boy?"

They looked to M in secret conspiracy and then—flat and colorless—at me. Where were the bright lights as my fever seemed to shoot up each night?

Juno stood to speak, placing her teacup on the thin wood ledge behind us that served as a table. Thank God, story time. The flames rose behind her as if she were the mother of dragons, lifting all the gray away. I came back to myself, and the ladies looked again like Madonnas, and Boy a beaming cherub. Hmm. The magical paradigm-shifting Juno effect.

"It was early spring when Grace came to see her father at the Deeksha after finishing a Bollywood movie in Mumbai. Dylan had been so eager for her to spend time at the Deeksha. Grace's opening petals, balancing yin and yang, were as beautiful as the blooming flowers welcoming grateful bees."

Juno's words and cadence were poetry. She could have been reading a shopping list, and it would have been Keats to me.

Juno loved speaking about Grace—loved Grace. I think she loved everything and everybody.

The almost always silent Boy, his gaze normally distant, sat up straight, eyes focused, each time Grace's name was mentioned.

"Grace told us something to the effect that anyone who comes to the Deeksha with an open heart cannot fail to have it illuminated," I said, trying to gauge M's reaction without looking at her outright.

Juno, not one to rise to a compliment, smiled, apparently taking pleasure in this account or in my clever way of reminding M that it was time to turn her love light on for me.

YaLan said, "We were immediately three sisters of remarkable hair—none, short, and flowing. Grace had just played the part of a boy, Kim, in Kipling's *Kim*, a big Bollywood production."

M ran her fingers through her own hair as she said, "She was perfectly cast with her short hair and tanned body as an Irish orphan pretending to be an Indian boy, but a Western woman playing the lead in an Indian production based on Kipling's colonialist history caused quite a stir in the West. The Western thought police jumped into hyperdrive, yelling *foul* because of contorted logic that said such a thing wasn't proper. 'Another form of colonialism in ole Bombay,' they cried in a mistaken accusation of cultural appropriation. Or maybe Grace's acting had fooled them into thinking Kim was a real Indian boy.

"For her part," M continued, "Grace's acting demonstrated the universality of being and the community of spirit, as she inhabited Kim as she did her own skin. And despite the controversy, Grace won India's Screen Actress Award for best actress. India's public and critics had no problem with a Western star or a young woman playing a boy."

"If we applied today's standards," I said, "Shakespeare would be banned for political incorrectness. In his stories he loved to dress the ladies as boys, and since in the theater of his time men played the ladies, the plays were all quite gender fluid."

"And biased," M said.

"How so?" I had to ask.

"No female actors," M said.

Astri picked up the story as Juno, silhouetted by the fire, hovered like an angel over the scene. "Grace spent time at a women's shelter while in Kathmandu, a charity for community outreach that had successfully brought an end to the barbaric practice of *chhaupadi* and now focused its efforts on pregnant women and postnatal mothers. Our mother is the patron founder of this charity, Awaken, Nepal."

Chhaupadi? I didn't want to appear insensitive and ask, even as M shook her head in knowing disgust.

YaLan continued. "And Grace produced an Awaken video that, based on her fame and talent, went viral and raised significant money and awareness for the shelter and to assure safer births and postnatal care throughout Nepal. Astri and I were the camerawomen, using Grace's phone at her direction."

YaLan, with a smile of tacit consent from Juno, pulled up the video on her phone to show M and me. YaLan and Astri shared a compassionate glance as Boy moved closer for a good look too. I had come to think M was right and that Boy was an asexual human being. He had said as much in few words. However, it was clear he was deeply in love with Grace in a spiritual romance, dispelling my shallow assumption that love always led to sex. But of course the compassionate and selfless Boy would love passionately in his way.

In the short film, Grace stressed the lack of awareness of the complications and death associated with the most primal and basic human passage, that of childbirth.

In one short, telling scene, a local constable came to the shelter. In an effort to appear helpful and avoid unpleasantries on his watch, he warned Grace, "It is not safe for you here, and you should stop filming and go back to the Deeksha immediately. Otherwise your life is at risk, and I cannot protect you."

YaLan paused the video to say, "We told Grace of the risks before she went to the shelter. Mother had been threatened many times for her work there. Yours is not our first death threat. There are still men who don't approve of women doing anything they don't control."

Juno settled YaLan with a squeeze to her arm, then continued her story. "YaLan and Astri are the celebrities here in Kathmandu, where most have never heard of Grace. The three are now sisters, since Dylan was a father to them all. It was decided that the twins, while visiting their young Americans in Portland, would also stay a time with Grace in LA. Grace insisted. She also wants Boy to join her there, but Boy has so far refused."

We looked over at Boy, who may have hidden a blush in his ruddy complexion.

I said, "It will truly be the City of Angels. Boy, how could you miss that trip?" I immediately felt guilty for putting him under the spotlight he so consciously sought to avoid.

He rose to the occasion and said, "I have responsibilities here and a happy life without more. Grace, however, is an amazing, accomplished young lady. She went with Dylan and me on a difficult day hike up two mountains that she summited easily, like a gazelle. It was Dylan's strong desire to show the great Himalayas to her. We had the most spectacular day. Grace is—" Boy didn't need to finish, or maybe he was overcome, but his eyes declared his love for Grace.

"A marvelous picture that you probably took on one of the peaks now hangs above the fireplace in Dylan's town house in New York," M said, ensuring that Boy's special moment was made even more special. "They both look so happy being there with you."

Boy smiled, knowing his secret was out, before returning to his natural state of shy reserve and directing his gaze toward the ground.

Out of mercy, Juno moved on. "Grace is, despite her celebrity, a humble, sweet, and honest girl. Dylan's daughter. He was so happy with Grace here. His joy in seeing her overflowed and made all of us happy at their celebration of love. They had not had the opportunity to spend extended time together for the past few years. Grace accepted her fame with humble gratitude. Here she was just a girl with her father. They went together to visit Yogi Mangku and had a wonderful time, just the two of them. Grace said the yogi reminded her of the lama she had befriended in India. Dylan was happy that she shared a bond with and had received the teachings of the real Tibetan lama who played the part of the lama in the movie. Do you know the story?"

"I read *Kim* as a boy," I replied, "and M has seen the movie."

YaLan said, "We will see the movie as soon as we get a chance, and we don't want to spoil our friend's movie by reading the book first."

"I couldn't spoil the book or the movie," I said. "My memory is dim about the spying and murderous intrigue Kim faced, and about the muddled quest of Kim and his lama for the hidden Fountain of Wisdom from which a river flowed—where the Buddha's arrow had fallen. Strange, I remembered enjoying the story immensely as a boy, but I can't recall now whether or not they succeeded in their quest. Oh, I do recall one important detail."

"What is it?" Astri asked.

"Spoiler alert? I do remember being sad that the lama died in the end."

YaLan and Astri looked sad. I had spoiled the movie for them.

Juno said, "Well, we all die in the end. Or at least our bodies and stories do."

With that rhetorical flourish, she finished her story and then punctuated that ending with silence. She stood graceful and still in a delicate mountain-flower pose. The peace of teatime flowed through the family as the day settled deep into night and the bonfire burned to a pool of glowing crimson embers. Juno's chameleon eyes were dancing in many colors, blessing her family in front of her while the fire died behind her.

The silence, the stillness, and the beauty of the night were shattered by what sounded like a hundred whips snapping right at the ears. An automatic weapon's rapid fire had erupted out of the darkness behind Juno. I tackled M, taking her to the ground hard. The family scattered at the staccato shots breaking the sound barrier as they burrowed into the brain. I wasn't sure what to do other than lie on top of M and take a bullet for her. I raised my eyes just enough to look for the attacker. Bullets were hitting around the firepit and around Juno's feet, a constant barrage of little explosions—bullets fired from a location I couldn't identify. I scanned the far side of the fire for Dick's grin and his rattling submachine gun.

Juno didn't even flinch but turned away from the firepit and the cracking flashes and back to her family. Waving her wand hand with a flourish, she calmly proclaimed, "Fireworks."

M was looking up at me, since I was still on top of her. She managed to get enough air to chuckle and gush, "My hero."

CHAPTER 44

THERE WAS NO INVESTIGATION of the dramatic end to Juno's story. The family assumed it was childish play, but I blamed Dick or Comrade for the fireworks and my humiliation.

Doubts and flaws began to riddle my new secret plan to return to Kathmandu and find the ToE. The fever's flood of what-ifs always concluded with the biggest what-if—what if the ToE wasn't with Yogi Mangku after all?

Life moved on, measured by me from the death threat to the time left before our flight home. Three more days. My fever, which had come on in fits and starts, now remained unabated and high, but I kept it secret. I was an unsung hero in my mind—a suffering stoic artist under the edict of a death threat morphing into a death sentence. I thought the fever might do Dick's work for him.

Time was also measured by the flows of water in a refugee camp. A couple of days before the death threat, the water had come back on at the Deeksha, to great celebration around camp. Waterworks were critical. Fireworks were not. Running water reduced significant sanitary concerns and my fear of cholera. I was glad my Google search told me fever was not a symptom of that deadly disease. And I was pale, not blue.

Yet even after the water was restored, the adults continued to go to a nearby stream where there were pools of rushing water, very cold and fresh from the mountains. The snakelike route of the large stream allowed for separate men's and women's pools, where each sex would bathe naked.

Living in a refugee camp and sleeping in a room of six left M and

me precious little time alone. And though the Deeksha was an incu-
bator for Big Love—at least that was my take, although I hadn't yet
received any benefits of that love—the crowded nature of the camp
made the physical act of love between two people an impossibility.
Bath time provided the only moments we could leave Xanadu's walls.
Not only were love and the quest cut short, we were forbidden by
death's threat to see the sights or hike as we had planned. Our short
walk to the bathing areas was a private ritual that brought us together
in solitude, even while we peered over our shoulders in search of a
stalking, gun-toting Dick.

Each day at the fork in the path to the men's and women's bathing
pools, we would share one short hug before going to the pools, and
another hug, a long one, upon returning from our segregated baths.
You would have to be in love or clearly remember first love to imagine
how my consciousness mingled with her consciousness. And how can I
describe her bright presence and spirited brilliance? I was determined
to keep my midlife love and its crazy river of desire flowing, creating a
bridge between us by any means possible.

The strange and childish courting ritual allowed me, in those
moments of M's sweet embrace, to forget the dark days of the death
threat as they flew by like Zeno's arrow on its sure path toward the
inevitable end: failure.

I had come to see my fever as a symptom of my burning passion for
M that would consume me in its heat. M didn't see it in quite the same
romantic vein when I was no longer able to hide it from her after we
bathed and hugged that day.

"Sean, you're burning hot. You have a fever."

"A fever for a girl—"

"Don't joke. You need to tell Juno; she probably has something you
can take. And you need rest. You need your strength to find the ToE."

I was glad my secret was out, but its expression made me wobbly,
and I almost fell to my knees.

I didn't understand and didn't want to question the way M continued to speak about the ToE. Her words implied the quest was still alive.

Her goal was still clearly in her mind. I feared she would be devastated, as every night brought us one day closer to heading to the airport without the theory.

As we walked home, M held my arm as if I were her grandmother who she was afraid might fall. I didn't want to pull away, but her considerate aid made me feel even worse.

Back at the Deeksha, I insisted we get back to work. Seeing M—a quantum cosmologist—putting her heart and soul into service had led me to love her even more. I was inspired to follow her and work untiringly in that service too—for our guests.

The novel was stagnating. In my current state I couldn't think straight enough to conjure an image, much less a scene, or even produce a string of words to line up in a sensible sentence. Physical labor was only slightly easier, but that service was an expression of love for M and an extreme effort to impress her.

I think M was impressed. Before tea she said, "You know what Gandhi said: 'The best way to find yourself is to lose yourself in the service of others.'" She put her hand to my forehead. "But you should get some rest. You must feel miserable; you haven't had a beer for days. I should have realized you weren't well."

Admitting defeat, I went to bed before tea was served.

CHAPTER 45

ANOTHER DAY PASSED, and we were still without a theory. Sick in body and sick at heart, I ventured beyond the sand pits—the spot we'd used as a number-two toilet facility before power was restored and before the general's team provided porta potties. I planned to lie atop an undisturbed sand dune in the sun to bake out my fever. I lathered up in suntan lotion and wrapped a white turban on my head to hide my thinning hair and fevered brow from the high noon sun.

Time remained a blistering fear, and I imagined it reflecting off the red sands, forcing me to close my eyes. Speaking to Dylan, I said, *Well, here's another fine mess you've gotten me into. I think it's 102 degrees.*

The wind sounded like music over the hot sand, and when I opened my eyes, I saw smoke signals in the sky. I heard music—jingling folk music. And the smoke wafted from a fire whipping up over the sandy hills.

Woozy but imagining myself intrepid and unbowed, like Lawrence of Arabia after crossing the desert, I trudged to the top of the highest dune to survey the scene, blinking at what might have been a mirage. It must have been 110 degrees. I dropped to my knees in child's pose, praying to Mecca for answers, and closed my eyes in the swooning heat, wishing I'd brought some water.

As I raised my head and blinked my eyes, I saw what looked like a Gypsy caravan about four hundred yards away nestled into a meadow cul-de-sac, where the desert reached the forest that rose into the mountains. The irregular semicircle of a nine-wagon caravan that looked like a colorful, perhaps poisonous, snake in an oasis where I could get some water.

Were they Gypsies or Gipsies? It was "The Scholar Gipsy" by Mathew Arnold that led me to my love and fear of that magical folk who might whisk me away. Either way, I followed my curiosity over the next dune and down to the woods.

A line of Nepali, arms outstretched and hands filled with gifts, were being directed one at a time to different ornate wagons. One held a baby goat, one a carved ornament, one some produce, and one some milk spilling over an open pitcher as they moved forward in the line. Each followed the directions of a ringmaster and entered with their tithe as another seeker emerged empty-handed.

I assumed they'd come to provide an offering in hope of receiving guidance on how to proceed after the devastation, or were looking to contact a recently deceased loved one. Gypsy business is inversely correlated to the fortunes of the locals where they camp. Yeats believed Gypsies were able to work with the simple openness of rural folk everywhere, who are more connected to nature and therefore to the magic of life.

The ringmaster was dressed like Dickens's Artful Dodger. He was also the leader of the band that played the toe-tapping folk music for the entertainment of the waiting pilgrims. He might have been fourteen or forty-four; it was hard to tell from a distance, and even as I drew closer, the range only tightened to twenty to forty. His colorful dress of royal-blue vest, flowing rainbow scarves, and top hat made him the spitting image of Jumpin' Jack Flash.

Just as I was turning to go, the Artful Dodger caught sight of me and came loping across the meadow with arms outstretched. His stride covered twice the ground it should have, and he was in front of me in a flash, offering a big hearty grin and an outstretched hand.

"Greetings and salutations, my friend. You've brought your questions?" He handed me a bottle of water and waited while I drained it. The best drink ever, it must have come straight off the mountain with that slightly mineral taste. It totally quenched my burning thirst.

I shook his hand, or more the Artful Dodger shook mine, as if he were pumping a well with more than the usual up-and-down strokes needed for priming. I told him I'd just come for a drink and would be leaving now. If only I could, as the Artful Dodger still firmly held my hand.

"Oh, no, no, no! Queen Mab will definitely want to meet you, and we all serve the queen!" He spoke with a cocked smile that said *I may be joking* and a cockney accent that reinforced the name I'd given him.

I tried another stab at protest, saying there really was no time and gesturing at the line of patrons. Without any hint of irony and while still holding my hand, he said, "Such a great sahib must not wait in line."

I felt silly in my turban and hadn't dressed to meet a queen. My flight button had been pushed, and I really just wanted to go.

Next thing I knew I was following the Artful Dodger—by necessity, since he *still* had my hand—and jogging to keep from being dragged. In any other situation, the fact he held my hand captive would have been rude. Here it was just overly friendly. I recognized that I was getting the royal treatment, and I had only the equivalent, in rupees, of a ten-dollar bill in my pocket. I hadn't thought to bring a baby goat to this surreal scene by the woods.

He led me to the biggest and most spectacularly carved and painted wagon; four other vessels fanned out in opposite semicircles from either side to form an S. The Artful Dodger finally released my hand and said, "I'll announce your arrival to Queen Mab," as if I was expected for a royal tea. He went alone into the wagon, closing the wooden door behind him.

The excellent craftsmanship and artistic painting on the wagon were museum quality. It brought to mind the craftsmanship of the Pennsylvania Dutch that I'd seen in my youth.

Was I crazy to enter the belly of this snake? I was about to start running when I realized how silly I would look and how the Artful Dodger would easily catch me in half my strides. So I waited, feeling the fear and desire for flight settle into a heightened sensibility, like that brought on by a mild hallucinogenic. Maybe the Gypsy water? It was all so *Alice in Wonderland*.

Taking a deep breath, I assured myself I wouldn't be set on fire in the daylight. The great caravan doors opened. The Artful Dodger stepped out while simultaneously ushering me in, into an infinite tunnel of an eight-by-sixteen-foot space shaped like a giant mailbox. By way of introduction and farewell, he said, "And here is my queen."

The ceiling above the center passage of the cabin was about six four, so I cleared it by just over an inch. The yellow submarine interior was drenched in beige, brown, and burgundies. The space was a dense and heavy cylinder filled with portent. At the back were two small oval eyes for windows, whose painted irises let in colorful slants of light that landed, swimming, in a pool at my feet. In the back of this stagecoach, between these eyes, on a large well-cushioned seat, sat Queen Mab. I wished my Juliet was by my side. M loved an adventure, and this was a doozy. The queen's seat could be called a throne, one that doubled for a monarch's bed. Isis's lair.

The adrenaline flow had time moving slowly, allowing me to notice each rich detail. Every space was densely covered with antiques, elegant tapestries, Oriental rugs, art, and urns. And books with poets from every century—Shakespeare, Shelley, Yeats.

The air too was dense, pungent and sweet, and seemed as solid as liquid, like Tibetan butter tea. In this intense cave, my breath was slow and deep, like that of a scuba diver at a treacherous depth.

Queen Mab seemed to appreciate my attention as I swam silently and slowly toward her. She didn't rise or speak. She, like the Artful Dodger, was of uncertain age—anywhere from forty to over sixty, depending on the angle and light. Still a beauty, but I could only imagine the beauty in her first few blooms. She dressed like Gypsy queens do, a Stevie Nicks with every stitch perfect and of the finest quality. On her stately head sat an unobtrusive crown made of feathers and jewels. Perhaps more Egyptian than Gypsy, but I had never met any queen before.

When I had traversed the full expanse before her throne, she offered her hand—to kiss or to shake? She had an otherworldly smile. Her crystal-blue eyes read my indecision as I shook her hand. A strange current of energy passed through her delicate and cool grip. She gestured royally for me to take a seat on the cushions in front of her. I felt like a kid being seated for story time.

"My boy was right in this: You do have power unrealized and a blessed life filled with some very dark chapters. Now it is good we two queens meet."

Her lips curled into a knowing smile at this play on my surname and not a secret penchant for women's dress. As if following my thoughts, she said, "Yes, your family name is not yet published, but why the reserve? I assume there's no relation to the dead actor?"

I shook my head, unable to speak. She'd mentioned the actor I had so identified with in my youth as he jumped fences on his purloined motorcycle with Nazis in hot pursuit. Just like Papillon, he was always escaping and being caught again.

This name game was offered as a token of her magical powers. Bothered by the small offering in my pocket, I was finding focus difficult. By way of confession, I removed it, holding out the bill and mumbling, "This is all—"

I stopped talking when a storm raced over Queen Mab's face. But her expression quickly reverted to its earlier calm. It was clear the offering was out of place. I put the money back into my pocket with some effort, squirming on the cushions below her. She was not a seal to be thrown a fish for performing a trick or a coat-check girl to be tipped. Like Juno at the Deeksha, Queen Mab ruled the caravan.

She smiled again and said, "I will tell you some Gypsy history—if you would like?"

I would.

"I was born into a lineage dating back to a time before anyone can recall and into the ruling family of the clan."

She went on for some time through the most fantastical history of her clan and herself, rich in Shakespearean tragedies and comedies of death and marriage.

"My gift has been realized by certain members of my family throughout the years and at times skipped a generation." She paused. "What's a gullible Gulliver?"

I had just told myself I was not one. Perhaps I'd mumbled the playful syllables out loud.

She continued without waiting for my answer. "In any event . . . My sister was a squanderer of the gift. She was known as a woman of great power, but she used it against her enemies rather than to help her friends and those in need. She died alone and miserable after many years of suffering from all the curses she had placed on others. While she was being given last rites—by a priest, no less—she cursed her gift before departing much too young."

Queen Mab closed her eyes, perhaps in trance or perhaps in communion with her dead sister. A few seconds later, her eyes flashed open on me.

"The gift arrives without rhyme or reason but only stays and develops through attention and appreciation and by serving its benevolent purpose. The choice we all have is to live in the world of men and thought—the great illusion—or among those who know of magic. I chose very young to walk among those who know the magic and to live in that fellowship and sublime solitude, connected to the source."

If only priests spoke this way, I might have gone to church more often. She spoke with such conviction and belief that I had no doubt in her gift.

She told me, "One should not speak of magic openly—why this is, I don't know—but with you I feel compelled to do so. Magic is misunderstood and isn't magic at all to the extent it is real. Telepathy, healings, reading minds, remote viewing, and the ability to see the past and the future all are real. The ability to speak to the dead is more complicated, since their communications come from the universal mind revealing what that person would say, just as anyone can hear anyone else in their dreams or know what they're thinking. All these gifts can be diminished into parlor games and weapons if not used properly."

She sounded a bit like the chairman's Guru. She frowned. "I'm not him."

"I know," I said out loud. "You're good." More like Juno, I thought.

"I'm not her either."

I stopped thinking as she went on telling fantastic stories of magic from her history with the universal mind.

"You can see why people are afraid of those with the gift that comes from the bardo between death and life—its potent mixture of telepathy and hypnosis can be greatly abused—but its proper use is to provide healing and guidance to the afflicted. Or, as in your case, guidance to one finally hearing the call to life's true purpose after having been lost in the illusion."

I wondered whether I was under a subtle hypnotic spell, because I believed every word she said and felt pleasantly relaxed and fully at ease in the company of the queen in the belly of the snake. Her belief in and ability to tap into the universal mind resonated with my Jungian philosophy.

It was as if she read my mind, which allowed me to keep silent throughout our conversation as she revealed her messages for me.

"I know your questions. You are healing, and you may perform a good service in the world, a service of some real importance, and that is why I am led to share these secrets of hidden things with you today. But you are in great danger too. Hidden truths do not come out into the light without the dark putting up a fight and trying to conceal the light. There is darkness looming in the East and in the West. It comes and then comes again. Be fearless in your response and remain awake. If you cower or sleep, you will fail, and you, your dream, and your love will die. Stay awake!"

The queen paused, head cocked, as if someone whispered in her ear. "She wants you to know she has evolved and is in a blissful state that your full power of imagination can also conceive; you can join her there. She says to proceed in love without fear or looking back. Em is good. She will truly love you too."

And then the session was over. The Artful Dodger opened the doors, and Queen Mab offered her hand to say goodbye. I kissed it this time without hesitation. She smiled at my homage.

Then abruptly, as I turned to go, she demanded, "Wait!" Following a pregnant pause, with my mind a blank slate waiting for her words, she said, "There is another—a man—who simply says, 'Follow the poetry of life and face your biggest fear without fear. Card N-E-O!' And now, with a chuckle, he is gone too. Cheeky fellow. Know these messages come to you from the universal mind. Keep looking for signs and trust your instincts."

Then, as if a veil dropped or a bell was ringing, the theater curtain fell, and the Artful Dodger ushered me out of the vessel tunnel.

There in the light, I felt released from a not unpleasant spell. The Artful Dodger warned me that it was important I not speak about what Queen Mab had shared with me. He gave me a big bro hug and insisted on a selfie with me before returning to his small Gypsy band.

As I floated up the steep dune, high from my audience with the queen, the band struck up a reggae beat. In my honor the Artful Dodger was singing a Tosh and Jagger duet—"(You Gotta Walk and) Don't Look Back."

I made it back to the sand dune where I had started, with a raging fever I no longer felt. At the top, I lay down to rest.

I awoke to a circle of family faces, looking like angels, above me. Boy was attempting to lift me.

I smiled, pushing his arms away. "What's going on? Can't a guy go to the sand pits in privacy?"

M, shaking her head, seemed relieved. "Sean, you passed out. It's been almost two hours. You could have died out here. What if Dick found you and not us?"

"Well . . . I'm glad I put on sunscreen and a turban." I was reorienting myself and was embarrassed by all the attention and fuss.

M put her hand to my forehead. "It's hard to tell with all the sun, but you don't feel hot from inside. How do you feel?" She passed me a bottle of water.

Delirious but happy, I confessed, "My fever broke! Did you see the Gypsies?"

I didn't know why they all laughed as they started leading me home. I was disoriented, but I felt pretty good.

It only became clear to me later that they thought my encounter with Queen Mab was a fever dream. I was unsure. It had all been so clear, so vivid. And I remembered so much dialogue for a dream. But her name had me wondering if it was all a literary dream.

When I went to bed that night, emptying my pockets on my small table, the ten-dollar rupee note was gone. Now that was magic.

CHAPTER 46

MY AUDIENCE WITH QUEEN MAB only slowed time for its duration; each minute had resumed its normal speed toward our departure and my defeat. T minus one. Zeno's arrow continued on its path.

That next morning before yoga, with fever gone, I returned to the sand dunes. When day broke, I saw the meadow oasis below, but the Gypsy caravan was gone. Back at the Deeksha, I still wanted to believe the magical encounter had been real. Real or not, it had cured my fever and given me a ray of hope.

At the end of yoga, after Juno's bowls had sung, I turned to M on the mat next to mine with a post-yoga buzz.

"Even if it was dream, it wasn't an ordinary dream. It came right out of my subconscious. The queen called it the universal mind. Never mind. The dream convinced me we aren't out of danger but that we still might find the ToE. Convinced me that there's a way."

M stood up, still wearing her yoga glow. "I like your enthusiasm, and you know I remain determined even with our flight home tomorrow." She rolled up her mat. "But I need to start packing. I'm just glad you're back and feeling yourself again." She left me to pack, to leave, to end our quest, with a sad smile that shredded my heart.

I stood there on my yoga mat, willing blood tears to come to ease the pain. Comrade passed me like a buzzard and strutted arrogantly up to Juno, who was still on her yoga teacher's perch, to confront her as she answered some of her guests' questions about meditation. Failing to acknowledge the native tongue of the Deeksha, he made his demands in Mandarin.

"Good morning," Juno responded in English. "You mean the hotel where the general is a guest? Sure, I'll go with you to see him in just a minute."

I watched as an impatient and angry Comrade weighed his options, but he had none other than to wait until she was ready to go; he couldn't manhandle her at the Deeksha. Always wary of the man, I left my mat and moved instinctively closer to protect Juno. She continued to speak to the guests, her British tones accentuating the calm she projected in all situations.

When she finished speaking to her audience and was coming down the three steps, I ignored the lurking Comrade and asked, "May I go with you to see the general?"

"Thank you, Sean. That's very nice but unnecessary. And it's best not to provoke a man like him unnecessarily."

There was no debating with Juno, and I knew she was more than a match for the general. Still, I didn't like his position of power, as general and drug dealer, and his continued pursuit to take over at the Deeksha. I assumed a British accent and said, "Well, do try not to be too hard on the man."

With that, Juno was off, Comrade behind her, a smirking ghoul of an escort.

Juno returned about an hour later. Comrade tried to shadow her, but she dismissed him and went into her room and shut the door.

"That's odd," I said to M. "Juno looked shaken."

"Yes, and she never does. She shut her door too."

We waited outside, hoping she would come out and explain. After a while, M knocked and was invited in. I was not.

Good. Some timely girl talk. You there, Dylan?

Two ladies to admire for their spirits and minds as well as their bodies.

Well, haven't you become the sensitive one?

Death does give one a fresh perspective on life.

I didn't like to admit it, but Dylan was right. I loved these ladies—each so accomplished in thought, speech, and action—for their bright lights.

M and Juno came out laughing after about fifteen minutes.

As Juno went on with her daily routine, M said, "I taught Juno the shake-off dance. The wonderful news is your dream queen was right— there is a way for our quest to continue!"

"What? How? What's changed?"

"Juno was shaken because Dick is dead! Killed somehow—perhaps in the earthquake or an aftershock. The general didn't explain."

Dylan's words and Dick's death stirred my love for this most amazing lady, and I boldly took hold of her hand. "Let's go sit by the Buddha to discuss this great news. Well, you know what I mean. I want to hear everything Juno said, and we need a plan to continue our quest."

She let me lead the way, her hand in mine, to the lotus pond and our cozy seat before we shared another word. My desire to kiss M there and then was wetting my lips. I imagined the compassionate Lord Buddha approved of this holy pent-up desire bursting in joy, freed from all restraint.

"Juno felt she had judged Dick and that her negative thoughts about him somehow contributed to his death or to him not going peacefully into that good night. As you know, for Juno, the world is one interconnected, ever-shifting field of energy experienced as relationships, so in her universe, that makes perfect sense."

While I adjusted to what amounted to spectacular news of a man's death, M added, "The general showed Juno photos of Dick, and in one, he was dead. I take it that the image was quite gruesome. His face had been crushed, and his beard had been half blown off by whatever hit him.

"The general said Dick was some sort of agent for the US and had been watching the Deeksha. He implied that we Americans—you in particular—may be involved. Juno said she knew the general's type and that it wasn't beyond him to have fabricated some or all of the story as a scare tactic to get her to give him control of the Deeksha and to sow suspicion inside the family. He apparently tried to bully her, not knowing her very well." She mimicked Juno's wave of the wand into the air.

I was perplexed. "That's so strange . . . I saw Dick alive after the earthquake, bloodied with a gash but not crushed, when I set out looking for you. And the postmaster saw him too. If he died from nat-ural causes, it was during an aftershock, not the big quake." I looked down, trying to think. Maybe he too was murdered?

I found myself vigorously rubbing my face with both hands—that nervous tic of mine—but now that I knew it made M laugh, I didn't hold back. But a horrifying thought wormed its way into my brain. I dropped my hands solemnly and caught M's laughing eyes again. "Juno can't think—"

"What? You mean you?" She shook her head. "Of course not. Doesn't fit your MO. Now, if he died in his sleep, that would be another matter. Juno said that nothing the general told her should be assumed to be true. I love that monkeylike rubbing thing you do, but you might break your nose if you're not careful."

"Coo coo ka choo," I said, using an expression of my childhood for *All is good*, which sounded like a sneeze. All was good, but I was con-fused by the news and conflicted about being relieved, and though it felt wrong, I *was* celebrating that Dick was dead.

I asked, "So we can't even be sure Dick issued the death threat, since he may have been already dead?" Was our true enemy nameless and faceless?

"Juno believes the threatening note may have been a game the *gen-eral* played, directing Comrade An to place it under your pillow in an attempt to scare us away and to drive her to ask for the general's help. Juno is sure they won't harm us—two Americans—considering who her uncle is. She insists we delay our flight home, and she'll take us to see the yogi as planned when our service to the refugees—guests—is completed. I agreed, assuming you would agree with me."

I shouted, "Quest on!" and then less full-throated, I said, "God bless Dick, may he rest in peace. I hope he had no hand in taking his own life."

"Okay, Father Bishop. That's quite enough of your blasphemy."

Full of hope, we laughed in relief.

My conflict and confusion over Dick's death were compounded by guilt. I knew joy wasn't the right reaction to death. I also didn't know how his death would play in the novel and where it would lead; was it another dead end? Hmm . . . And another mysterious death.

Dick was dead, killed by a brick to the head. And it was Dick who was dead, not the entire CIA and his Guru. Still, my confusion was overridden with elation that the quest was back on, providing a way forward to consummate my love.

M picked up a stone and turned it over in her hand. "Juno's confident the need for the refugee camp will be coming to an end soon and that we can see the yogi by the end of the month. The number of tents is already down by over half, and our guests are leaving on an accelerating basis. So I'll call the travel agent and delay our flight until August first, okay?"

"Sounds good, concierge!" But . . . "What's today?"

"July twenty-first all day!"

"I'm so confused. The sooner the better in case the Guru sends more Dicks."

I was thrilled to have more time with M in the increasingly less crowded Xanadu, with our quest back on. In my mind, the image of Dick lurking in the shadows, pointing a gun, was replaced with an image of the yogi standing in bright sunlight, holding the pages of the ToE.

"We didn't know Dick," M said. "Who he was or what he did. We do know there was another death, of a man we'd seen once or twice. It's okay to rejoice that our quest is back on."

She stood, handing me her stone to throw, saying, "I told Juno I'd help her with a guest matter after I updated you. We can discuss everything more later. Bye, buddy." She smiled that tender smile of hers when she delivered the *buddy* moniker, a needle prick to my passionate heart. *Plunk* went the stone into the pond.

I was of two minds. Dick's death meant that Dylan's death might forever remain a mystery. And yet if he did murder Dylan, my joyful reaction to a man's death might be justified. I didn't adhere to an eye for an eye, but if the gouger happened to also lose his eye, who couldn't see the justice in that? That version was more the solace of karma than the grim glee of human vengeance.

It was remarkable that the love seat in that perfect setting, where I now sat alone, was always left vacant in the crowded refugee camp. I believed the others stayed away knowing it was where M and I came to talk in some semblance of privacy. The refugees were united in supporting my quest for love. I could not let them down.

I googled *American killed in Kathmandu earthquake* and found a local paper that morbidly posted pictures of the dead. One showed a grainy passport-size picture of a man without a beard, with *American* in the Nepali caption but no name. Hmm . . . Creepy Google knew where I was and supplied me the local news of Kathmandu? With the poor picture, it could be Dick from the Quaker wake or Kathmandu Dick with a shave or both or neither.

I wanted the man's real name to send to Detective *Mulhearn* in New York so he would perhaps consider reopening the case of Dylan's death. It was a half-baked idea, and I was unsure how much to confide and to speculate as true to get the recalcitrant detective to reopen the file. And I hoped to gather more background material on Dick for my novel, to make him more than just a spook who went poof.

Without having a real plan or consulting with M or Juno, I quietly left the Deeksha.

It was my first time back on the buckled busy streets of Kathmandu following the death threat. The big village was slowly healing, and the odors were the first to recover.

I took a meandering path dictated by fresher air and the resumption of moving traffic—and crossed a few roads filled with drivers even wilder than those in Manhattan. Here the only rule of the road for pedestrians and vehicles of all sorts was *first to the spot*. And due to the gas rationing limiting the number of cars, they now moved with unaccustomed speed. But I made it safely to my destination—the US embassy.

The embassy was housed in a square concrete bunker of a building that had survived the earthquake with just a few visible cracks. Cracks that would likely remain, as it had been run on a shoestring budget, according to my research, since opening and being furnished in the 1970s. It remained Nixonian in both architecture and décor, an ugly contrast to the ornate and playful buildings that rippled down the streets like colorful prayer flags, many of which now lay like crumbled sandcastles along the way.

The first clerical official I met with was far from helpful when I inquired about an American killed in the earthquake. The man asked to see my passport, and taking it, he said, "Wait," as he went into a back room.

I wondered if I'd stumbled into the Russian embassy by mistake. But above the door hung the American flag. Still, the lack of welcome and the atmosphere suggested I shouldn't be there. A high-tech camera, which looked to be some type of artificial intelligence, perhaps facial-recognition technology, pointed at my seat. I shifted sideways and turned away from its gaze.

Was the novel so important? Was how Dylan died so important? Important enough to put M and Juno in jeopardy? I was acting as though I was fighting city hall and not the CIA, an agency I was certain was behind Dylan's death. Another case of self-sabotage when my mission to win M's love and find the ToE were all that really mattered and the path was finally clear. This misguided escapade served neither end and might just bring more trouble.

I was prepared to walk out, but I couldn't without my passport. I decided playing dumb was the best course of action; however, even the dumb would have a simple answer to explain why he was there. I had none other than the truth.

My mind was racing for a story when an evidently more senior official strode out from a back room, firing questions.

"Was he family?"

"No."

"A friend?"

"No."

"Well, how did you know the man?"

Luckily, I could reply, "I saw a picture in the local paper that listed an American among the dead."

This embassy official—whom I immediately dubbed the *Inspector* for my story—then asked, "What are you doing in Kathmandu, and why are you inquiring about a dead man you didn't even know?"

Here I was, only now realizing I was inquiring about a dead CIA agent and likely to be arrested for suspicion of murder—if he was murdered. Or at least to be interrogated and draw the Guru's attention further.

The other embassy man, who hadn't so much as greeted me when I got there, was making a copy of my passport. "Just in case something happens to you too," explained the inspector.

I lucked into a plausible story that suited my desire to always hew to the truth. "I'm a literature professor from NYU writing a novel. A dead fellow American in Kathmandu who died in an earthquake might afford me some good writing material."

"Why do all books and movies focus on love and death? Death's okay in a good war story or Western. Okay, Stephen King, where are you staying?"

When I said, "The Deeksha," I felt I had betrayed something.

"Weird name, Dyke-sha. Some kind of ashram with a popular restaurant run by an exotic Chinese lady, twin beauties, and a pretty boy?"

"Something like that."

The inspector handed me back my passport. "You're free to go, but without the name. I'm only at liberty to give it to family, and they don't need it, do they?"

"Free to go? And you can't tell me anything about who he was or how he died? For my novel?" I asked.

"Yes and no. You know curiosity killed the cat."

"Thanks. I'll use that line in my novel, if I may?"

Upon returning to the Deeksha, I confessed the whole story of the ill-advised excursion to Juno and M. The women laughed at my playing the confused American tourist and bumbling professor writing a novel. M noted, "That role so suits you."

I agreed. I was an idiot for going. We started to prepare for the evening meal. All was forgiven. I was determined to be less a bungler in the face of future challenges and dangers. Despite the image in my head, I was no Sherlock.

That night Astri, enjoying the lighter mood of Juno's hostel room, asked that I start telling stories again after the candles were out. That night's story was of Dylan and my adventures to find Shakespeare's long-lost play, *Cardenio*. I was the undaunted hero, with Dylan still guiding me on a quest that might never be fulfilled. I left the story with a cliffhanger to pick up on each succeeding night.

CHAPTER 47

WITH DICK DEAD, PEACE INFUSED our extended stay in Xanadu. We would soon visit Yogi Mangku and unearth the elusive ToE. I hadn't felt so confident since before the earth's seizure shook my world upside down. The earth was solid again beneath my feet.

I was also back to writing my novel. Writing, yet not reading any of my beloved books. I was living in my own fantastic adventure and had no need for fictional worlds. I also saw myself at the Deeksha more in the role of a student of Big Love rather than a man playing the part of a professor of literature. Still, all the great authors' and poets' words were with me. As was Dylan's voice.

New York City, tolerated with coffee by day and wine by night, existed still, but light-years and a lifetime away.

The third night following the news of Dick's death, I prepared to shift from beer with dinner into the relaxing pre-sleep harmony of the tea ceremony. If there were fireworks, I wouldn't duck for cover, knocking M down, but I'd take her breath away by seizing the startled moment to steal a kiss.

As Boy was preparing the tea, Juno said, "Boy has an idea where the ToE might be found. He thinks it's far-fetched but wants to tell us over tea."

Astri and Juno were waiting with M and me as we took our rock seats and adjusted our meditation cushions for comfort. Behind us was the wood bench, on which we placed our cups. YaLan was on the other side of the firepit playing with children in an ecstatic mixture of dance and yoga. The music was too far away to hear, but I felt the melody and rhythm in YaLan's graceful fire dance.

As I enjoyed the charming play of YaLan and the children, M said, "So, lotus-eater and beer drinker, it's almost time now."

"The time is now. And if it was wine, you'd be just as full of the lotus too. Don't worry; I'm ready. And perhaps Boy does know where we'll find it." I was enjoying my beer buzz and the company.

M turned to Juno. "When do you think you'll be able to go into the solitude of your sanctuary? I'm excited to meet Yogi Mangku. I believe he must have the ToE. And even if Boy helps us find it first, I'd still like to meet him. And by the way, thank you all. With all your responsibilities and with working round the clock, you still found time to support us on our mission."

"It is our pleasure," Juno replied. "Dylan's last wishes are our wishes. As a person to be trusted, it is an honor to play a part. Tomorrow we'll start our preparations to transform the Deeksha back into a meeting place and teahouse. In a couple of days, the end of July, the Deeksha will be settled, only a few of our guests will remain, and we can be on our way. Your flight is postponed till August first, midnight, I know. Are you okay with a day trip on the last day of July and going straight from the yogi's compound to the airport? It is not so far away."

"Yes, we have our guest to see off before we go. Next visit, I hope we will have more time with your yogi though and to hike," said M to our concierge.

"Ah, and here comes the man of the hour," I proclaimed. "Boy, who brought us daily gallon-by-gallon gas so that our quest could continue and who now has a theory of his own." He was carrying out the tea.

Boy shook his head at my silly welcome and silently served the wonderful Deeksha tea, his duty always performed joyfully. That night he was clearly excited to tell us where he thought the ToE might be found; he didn't look down but engaged in eye contact with each of us. The family was infused with anticipation.

"Is YaLan going to join us?" I asked.

"She's been banished," Astri said. "She dared to pull my hair too hard. I almost slugged her."

It was sometimes hard to tell when Astri was joking, or at least how serious she was about a sisterly rift.

Juno mused, "We only hurt ourselves when we don't forgive."

Most nights I visited the pee rail after tea and right before bed, but I'd drunk more beer than usual. I couldn't wait, saying, "Please excuse me. I'll be back in a minute. Boy, please wait to tell us your idea for the ToE hiding place. Regardless of how far-fetched you think it might be, for having an idea, you win Astri's competition."

Boy's amber complexion turned a darker hue with my words. The mischievous Astri's words followed me. "I think Sean needs to wipe the dew from his lily before tea." The family laughed as I took my leave but couldn't see that I had blushed too.

As I walked to the railing, I had to pass Comrade. I was glad he turned his back so I didn't have to interact with him. Comrade wasn't lurking more than usual, but I had changed my schedule. I wished he would return to his old schedule of being in his dark lair by teatime and my bedtime pee. His presence always brought an unwanted smell that lingered even when he was no longer around.

He stood silhouetted by the black screen of night. I felt his dark eyes following me as I passed him. He was mumbling something in nursery school English about red being good and blue being bad. It was sad he had no one to talk to.

When I returned, creepy Comrade had moved closer to the fire, although he stuck to the shadows. I didn't like the way he glared upon my family like a gargoyle keeping watch. There was no easy way around him, and I couldn't pass undetected, so I stopped about ten yards behind him and waited for him to leave. I was able to ignore him by not looking at him. I liked the vantage point to watch M as the flickering firelight played over her face. There was never a moment she wasn't beautiful. I didn't mind waiting, savoring a scene I enjoyed so much each night and that would soon come to an end.

A line of three little girls waited for Juno; the line got shorter each night as more guests left. Juno laid hands on the next angel's head for a good-night blessing before the little girl ran back to rejoin YaLan's dancing fireflies. I returned my attention to YaLan's graceful ballet of warrior poses with the little spirits flitting around her, and I smiled when one little girl plopped unexpectedly to the ground.

And then it started, a material shift in time and a disturbance of space within the Deeksha's energy field. It happened fast, so it may have been the flickering projection of light from the fire that moved the scene forward in slow motion, like a car accident or the Zapruder film.

Astri playfully and surreptitiously flipped her sister the bird. YaLan shot up like a flare, her eyes burning bright, all harmony gone from her movement. Her mouth was contorted in a shout that was lost in the distance and noise of the playful night. She darted toward us in a desperate sprint. She was really pissed at her sister, and there was going to be a twin fight.

I turned back to the family. Other than Comrade backing away, there was nothing new to see.

Juno was smiling as the final little girl ran off, and turned to her cup of tea, every movement mindful and graceful. Her fingers picked up the cup and moved it with a slow tennis swing—the images flickering, flickering—to her lovely lips.

Astri, sitting to Juno's right, twisted from the firepit and her sister's line of attack and toward Juno. Swinging her arm in a violent volley-ball spike, she knocked Juno's teacup to the ground with such force it shattered. Juno's lips, which had been pursed for a sip, curled into a quizzical smile at the startling break of teatime decorum.

YaLan arrived, a livewire of energy, at the center of the disharmony. I hadn't moved, a frozen witness, scared for no reason other than seeing the incongruous scene and the violent actions of the twins. Perhaps it was the crashing teacup that upset me. M looked on incredulously. Boy stood dumbfounded.

Juno reached out a hand to both of her daughters. YaLan pointed at Comrade An and said to Boy, "Search his pockets for a vial or tube. He dropped something in Mother's tea."

"I'm so sorry, Mother," Astri said. "But seeing YaLan's reaction and shout through the fire, something told me to slap your cup away."

YaLan said, "I'm glad I had my one eye—"

Comrade yanked a gun from the crotch of his pants and jammed the barrel's eye into Boy's face, a wild, wounded animal not wanting to be caught. Boy froze in his approach, suspended by imminent death held by an unsteady hand.

Comrade bellowed like a harpooned whale, screaming, "Juno, a traitor to the People! Juno, a traitor to the People! Juno, a traitor to the People!"

I was in shock. But when I caught Boy's eyes over the barrel of the gun, we shared an instant communication.

There was no time to think as Comrade's lizard mind flooded with adrenaline, and his body, including his trigger finger, started to shake. His wailing refrain grew louder, goading him, I was sure, into pulling the trigger.

I didn't want to startle Comrade and get Boy and perhaps the entire family killed, so feigning a nonchalant stroll, I started to hum softly, then gradually more loudly sang, "My oh my, what a won—"

Comrade swiveled his head and the gun's eye toward me. M shouted, "Sean!" startling Comrade midtwist. *Bang! Bang! Bang!*

Boy pounced like a panther, taking Comrade to the ground. Heat seared my temple as flashes went off in my eyes. Stunned but still standing, I kicked the gun out of Comrade's outstretched hand. I fell to my knees, waiting for warm blood to start flowing down my cheek from the burning shot to my temple.

M rushed to hover over me, searching me for bullet holes like Jackie Kennedy had done to JFK. My mind was spinning, and I felt myself rising out of my body to watch the tragic scene from above . . . only to be pulled back by my love saying, "Thank God, you're not shot! But you have a flash mark on your face. Here." She stroked my burning skin.

I was relieved to hear her diagnosis, as my ears were still ringing and fire pulsed against my right temple. M's cool fingers soothed the heat where one of the shots had scorched me but not punctured my brain.

The twins handed over some rope provided by the gathering

refugees. Boy held a shaky gun on our prisoner as I tied Comrade's hands in a secure though unartful knot. We allowed him to sit up. Boy removed two vials from his pocket, one with a red label and one with a blue label.

Comrade looked like a beast that had been beaten on the way to the slaughterhouse. A beast conscious enough to know exactly what was coming. His face had dropped all shadow of menace, and I imagined that he wanted to disappear. Strange, but I felt sorry for him until a flashback of his shooting at me a moment before sent me crumbling to my knees.

Juno took charge and, with Boy and a few other men as guards and escort, started marching the miserable murderous misanthrope to the Deeksha office. Boy held the gun as if it were a dead rat or a hand grenade with the pin out. They paused by the spa door, and Juno gently relieved Boy of the gun, which she carried much more steadily from there.

M cradled me in her arms like a newborn. When I play back comforting and nurturing moments in my life, that moment will feature in the highlight reel. I was reborn, with a fresh birthmark as proof.

She said, "You're so lucky—*we're* so lucky—and such a handsome reminder of you truly being my hero." She again soothed my temple with her soft hand's kiss.

My precious angel holding me, perhaps sensing more danger, suggested we stand vigil outside the Deeksha office; a concerned crowd of refugees had already followed the family's procession inside.

I checked a mirror on the way to examine the slight and inoffensive red mark, about an inch long, just below my hairline—a small sideburn or crescent-shaped birthmark. I hoped it wouldn't fade away.

Juno soon emerged from the office, with Comrade and her guards led by Boy. She said, "Comrade An is to be shown out of the Deeksha and not allowed to return. If he does return, please call the police. I say that only as a formality. He will not return—of that I am certain. It is over, and no one is hurt, so, everyone, please rest assured you are safe, and sleep well."

She was the calm following the poison and pistol attack. But I was confused; why let the man who tried to shoot me go?

Juno took the gun to the firepit—with all of us following again—and removed the clip, checked and emptied the chamber, and threw the gun into the fire.

CHAPTER **48**

IN JUNO'S ROOM NOT HALF AN HOUR LATER, the family were all more than a bit shaken—or in my case, shaken and stirred—as we readied for bed. Juno, however, still carried on as if nothing had happened and our would-be murderer wasn't on the loose.

I *really* wanted to crawl into bed with M just three feet above me. I was a bit of a hero with Boy, and to the hero go the spoils.

Of course, I remained in my futon bed, but that didn't stop a film from playing in my head—my momentary heroism and dashing battle scar leading to a passionate love scene with M.

I asked Juno to be the storyteller that night. We all wanted to hear every detail of Comrade's confession. Juno waited until all the candles were out to start to speak. I put my love scene on hold.

"He said it was a date rape drug and that he was going to lure me out of the garden before it took effect to—can you believe he used these words?—to 'make love' to me."

I thought of the twisted rape scene I had drafted for my novel and felt shame for all men and my X-rated imagination.

"I said those were words I never wanted to hear from him, and I told him to tell me the truth or I would call the police, and he would be arrested and convicted quickly since he'd been caught red-handed in front of many witnesses. Nepali law is very harsh in cases of attempted poison, rape, and murder. And General Liu would be none too pleased with all the ugly publicity. I also reminded him who my uncle is and that, at least for now, he had more to fear from me than the general."

The family lay in the dark in rapt attention; no one was going to fall asleep.

"Comrade An decided to tell the truth. Sometimes, even for the dishonest, truth is the most self-serving option. He told me all of General Liu Feng's wicked plots, eager to prove he was innocent, was just following orders, and had no choice."

I imagined Comrade sitting with Juno in a confessional booth, wanting her forgiveness for his sins and telling her everything he knew.

"He was instructed by the general to administer the date rape drug. The general was awaiting word of my being stricken and would come to the Deeksha to *rescue* me, using his plane to fly me to Beijing for treatment under his command and *care*. Comrade was then supposed to plant the vial, along with another deadlier vial of poison, in Sean's bag. And then the Nepali police would receive a call from the general that the Chinese government had reason to suspect you and were demanding a search of your possessions."

I struggled to sit up. "What? My bag? Why me?"

The sheet and blanket rustled above me as both Juno and M tossed about, trying to get comfortable following the plot's articulation. M's hand slid down the side of the bed, and I wrapped one of mine around it. She squeezed tight. She was probably imagining what would have happened had Comrade been able to plant false evidence on me. I lay back down to enjoy our interlocked fingers.

Juno's voice spoke into the loaded silence. "Comrade seemed confused by which vial was which. 'Red and blue, blue and red, good and bad, and bad and good,' he repeated multiple times." She was quiet for a few seconds before adding, "Thank you, Astri. Thank you, YaLan. Thank you all."

Juno was a strong woman, but I heard the deep emotion in her voice, not fear but loving gratitude.

M said, "You and Sean both dodged bullets tonight."

"Yes, and Sean and Boy showed great courage."

M squeezed my hand, and I squeezed back with an audible *Mmmm*.

"It's a night to give thanks," Juno continued. "After mentioning Sean's bag, An paused, a liar's pause; I knew he was holding back. 'Tell me the whole story,' I demanded. And that was when he told me they'd been into Sean's computer bag once before, looking for information. They copied your files and found information about a dead man the CIA was involved in killing while looking to find some theory the man left behind. The CIA followed you here and believed you were seeking the document too. The Chinese think the CIA is after you, Sean and Em. General Liu considered planting evidence that you had killed Dick outside the Deeksha, yet decided the vials in your bag were enough for what they needed. And the general would film it all in a documentary he'd already entitled *American Poison*."

"Wait, wait, wait." I sat up, losing M's hand. "They read my novel drafts and notes and didn't understand they were fiction?" I cringed, thinking of them reading my work in progress and the note where Comrade rapes Juno. They didn't know I had scrapped that sordid plot twist. I felt like an unwitting accomplice to their conspiracy, but I didn't confess my imagination's role to Juno and the others.

"English isn't their first language, and I don't imagine they read much literature," Juno reassured me. "Please don't take it as a bad review."

"It must be quite realistic and well written," M added.

Astri jumped in. "I hope you mention my beautiful long hair that's not to be pulled."

"Yeah, sister," YaLan replied. "I was thinking we might switch hair-styles soon."

Boy said, "Or you could both have hair. I'd still know who was who."

"Astri," I said, "I did mention your beautiful hair and how your sister was no less beautiful for her smooth head. But . . . this is so uncomfortable. I may be to blame for the attack." To rid myself of guilt with a partial confession, I said, "I recorded the day of the general's arrival here as it occurred; I can't imagine he enjoyed his depiction very much. My notes even suggested what they might do next." Sitting up in the dark, I put prayer hands to my chest in gratitude and by way of silently asking for forgiveness. "I need a shower."

I saw clearly in that moment the little general in me, a man obsessed with M's body when my true affection was for her heart's light and its essential goodness. She was a brilliant quantum cosmologist and a most excellent friend. I performed a little shake-off dance for M. I think she heard me moving in the dark and gave a little wiggle too. With the dance, I let my guilt go. I had confessed enough about my role, and I forgave my little general.

"For his bad work," Juno continued, "Comrade would be rewarded by being put in charge of the Deeksha."

Juno snorted at the absurd possibility. And I couldn't help but snicker at the ethereal woman's snort. A moment later everyone was laughing. It took another minute or two for the contagious laughter to settle down, as it served as cathartic relief.

Juno and M rustled the bedding above me once again. I waited in vain for M's hand to fall.

Juno said, "When Comrade said he knew nothing more, I believed him. I imagine the general would have tried to gain notoriety and the attention of my uncle, becoming the director and star of a film that followed his heroic rescue and exposed an American's cruel betrayal."

"Diabolical," I said, impressed his plot had outstripped even my evil imagination.

"He knows my uncle, and now that we know his crimes, he won't make any further attack. So it is done and life goes on. Good night, all."

With that, in her unassuming way, the case was closed, and Juno slipped off to sleep. We all said, "Good night, Juno. Good night, all."

No one questioned her decision to let gunslinging Comrade go and not to pursue a case against the general. I, however, remained concerned that the general might still attack the Deeksha again despite the distant protection of Juno's uncle.

The refugees had set up a watch around the Deeksha to protect their queen, so we didn't have to worry that night. I figured I knew Juno and that it would be back to business as usual tomorrow, starting with yoga at break of day.

I lay on my futon feeling violated by the breach of my computer and my privacy. And I was angry that my fiction might have played a part in the events of the night. I could forgive Comrade for shooting me but not for stealing my novel drafts and notes.

Despite the violation of my art, I smiled at each twinge of my new sideburn. M had rubbed some cool face cream on it that had reduced the sting, but it pulled when I moved. Still, it was a *battle scar*. A small-tattoo conversation piece or short story with a hero narrator.

I closed my eyes and exhaled, letting go of the comrade and his general. With Dick dead, the quest back on, and me a hero, the prospect of love in Xanadu rebloomed in my heart. I returned to the love scene in my head but made sure it was tender and PG-13.

CHAPTER 49

THE NEXT MORNING, after the general and Comrade's attack, the usual supplies from the Chinese relief effort were left in front of the Deeksha. The supplies were delivered by the general's shy camera girl assistant. She also carried a satchel and a note from the general to Juno. Juno translated the Chinese on the envelope—*for Juno's eyes only*.

As soon as Juno took the bag, the nervous assistant started to hurry away. Juno said, "Please wait. What's your name?"

"Lien."

I saw Lien through Juno's compassionate eyes—a fearful, probably abused, young lady.

Juno hugged Lien briefly and then placed her hands on the back of the girl's head, whispering at length in her ear. Lien's expression of fear and apprehension turned slowly to hope and appreciation. They hugged again, and Lien left, apparently free of the weight of her oppression.

Juno opened the bag in front of us all, and a flurry of large-denomination US bills floated out and around her feet. Without a second thought, she gave the bag to Boy. I wondered if it was the drug money.

"Please distribute a hundred dollars to each of our guests and take the rest to the hospital. Tell them it's courtesy of the PRC. Please get a receipt from the hospital."

A few hours later we received word that the Chinese aid team had departed for China. All the aid teams were leaving, as international media attention had moved on to other tragedies, but we knew the Chinese were escaping scandal because the attempted coup had been whispered about in town.

That day, Juno penned a letter to her uncle. With Juno, one didn't ask what a private letter said. She shared only what we needed to know. M gave me a quizzical look, to which I Socratically replied, "The only true wisdom is in knowing you know nothing"—although I really wanted to read that letter.

Before Juno licked the seal and asked Boy to post her letter, she called a family meeting, a huddle around the Buddha pond.

"I know Sean well enough to know he wants to know what is in my letter, and I think you all should know so we can move on and let go of the gunfire within the Deeksha garden." And then she read her *Dear Uncle* letter to us, translating from the Chinese.

She matter-of-factly relayed the story of the attempted poisoning and the plan to capitalize on the manufactured tragedy and publicity through a documentary film. And An's firing his pistol point-blank at me. And the general's plan to frame me. Juno knew how those things were handled in China.

She asked her uncle to look after the general's assistant Lien, to assure she was provided a safe post away from the abuse of men. She thanked her uncle for the cash support of nearly two hundred thousand US dollars. The refugees and the injured at the hospital were surprised and grateful at this novel form of disaster relief and the generosity of the Chinese people.

She could be impish but always polite.

Juno knew the letter would silently end the general's career, but she couldn't allow him to go free with impunity to attack others. Now the general and Comrade An would be dealt with harshly by the system that had created them, a system that had become so foreign and anachronistic to Juno. She felt sad her letter would land them both in a box—a prison cell or, more likely, a casket.

She concluded her letter with a postscript imploring her uncle to be merciful and suggesting prison, with the hope of redemption for "the two wickedly ignorant men." She then led the family in a silent prayer of forgiveness.

Juno licked the seal and handed the letter to Boy, who was off to see our friend the jolly postmaster. And with that letter, all was set right with the world. It was time to get to work and find the lost theory.

CHAPTER 50

THE CURRENCY DISTRIBUTED AROUND CAMP that evening brought the energy of the guests to a communal peak. Following the earthquake's disruption of jobs and services, a hundred dollars to a refugee was cause to celebrate. Beer flowed alongside songs and a guitar played by accomplished fingers. "Sweet Caroline" rocked the Globe Theater in its final sing-along curtain call. Mostly there was a communal sense of gratitude that the queen of Xanadu was safe.

After a busy day of routines and mopping up from the attempted insurrection, and after the festivities and over tea, I reminded everyone we were yet to hear Boy's revelation as to where the theory may be found. "We all agreed to wait till tonight, but now, Boy, please tell us your idea about where Dylan may have hidden the ToE. We never got to hear that last night with our having to save the ladies." The ladies collectively rolled their beautiful eyes.

Boy's excitement overcame his reticence, and he jumped up, his face lifted to the near-full moon and one finger pointing at the mountains silhouetted in the distance. "I don't think it will be found there, but it's a possibility. The idea came to me after we spoke about Grace hiking with Father and me."

M said, "Well, the only other hope is that Yogi Mangku has it, so please tell us what you have in mind. We'll follow any lead."

"Dylan had a favorite hike I showed him of two mountains—the same hike I took Grace and him on while she was here. He would go once a month or so. One day not long before he left for New York the last time, Dylan made the hike alone. Before he left, I saw him packing prayer flags and thin flagpoles. He said only, 'A spiritual hike for giving thanks. I'm so blessed.' I didn't think anything of it; it's quite common to hang prayer flags on the mountain peaks."

YaLan said, "Often the flags have spiritual texts, so maybe—"

"So maybe he wrote his theory on the prayer flags," I said. "So fantastic, so precarious, so impermanent, but so Dylan!"

M, her face alight with hope, stretched out her arm and clinked teacups with me. "Maybe it's too impossible to believe. But either way, let's hike!"

CHAPTER **51**

THE HIKE WAS SET FOR the day before we would leave the Deeksha to see the yogi, which left a couple days to first enjoy the peace of Xanadu. I wrote and meditated.

I played with the novel's plot, allowing the general's plan of poisoning to succeed and send Juno to a hospital bed in Beijing. I trembled to even imagine Juno alone and helpless there and what the real general might have done.

The day before the hike, sitting at the Buddha pond, I outlined what was to happen next.

James was arrested soon after Juno's poisoning. As he was hauled away, he had time only to yell to Brigitte, "I'll write!" The next day he was extradited to Beijing and placed in a nasty Chinese jail to await execution, wondering about the international scandal and whether Brigitte could possibly believe he'd intended to rape and/or kill Juno. Brigitte knew of James's insatiable sexual hunger; perhaps he had gone mad with a fever after hallucinating about a Gypsy queen handing out fortunes and poison potions. And perhaps he had become psychotic and still heard the evil queen's voice directing him to poison the good fairy queen.

James was confined with a crazed artist of ancient Chinese landscapes marred by the wheels of progress, a man who hadn't seen a dentist in a decade but who enjoyed playing host to his new foreign roommate. I began to like the dissident and unnamed prison-mate. He was the only entirely fictional character I'd created. That gave me freedom and allowed me to have him eat his own toenails, grinning and repeating "collagen," one of the nine English words he knew along with *tits, food, piss, shit, interesting, sweet,* and *pig's feet*. There would be a lot of *interesting shit* and *sweet tits* in his dialogue.

James had no way of knowing that Brigitte had started an international effort to free him despite the damning evidence found in his bag. She knew poisoning wasn't James's MO, unless of course Juno died in her sleep.

Brigitte was able to get Juno's uncle to agree to reconsider the case and move for a stay of execution, in the hope that Juno might recover and be able to testify. This reprieve was short-lived, as the Guru had the State Department drop all US pressure on China to return its citizen alive, and the general rushed to have James shot dead by a firing squad.

The dramatic march to the red brick wall, the blindfolding, James's last words: *Brigitte! Big Love I wrote yo*—And the twelve shots to James's chest and head—all captured on film for *American Poison*.

The night before his execution, James would pen one last heart-wrenching letter to Brigitte and leave it in secret with the cellmate to hopefully be found someday—*interesting shit*.

I discovered it took courage to write exceedingly dark scenes. I wondered what my readers would want me to do and started to think about a sequel where Brigitte, heartbroken, finally finds the ToE. Dylan had posthumously posted the ToE in a letter to Brigitte through a site that sends messages, in case of death, based on instructions left by the deceased. With the help of Juno's uncle, she would gain access to James's prison cell to look for his promised last words. There she would meet his charming cellmate, who would give her James's dying letter. *Sweet tits*.

Concerned that my writing was hackneyed and overly dramatic, I closed my laptop, ready to give my childlike imagination a break— though it was only YaLan's *one eye* on Comrade that had prevented it all, more or less, from becoming true.

As the garden was now mostly quiet, twice a day I'd sit in meditation, like Buddha, under a large secluded banyan tree. I headed from writing at the Buddha pond to reflecting by the Buddha tree.

The grand old tree, Juno told me, was really two trees. "One, the host that grows from the roots in the ground to reach upward for the sky, and the other the banyan, whose roots stretch from the sky toward the ground, consuming the host tree it will cannibalize for its life." In my novel, the banyan would become a metaphor of perfect symmetry.

My novel's tragic and comical turn was in stark contrast to the peace that now flowed in waves into Xanadu. By the last days of July, the number of tents had decreased substantially. Life in Kathmandu was slowly returning to some semblance of normal as the noise, the odors, and the mirth returned to that dirty and dusty and delightful town.

Homes had become habitable, and the fear of cholera was gone, leaving only the normal odor of burning cow dung and pungent spice. Songs and laughter had returned to the streets.

With each departing refugee, our anticipation of resuming the quest and finding the ToE grew. For M it was a question of belief. For me it was the answer of love.

I now had time to reflect on all that had miraculously occurred around me and in me. My whipsawing emotions had gyrated around a calm center held in place by the Deeksha's ceremonies and celebrations of innocence. And now I was sensing something new—perhaps Big Love—being born in me.

As I sat cross-legged and looked up at the bright sky through the abundant leaves of the swaying banyan, I realized the kaleidoscopic nature of reality—a consciousness behind the eye, the turning hand, the shifting forms. The constant instant of creation—in our perception—becomes the illusion of time, illuminating the films playing in our minds.

The Deeksha was a floating dome of meditation, yoga, art, music, and joy created by Juno. Each day was a fresh blank canvas for Juno's art of living. And each night, though the nighttime bonfire burned out and only a small fire remained, the warmth and energy spread out like ripples from a stone. Like its namesake, energy at the Deeksha was always being transferred and dispersed from the inexhaustible well of its creation, a source known by Juno and which the family was learning. Throughout the tragedy of the earthquake's aftermath, Juno maintained equanimity as the queen of Xanadu.

Before quieting my mind to go deeper into meditation, I reflected on myself under that banyan tree. I wondered whether time and distance from the Deeksha would pull me away from this emerging, more authentic self. Like the opening to the infinite and expanding big bang, the black hole of my comfort zone back home had its inevitable draw too.

I had learned that meditation and yoga didn't stop when we uncrossed our legs and rolled up the mats. All of life was a "practice" in letting go into the flow and trusting what the universe directed us to do. Death was the denial and not the opposite of life.

I closed my eyes, feeling that truth rush through me. *Death was the denial of life.*

To that view, I saw Dylan not as dead but as evolved, as Hope had said through Queen Mab. Dylan was certainly still alive in the Deeksha family, as well as to Natalie and Grace. I heard him speak and knew he heard me—how much more alive could he be?

Learning how Dylan died, writing my novel, and finding the ToE were all less important than the love springing from my heart. And that love alone was worthy and worth pursuing. The Artful Dodger was wrong; we were meant to serve love, not the queen.

I flowed along my muse's stream, reflecting next on love. Juno was above romantic love. She had Big Love, in which I had come to believe but didn't yet fully understand. M didn't believe in romantic love but loved the Truth we had yet to find. I was somewhere in limbo, suspended between Juno's love and M's love. As my spiritual practice was elevated, my love grew brighter and focused on M. It was the same love I had known for Hope but somehow less exclusive and bigger. M's presence just made it so very, very easy to access.

Despite my practice imposed by circumstance, I was no monk. The woman who slept next to me was not a sister to me. Her sleeping face was perfect, with the hint of a smile playing over unkissed lips. My being wanted to commingle with her being and never return, or only return so we could comingle again. Hand-holding and hugs were a touch of honey; I wanted the taste. I wanted no boundaries to an infinite and eternally expanding circle of M and me. I wanted the ecstasy!

I wondered about the correlation between strict celibacy and spiritual awakening. In Juno's crowded room, there had been no opportunity for self-indulgence. And more and more I recognized my own deep social conditioning that always first invoked the primal and turned love's focus to expressions of lust in my mind, despite the connection of true love, despite the recognition of all M's talents, and despite our friendship. The root had been buried deep, but I wouldn't let it direct my actions any longer.

It was time to quiet my mind and all its desires—to focus with single-minded desire on the heart of love, as was my practice underneath that nurturing banyan tree.

With Dick dead and the general gone with his Caliban, I felt no fear losing myself in the bliss of my own private Xanadu, protected by the branches of the banyan.

When I finally opened my eyes, I saw with clarity, in the distance, tomorrow's mountains to climb.

CHAPTER 52

THAT NIGHT, AS WE SAT AROUND the now-small fire with our bedtime tea, Juno said to M and me, "I pray you will find on the mountain what you're searching for. Remember to enjoy each step, and you will reach the peaks. And then we will go see our yogi."

Astri added, "Yogi Mangku is often spotted in the mountains. Maybe he'll bring Dylan's theory to you."

"That would be a miracle," said my enthusiastic M. "We'll be on the lookout for him. I love a long hike, sinking deeper with each step into the beauty of nature."

"The supposition that Dylan wrote the theory on a series of prayer flags to be found, or not, blowing in the wind at the top of some mountain seems improbable on its face." I felt the unintended heaviness and downbeat nature of my words and attempted an uptick. "But still, the poetry of it, the embrace of Buddhist spirituality to post the Truth, is something Dylan might do—allowing his answer to be found 'blowin' in the wind.'"

"You're full of songs from the 1960s," M said. "Let's enjoy the wonderful day and nature to the fullest without looking for anything else. No more talk of finding the ToE there, please. Let's just see what comes."

"Okay, but 'Zip-a-Dee-Doo-Dah' is 1940s, I believe."

"What?" M asked.

"*My, oh, my, what a wonderful day. Zip-a-dee doo dah* . . . I started to sing it, to save you all from being shot by Comrade," I said, cuing more eye-rolls.

The prospect of mountain beauty, mountain air, and M in that native habitat was a dream to me. But I felt some reservations about the hike's challenging level of difficulty.

Boy said, "We will leave at dawn and return just before dark."

"Truly a day hike," I noted.

He pulled out an old-school map. "Our path is about thirty kilometers, with two four-kilometer peaks and lunch at a high-elevation lake in between. A magical lake of dreams." He wouldn't need GPS. Boy knew the way.

I was alone in my reservations about the twelve-hour-plus hike and in thinking one peak might be enough. If we found the ToE on the first, I knew M would want to do the second peak regardless. "Who knows? Maybe there's more," she would say. And if we didn't find the ToE on the first peak, we would of course have to look on the second. In either event, I wouldn't have the heart or strength to argue with her. We weren't speaking about finding the theory, but I was thinking about it, afraid M might become despondent if it wasn't found on our last day in Kathmandu.

Boy, perhaps sensing I was on edge, started teasing me. Well, I hoped he was teasing.

"Sean, don't worry. I'll have headlamps for us in case it gets dark before we get back."

That night in Juno's room, I concluded the story of Dylan and my quest for *Cardenio*. I unearthed it from a chest, after Dylan whispered to me where a theater critic had buried it in 1666, under a windmill on a hilltop outside Stratford-upon-Avon. It was a little too pat and trite of an ending, but I think Astri enjoyed it from the tone of her *good night*.

The next morning, just before dawn, we met in the great room of the Deeksha, M and I wearing our hiking shoes for the first time. Juno supplied porridge and tea. YaLan and Astri supplied loving energy and helped us stretch. Boy supplied our packs, and he was to carry a much larger one. We were well stocked with water, strong Juno-made tea, and grainy honey-soaked goo in tubes for energy, and Juno had prepared a feast for lunch. This was going to be a first-class hike, courtesy of the Deeksha family.

Boy presented two weathered artisanal walking sticks to us, saying, "These were my parents', so please don't leave them on the mountain."

The staff in my hand conjured the courageous in me. They were carved with knotted and scrunched wooden faces with big Western-wizard noses. I was ready for the magic to come. I twirled mine in the air like Juno waving her invisible wand. She smiled and repeated her familiar gesture, ending with her hand pointing at me. I swear I felt a zap of energy.

It was a beautiful, crisp dawn that followed the night's torrential rains. In christening the new day, I said, "Auspicious is the day!" At hearing Dylan's catchphrase, the family smiled, and Boy, M, and I were off to hike.

M was stoked. She led the way along the initial forest-jungle path on a relatively easy incline approach to the mountains. The morning sun soon dried our rocky path. Romantic poets with their love of nature would find an ode to beauty at every turn and vista. I felt the miraculous rising in me and all around us. If only I had Wordsworth's sensitivity and imagination to express that beauty.

Inspired, I shouted to M, "Nature never did betray the heart that loved her."

"That's sublime. You're a great poet!"

"I wish," I said. "It's Wordsworth, from 'Tintern Abbey.' I teach it . . . but still I can't . . . remember . . . the full name . . . of the poem. I'm not . . . good . . . with names." I was already short on breath.

"I know," she said.

Following rolling foothills through a forest, we came to a clearing with a swelling stream fermented by the night of rain. A rope bridge across provided us with an excellent view of the two mountains we sought to peak. The elevated valley between the two tips was where the lake hung suspended, the site of our midpoint lunch. I figured that if I made it halfway, I would make it all the way. So I focused on getting to that lake, putting out of my head the countervailing thought that once we reached it, there would remain an amount of hiking in front of us equal to what had passed behind. It was easier for the mind to conquer extreme challenges in smaller steps. I was embracing Zeno's paradox, arousing myself to go halfway in order to make it all the way.

Maybe we were lucky—or more likely, it was due to the earthquake—but our trek's path and the scenery were empty of other
trekkers. It was just the merry three from the Deeksha family on the
narrow trail. M set an eager pace. She had learned to walk at the same
school as the Artful Dodger. Hers wasn't a girl's pace. "Oh, WOPA!" I
spontaneously uttered.

M pivoted and said, "What?"

"Nothing," I replied. "Just chastising myself."

"Don't be too hard on yourself," she said as she picked up the pace.

M could go twice as fast and twice as long, but I wouldn't be a
crybaby. And I found that following M up the gradual and then steeper
narrow jungle path inspired me with rhythmic energy as my eyes followed her graceful gait and the rise and fall of her shapely shape in
formfitting hiking pants. The motion was a sensual hypnosis. Something
about nature arouses primal urges and stills the verbal mind.

I was glad that Boy was our guide; alone we would never have been
able to follow the mostly unmarked trails, some as narrow as deer paths.
M would pause every two hundred yards or so for Boy to confirm we
were still on the path. The forest-jungle was lush and extraordinarily
vibrant in the sunshine and clean mountain air, and it was quickly
reclaiming the path after the disuse following the earthquake.

We came to a deep crevasse that dipped steeply for about twenty
yards before we could continue our ascent up into the mountains.
Going down was always easier and more dangerous than going up. I
was daydreaming when I slipped and knocked a baby boulder, which
bounded directly downward at M.

"M!" I shouted, afraid I'd crippled or killed her.

With great agility M pirouetted to avoid the bouncing meteor. The
projectile winged her walking stick, which flew into the air like a javelin.
Seeing we were both unharmed, she laughed. "You know, the subconscious mind can process faster and better than the thinking mind the
placement of the next footfall. Maybe practice hiking meditation and
let your intuition be your guide."

Relieved, I took her admonishment in stride and her advice to heart. She was right, of course, that hiking was a meditative art.

She bushwhacked off the path to get her walking stick and showed us it was also unharmed. I hadn't hurt Boy's parents' memory.

We then proceeded with the ascent and had to add a fleece layer we'd been carrying in our packs.

When the first mountain peak finally came into view, the perfect dome was still coated with white and reflected the sun's brilliant rays. The temperature hovered just below freezing. With the steep path covered with snow and ice, we wouldn't be able to reach the summit only a half mile farther up. Hands on hips, lips pressed tight, M had the look of one peering into a full mailbox that couldn't be opened. Watching her shoulders droop, I contemplated crawling up the icy slope to look for Dylan's prayer flags.

Boy said, "Each year the snow cap retreats more," perturbed that the snow didn't start lower down the mountain as it had for most of his life.

He then told us that we had microspikes in our backpacks. The clawlike booties were easy to put on. Hiking on the snow-ice combo wasn't too difficult with the spikes penetrating the ice and preventing any forward or backward slip of the foot. We'd be able to summit!

Halfway up the last half mile, we could see prayer flags fluttering in the cold, clear breeze. I felt M's anticipation rise so palpably it aroused every cell in me.

We rushed on, hurrying like children to the maypoles.

At the summit, it was always the first day of creation. Standing on top of the world, I flung my arms wide open in celebration, ready to take flight. Just a moment earlier I'd imagined myself yelling when I hit the peak, but I was silenced by awe. *We* were silenced by awe. We were three beings atop the peak of nature, posing on the crown of the earth with prayer flags encircling us and flapping and snapping in rhythm with the writing on each whipping sheet. The wind in the flags was the only measure of time, which otherwise stood still.

I don't think any of us wanted to look and disturb that perfect moment. But the time had come, and I bent the closest prayer pole toward me. "It's a poem. 'Golden Rabbit.'"

"I'm so sorry," Boy said.

I turned. Boy's long face said it all. He was crushed that his winning hunch hadn't paid off. I'd never seen Boy at anything but an even keel, emitting a mellow joy, and yet now he was deflated and defeated, believing he'd misguided us. He must have really thought we'd find the ToE on that mountaintop.

M didn't register disappointment for herself, but she tromped over to Boy and hugged him. I dropped my impatience and joined her in celebrating the moment of poetic discovery at the top of the world.

I sang out the words from the first pole—"Golden Rabbit"—putting out my hand for M to join the song and to cheer up Boy.

She laughed and spun around me to the second maypole. "Auspicious is the day!" she sang.

I danced around her to the third pole. "With all the stars aligning—"

"You to year—to birth—to day—to innocence alighting—"

"On fur of golden dawn—"

"Skipping lightly across the lawn—"

"Into your sleeping garden."

"Just then, before you're gone—"

"I catch you by the foot and sing you my lame song—"

"'Forged in golden metal and cooled in alpine wood.'"

"But now I must let you go—"

"To follow you silently down—"

"Your rabbit hole that echoes in your sight, your scent, your sound."

As our song and dance concluded, Boy joined us in the center of the spiraling flagpoles. At the top of the world, we lifted our faces to the sun.

To the Dylan in my mind, I said, *Nice setting for your lyric. Is this what you meant by "following the poetry"? Did you bury the ToE like a pirate, in the frozen earth beneath our feet in a chest like the long-lost* Cardenio?

I heard his laugh and mocking refrain chasing the wind. *Tao . . . Tao . . . Taooo.*

M said, "Boy, thank you for bringing us to this place of beauty filled with Dylan's memory. This is a great find." Boy's buck was back as he raised his arms in salutation to the infinite blue above us. M's resiliency and joy were infectious. She hadn't lost but gained enthusiasm on that mountain peak. All thought of the ToE being lost was banished from our minds in full appreciation of the poetry at the top of the world.

We witnessed the scattered, billowing clouds spread out below like the ripples of a vast ocean, and the blue sky infinitely high above. The air was thin, clear, and sweet tasting, without pollution or corruption. Body and lungs paid attention, concentrating on converting each crisp breath into energy from the limited oxygen in the air. Maybe that was why sages were found in the solitude of mountaintops, where one must focus on one's breath. The awe of nature naturally quiets the mind. I could understand how one might see their yogi there in the thin air.

We were ahead of schedule, so there was time to drink in the view. Everest loomed like a Mount Olympus over this child mountain that bowed in respect. Though still many miles away, its mass exerted a gravitational pull, and its presence felt like a tidal wave suspended overhead. It was a majestic spot often depicted on works of Asian art: dramatic nature on delicate porcelain.

An eagle circled overhead three times before flying off. A symbol of my liberation. When the large bird was gone, we drank warm tea along with the goo, which together provided liquid and semi-solid energy that replenished our systems.

As we descended a winding path, the wide expanse of a crystal-blue lake passed into and out of view below us. The late morning's sun brought a lovely, perfect day, warming with each step down the path. Perfect rhythm of footfalls, perfect sounds of nature, majesty all around. I was in a monk's mind—or Emerson's—with fresh and magical thoughts coming to me from some higher source and not from the routine chattering of my own preconditioned mind.

My freed mind was seeing the vibrancy of nature in a new light. A divine light. The mind for the first time saw so clearly the miracle of creation in the waving of the trees, dancing deities playing in yoga poses and swinging in the breeze. Two little birds—one yellow, one red—danced and sang from the branches of the yogis above, piping a loving tune into the splendid sun of the azure noon. The air was thin, and my head was light as my body floated down.

Three trees had been set apart from the rest. The two smaller barren sentries looked like crucified thieves. The larger center tree stood in full bloom and commanded attention, its network of abundant branches reaching for the sky like a frozen plume of fireworks, each branch a finger in the Sistine Chapel. Tuning in to God, I saw each branch, high and low, receiving life as dictated by its frequency—vibrating in the desire to touch its source. The love being transmitted, given as well as received, was determined by how open we were to it. Why allow limits to be placed on our connection to all of life, to all of love?

I imagined M was tuning in to the same joyful, nonlinear frequencies.

An hour later, tired but cheerful, we'd made it to the tranquil lake, the halfway point. There was more oxygen at the lower elevation, which grounded me and made me hungry.

The approach to the lake was green grass dressed with wild mountain flowers that spread out like a beach around the lake's circumference. Two large elk, one with a big rack, greeted us there. They lifted their magnificent heads from their drink and then, unconcerned, finished before turning to face us.

Boy said, "It's mating season. Be still so that the bull does not attack us for interrupting the rut with his lady."

I cringed at the image of an angry and horny bull chasing me around the lake or me having to stand my ground to defend my own love. Either way I didn't stand a chance.

Luckily, they turned away, loafing off into the trees to rut in privacy. I wished human nature was so natural and M and I were Adam and Eve in this Garden of Edens, about to discover the apple of forbidden knowledge.

Boy showed us the nearby spring that fed the lake and which served to quench our thirst with the best water I ever tasted.

Our small company then found a grassy knoll, and Boy, as Sherpa, emptied out his pack, providing a comfortable blanket for us to lie upon. He spread out the meal prepared by Juno, a meal of exotic spiced vegetables, tea-infused couscous wrapped in spinach leaves, and pickled fish accompanied by fresh sweet-and-salty bread. Our lunch was a Michelin-star meal eaten on a mountain vista, the wind jingling over the silent lake for our music. The meal's taste perfectly matched the tea Juno had prepared with a bitter root and a touch of sweet local fruit.

We ate in silence and with smiles, immensely enjoying the food and company. When she finished, M lifted her teacup. "To Juno, in gratitude for this wonderful feast in the beauty and serenity of mother nature. And to her tea, which we treasure here and now more than the best of Burgundy. And to Boy—the best possible guide and family!"

Boy's doe eyes burned like a mountain cat's. He said, "I have not been to this lake *alone* since I used to come to this spot as a little boy with my parents."

I reached for the walking stick that lay beside me. I was glad Boy felt "alone" with us. We were together in the harmony of communal solitude.

Dear, silent Boy then spoke more than he had since we met him on the first day.

"My parents died in these mountains after an earthquake. They were highly experienced mountaineers and guides, and they volunteered to rescue hikers stranded on a precipice in the snow and ice after the earthquake removed part of the mountain's face. I was almost fourteen years old and already a climber. As they said goodbye, I begged to go with them but was told no. I obeyed their final command.

"My mother and father saved over twenty stranded trekkers before the two of them died together in a fall trying to save even more. I knew instantly the moment they fell, as a rush of love like I'd never felt before washed over me. I knew it was my parents' spirits, and I knew in that instant that they were dead. But I can still feel their love from that moment anytime I tune in to my heart's core."

Boy, seeing the tears on M's cheeks, smiled broadly. "Please don't be sad. I am proud. My parents are local heroes, and a hero's death is the best death of all. And they came to me in that moment and never left.

As a young girl, Juno met my parents as her guide on her first trip to Kathmandu, and they had remained close ever since. I was orphaned but still blessed by my most wonderful godmother, who is now my mother too."

We honored Boy's memories with a shared silence.

Then, without words and in unison, we sat cross-legged and half closed our eyes to meditate on the shimmering light coming off the lake. I held the wizard's staff, Boy's biological father's walking stick, proudly between my legs as a talisman.

My mind followed the sparkling lake's surface and then sank into the depth of dark blue waters. At the same time, a pure radiant awareness arose in me, shining into the sky of light blue. I merged with the expanse of every hue of blue in all dimensions, in ever widening spirals, until with a *click*, limitless white-light energy cascaded through the crown of my head. Silence, space, peace, and bliss . . . Love . . . The love of love . . . Loving . . . Flowing.

I was one being, but M's being was there too, with me, part of me—or me a part of her. And then the being of Boy joined, followed by Hope, Dylan, YaLan and Astri, and finally Juno. Then another *click*, and all was still, and all of humanity, nature, and the universe became one. This wasn't a thought but an experience and a knowing, a union with the One where all is known and understood . . . a rushing stillness of loving energy that cannot be put into words . . . each one with the lake, one with the mountains, one with the sky, and one with each other. Time passed but didn't move in us as we traveled with it, suspended in the speed of light. All time and space collapsed in that moment, and in that moment was every moment. And in that, One was everything and nothing.

Boy, by starting to chant *aum*, gently signaled that it was time to return to our seats by the lake. As I reentered my body and mind, M and I joined in, one last *aum* in three-part harmony. Smiling, we namasted each other.

There was still another mountain peak and a long trek home, but I now had unlimited energy.

As M and Boy started packing up our lunch. I had to remain seated for some time. My bliss had left me fully lit, a lightning rod still glowing, with all my senses, organs, and sinews completely aroused and vibrating at an ultra-high and subtle frequency. Perhaps certain aspects of the sublime experience were underreported in the accounts of sages and poets. Words certainly failed me at that moment.

But that wasn't the only effect of the experience. The animating force of Big Love that came in through the crown of my head had illuminated every cell of my body with blood and energy until the vessel—me—could no longer contain it and merged with the infinite. I had experienced the omnipotence of Queen Mab's universal mind. Enough clarity remained to understand it could not be understood.

Lunch was cleared and packed before my vibration finally calmed to a shimmering hum, allowing me to stand while adjusting myself to my body. Slowly, my mental and motor skills were returning to some semblance of normal.

M and Boy were kind enough not to say anything about my delay and my failure to help. It was just past one, and sunset would be at seven, so we were still on schedule.

My belief in Big Love, now experienced, was now unshakable. Big Love, once only two words, was undeniable and unbelievably true.

CHAPTER 53

I TRIED TO PROCESS THE FLOOD of love that flowed through me from the unfathomable experience by the lake. Even though all comparison was inadequate, the only analogies I could imagine were perfect sexual union and perhaps conception itself, both of which I had long ago forgotten. I didn't want to forget the moment of oneness that still vibrated through me.

After a half mile or so of hiking toward the second peak, M said, "I felt that you experienced something special during our lake meditation."

My mind was immediately locked in conflict over an experience both personal and universal, indelible and ineffable. One I didn't understand or have words for, and one I didn't know how to share. I responded with a tepid, "It was quite pleasant," and attempted a knowing smile.

I let the moment pass without revealing the intimacy of my experience, which might only be described as a communion with God. I feared I'd sound either pompous or silly or, more likely, both. A Queen Mab discretion for such a miraculous transcendence was best. Big Love could only be experienced; I had no words. Words were forever failing me. One shouldn't share such moments of grace other than in sublime poetry—and I was no Shelley, Yeats, or Dylan—or in saintly spiritual texts, and I was no Christ, Buddha, or Juno.

And Boy was there too, so it wasn't an exclusive moment of love I could share with M alone. Still, I was troubled by my response and the dishonesty inherent in my casual, off-putting reply.

Yet, however that bliss was to be described, it left me full of energy for the next ascent. On the second summit, more prayer flags bearing Dylan poetry danced in the breeze. M and I spun around each other in another duet, this time reciting "The Gift," a sonnet. Boy enjoyed our second performance too. In Big Love's afterglow, I wasn't impatient or even disappointed that our quest remained unfulfilled. I was undeterred and remained fully confident.

M repeated the poem's ending. "And wills for time and space to make amends / Renouncing all distance between true friends / Sharing in the speed of light one slow kiss." She then closed her eyes in rapture, as if Dylan had reached out from heaven to beat me to a kiss.

M stood suspended in the speed of light, so radiant in meditation that I thought she might rise like Jesus into the sky. She was peaking on this second summit, her mind connected with the universal mind. She was sharing the wonderful transcendent experience I'd just been blessed by; I could feel it in my heart. In that oneness was a reconciliation of opposites. Boy and I honored the sacred moment with silence and basked in her radiance.

Returning to us, M looked at us with Christ eyes and her sweet Buddha nature radiating in all directions. As tears streamed down her face, she shared, without holding back, so simply and truthfully, "Oneness, love, such bliss . . . Truth . . . Beauty . . . Thank you. Thank you. So that's Big Love!"

Her eyes at that moment I will never forget. People say sages' eyes are lit from within, but hers were mirror wells reflecting the light all around. The prism of her soul radiated the colors of the rainbow that illuminate the forms of the world we see. With her light shining on me, I saw my desire to obtain M's love was vanity, an impossibility. It was impossible to possess something that was totally free. Through her eyes I could see beyond the mountain peak, love as liberty.

From that peak the world spread out beneath our feet in a 360-degree view. Kathmandu shimmered in the distance, and the Deeksha too, a small circle of a colorful mandala, its golden dome and stupa set in a network of concentric domes and stupas that stood between cobblestones of destruction. The wombs and tombs of Kathmandu.

The poetic view from our high vantage point evoked both sorrow for beauty lost and faith in the beauty that remained and would rise again. Compelled to share, I recited a couple of lines of poetry for my travel companions. "'All things fall and are built again / And those that build them again are gay.'" So strange, I knew the lines so well, but in that moment I could not recall the poem or poet's name.

As we started the second descent, I shared M's high. The exhilaration of the hike and its exertion brought inspired thoughts into my mind from Queen Mab's universal mind, as if my mind was a radio receiver tuned in to God's frequency—Juno's definition of a meditative state. Instead of repetitive thoughts that replayed from within my own mind, these were new and fresh, inspired with vibrant truth and perhaps coming quietly into other minds—M's, for example—at the same time.

One message that came to me was so trite and yet so true—that the biggest challenges of life weren't extreme hikes, bridges falling, the earth's quaking, the evil heart of some men, or even death but the limits one places on one's own spirit and heart. From that vantage point, I saw my limits: the doubt and fear that led me to withhold from my fellow travelers, including the woman I loved, the transformative touch of Big Love intimacy I experienced by the lake. Withholding true witness from your beloved, who seeks only Truth and honest communication, not romance but the source of all love that just graced you—that was betrayal. I would not be a Judas of Big Love. I had to speak my piece.

I stopped in my tracks, planting the tip of my staff firmly in the moist ground. The moment of truth. As saltwater dripped from my eyes, M and Boy looked on wide-eyed, surprised that boys do cry. I then told them my experience with Big Love without reservation or filter and using every cliché in the book. It sounded so much smaller than a moment of oneness should. M and Boy knew walls had come down within me, as only truth and beauty remain in the light of Big Love.

Then it happened. M looked deep into my innocent eyes and straight through to the infinite space within my heart, and with Boy as our witness, she said, "I love you, Sean Byron McQueen." I responded with the words she already knew. She marched on as if nothing had happened. But to me all was new.

CHAPTER 54

WE WERE DESCENDING, on our way home. I walked in a lucid dreamworld, listening to one repeating loop of *I love you*. It became my marching mantra, a tune that led me onward, out of the past and into a world of magic and miracles.

We soon entered a subvalley shaped like a large amphitheater hollowed into the mountains. Such a place I imagined Wordsworth's shepherd, Michael, had lived in.

The hidden valley resonated with sound—ambient and growing louder as we strode toward its center. The sound was real, pipe music increasing in intensity. Music arising out of thin air. We looked up. On a rock cliff jutting out high above, a sole sentry in full kilt and sash marched back and forth, playing bagpipes. I imagined it was a cliff similar to the one where Boy's parents had saved many lives.

The barrel-chested man, his broad smile framed by a red beard and flowing hair, stopped to give us a big wave of both hands and a salute. That I could see that smile, so far above, seemed implausible, but it was so.

The Scottie then picked back up his bag of pipes and began to play the most spirited marching tune ever played. A tribute fit for Kipling, it was all "Din! Din! Din!" As we marched along, the natural amphitheater and crisp mountain air set the sound vibrating from every point, and in reaching us, it lifted our steps. Thus we left the amphitheater on a levitation of sorts, with the vibrations of the musical air fading into the background.

Love makes all happenstance miraculous. My bagpipe heart was full and pleasantly bellowing with certainty that following the Tao would lead us to a yogi and the ToE.

CHAPTER **55**

BOY HAD KEPT US RIGHT ON SCHEDULE, and we were within an hour's hike
of the Deeksha when we hit an obstacle that barred our path home. An
uncharted raging stream, or wash, flooded our path, and there was no
way around it.

"Global warming is causing flash floods like this more and more
often." Boy had never expressed anything near to anger, but he sounded
angry now.

I knew climate change would kill me someday—even with finding
Big Love and M's love, there were still challenges the illusion would
create. Challenges that might kill.

I looked down at the tips of posts the stream that had become a
river crashed over and realized that underneath was the rope bridge
we'd crossed that morning. There was no way around, and night was
approaching fast.

Summoned by the power of nature—the intensity of the waters
and the mist shooting into the air in the slanted light of dusk—an even
more primal danger waited for us just ahead. Not more than thirty
yards down the raging stream bank from where we stood, a large and
regal snow leopard stared at us, its improbably long tail sticking straight
up. It was so elegant and powerful that it evoked awe rather than fear.

I knew from the travel sites that praised the wildlife of Nepal that
the snow leopard was a rare and endangered gem of the wild kingdom. I had seen from a distance bears, bobcats, and coyotes while
hiking in the West, and now a horny bull elk and his mate in the East,
but never had I been so close to such an imposing and exquisite force
of nature.

Boy seemed alert but not scared, and M, of course, registered no fear. In my new state, fear held no power over me.

"We are blessed," Boy said. "She is the ghost of the mountains and very rarely seen. She is well-fed, and they attack their prey only from behind or to protect their cubs. They rarely attack humans and never without reason. So we have little to fear."

Little? The big cat set off down the bank and away from us. I thought we'd go the opposite direction, but Boy chose to follow the ghost.

The elegant leopard would pause and look back at her fellow travelers every twenty yards or so, then look out over the "boisterous brook" and let out a *puar*, the sound midway between a cat's loud purr and a lion's soft roar.

The large cat's eyes were green stillness in a vortex of ferocious power. Brahma and Shiva prowled in her, and she was protected by the mountain-jungle, Vishnu.

Kali was my pet name for her. As we mirrored Kali's pace and kept a constant distance between *puars*, M and I took turns softly cooing, "Good Kali," "Well-fed Kali," "Pretty Kali," "Keep going, Kali."

About a mile downstream, we encountered an old-growth tree with a long fat trunk lying across a narrow and even more dangerously churning part of the stream. The fallen tree had been torn from its roots by the floodwaters. Kali jumped up onto the tree trunk and was quickly across. As soon as she got to the other bank, she let out one long *puar*. Two cubs emerged from the woods and rubbed up against her. The ghost of the mountain looked back once more before she disappeared, with her brood, into the woods. I was strangely sad to see Kali go.

"Goodbye, Kali," M and I intoned at the same time.

The agile cat with its claws and low center of gravity, not to mention its athletic ability, instincts, and practice, had made the crossing look easy. However, upon closer inspection, the crossing didn't look easy at all. Our bridge was a slick, uneven plank covered in moss and broken limbs, about twenty feet across and only a couple feet above the raging waters that were rising fast in a race with the setting sun.

The light, in brilliant waves of yellow, orange, and red, rolled both toward and away from us over the jagged mountain peaks that formed the now jeweled crown of the earth. M saw the spectacular light show too and smiled a sunset at me.

There was little time to think, as the last waves of light were retreating behind the mountains. We put on our own sets of claws, which made us catlike for the scurry. Boy pulled a rope from his pack; he must have been carrying fifty pounds to my twenty-pound load. He gave me one end of the rope to hold and explained the plan. He crossed, as easily as Kali, with one end of the rope in his hand and the other held by me on the near bank.

Chivalry still ruled under duress in the wilderness, though in a pure egalitarian world, I, as the weakest camper, should have followed next. M refused my offer to carry her walking stick and pack, but she knew there was no time to argue about who would go next, and with the rope guide held securely by Boy and me, she started across. Her yoga-trained body held each step, and the rope, connecting the three of us, served as an unnecessary safety cord as she too made the crossing look easy.

It was only a few minutes since Kali had crossed, but the dark side of dusk was coming on fast, making it harder to see the log, and the waters were still rising and now sometimes splashing over the tree trunk.

I fastened the rope firmly around my waist, as Boy had instructed. I knew thought was my enemy, so I banished the image of my body flailing in the fierce, frigid water, a bobber smashing against rocks. I was worried about humiliation in front of my love when I should have feared death. My experience at the lake, however, had made me less fearful of death with the realization that the animating force in each of us—our essence, the God in us—can't die. One of Juno's catchphrases repeated in my mind: Love is the absence of fear.

I shut down all thought.

I opened my mind again, a minute later, when I was safely across. I insisted on a group hug. I held Boy by the shoulders and said, "Boy, I love you."

He smiled shyly and said, "I love you both too."

By the time the rope and claws were packed, we were in total darkness and now well off the path. And we weren't home yet. As bravely as the words would allow, I asked, "Are we lost?"

Boy said, "No worries. I can get us back to the Deeksha from here."

M said, "Any true hiker knows you have to get lost before you can know the joy of being found."

I chose to interpret her words as a metaphor.

Boy produced the promised headlamps, and we set off upstream. Somehow the combination of knowing you weren't going to die soon and that you were in love and were loved by the one you loved could make even the most challenging situation joyful. As our strobes danced ahead of us and onto the garden floor of the forest, M and I quickly learned not to look at each other. Our first attempt at eye gazing had left us momentarily blinded by our love's light. A rookie mistake. We laughed as we regained our sight. From then on we kept our eyes and lights straight ahead and focused our hearts on each other.

The dark of nighttime made the prior thirteen hours of trekking in daylight register as one hike and this night hike a second one—a new start, with new body, fresh legs, and elated mind. The Deeksha, a fire, food, and the rest of the family were not that far away. With each step, love rose up to meet me, and halfway home was getting shorter.

Boy returned us to the path by following the floodwaters back to where we had lost the trail on the other bank. A simple navigational trick, but I felt grateful Boy was there and had mentally marked the spot of the path, now impossible to discern in the dark.

As we approached the Deeksha, the fire, Burning Man bright, greeted us from the garden. In celebration of the last night at the Deeksha, the fire had been returned to its full bonfire glory. Juno and the twins welcomed us with hugs and a total absence of concern.

YaLan's and Astri's welcoming smiles were all-knowing, blending innocence with a keen instinct for love. No one mentioned the ToE.

M and I used Juno's shower—in sequence, not together—before changing for dinner. It was the first time I'd used a real shower since the earthquake. And it was the best shower ever. I felt baptized, forgiven, and ready for love.

The family shared a last supper. Juno's dishes were always a recipe of delight for the senses and the soul, but that night—after hiking for over twelve hours, experiencing Big Love, and hearing M's *I love you*—it simply was the best meal ever.

I had taken pictures of each poetic prayer flag. With our tea by the fire, M and I performed our duets of "Golden Rabbit" and "The Gift," pretending to be imaginary flagpoles and twirling around one another.

When we finished our dance, I said, "Prayers do come true."

M and I then told the family of the oneness and the bliss we experienced that day.

Juno clapped her hands. "So wonderful. You had miraculous moments of grace. Big Love is not a memory, so don't now start looking to recreate that experience. Big Love is always present in your radiant awareness, through which all experience parades. We are not special. We all are that radiant loving awareness."

I said, "Sounds like constant creation. I'll have to find that."

"Yes and no." She smiled as she clarified, "We *are* that."

Boy presented the tale of our adventures; the hike had opened his throat chakra. His telling of hiking with Kali to find her cubs and the story of the Scotsman and his bagpipes already sounded like campfire stories.

When he concluded the story of the bagpipes playing in the valley, Astri said to YaLan, "Our yogi? It fits his reported ability to take on any human form!"

YaLan's eyes lit up too. "And to play any musical instrument! Maybe! Mother, what do you think?"

Juno smiled and said, "There was a man playing bagpipes. Our yogi's only powers that I have seen are absolute Truth and unconditional love, and that is more than enough."

The twins' suggestion was a magic too far-fetched for me to believe, but I hadn't yet met their yogi.

I said to M, "If Boy and you weren't there, you'd swear I made it all up."

M teased, "We know your tiny Gypsies and queen are real too. To you."

Boy then made me the hero of the raging stream for crossing last, a kindness, since everyone knew he was the hero. For me, everything danced in clarity and mystery, as it did for runners after a marathon and children with a big secret. Mine was a secret shared by Boy, Juno, the twins, M, and the entire universe.

I whispered in M's ear, "You really should believe me. I will find you the ToE, my love."

She smiled in her we-will-see sort of way and spoke with the clarity of her freshly illuminated mind. "Not our love but Big Love."

Between the bliss of transcendence by the lake and M's declaration of love, I wasn't my old self; my every thought was of love. I envisioned us finding the ToE and reading its vows to consummate our one big God-given love.

Just one more night in Juno's room with M hovering above me in the bed. My none-too-subtle short story for that last night was stolen from the pages of the master, Gabriel García Márquez's *Love in the Time of Cholera* when decades of unrequited love were finally rewarded. After that, I didn't sleep, dreaming of what would follow now that love had found me.

CHAPTER 56

THE FOLLOWING MORNING, my middle-aged legs were sore, but my age-less spirit remained elated. I had lain in bed primed and awake for what seemed the entire night and was waiting for Juno to arise for her morning meditation.

Juno hadn't slept more than a couple hours a night since the earth-quake. She was always the first up for an hour of silent prayer and meditation in front of the shrine alcove in her room. Her practice—sit-ting peacefully still in the dark as the dawn was being born—allowed me to begin my own day with a humming heart.

On this last morning in Xanadu, not being able to sleep in any event, I joined her. She didn't say a word but pulled out another meditation cushion from the basket, as if I was expected. As we settled side by side, my mind followed her mind into a state of peaceful surrender. I didn't know if it was Juno's energy being transmitted, but I was left with the impression of a great insight flowing from her to me. A silent blessing of the love that M and I found on the mountain and which now con-nected our hearts.

In no time it was six and time for morning yoga. My mind and body were refreshed and ready for the day. Even my legs were limber and ready to go.

While I listened to the vibrating bowls at that last morning yoga session, the insights from my meditation with Juno started to crystalize.

M had declared her love for me, much like she'd declared her love for Juno. It was Big Love we'd found on the mountain, and that made all the difference, but it wasn't to be possessed. It flowed through us in constant creation and wasn't the end but a constant beginning.

Our dream to discover the Truth by finding the ToE and releasing it into the world was soon to be or not to be. It had to be—without question. Otherwise, M would keep searching on her own, determined not to allow the Guru to find it first, and we wouldn't be able to consummate our love. Celibacy had served its purpose and led me to the mountain peak, but I wasn't ready to take its vow.

After yoga, the remaining guests came to say individual goodbyes to Juno, M, and me. We hugged each, the final lesson being life moves on. It was good—for them and for the Deeksha—that the German trekker singers were packed to leave that day too. Oh, Sweet Caroline, they smelled of teen spirit, that pungent mix of old fish, stale beer, hashish, and not washing after sex.

Juno's jeep was a fast UTV, a Polaris Ranger, with roll bars for a roof and a full tank thanks to Boy. It was quickly packed for her month of solitude in the jungle. The Deeksha was set for the absence of its fairy queen.

As I said goodbye to Boy, my eyes once again met his and held, an experience we'd shared many times over the last couple of weeks and once over the barrel of a gun. The love we'd shared on the mountain made him forever family. Forever a friend. Heterosexual shackles be damned, Boy was a beautiful man whom I loved.

YaLan and Astri were crying, so M cried too. I started to cry, and then Boy joined the family cry. Strange that now the floodgates had opened, the tears flowed so freely, cleansing my soul. Juno was joyful and smiled at the rest of us. I was overwhelmed by the wonder of my Deeksha family and the love that had found me in their Deeksha home. *Goodbye, Xanadu.*

YaLan touched foreheads with M. "Teacher, we'll miss your course on consciousness, but thank you for all your blessings and lessons."

M said, "You and Astri are welcome to come to Columbia and attend my course and live with me. I'll write, explaining a new college I plan to start soon. We could use some brilliant yoga teachers there if Juno could spare you. Thank you all for the Big Love—the nature of universal consciousness—that we found here."

"Yes, let us all focus on Big Love," Juno said. "And let's go meet my yogi."

Using all my literary flair, I added, "Big Love, let's go!"

CHAPTER 57

M AND I INSISTED WE GO to Juno's sanctuary to help her unpack and prepare for her retreat before heading on to Yogi Mangku's nearby compound. As we started driving out of the Deeksha entrance, I wondered how different Juno's sanctuary would be from my Chelsea tower library of books in the big city and how different I would be upon my return. My past was another life and a fading dream.

The ToE quest could wait one more hour now that its end—I hoped—was so near. But we were curious to see Juno's mountain-jungle retreat, where the ToE had been revealed to Dylan. M and I knew this was a place Juno didn't share, except perhaps with those who knew Big Love. We were on a pilgrimage to a holy site.

There were sixteen hours until our midnight flight home. August was arriving after a long, wonderful, and tragic month of July. And with me in my new state of miracle readiness, August held all the promise of the unknown. So much potential turned ever faster in the vortex—discovering a theory of everything, its release, love's consummation, and a novel to finish. Rooted in love, I had no fear.

Boy had said it was an hour-and-a-half drive to the tiny village of Badhrahni, but it would take Juno only an hour to traverse the rough and mostly unpaved mountain roads, which were unusually *uncon-gested* with all the tourists gone. She drove like a race car driver, a Chinese cowgirl with a fast horse—she was born to ride. Given her skill and dexterity, our ride was more sporting than dangerous. An incongruous twist for this ethereal being of peace was that she was so mercurial too.

She was free, celebrating release from her responsibility for the

333 refugees. My fear reflex was turned off, supplanted by the thrill of speeding with the wonderful M and magical Juno into the remote wilderness of Nepal.

I was seated in the back middle, without my seat belt on, so I could lean forward between the front bucket seats. I was a child who didn't want to miss a moment as the exhilarating mountain scenery flew by.

I had the passing thought my novel should include a car crash but dismissed it as too pedestrian and dark.

Juno, with her windblown hair highlighting that holy, divine face, spoke of Dylan for the first time since the earthquake. "Although Dylan's body is ash, although there is only silence and space, I feel his presence unchanged and even more so now. He is there in the source of love. He is still here as the beloved."

That was the first time I could remember Juno becoming self-conscious, as if she'd remembered some extremely intimate event.

She laughed, releasing us from the earnest silence. We joined in, all of us laughing at nothing in particular other than the shared joy of life.

We sailed through deserted roads and into the mountain-jungle. I didn't know how this adventure would end and whether it was already determined or could be cocreated by acts of free will. M believed with all her heart in the pursuit of the theory of constant creation as the ultimate goal and destiny of mankind. Destiny that required it be found not too soon and not too late.

I welcomed the unknown as we twisted along the mountain roads, traveling at the speed of light. I prayed, with all the certitude of Big Love, that now was the time.

As Juno's race car slowed to turn onto a long, narrow dirt path, a palpable calm came over her. After a quarter mile, a small secluded temple appeared ahead, a very private property without trespassing signs posted or any demands to keep out. Like Kali's, this lair was protected by Lord Vishnu and nestled in his jungle nature. A fitting birthplace for the ToE.

The cottage temple was another study of unique architectural design, a beautiful face with large golden wood doors for a nose and large windows for eyes. The round temple sat within rings of nature fanning out from its center. A smaller circle of space sat like a white beret on top, and that pearl was capped by an elegant dark red Gaudí-like tower that twisted up, like Juno's wand, until it touched its final point and disappeared. Two white concentric stone circles flowed like gem pools from that maroon funnel, channeling the energy out of the blue sky.

The artistic architecture and craftsmanship could never be replicated in another setting, and its impact on my emotions was impossible to describe. This was Juno expressed in architecture, a delicate yet strong lotus temple of nature fit for a fairy queen. This was both the manger of Bethlehem and the bodhi tree of Big Love.

Juno opened the large wooden doors without a key, as if they knew her touch. They opened into a large circular artist's studio awash in light from the large windows.

And in the center of that studio, in that light, stood Dylan.

In a room of paintings, my eyes—the eyes of us all—were immediately drawn to a large painting of Dylan standing in front of a waterfall. The lush jungle waterfall cascaded down a mountain crevasse, bursting into wild jungle flowers in a splashing pool of flora around the man. Set upon a large easel, the investment banker had become a life-size Rousseau or Gaugin. The lights and colors of the painting emanated from him and encircled him in nature. Although modern, it was also impressionistic, and somehow Asian in its use of colors and lines in the romantic and natural mountain setting.

My reaction was the same as on first seeing the snow leopard by the raging stream: The power of art in nature—or here, nature in art—stopped my mind. I was overcome with a sense of Dylan's presence. *You were with me then—you are with me now—always will be.*

As awed as I was by the beauty and power of the painting, Juno was moved to tears.

We approached the painting slowly, as if it were the great and powerful Wizard of Oz. I half expected Dylan to step out from the canvas and join us.

Standing in front of the painting, Juno composed herself and said, "I was inspired to leave the Deeksha one afternoon, to come here to this sanctuary. It was a strange compulsion. Listening to one of my favorite songs for the guzheng, a cup of tea at my side and wondering why I was here, I was moved to dance. As I did, I felt Dylan's presence. He whispered, 'You are here to paint. But let us please finish our beautiful dance.' He then fell silent, but his presence remained, and it is still here.

"Only at sunset did I realize fully why I was here, when a completed painting came into my mind's eye exactly as you see it now. In joyful mania, I painted, inspired by the vivid image. It was a labor of love. I lost myself in a dream of a rainbow as a showering beam of light passed slowly through the canvas, leaving this painting behind."

Juno paused for a long time while we stood communing with Dylan through the painting. I was about to reach for M's hand, but I also wanted to hold Juno's hand, and yet I didn't dare reach for either. I couldn't bear to hold both those hands in this, her sacred space, with Dylan watching me. I thought I would disappear into the infinite if I did.

So my hands remained empty, and I started rubbing my face. That reflexive gesture prompted Juno to continue her story.

"At the time it was strange to me. I'm not the sentimental type, but I was acting sentimental. Dylan had come and gone many times. He had just left for New York. But I followed my heart and did as the universe swayed me to do. The painting was completed by the second morning, and I left the sanctuary to return to the Deeksha from an absence I had not planned.

"I learned only later, in a letter from Grace, that I painted around the time of Dylan's death. This is my first time seeing the portrait since I left it here. With his death and the earthquake, I didn't think of it again until driving here and speaking of him."

Dylan's portrait was a wonderful presence, and surrounded by other impressionistic landscapes, it set a calming and joyful mood for the room. The other paintings were exquisitely balanced around Dylan and the waterfall, though they'd been painted by Juno before the portrait. Like everything in her world, perfectly curated.

Juno wouldn't be alone in her sanctuary after all.

I recognized Juno's painting style from the art I had become so familiar with at the Deeksha. I'd assumed the paintings were from some local or international artist; none were signed. I'd forgotten to inquire about the artist's name. There had been so much at the Deeksha out of the norm, shaken by the earth, that only the essential questions of survival and spirit had been asked.

At the Deeksha, the art, design, people, and ceremonies—collectively, the energy—had inspired the community of refugees to heal. There was something of the same energy here in the sanctuary, but it was private and personal, more hushed and focused.

The large circular studio had a comfortable kitchen and a sitting area, and only two other rooms. One was a large oasis bathroom with a waterfall shower and large marble tub and sinks. However, this impressive functional space was all prelude to the upper chamber—the pearl with the spiraling tower we had seen from outside.

Two rich crimson silk curtains covered the entrance to this holy place, extending down and out like a reverse train on a gown. The pair of tapestry lips draped into the exact center of the room behind the painting of Dylan.

As we followed Juno, the red silk provided a soft tactile passage, a full body kiss as we slipped past them into the hidden space behind. There we found a circular marble stairway, each step inlaid with lapis lazuli, leading to a portal that provided the light needed to ascend. Only nine steps up to Juno's inner sanctum. With each step, my breath deepened and more peace enveloped me. We emerged, at the top, into the nexus of Juno's energy and space of creation.

This private nest was a mesmerizing spiritual stage, with one small bed draped in luscious white linens and a rich burgundy comforter, and two meditation cushions on the floor. The space was almost an altar, but more personal—delicate and more artistically feminine than religious. Juno stood in the center of this room and its vortex of the spiritual and the artistic.

The Deeksha, the art studio sanctuary, and this inner sanctum were the nautilus chambers of Juno's heart. In each spiral, Juno's heart and soul became more clearly manifest. Each chamber of her creation reflected the universe within her more deeply.

I imagined she rarely shared this space, the queen bee's castle keep. With its pure energy, any thought but love would be out of place. I felt like an intruder being forgiven for my trespass and transformed into an anointed one. And in that welcoming absolution, my mind became totally settled into the peace of Juno's inner space.

The final remarkable architectural touch was the absence of windows. In the center, however, was the twisting tower that rose over twenty feet to a large round skylight, which provided a shower of light during the day and became a planetarium telescope at night.

Under the gyre's light, Juno was transformed into a young, innocent, fearless, and radiant girl. She was a chameleon in her ability to look different in ever-changing settings and lights. Her eyes were those of an innocent child at dawn, an awakened Buddha during the day, a wild-eyed poet at twilight, and an angel at night. Here in her inner sanctum, she was all incarnations at once. And I was undone.

Juno spoke from the silence, her eyes changing colors with the light.

"It was here where Dylan and I sat in meditation, at sunset, in the lovely shifting glow from the slanted twilight rays above. As we meditated together, I was visited by a voice, a voice that came through me in waves of poetry far more celestial than what I might have thought possible in my second tongue. As I sang in a trance, Dylan listened in rapt attention. Our eyes were on each other; we were transfixed. It seemed the words came from him but through my lips. Boundaries fell and borders did not exist—in that love—limitless.

"We sat in silent mediation for a long time, until a full moon directly above us shone down in benediction and atonement. It was the rapture of revelation." She paused with prayer hands to her heart and the eyes of a magi.

"Dylan told me afterward that as we glowed in the hum of the moonlight, he'd been blessed with a simple truth and that he was charged with that truth. A truth that would bring science in line with the universal spiritual truth. A theory of everything. From that point on, he was filled with passion and worked joyfully on the theory. That evening the theory of constant creation was born in the light of Big Love."

M and I were speechless. M looked again as she had upon the mountaintop—like Christ played by Brigitte Bardot bathed in white light. Hearing other's experiences with the ineffable confirmed the magic of the mystery for us, reminding us of our own embrace by oneness.

Juno broke the spell by laughing at herself. There was nothing left to say. With extreme gratitude, we thanked Juno for sharing the vision with bows, a chorused namaste, and smiles from the heart.

Then we reversed our steps and returned to the art studio, reborn, emerging through the red silk lips. I turned and looked into Juno's eyes. In those turquoise whirlpools I saw the full beauty of her nature. A nature felt by everyone and everything her gaze lit upon.

We each said our goodbyes to Dylan. *All the people to be trusted still love you.*

Juno, eyes dancing, said, "Yogi Mangku awaits. Time to go!"

I heard M think, *And find the ToE!*

CHAPTER 58

M WAS SMILING AT ME, thrilled to finally be on the way to see Yogi Mangku. It was the same smile she'd always had, but now I saw her love behind it—the love that had always been there. I just couldn't see the holy light until my heart was opened by Big Love. Our eyes met, our gazes dancing between us in anticipation. We were in love and on the verge of fulfilling our quest. I prayed from the heart that we would find the ToE in this final stop on our search. I couldn't imagine where else it might be and believed it must be found there.

Unless it was incinerated in the inferno with your photographic memory?

We quickly unpacked Juno's provisions, and then she drove us slowly, in serenity, to meet Yogi Mangku. His "compound" was only ten miles away on a long winding dirt road lined with green foliage. The slow-motion scenery was dramatic: a lush green jungle covered in moss, with spirited streaks of sunlight angling through the green dew. Wildlife and fairies hid behind each tree, an unbroken column of banyans that stretched for miles and led to a greenish-blue lake. In the distance, a dramatic waterfall cascaded down, feeding the forest creatures' big swimming hole. I imagined the outlaw Robin Hood and his Lady Marian slipping in for a naughty swim.

Near this jungle lake we stopped at the yogi's compound gate. Juno rang the bell, a cowbell, which surprisingly sounded like a crisp tingsha cymbal. It awoke the surrounding jungle, scattering birds from their nests and fairies from their hiding places.

The yogi, summoned by the vibrational tone, greeted us wholeheartedly. "I've been expecting you!"

I didn't know what I'd been expecting. Probably not this powerful man dressed in only a loincloth. Though imposing and nearly naked, he immediately put us at ease. He gave Juno and then M and me hugs of great warmth and abundant skin. He wasn't overweight but large, with a strong, stout belly. Despite his age, which must have been over eighty, his skin was smooth like that of a child, and his eyes sparkled. His commanding physical presence had me imagining him as a jolly living Buddha or a panda at play in his jungle compound.

He and Juno touched foreheads in a joyful family reunion, hands lightly clasping each other's temples, meeting eye to eye. My heart smiled at seeing them together.

Yogi Mangku then took M by the hand and draped his arm around my shoulders, leading us into his compound. His presence and spiritual scent had the same calming effect on me that Juno's presence did, even though we had just met.

The place we hoped would lead to the consummation of our quest was a modest square space of ancient Asian architecture. One large interior room for receiving visitors also served as a yoga and meditation hall. That room had two large sliding doors that opened onto a balcony, providing an unimpeded view of the lake below. The other rooms were his sleeping quarters and a small study. There was an outhouse and a rainwater shower a short distance down the hill and closer to the lake. The three main rooms, with the gate and tall stone-wall entrance, squared off the compound's courtyard.

As a man of letters, I'd never considered myself a spiritual man, though my old concepts of self had altered radically since meeting M and arriving in Kathmandu. My one prerequisite for a true spiritual teacher and a genius writer was that they had to be dead. But now—setting Queen Mab aside—I was open to spiritual teachers being alive and real. Juno certainly was a transcendent woman; I imagined the yogi was equally or more gifted, although I couldn't imagine anyone more accomplished than Juno.

The two of them together produced a powerful union of spirits, a unity of yin and yang, whose potent currents had me buzzing like a fluorescent tube. I saw M in that same radiant light.

Yogi Mangku served us tea in the yoga studio. He understood we were friends of Dylan's without being told. I wondered how he had known to expect us and how he knew Dylan was dead, since he had no means of electronic communication or phone. He picked his English words carefully in a blessing and benediction as he slowly poured the tea.

"Though we may miss your funny words and lovely smile, we do not miss your spirit, which remains with us undiminished. Dylan, with your friends all here, there is only love. We are grateful for your presence and call upon your guidance."

He still speaks to you too, old friend.

The yogi caught my eye and bowed his head, as if agreeing with my Dylan-chattering mind. I wondered if, like Queen Mab, he would respond directly to my thoughts.

He said, "I know you are wanting to know about Dylan. He and I spent the last year in joyful practice, few words, and much laughter. He did not want his body to die but was prepared to leave it." He sipped his tea, and I followed his lead. It was very good tea.

He said, "Dylan, Juno, and I communicate without words even when apart. Fortunate, as my English is not so good. You see."

I asked naively, "Is this communication through a sort of telepathy?"

"I do not know how such things are done." He offered a wide, joyful grin.

To Juno, he said, "I've been sending prayers of protection for you. Some days after the earthquake, three dark Chinese men visited here. They wanted writings from Dylan and demanded to search my home. My computer and phone. I told them I do not read English and have no computer or phone. Since they were brutish and would search anyway, I told them to please look around. They said I would be beaten if I lied. I told them that would be no problem. I meant the lie, but I think they thought the beating. The one with most fancy military dress and medals wore a gun that he kept gripping at his side to make sure I didn't miss it strapped there. I got the sense he would like to use it."

I knew Juno and M were thinking *the general*, as I was, but none of us spoke.

"I do not meet men like that, and I found it interesting and was sad for them. They were so dark and fearful in their thoughts, so narrow, leaving no room for the love hidden in their closed hearts. They searched two hours, even opening cushions and bedding. And the outhouse and the shower. Cursing me. 'You have taken a vow of honesty! You cannot lie! Where is it, you old fossil?' I didn't know what a fossil is, but one of my students explained later. They must have been angry geologists, he told me."

My laugh got him laughing. He reached into a bowl by his side and pulled out two beaded necklaces with a lovely tassel hanging from each. He got up, handing one to M and one to me, saying, "A blessed mala of one hundred and eight beads for prayers and to count your mantra." He whispered in my ear, "I am infinite consciousness." And then he whispered in M's ear. We put our gifts around our necks and namasted in gratitude. I loved my new necklace. *I am infinite consciousness.*

I thought of M's jingle-jangle bracelet that rested in my writer's bag. Two treasures for a man who never had jewelry before, not even a watch.

"Now, back to my funny meeting with the angry Chinese geologists." He winked at our shared joke, which I didn't know if he understood. "They seized papers and a book but were not satisfied. They were not convinced there was no computer or small phone here and thought I must be hiding them. They really wanted Dylan's theory and were sure I had it hidden somewhere. And they also had an advanced practice to teach me in witnessing my own death."

My heart swelled, and either I followed M or she followed me as we both put our left hand over our mala's center and pressed the fragrant tassel against our chests.

"They marched me to the lake. Such a lovely day. The two younger men held me to a fallen tree trunk with my head hanging down, faceup. The senior man with the gun used my bucket to fill from the lake and placed a towel over my face, demanding again my computer and phone. 'Ask me,' I said. 'I cannot lie. I told you I don't have a computer or phone.'

"Then I am drowning. I see an image of a prior life, sinking at sea after a shipwreck. Waves of terror flowing over me. And then peace, floating in a most peculiar way."

My hand and the mala tassel were all that held my heart in place, now breaking for this man who suffered such cruelty.

He continued, "Then my head jerked up, still in the dark, and they demanded, 'Where is the computer? Where is the phone?' When I said, 'I don't have any,' they replied with the wet towel to my face. They stopped, waiting for me to speak. I think they thought I would at least lie.

"Their work gave me time to see this as a practice death. The water came, and I watched the panic beside me, aware but not afraid of the mind's reaction to my lungs taking water and gasping for breath.

"Again my head was jerked up to the same question and same answer. After the second drowning under the waterfall, there was a cold steel ring on my wet chest and the cock of a gun. The same demand was made as I remained silent and prepared to leave my body without regret." He paused, smiling upward like a saint to his god. "Ahhh, to be welcomed home into divine love. Then the shot went off, a bang of death, but instead of Nirvana blazing into my chest, they put me back under the waterfall a third time.

"Lifting my head, either they saw it was ceasing to have effect or they believed me. They left cursing me, my ears still ringing. I think they had shot the earth next to my head, though it may have been the sky. All that for some papers and a small book from Dylan's room they had already taken. Giving thanks, I walked into the lake, where I floated with my face to the sun, breathing the holy air. What a practice that was."

Finally releasing our hands from our hearts, M and I shared bittersweet tears for the unrelenting evil of evil men.

He lightly pressed one hand to M's head and then to his own heart. "They left no mark on me."

M wiped the tears from her face. Juno hugged Yogi Mangku, and then, eyes locked, the two yogis once again laid their hands on each other's heads. Even though I wasn't touching either of them, I felt the power of their connection as it filled the space around us. And even after that moment of healing, I still felt horrible that such a kind old sage could be treated so heartlessly.

"I'm so sorry," I said.

"No sorries," he said. "Though drowning is not a yoga practice I suggest for any except the particularly adept. I've practiced many years and have long ago accepted my body's death. I am actually grateful to see I was ready."

I took one of M's hands and squeezed it between mine. "I'm so sor—" She held a finger to her lips to hush me, but I said, "I promised you."

"We'll still find it, even if I need to rediscover it myself. I mean with you, of course."

The yogi smiled at the lovers' sidebar.

Juno said to him, "I apologize for my countrymen. The danger is passed now. I was lacking clarity not to see you might have been disturbed."

"I may be responsible," I said, rubbing my face. "They must have found your name when they hacked my computer. Dylan left a list of people to be trusted, and you were on it. We were—*are*—also looking for a piece of writing by Dylan, what he called a theory of everything. Do you know anything about it? Do you think that might be the papers the Chinese took?"

"Yes," the yogi replied, "Dylan explained the theory to me. It was so simple, 'the truth expressed in scientific words.' He meditated, and then full of joy from cocreating with God, he wrote out the theory." He shook his head. "I think the papers the Chinese took were poems Dylan was writing, left on his desk."

"We were so sure we'd find the theory here," I said. "And although it doesn't sound like it, perhaps the Chinese found what we've been searching for."

The yogi said, "Don't give up hope. They did not find what they looked for without guidance and with closed hearts. You may still."

He tipped his head toward M. "So, lovely lady, you are also a scientist?"

"Yes, a quantum cosmologist; how did you guess?"

He didn't reveal his source but engaged M in an animated discussion of quantum physics. M elicited what the yogi knew of the ToE, and they went into a long, naturally flowing discussion of consciousness, the quantum reality, and spiritual oneness. Surprisingly, the yogi was familiar with the concepts of quantum physics, which he probably picked up from Dylan. He asked insightful questions in his broken English as he sat cross-legged and nearly naked—a wise old child. M looked like a radiant child too, and they exchanged roles as teacher and student each time they spoke. Juno and I were content listening to the back-and-forth flow. M hadn't given way to desolation. She was clearly enjoying the moments in the yogi's company and their lively discussion.

"Where did Dylan stay while studying with you?" M asked. "We'd hoped to find a copy of the ToE there, but even if a further search is pointless, we'd still like to see the room."

She was praying that the yogi's torturers had missed something. I was too, though I was finding that Big Love provided a perspective that transformed failure into a lesson. Juno had cautioned we mustn't demand the time or way to realize our dreams. I'd learned my lesson. My impatience for M's love had served no purpose other than to delay its expression. And I still believed we'd find the ToE that the general had failed, through waterboarding, to find.

The yogi led us to the third small room of the spiritual compound. As he opened the door, I experienced a palpable sense of Dylan in the air and ambiance. A chamber bathed in late-afternoon mountain light, it looked like Van Gogh's colorful bedroom with its wooden chair and simple desk and single large window onto the lake. The room was comfortable, with Asian tapestries on the walls and a small wooden bed. Above the desk was a large bookshelf, books haphazardly lying on the shelves as if they were always snatched and replaced in excitement. Or perhaps they'd been shaken by the earthquake miles away.

M and I studied the books to see if the ToE was in or among them.

The yogi said, "The Chinese could not read the books, but they shook every book and left them like that."

After surveying the books, Juno asked, "Was the book the Chinese took little and red?"

"Yes."

"That's one mystery solved. I gave Dylan my vintage copy of Mao's little red book, a rare edition signed by Mao. My uncle gave it to me as a child. I knew that Dylan—like you, Sean—liked books. It's not here. Quite valuable, yes, but not precious like his poetry or the theory they may have taken."

I tried to imagine the value of that autographed little red book that was so easily given by Juno and then lost. Not as taboo as a *Mein Kampf* signed by Hitler, or as holy and miraculous as a bible signed by Jesus, or as much to my liking as a *Ulysses* signed by Joyce, or as personal as a young woman's diary signed by me. Mi Na! Her name came back to me. A miracle that I remembered.

Juno and her yogi stepped out, leaving M and me to continue our search of Dylan's bookshelf. We exchanged a sad look as their uplifting energy left the room. We turned to the remaining volumes, books of science, spirit, and poetry. The science books ranged in topic from the big bang to string theory and quantum physics: *Feynman's Lectures on Physics*, *The Age of Entanglement*, *Black Holes*, and *A Briefer History of Time*. All books well-known to M.

I pulled down one science book—a picture of a grinning elf statue on its cover—from my own past. Praying that my fiction had come true again, I opened the book, expecting to find the ToE folded into its pages.

No ToE.

But there were more books to check.

The spiritual texts included the *Upanishads*, *Bhagavad Gita*, *Autobiography of a Yogi*, and *The Power of Now*. *A Course in Miracles* was ironically there too, with an inscription by Grace. *To my father, who taught me the miracle of life.*

No ToE.

And finally there was an abundance of poetry books. *Follow the poetry* . . .

No ToE. No ToE. And so it went, poetry book by poetry book, M and me in somber chant and response. With each refrain, the reality that the ToE was lost sank deeper into our hearts. This end I hadn't imagined—couldn't have imagined—since we had found our love on the mountaintop. How could we fail to find the theory after finding Big Love, after declaring our love for each other, after surviving an earthquake and a homicidal CIA agent and overcoming a powerful Chinese general and his crazed subordinate? How could we fail? No, how could *I* fail?

When the final book was shaken and the room had no other hiding places, I retreated to the window that overlooked the lake, where another torture in pursuit of the theory had been inflicted on the most innocent of men. I didn't want M to see my face or read my thoughts. Despite all my learning, I remained unworthy of love. I'd broken my promise and failed in our quest.

I had nothing left to offer. I was a middle-aged man, getting older, who would return to comfortably reading the same books again and again in his book sanctuary. I was fit only for grading papers and correcting the musings of uninterested students on the big ideas of bigger men, writers with conviction who had accomplished their goals.

James dying by firing squad after penning his last love letter? What rubbish.

My body was rigid and shaking uncontrollably, imploding from within. All the planning and misgivings and drama had led to an anticlimactic end—no treasure found, no triumphant hero hoisting the theory to end all theories over his head. No outrageous joy and shared sense of accomplishment for a quest hard won. No ecstasy. I was only a Don Quixote, beaten and battered in the end.

Needing to escape the loss of my beautiful delusion, I opened the window in front of me, prepared to climb out and run. A fresh lake breeze smacked my cheeks, startling me.

I felt a presence bracing me, holding me back. *Dylan*, I imagined in disbelief. I expected that he might slap me Bogart-style for my unseemly hysteria and failure to accept my fate. Instead, he simply said, *Turn around.*

M was slumped on the bed, her sad eyes swimming with pain. He was right; there was a bigger loss if I wanted loss.

Reading M's tearful eyes, I offered her my own sad smile and tears. Then I offered my arms. When I wrapped myself tight around her, she started sobbing, and in those ebbs and swells, our hearts were one. I comforted her by reminding her of my and Dylan's lifelong quest to find Shakespeare's lost work of *Cardenio*, and how a quest was never done. I reminded her that the Holy Grail and Maltese Falcon were never found.

Through the easing sobs she managed to say, "And they never gave up?"

"And they never gave up," I echoed.

"And I think . . . they think . . . they finally found the . . . the Holy Grail . . . just a few years ago." She let one last sob pass into a laugh of resignation.

I pulled back for our tearful eyes to meet. Her face was wet, but she was smiling. The joy of defeat. The powerful acceptance of all—the good, the painful, the everything—that comes with Big Love.

Dylan was smiling at me as though our quest, like all of life, was one wry joke, with meaning lying just beyond our grasp or available only in small glimpses of grace like the ones we'd experienced in the mountains. I didn't understand how, but even a touch of Big Love made despair impossible. That knowledge left me equal parts frustrated and infected by Dylan's good humor. I took Pollyannaish comfort in the fact that the ToE would remain M's and my *Cardenio*, even more magical and compelling in its loss and absence than in its discovery. We would always believe with all our hearts that someday the theory would be found.

Juno and the yogi returned from the other room. M looked resolute and bright, so I put on a brave face too, though our puffy eyes remained telltales of our moments of doubt and fear.

Juno pointed to a picture on the desk—Grace and Dylan on a mountain peak. "Boy took that picture, and Dylan loved it."

I recognized the picture as the one hanging above the mantel in Natalie and Dylan's town house, and the mountain as the one where M was kissed by Dylan's sonnet and where she found Big Love.

Also on the desk were an Asian urn and a Buddha. The urn was painted with busy bees swarming the porcelain hive. I picked it up, and holding it out at arm's length, I shook it. But no ashes shifted with the shake. It was an empty vessel.

The yogi said, "That was my gift to Dylan. It is Buddhist practice to contemplate one's own death." He gave us an all-knowing smile, the way sages do.

"Bees. I know I should like bees, but as a young boy, while climbing a tree, I put my hand through a nest on a branch above me and was stung over and over again." I placed the urn down gently and picked up the healing Buddha. My redundant memory of thirty-five years ago held more current pain than the yogi's torture of maybe just a week ago. I felt silly looking into his compassionate eyes.

The small Buddha had a beautiful, serene face. It was an identical bookend to the one Dylan had sent Natalie. I shook the Buddha too, but like the urn it was a sealed and empty statue. The yogi had the same face and peaceful features and might have been the statue's model. The Buddha spoke to me of entanglement and Zeno's paradox but didn't reveal to me the location of the ToE.

The only other personal belongings were meditation cushions and blankets on the bed and singing bowls on the floor. The bowls formed a sacred space with another meditation cushion centered in their arc.

Juno bowed to the bowls. "I taught Dylan to play."

Despite my heart's continued prayers to discover a miracle, my head said that there was no ToE to be found. We had reached the end of our searching.

CHAPTER 59

M TOOK MY HAND IN ONE OF HERS and waved Juno's invisible wand with the other, saying, "We still have Big Love, and we *will* rediscover the ToE eventually based on where I left off with Dylan and what we've found together here in Nepal."

I squeezed her hand. "I will quest with you until the end of time or until we find the ToE and set it free or die trying."

The yogi opened the window even wider than I had, letting in the cool breeze and the music of the lake water licking the shore. Two elegant long-legged herons, red from the sunset, stood sentry to the lake. A symbol of longevity.

I saw the Buddha in our family's yogi, a man who could bear and forgive torture in the very moment he endured it, the way I imagined my wakening might now allow me to handle a traffic jam.

He said, "I see your conflicted energy at not finding our friend's theory in the place of its sweet labor. Let's have a cleansing and uplifting meditation in Dylan's honor here in his space. Please take a cushion seat on the floor. Juno, please sit among the bowls you play so pretty."

We formed a circle on the floor. There, in the evening light, Juno looked like a Monet fairy princess surrounded by lotuses rather than lilies. She mused, "All Dylan's people to be trusted, together in his room."

Brother, your family is looking after me. I just wish you had stayed around to show me your theory and to push the poetry of our literary collaboration. Or at least that you would have left us your photos from your graphic memory before saying goodbye.

Remember, Big Love is not a memory, nor am I, came his cool, cryptic, rhyming reply.

After a long silence, the yogi said, "Please close your eyes when you are ready." He led us, saying, "Letting go . . . inward . . . more and more into your deep heart's core." I breathed rhythmically with the rise and fall of my heart's beat as he repeated, "Relax and love. Relax and love."

His words floated in and out of my consciousness for some time, and then he said, "Everyone, please lie on the floor and place your cushion under your head."

I was a hollow vessel in dead man's pose, liberated from myself in the devastating beauty of a quest unfulfilled, and surrounded by Big Love. My outstretched index finger touched M's, making us one current of energy.

"Here, now," Yogi Mangku said, "we remain in silence in this infinite space and in stillness in this eternal time. Relax and love. Infinite consciousness—eternal love."

As I floated, time was hard to gauge, and a feeling of silent communion entered the group. I repeated, over and over, my new mantra.

An even deeper taste of transcendent bliss came when Juno started playing the singing bowls. I found my energy shifting in tune with the vibrations and transporting me out of myself—up and up—a satellite of love.

The bowls' tones, accompanied by the lapping lake, set the room into one harmonic buzz, our four consciousnesses blending. After one long vibration stretched out, Juno started singing, a mystical songbird. This otherworldly invocation flowed into our circle of magical bliss.

I peered at Juno through half-closed eyes. In a trance, she was channeling the most wonderful poetry I had ever heard, the lines streaming through her, not from her, in waves of complete rhythmic verse. It was her voice but not her words. Each word was ordained for its place, destined by the flow dropping in perfect metrical footfalls. The stanzas broke rhythmically upon a shore, until, as with the very end of a dream, the waves quickened their pace, breaking all poetic form.

"We invited silence / Silence came / Summoning you / The portal is open / Welcoming you / The time and way / You choose / Leave open the door / Behind you."

Bang!

The loud bang, what sounded like the end or the beginning of the world, silenced the singing. We all sat up to find that one of Dylan's books had fallen to the floor from its high bookcase perch. The vibrating bowls must have given it the final nudge from its precarious lodging.

The old book sat cracked open, facedown, right next to me. It had just missed my head. I picked it up, wildly hoping it might contain the ToE in its pages. It was a well-worn hardback edition of Yeats's poetry, no ToE. Yeats was a prolific poet over many years, hence the big bang. The volume was splayed open to "The Lake Isle of Innisfree."

Dylan loved Yeats, always reciting for me all those lines of towers burning and gyres turning in Yeats's poetic vision. Dylan even went so far as to suggest that he was the reincarnation of the Irish bard. He made the boast in jest, I imagined. But I wasn't completely sure he didn't believe his claim. Yeats couldn't spell and may have had dyslexia, so I argued he was more like me. The book's intrusion was a fitting ending to the spell that Yogi Mangku and Juno had cast. Yeats had always loved a good séance.

It was dark outside, and an hour, not minutes, must have passed. It was time to say goodbye and catch our slow train back into Kathmandu, then a taxi to the airport in time for our midnight flight to Dubai. After that, it was on to Athens for M and NYC for me.

I rubbed my face, torn between my heart's calm beat following the yogi's pleasant hypnosis and my mind's insistence that I had failed M in not finding the ToE, my promise broken, my quest unfulfilled.

M pulled my hands down, holding them and studying me. She didn't say a word. Her expression was one of resolution, not condemnation or despair, and her eyes still shone only with love. I was determined not to let fear in and to support her resolve in finding the ToE, however long it might take.

It was sad to leave the yogi, a member of our new family, so soon. We were buoyed when he said, "You will return." Even though it seemed unlikely, I already wanted to return, to explore and hike remote Nepal as M and I had planned.

M said, "I hope we will, and thank you for your kindness and the transcendent meditation and, Juno—wow—what an incredible song."

The yogi handed me the fallen book. "I think Dylan wanted you to have this. Remember all discovery is found in the last place we look."

I couldn't argue with that. I was glad to have a book for the long trip home. I hugged him, and we stepped outside, leaving Juno and the yogi a moment alone.

As we headed to Juno's jeep, M said, "If Dylan was right and there was no first cause, then there would be no last cause, and given eternity, the ToE would come to light eventually. There's a terrible beauty in that, that some of the most sublime works of creation are lost."

"*Cardenio! And those that build them again are gay*," I said, now remembering that the poet was Yeats.

CHAPTER **60**

JUNO ACCOMPANIED US to the small train station only a mile away. She helped us purchase tickets and waited with us on the platform for our train to come.

I asked, "Would you be able to send me the words of your incredible mystical poem?"

"It came through me from the source," she explained. "I am no English poet and can now only recall the sense and feeling of the words. And Dylan's presence."

I regretted not recording every word she had said from the moment we first met, as nothing else could capture their full beauty and tone. Even a recording, absent her presence, wouldn't do justice to her lyrical voice.

As Juno walked beside me for boarding, I realized fully, for the first time, that I loved her and not just her words. Of course I did! I had held her above such a personal connection and intimacy in her Big Love, but Juno taught only love, and love wasn't love if limited. I now realized that Big Love and love of her were all part of one love. Here was the final release—I was worthy of even her love's reflection, and of loving that love in her as she loved mine in me.

I looked into those eyes one last time, and as I was saying, Juno was saying—*we* were saying—*I love you*. Instantaneous communication. Love received in the giving. Juno then put her prayer hands to her heart and said, "Love loves."

"Love!" I pressed prayer hands to my chest. We bowed. We embraced. And in that hug, Big Love was sealed in forever, with me knowing now that it had always been and would always be there. M joined the hug, and tears fell all around us, the dripping currency of love. I had inside me a fountain that tapped into an infinite sea.

Juno gave me and then M a kiss and whispered her refrain, "Nothing real is ever lost."

The train whistle blew an end to our farewells. M and I stepped aboard. As the train pulled away, Juno stood in bowed namaste on the platform, her soft white-cotton dress fluttering in streams of smoke billowed by the wind. She looked like an angel, hovering there with clouds passing around her feet as our train carried her away. She disappeared, leaving only "the illumination of love that animates us."

We sat on wooden seats that rattled in time with the tracks beneath us, on a bumpy, dilapidated train motored by steam and dating back to the British Empire.

We shared the silence and stillness. The glow around us caused the few locals to look with curiosity at the couple so deep in love. M would still love me now and always, even if we never found the ToE—no theory of everything, an end to all the places of possible discovery, and a goodbye to the people to be trusted. But we had been touched by Big Love, the source of constant creation.

I brought my left hand solemnly to the right side of my chest. "I pledge to you my heart." M smiled at the grand gesture of her earnest Lancelot and his dyslexic heart. When she wetted her lips with a lick of her tongue, I wondered if this was the time for our first kiss.

"Perhaps it wasn't the time for it to be found," she said as the moment passed. "No doubt, whenever it *is* discovered, bad men will look to use the source of all creation to destroy creation. Maybe they beat us to it, but if so, it'll come to light. Now the Chinese are looking for it too and are willing to torture an old yogi full of love to find it! I know I shouldn't be mad, but still. Sounds like the general with his gun."

She put her left hand to her lovely right chest, returning my gesture and naturally drawing my attention there. "Sean, my eyes are up here . . . Let's use all of this, all their actions and our disappointment, to make us more determined not to back down in the face of generals with guns and gurus with artificial intelligence."

She hadn't lost any enthusiasm, and our quest was still on. And I was still a man, but learning. Like Sydney Greenstreet and Peter Lorre at the end of *The Maltese Falcon*, we weren't going to give up our quest.

Idly turning pages in my notebook, I tried to recall the words of Juno's sublime song, but only some vague and dim recollection remained of the general import of the vision. I could bring to mind only a few scattered word fragments, brief pieces that lacked the power of the poetry that had come from her lips. I felt like Coleridge trying to remember the full opium dream of "Kubla Khan." In my notebook, I composed a rough approximation of five lines I half remembered.

JUNO'S SONG

(A Short Fragment)
The Almighty eye flashes open
Kai Wu!
The shell of oneself is broken.
And all is new
As one becomes two.

I showed M my poor attempt to bring down to earth Juno's ethereal song. She smiled and then sank warmly onto my shoulder and fell asleep. M's hour nap was the most intimate prolonged physical contact we had shared since our meeting a month and a half ago. The intimacy recalled for me our hand-holding behind the Shangri-La silk screen, our near-naked spa, the hugs before and after bathing each day in the cold river, and her cradling me after I was sort of shot in the face. The rhythm of her breath and the rattle of the train resonated with the vibrating bowl of my heart.

Enjoying the warm body of love pressing against me, I quietly opened the book of Yeats's poetry to read "The Lake Isle of Innisfree." I marveled at its beautiful simplicity, at the magic of hidden things in simple words strung together by a master wordsmith, a mason placing small cobblestone steps that sit inevitably, one after another, on a well-worn path leading somewhere profound. I was a tinker of words, and Yeats was an alchemist. I closed the book and my eyes.

It was nearly ten at night when we got to the Kathmandu train station, where a byzantine market of few travelers and many vendors created a cacophonous hum. Here one must ignore all vendors and smells or gain the attention of all vendors and not be able to shake the odors from one's nose. But one particularly nagging old woman kept peddling a jar of something that smelled sweet. The words she repeated at first sounded like "humming of the trees" and then "honey of trees."

No, she was saying, "Honey from the bees."

Just as I was thinking that she might sell more honey if I taught her the proper pronunciation, I stopped moving with M toward the exit— stood statue still—while my mind became lost in a spiraling epiphany. In that moment the world stopped, in synchronicity with me, as the menagerie of humanity continued to swirl madly.

M looked back, incredulous, as I bought a jar from the old lady and repeated slowly for her *honey from the bees*. The other vendors swarmed, which made it difficult to communicate. M had to shout over the din of sellers offering their best bargains just for me. "Have you gone crazy? Honey?"

I didn't know how to explain and was sure I looked silly, but I shouted over the din, "I have to return to Yogi Mangku's compound. You go on, catch your flight as planned. I'll text and explain. And yes, I have gone a bit crazy."

"You know me better than that," M shouted back. "I'm with you."

She didn't ask for an explanation. I knew she couldn't be convinced to leave me, and I didn't want to let her go without a kiss. But what if I was wrong and we missed our planes for my flight of fancy?

We checked the big train board; there was a ten o'clock train back to Badhrahni, the last train of the day, and it was already boarding. It was the same train we had come in on. So we jumped on board and hoped they sold tickets on the train. When we were seated, in a coach with only a mother and her small child, the conductor appeared. He let us proceed without tickets and without taking our money. The easy-pass of love.

M sat in amazingly good spirits, waiting patiently, I assumed, for my explanation, though she might already have figured it out.

We washed our hands and faces with wet wipes and the bottled water we carried, as refreshing as a waterfall after two hours on a dusty old train.

M sent our travel agent an email. Leaving Kathmandu was no longer difficult to rearrange, as most of those trapped had escaped and few dared to enter, assuming that lightning does strike twice, or at least that earthquakes do. Although my pulse quickened with excitement, a tremor shook me to my core, my intuition ricocheting against pangs of doubt that screamed I was crazy sitting there with a jar of honey, a book of Yeats on my lap, and my Irish Gypsy belief in synchronicity leading us back into the unknown. Was it Jung or just dumb? Was I gambling M's love? Would she love a fool who dragged her into chasing windmills in the middle of the Nepal night?

I decided the best way to share my wavering conviction in a hunch—a hunch based on what I believed to be a message from Dylan—was by handing her the book of Yeats open to "The Lake Isle of Innisfree." She read it and tilted her face up to mine. I worried that she was remembering Queen Mab and questioning my sanity. She read it again. And then she gave me that knowing smile that said, *Well, maybe. Yes, we'll see.*

We had forgotten to eat, and there was no food on the train, so I opened the jar of honey. Having no utensils, we dipped our fingers into the pot. On our first dip, our index fingertips met inside the honey, so sensual a touch. Following that, each dip sank us deeper into the erotic opium bowl. Our movements became synchronized, every plunge and twist finishing with the sucking of our fingertips. My mind went blank as M and I disappeared into that sweet nectar.

Our dance was done in silence, only eyes and fingers meeting—first the tips, then interlocking, then back to the tips—until together we would take the sweet finger to our lips.

We kissed the first—the sweetest—kiss.

Just as I was about to gush and blabber, my enlightened tongue and lips spoke most true—with another long, deep kiss of honey.

CHAPTER 61

THAT SLOW TRAIN COULDN'T MOVE slowly enough for me, but it got us back to the yogi's village near midnight.

Starting down the dirt road, rattling our luggage wheels to Yogi Mangku's, we were a strange sight in the full moonlight. While my mind hungered for more honey, my body was a circa WWI German hand grenade with the pin pulled, about to go off.

We didn't discuss the lack of social graces in showing up, even when on a quest, so late and unannounced. All thoughts and words still sounded like blather to me in the aftermath of those kisses and in the prologue of what I was imagining to come. We didn't speak.

Three men appeared on the dirt road ahead of us, emerging from the jungle, and started marching our way.

I imagined the four horsemen of the apocalypse had dismounted, leaving one in the shadows to menace unseen as the others advanced. Because of the darkness, the late hour, and my glazed mind suffering exhaustion, I became lost in the illusion. I puffed my chest to look larger; it works for bears, so why not men? I signaled to M to fall in behind me as I prepared to do battle. She either didn't see or ignored my military command.

Their age, the time of night, their rough peasant appearance, and the sticks or guns in their hands meant they must be thieves.

No! The three cruel Chinese torturers had returned!

M waved hello. To her, they were three strangers in a friendly land. I was reaching for her arm to pull her out of the way when the trio waved in return and continued across the dirt road to the field on the other side, and then they were gone.

Probably looking for a tiger. I had the good sense to hold my tongue and record the imaginative stream of thought as fodder for my novel.

From the perspective of Big Love, one sees the illusion as it arises, like a motion picture of a dance or play—God's work of fiction that we cocreate with our minds. My brain was overtired and searching for some last big impediment to bar the door to the fulfillment of our quest. My body, on the other hand, was on its own secret mission now before it would allow for sleep.

When we arrived at Yogi Mangku's compound, we were glad to see abundant candlelight. We sheepishly rang the cowbell at the gate. The cymbal-like sound brought the night to attention as giggling fairies and wild nocturnal critters scurried into the jungle brush.

Yogi Mangku, with the moonlight as his lantern, soon met us and smiled, repeating his earlier greeting. "I've been expecting you!" He gave us his warm hugs in his same state of undress.

We offered abundant but unnecessary apologies, as he was truly glad to see us again so soon. I asked if we might return to Dylan's room. He eagerly agreed and joined the party.

We entered the séance room so full of Dylan's spirit. The yogi lit candles to assist the moonlight streaming in the window. By way of explanation, I showed Yogi Mangku the Yeats poem and then read the first stanza out loud, since he wasn't able to read the English.

"I will arise and go now, and go to Innisfree, / And a small cabin build there, of clay and wattles made; / Nine bean-rows will I have there, a hive for the honey-bee, / And live alone in the bee-loud glade."

He said, "I hear it in the deep heart's core." He gave me his all-knowing smile. He knew the poem by heart.

After inhaling a deep breath and taking three steps, I picked up the bee-covered urn on the desk. I turned the hive over and around, inspecting the Pandora's box. There was still no way to open it, that Maltese falcon covered in vengeful little bees sporting deceptively harmless yellow jackets. I exhaled and looked into M's eyes and then into the yogi's eyes.

He said, "Once sealed, there is only one way to open it." His eyes, dancing in encouragement, held mine.

I asked for Dylan's approval and intoned, "Auspicious is the day!" letting the urn drop to the stone floor to shatter in another big bang.

The moon shining through the window illuminated the destruction *and* the discovery, as the fragmented shell revealed the once hidden pages now unrolling at my feet.

M snatched up the sheets of paper. The verdict was swift, and she jumped up, wrapping her arms and legs around me as though I had just sunk the buzzer beater from half-court. "The theory, it's the theory of everything! As you promised, Sean, the ToE!" We kissed again before realizing we were not alone in our moment of discovery.

But Yogi Mangku was sharing our joy, saying, "When we sealed it in a ceremonial death, Dylan had me vow to tell no one. I trusted you'd find it in your deep heart's core!"

He'd known all along. I wondered briefly about absolute truth versus relative truth. I would have manufactured *a* truth as a way to break my vow. But in Yogi Mangku's presence, I felt absolute truth was all there was.

I said, "You knew and didn't tell the Chinese when they tortured you."

He smiled. "I did not lie—I don't have a computer or phone. It was my lesson and practice. It was harder not telling the two of you. We did guide you, though."

M laughed and squeezed my arm. "We found the theory and a man of complete integrity." She hugged Yogi Mangku before returning to me and twirling us like dervishes until we were both dizzy. "My heart is whole!"

We were elated, each holding several pages of the ToE.

Although we had no choice, the yogi insisted we stay in the single bedroom for the rest of the night. He brought us food, drink, a basin of water, and towels before wishing us good night. All fatigue was gone in the light of our discovery. We were up until the dawn reviewing and discussing the handwritten pages. We'd found Dylan's buried treasure:

each word a diamond; each sentence a strand; each paragraph a constellation; and the whole, Indra's net of jewels.

M sat at Dylan's desk with my pen and blank paper, rewriting and explaining every line. It was both a very universal and deeply personal manuscript, as Dylan's draft theory contained references to M and me. She got more honorable mentions than I did.

"This is how I learned eureka science from Einstein and others, by getting into their heads, by rewriting their ideas word for word." She studied science in much the same way I studied poetry, learning by heart, word for word, from the best and recording their sublime moments of inspiration in re-creation.

When she finished her rewriting of the entire ToE, we had her handwritten copy and Dylan's. We lay in his single bed, each with a copy. I took hers, and she took Dylan's. She instructed me in the theory of constant creation. As we lay there, it was clear to me that what I'd always loved about her from the first lecture at Columbia to now was that sexy intellect illuminated by an enlightened spirit.

"Dylan was right—it's a simple and elegant theory of everything." M was excitedly reading and CliffsNoting for me. "It explains Einstein's spooky action at a distance—our favorite entanglement. Each instant, instantaneous communication may occur at once in the omniscience of oneness. Let me try to explain. As you know, Einstein postulated that all things are traveling within the speed of light and that time stands still at the speed of light. The answer was right there, in those realizations, but he didn't see it. Dylan then leaps to the logical conclusion.

"All things travel at the speed of light, and time stands still at the speed of light; therefore, all things collapse and reemerge each moment of creation—expanding out in all directions, from each point, in a flash of light. We are rays of light from a single source. Instantaneous communication occurs within that constant singularity of now—faster than the speed of light!

"A constant singularity with each instant as an omnipotent event horizon. The moment Zeno's arrow strikes the target, it shatters the illusion of time and space and moves on through the singularity to the

next same moment of singularity. With time stopped and space collapsed, all is One in the illuminating source. Flickering like a film. Big
banging, not a big bang.

"Think of it this way: In the mind of God—the universal mind
or consciousness—time has stopped, and information can be shared
instantaneously. The universe even looks like a grand neural network,
but that's just the way consciousness appears in space and time interpreted by our thinking minds." She paused and seemed to be tapping
into that omniscience of God's mind.

I exclaimed, "Eureka!" since the word seemed to excite her as much
as Zeno did me. And she was already beyond excited at untangling
entanglement for me. And I was beyond, beyond excited having her
explain it to me.

She laughed at herself. "I sound like Juno with a scientific degree
rather than degrees in spirit and poetry. Well, it'll take some study and
testing, but it sounds cogent to me."

She then walked me through it as though it were elementary physics.

"The procession of beauty reached from Newton's time as a
mathematical march through a finite universe . . . to Einstein's relative time ticking faster or slower, depending on perspective, in an
infinitely expanding universe where there is no now . . . to the ToE's
constant singularity of now, projecting an infinite and eternal universe
from perfect symmetry—where in each instant of creation, no thing
becomes everything."

Lifted by her contagious effervescence, I repeated, "Eureka!" even
though I only vaguely understood. I didn't need to know what she knew
to intuit it and share her joy. This was M's moment of ultimate discovery, and I was transformed into a patient and confident lover wanting
her full measure of pleasure to come first.

M was beautifully lit from within, and I followed her metaphysical
flow of words while in what can only be described as a mentally, physically, and spiritually aroused state.

"It actually all makes sense. At the source, all is One, connecting
everything to everything else while traveling at the speed of light each

instant. And that source shines like an infinite sun of infinite energy that is constantly entering the physical world as the next *now* and propelling forward everything we perceive and measure with our minds."

She was becoming more excited epiphany by epiphany. The less I understood, the more I believed in her Truth.

"It invokes the thought experiment of an ambiguous image of the universe. An image the mind can't see both ways at once, like . . . like the two-faces-on-a-vase image. Constant creation theory takes each lynchpin of the standard model and turns it on its head."

She then went on to explain, point by point, the second law of thermodynamics, black holes, the Higgs field with its God particle . . . all as seen from the standard model and then completely differently from the perspective of constant creation theory.

I more easily grasped the simplicity of the images cast by constant creation theory. To each image, I offered my *eureka* refrain. "Everything emerging from all points as a constant singularity, each instant a big bang. The big bang is just our recently obtained ability to observe this phenomenon at one point of time and space fourteen billion years ago!"

To M, the ToE was God-given poetry. She paused, perhaps realizing that while I was enlightened by her words, I only half understood the concepts. "This energy entering the world from an omnipotent consciousness—it's love."

Eager to share in the moment of celebration, I said, "The ToE is a manifesto of Big Love? Creation as a constant act of God's unconditional, unlimited love?"

It was the truth M had been looking for. We were lit by the same light. My being, her being, our being, we were fully alive and traveling together at the speed of light, where our thoughts were one with God.

Though we were alone, she held me and said, "Sean Byron McQueen!" and brought her excited lips close to whisper in my ear exactly that which I needed to hear. The soft cooing came as the dawn light slanted through the window. A new day.

I licked another taste of honey from her lips before we stripped each other down to our malas. Her 108 beads streamed down her neck to nestle between her soft and firm breasts, with the tassel point-ing down to *infinite consciousness*. We laughed, not knowing what to do with the beads, so we kept them on and whispered our secret self-same mantras to each other. We laughed again as our mantras merged in *infinite consciousness*.

We became two particles in that beam of morning light, entwined and entangled. So naturally we fell into that sacred tantra of constant creation and its main tenet—big banging. Our bodies, minds, and spir-its followed our fingers and lips into a primal dance to the songs of innocence and experience, M inhaling, "Yes, yes, yes!" and me exhaling "Mmmmm, mmmmm, mmmmm!"

Zen-ureka! The old German hand grenade finally exploded, and a new universe was born.

CHAPTER **62**

WE AWOKE AROUND NOON to brilliant, blissful sunshine embracing our bodies in our new ritual of love—communing in light. As at the Deeksha and in my heart, there were no curtains or locks in Dylan's room. M defied physical laws by becoming even more lovely as a lover in the bright light. She was light after all and especially when we made love and became one light.

Following one singularity after another, we eventually returned to this world and the yogi's spiritual compound. There we found our yogi in his large yoga studio, standing on his head without using his hands or arms. Just on his head. Quite a feat for someone half his age. He smiled upside down, but there was no mistaking the expression for a frown. The yogi was sharing in our love. Righting himself, he had us sit for tea and warm sweet bread and mango juice. Our bodies were hungry and grateful.

After eating, the yogi suggested we all go for a swim in the cool fresh water of the lake. The yogi's compound had no Speedos, so we returned to nature. There we played like children for an hour or more. My newly woken passion was kept in check in front of the yogi, and the physical instrument of love retreated from the frigid water after all its hard labor at the break of dawn and high of noon celebrating a decade of pent-up restraint.

Strange, but the contrast of young and beautiful naked M and old and beautiful naked yogi was perfect. And somehow swimming nude with the old holy man was not uncomfortable in the least but a holy baptism of our love. This ritual of Big Love was done without thought to the imaginary past and the fictitious future.

After we were dressed and the yogi diapered, it was time to go. He asked that we wait a moment while he excused himself. When he returned, he presented us a neatly wrapped hemp bag holding the shards of the broken urn. It had cracked rather cleanly into fewer than ten large pieces.

He spoke with the joyful innocence of a child, saying, "I will be with Dylan soon," as if he had a dinner date. And then more seriously, "I may not predict the future, but you now should know death is only the end of the ego, the shattering of the illusion—like this urn releasing the truth. So you will never be apart from Dylan or each other or from me. Come now, no long faces. This is a day to celebrate and not worry about the future."

He reached out to me, putting his hands on my head for a moment, which brought a wave of Big Love and made me forget his words of death; there was only life in that love. Then he laid hands on M's head, and I felt another rush of Big Love.

In a final grand gesture, the yogi held wide his arms, making room for us both in a group hug. We embraced the now only *near*-naked man who was so full of the joy of life. I felt I'd known him for an eternity and that our paths had crisscrossed infinitely and inevitably as part of Juno's family.

It was time to go home.

CHAPTER 63

WE WERE BACK IN KATHMANDU in a taxi on our way to the airport. As I gazed out the window, saying my goodbyes to the still-healing streets, I wasn't entirely lost to the transcendental, the sublime of a loving union, and the insights of the ToE. In fact, there was nothing more humbling than a return to the illusion. Thoughts, doubts, fears, bodily functions, and challenges all continued their assaults, and sometimes they attacked with a vengeance. My thoughts were looking for some object of fear to focus on and some bogeyman from the subconscious mind to conjure as we prepared to leave Nepal.

The illusion exerted an inescapable pull back into the dreams that M and I had glimpsed liberation from. The illusion and its source are inextricably entwined in constant creation. But my new bird's-eye view of the illusion opened infinite creative channels and possibilities to tap into for my fiction.

In those moments, M and I both ignored the risk of possessing the ToE, assuming the risk was no greater than it had been in our search for the ToE. We also believed that by returning to the West, the first world, as citizens of a civilized country of laws, we'd be safer than we'd been in remote Nepal. A lot had happened with little time to sleep or think. We were enjoying each other's spiritual and physical company and didn't do a lot of talking.

As we pulled into the airport, M finally spoke more than a few words. She held my hand as if what she was about to say was vital to our mission. "Our yogi was willing to die for the theory of everything. Big Love truly is the absence of fear. May I be so brave on my dying day."

"You're so fearless. I'll be fearless too."

Our taxi stopped at the terminal entrance, and at the window of the cab appeared the always lovely YaLan and Astri. They had insisted on seeing us off. The twins were so excited, with the thousand questions of youth. They had to hold the paper Dylan had written the ToE on and see Guinevere and Lancelot again before the lovers left Kathmandu after fulfilling their quest.

As they took pictures of the ToE's pages, I felt paranoid about the email images of the ToE I'd sent to Natalie.

Somehow the twins knew we had made love, and they wanted to celebrate that too. They didn't say anything, but the twinkling turquoise of their virgin eyes let me know they knew.

I felt silly in the role of hero and lover, but in following the bread crumbs left by Dylan's ghost, it was as if we had brought Dylan back to life for the young, life-affirming ladies. We'd said goodbye only yesterday morning, but all had changed since then. It was good to see them again and share their thrill of our discovery.

Even in the age of heightened security, the twins, as royalty of Kathmandu, were able to walk us all the way to our boarding gate. Like their mother, they didn't suffer the limits that shackled most mortals.

As we stood by the gate, the dog ambassadors were on patrol, and all seemed drawn to M and some to me. It must have been her scent, which now was on me.

YaLan turned to me with her mother's eyes and asked, "What have you learned on your quest?"

Astri smiled, Puck-like, at the question.

In turn, I took a Juno-like pause to listen for a worthy answer. M was giving a look of encouragement—the sexy eyes of *come on, boy*—as the words came to me. "We either believe love and energy are limited and finite, and we seek to hold and get that love and energy from others— playing the zero-sum game of the ego—or we realize love and energy are infinitely abundant and increased in the giving, and therefore we choose a life of Big Love."

"Good answer, Professor!" M said.

Astri took her spritely turn, looking to M and asking, "And what have you learned, my teacher?"

M paused too, to look at me. My eyes were nowhere near as sexy, I'm sure, but they were full of love and desire. She said, "The truth expressed in the ToE is only valuable to the extent it's shared and accepted. We'll have to see that it's studied and tested in the light of many eyes."

"So our work isn't done?" I said.

"Never in constant creation," M replied.

The four of us shared an embrace and a cry before M and I said a final goodbye to Kathmandu and those twin towers of family and beauty.

Upon arrival in Dubai, we didn't see the whirling dervishes that had spun my love and set the wheels of our adventure in motion. I wondered if they always spun the same direction or if they'd be spinning counterclockwise now. I smiled to think of them as entangled particles that would always spin the same direction, one and all. I shook my writer's bag to jangle the bracelet packed inside. M looked confused until she heard the muffled ring. She shook her own more stylish academic travel bag until I heard her jingle.

After we passed check-in and more security, we decided to wait in a Palm steakhouse restaurant. M ordered a Burgundy Grand Cru. From the dress and bling of the fat-cat Arab and Western business patrons and the server's reaction, Domaine de la Romanee-Conti, Grands Echezeaux Grand Cru 2009 must have cost a fortune. M toasted our first sip. "To fulfilling our quest, and the constant creation of an enlightened relationship!"

We followed the finish into a new life together.

Over that most excellent bottle, we discussed our plans. We would work to release the ToE broadly before the Guru learned we had it. I would see Natalie the day after my return to the city and gain her permission to promote Dylan's constant creation theory. M was going to continue to study and test it, stanza by stanza, to learn by heart the implications and illuminations that I only dimly understood.

I insisted that Dylan would want M to annotate the scientific jargon and concepts. She humbly agreed. I would edit it for English, though the scientific jargon would limit my ability to make corrections without altering the fine-tuning of the universe. I would also write an introduction on the plane ride to New York. Within a couple of days, we would see that the handful of people who had the theory became a theaterful of academic colleagues, literary and scientific, and from there, there would be no burying the ToE. I thought Grace might want to personally deliver a copy to the tipsy Father Bishop.

M was enthusiastic about using her credentials to promote the ToE through the scientific community. She believed it rang true and answered many of the open questions of the standard model of particle physics and cosmology, though it lacked in scientific rigor and would need to be tested, experienced, and studied. She was open-minded, and her approach would be certain to spark debate in what she was sure would be a recalcitrant scientific community.

For my part, I would finish the novel as another means to promote Dylan's theory, as he'd envisioned in his letter. I would join M in Athens at the end of August for our final week of summer break, and then we would return together to NYC for the beginning of the new school year.

My layover was longer than M's, and I was able to take her to her gate and see her off. Before our last goodbye, I made her agree that she would write an email each morning from Athens. I would write one each night from NYC, and we would each wake to an email from our love. I was following the track of the twins' young runners in the practice of love. What might have been a sad parting felt like a joyful new beginning following a tragic but perfect adventure of discovery. That journey had ended in our unbridled love, and it would continue in less tumultuous chapters of our lives together.

As M made quantum-love talk, reminding me how entanglement worked—"The spin of one is the spin of two"—I went right to the theory of constant creation—"All is one in each instant of creation. Remember only love."

"Love is known by the absence of fear," she said, reciting one of Juno's mantras.

We hugged and kissed as Zeno's paradox of no distance raced in my blood. I felt her heart beating through the warm and firm flesh of her chest. We kissed, and she started to back away and finally turned to leave.

I watched her walk down the Jetway to her plane, standing with prayer hands to my heart that now overlapped her heart such that no distance could tear the two apart. I reached quickly into my bag, removing the Dervish bracelet she had given me, and started to shake it above my head like a Hare Krishna with a tambourine. She didn't look back but pulled her matching tambourine out and shook it in resonance with mine. Her head was bobbing, her back shaking—she was laughing as she turned the corridor's bend and disappeared.

Dubai was dry, and life quickly lost its luster, returning to black and white. After finding my gate, I bought a large bottle of water and a *New York Times*. The purchase of the newspaper felt like a betrayal, yet it was time to reconnect to the world at large, which ironically felt smaller than the universe we'd inhabited in Kathmandu. When you don't read the news, it doesn't matter what page your news is on, but I imagined that despite the editorial board's distance from the epicenter, the earthquake had made front page news before being replaced by more proximate bad news.

Perhaps the tipping point of prayers was coming. I skipped over the bad and read the report of women's marches held in almost every city and town across the US, as well as in several key international cities, the previous day. It was a quickening with which humanity was changing direction, a colorful banyan tree of enlightened womanhood growing down the trunk of a decaying white patriarchal society, with its roots about to touch earth.

I wondered what role the theory of constant creation might have in this accelerating and revolutionary emergence of humanity. I laughed aloud remembering M's joke: "Men of science will try to hold on to their single big bang, while women of science will more easily embrace constant creation."

I switched on my phone's Wi-Fi for the first time in days, since I hadn't needed to text or make calls while in Nepal. I only really texted with M anyway, and she'd been in my company constantly.

Ting ting ting ting ting. A couple of eager but unimportant texts came through from my agent. Dear Elliot had missed me. And there were three texts from Natalie. The first two were old news, but the last text, a long one, had arrived too late.

"Thank you for your last email. Sorry the mailbox there was empty, and no need to pay for the lawyer. Please do Grace and me a favor. If you see Dylan's urn with the bees on it, bring it home. Grace thought Dylan wanted his ashes placed there. She saw it at Yogi Mangku's. Good ToE hunting . . . Peace and love, Natalie."

The text caused me distress as I boarded my plane. I had shared the thrill of discovery and the ToE with Natalie in an email but hadn't mentioned where it was found or my shattering of the urn. No good deed . . .

My checked bag held the shards that Yogi Mangku had the foresight to collect. I'd see Natalie soon after returning, confess my vandalism, and ask her permission to publish the ToE. I hoped her reservations and fears for Grace, and perhaps anger over how and where the ToE was found, wouldn't prompt her to rebury Dylan's declaration of constant creation.

M wouldn't allow that to happen.

CHAPTER 64

MY MIND WAS BUSY, my body exhausted, and my bladder jiggling when the wheels bounced down with a hop and a thump—to the applause of passengers grateful to be alive—at JFK at ten in the evening. My economy-class seat didn't allow those over six feet tall to sleep. I'd been suffering Zeno's paradox in reverse—constantly moving twice as far away, flying back in time and away from M.

I'd spent a few hours after takeoff writing the introduction to the ToE that would help the lay reader see constant creation theory through my nonscientific mind. M was an excellent teacher, and I had been able to grasp the mind-blowing fundamentals of the theory. And my experience of Big Love brought constant creation alive for me. When the draft was done, I attempted to meditate on not wishing I could stretch out and sleep, and then I turned my attention to all the changes in my life. My mind was far from quiet.

The novel would be revised from the perspective of Big Love before my inspiration faded into memory, the way the sweet taste of a honeysuckled first kiss leached from parted lips. James was still stuck in a Chinese jail with an amorous cellmate and looking for a clever prison break, knowing the firing squad was being assembled and he would soon be served his last supper. He began one last letter to Brigitte.

At last, my love, the end always comes.

But first, I needed sleep.

At the immigration desk, I was annoyed at my annoyance that the inspection officer spent more time than usual at his control screen without explanation. The TSA had confiscated my letter opener a month ago, and now I was flagged for additional inspection. Or perhaps they were going to return that memory of Hope to welcome me home.

A man flashing an FBI badge invaded my exhaustion and my personal space, saying, "Excuse me, Mr. Sean McQueen. Please come with me."

My impatience gave way to loss of wind. I'd been sucker punched in the gut. My bed in Chelsea was being pulled out from under me, or at least being pushed much farther away. They could keep my letter opener.

"May I have my passport back, please?"

"Oh, yes, they'll send that to us soon. Don't worry." The agent ushered me along with the imaginary handcuffs of authority.

I tried to regain my breath and composure as the FBI man—"I'm Bill"—led me to a small, square, well-lit sterile room noticeably lacking color or smells. The absence of odor was so strong as to be morbid. The absence of color was highlighted by a bright white overhead light.

If a room could lack humor and humanity, that room was the archetype. A white camera with a dark eye was mounted on the ceiling and directed at me. The only objects on the white walls were a vintage white phone and a large round white clock with black hands and numbers, both circa 1970. I imagined a picture of Nixon had hung there once and would have been a thing of beauty in this mortuary of white tinged with black.

The lack of color must be based on a psychological study of confessional décor, or maybe it just declared to the detainee that *things are black and white in this room, this city, this universe.*

Bill offered me a seat on a cold black metal chair and said, "Please be patient. We'll be back to explain in a minute."

He left me sitting in detention with my carry-on. The bag held M's handwritten copy of the ToE and my handwritten introduction and my phone and laptop, which had pictures of the ToE pages I'd sent to Natalie.

I was having flashbacks to the fear and tension of school detention. Dylan and I were routinely held after school, me for going one step and Dylan for not letting me cross the line alone.

That isolation in such a sterile room made me realize just how much I already missed the colorful Xanadu, M, and the Deeksha family.

I attempted to text and then call M to tell her of my captivity, but the barren room allowed for no reception, prohibiting any love connection. Although the camera's eye followed my every movement, I wasn't starring in a lighthearted TV show.

One minute was going on thirty with no commercial breaks for my one-man show, and for each second the old clock ticked, my mind raced, wondering what the FBI might want from me. I tried the door; it was locked. I'd been kidnapped, and it wasn't so they could ask about my letter opener. The FBI wasn't the CIA, but my detention was no coincidence. My mind's hard drive pushed the panic button. The white walls started contracting.

To demonstrate a lack of concern and an innocent frame of mind, I crossed the room to test the vintage phone. I thought to call M and tell her not to talk. But the phone was just a prop: a rotary dial but no dial tone. I imagined my audience's cruel laughter.

Bill and another man entered the room, with Bill saying, "That phone hasn't worked for decades." They carried their own black folding chairs, though they didn't sit after unfolding them. The second man was Bob, a clone to Bill. Both wore Detective Friday suits. They flashed FBI badges with their likenesses and names, Senior Agent Robert something and Agent William something. Good—not the CIA. Still, their authoritarian manner made me feel even more alone in that room.

"Do I get a phone call?" My humorous opening salvo.

"You're not under arrest," Bob said. "Please relax. You've done nothing wrong. We just have some questions. Anything to drink?" he added, as if we were at a cocktail party.

I was parched from the flight and nerves, and though my bladder was full already, I said, "Sparkling water, please, and an explanation would be nice."

There was a knocking on the door, and Bill accepted bottled water from the hand and arm that extended into the room. This display, without anyone leaving the room or phoning, was to make clear to me that others were watching or at least listening. It proved that just because I imagined an audience didn't mean there wasn't one. If the intent was to be unnerving, it was successful. If the intent was to be responsive, it failed. The water was flat.

Bob launched in, saying, "I know you've had a long flight and must be very tired, but this is an important matter of national security. We're tracking a major security hack by the Chinese government and large trades in Bitcoin. Do you know anything about that?"

"How am I possibly involved in that?" I rubbed my face to stay awake, seeking guidance for how to play the scene.

"We don't think you're knowingly involved, but I'll let Bill explain, as he's an expert on cybercrime and cryptocurrencies. Bill, please explain to our friend in a way that even I can understand."

Bill said, "I'll make this simple. The Chinese have hacked, using the dark web, a demographically diverse set of computers around the world belonging to people who have traded in cryptocurrencies. By influencing investment sentiment and mining activities regarding Bitcoin currency trades within this group of computers in real time, they're able to manipulate the currency through algorithms and black box trading. We believe they beta tested this network manipulation and made an over-ten-million-US-dollar Bitcoin profit with a test that took them a second to execute and which they probably limited in effectiveness to avoid detection. As cryptocurrencies gain acceptability, we don't know if they plan to use this embedded and expanding network as a financial weapon or as a tax they'll collect on this emerging market. This is a win-win for them. In a more developed market, if they feared they might get caught, they could take a significant short position and await the crash or cause the crash themselves.

"It's like a metastasizing cancer that they're spreading through the blockchain. Let me explain."

He went on and on for another ten minutes. I knew Bitcoin. It was the logical extension of the theory that all currencies are an agreed-upon fiction, but I never understood the blockchain, which required genome mapping of the internet. They might as well have been explaining the Higgs bosun and field to my tired brain.

I paid attention again when Bob cut in. "There are also other ways they might use such a network of computers. So when it was brought to our attention that your computer was infected and in this network now, we needed to meet you and ask for your cooperation. So how might they have gotten into your computer?"

I was relieved this wasn't CIA and ToE related, but I was still wary. I didn't want to say much about my recent adventure and wanted to leave the family out of whatever this was.

I went with a narrow and convenient lane of truth. "I didn't routinely carry my cell phone during my stay in Nepal. And the laptop I was using, for a novel I'm writing, was also routinely left in my room. Someone might have gotten to it there."

I took a drink of water, expecting a response that didn't come. They also didn't show any interest in my novel, which struck me as a bit rude. So I said, "A Chinese military bureaucrat, Comrade An, who was staying where I was after the earthquake in Kathmandu—there were no locks—had access and must have been the one who did it."

Bob handed me the bottle of water I'd set on the white linoleum floor. I took another sip, and since they continued to stare, I continued to speak.

"I've dabbled in Bitcoin but not in amounts that would enable espionage on my salary. Perhaps they got into my computer that way?" I drummed my fingers on my chair. "No, I'm confused. It must have been that stinking Comrade." I wanted to show I was a patriot and wasn't fond of Comrade.

Bob said, "Probably. What we ask is that you leave us your cell phone and laptop tonight, and then tomorrow we'll be by first thing to check your home computer. We need to scan the devices to see how the network fans out from your breach."

I had the tired presence of mind to say, "Let me think."

If I gave up my electronics, I would still have M's handwritten ToE and my penned introduction, which I'd already typed onto the computer. My novel work was all backed up onto my NYU computer. I was on the verge of giving them what they wanted, but I wanted to email M on the way home, and I didn't want the FBI reading her first good-morning email to me before I did.

And my suspicious mind thought the CIA might still be behind this charade and looking to see if we had found the ToE.

"I'll certainly cooperate, but I'll keep my electronic devices for the evening. We can discuss their release, and my computer, when you come by in the morning."

Bob said, "You really can't use them without jeopardizing anyone you would contact. I think it's best you leave them with us."

His insistence brought on a firm resolve to resist. "No. Not unless you have a legal right to take them."

Bob said, "Bill, let's speak outside a second."

They stepped outside, again for minutes, not seconds. The FBI apparently couldn't tell time and wasn't concerned with my sleep deprivation and need of a bathroom.

When they returned, an older man—nattily dressed like an English gentleman—was with them: a cocky old Truman Capote with red hair, piercing eyes, and an incongruously crooked smile. He was as white as the walls of my detention room. I felt that I knew him or had seen him before. His cold hand shook my hand, and he said, "I'm sorry I'm late to the party. How are you, Sean? You must be tired. Would you like another bottle of water?"

"I'm fine. Who are you? Do you have identification too?"

"Yes, of course. I'm with these gentlemen from the FBI." He offered no identification, however, although my mind did, screaming out, "The Guru!"

"Bob and Bill have filled me in." He paced down one short length of the room and back again. "You know about the serious Chinese hack and currency manipulation you're involved in and how it's a matter of national security. My interest goes beyond that into how they'll use the internet and this network to control information and influence Americans. You can see that information and tech weaponization—the

ability to control, disseminate, and distort the truth—is the new bat-
tleground, creating a new reality for the many addled minds that live
in the dreamworld of the internet. AI will increasingly control their
thoughts. The Chinese are years ahead of us in establishing a national
blockchain—creating a new Silk Road of information from computers
to brains. Why, it's the practice of mind control in the modern era on a
grand and interconnected scale."

I thought he sounded like Queen Mab, but rather than tapping the
universal mind, he dwelled in artificial intelligence.

"The Russians and Chinese are more advanced than we are. So we
need all the patriotic help we can get." He nodded and then lowered
his voice, the avuncular uncle. "You can't imagine the embarrassing
information they have about you and anyone of standing. We're all
compromised, more or less. You just more so."

I said, "I really must insist I see your ID." I doubted it would say
Guru, yet I wanted to see *CIA* to confirm my strong suspicion.

"You know these gentlemen are FBI and wouldn't allow me to speak
to you without the authority to do so. I'm undercover and, by Agency
rules, can't use ID. Bob?"

"This is a serious matter, and you can rest assured our colleague is on
our side. Please cooperate."

"Thanks, Bob," the maybe Guru said.

I was being sucked in by the deep state but wanted to think this
was just FBI and all about a Bitcoin virus that stinking Comrade had
infected me with.

My red-haired interrogator was looking longingly at my bag, as
though weighing due process and wishing there were none. I assumed
my checked bag was now being rifled. Dirty underwear and a broken
urn in a hemp bag were the only compromising items they would find.

The nameless interrogator asked questions about M, Juno, the
Deeksha, and Comrade. An alarm went off when he asked, "Where is
Professor Emily Edens now?"

So they weren't just interested in Bitcoin. I'd mentioned only Comrade An. I couldn't fight or take flight. I'd have to arm my words. They

must know about her flight to Athens, so I went with a small truth. "Staying somewhere around Athens."

The interrogator asked, "May we have the hotel name?"

"I don't know the name." It was the first time I was glad I wasn't good with names.

"Well, okay. Would you please give us Professor Edens's contact information?"

"You don't have that already?"

"We do actually, but I wanted to see how cooperative you were." He smiled ominously.

From then on, I either dodged questions or gave the most benign replies I could come up with, trying to appear cooperative while still protecting M and the family. I was able to avoid risky revelations about the adventure only through some artful dialogue and word twisting; I understood it was a crime to lie to the FBI and, I assumed, the CIA.

Wordsmith versus master spook—I'd say we played to a draw. I celebrated by letting loose a long yawn, unconcerned about covering my mouth.

The interrogator said, "I know it's late and you're tired; do you have to use the men's room?"

I sorely needed a bathroom break, but I wanted to finish first, so I declined.

It was maybe a good sign that they all were playing good cop, but I was swimming in conspiracy theories while suspecting my nameless interrogator was the Guru. I reassured myself, saying my overtired mind was playing tricks of paranoia, because the Bitcoin hacking story rang true. A strong and sensitive imagination can be a blessing or a curse. The general and Comrade *had* been on my computer. Why didn't I change my password?

The interrogator said, "Before we go, let me tell you a little story." Bill and Bob finally sat. I frowned as they seemed to be settling in for story time. My bladder protested the further delay.

The interrogator went into a long description of the history of physical warfare morphing into technological, cyber-powered battles "where the terrain has changed and the goal is to control and change minds." The interview became a lecture, despite the promising ring of "before we go."

"Fire, the wheel, combustible engines, biology, chemistry, atomic physics, computers, artificial intelligence . . . Each scientific advancement has been used to make weapons even deadlier." He said "even deadlier" not so much as a regret but as if it were a worthy goal of humanity. "Death is just the blunt and final means of controlling minds by destroying them. The A-bomb quickly changed Japanese minds. Did you know the first supercomputer, MANIAC, was developed to allow for the creation of the H-bomb?"

Just when I thought his dropping of the H-bomb was the conclusion of the history lesson, I discovered he was just in the middle. The interrogator, now lecturer, started up again. "So you can see the importance of controlling information with our enemies out front on AI, quantum computing, and brain-computer interface. And where is this all heading?"

Unfortunately for my dozy brain and ballooning bladder, I was about to learn. As he went on projecting into the future about global espionage and war, he sounded like a twenty-first-century Dr. Frankenstein looking for alien technology to animate artificial intelligence.

". . . matter of time until AI is omnipotent—once we have the complete theory of everything. Quantum computers already can predict the probability of each possible occurrence, and we're looking to make the leap to knowing the outcome. We're in a race to control the world. A race I must win."

Wake up, McQueen! This guy is the damned Guru.

Instead of a pinching, I gave myself a good face rub and surprised myself, saying, "It's always the awe of paradox that distinguishes the universe and us from the metal and wire minds of computers and robots."

"Well, I'll be a redheaded stepchild! That is poetic, Professor, but just you wait."

He was gearing up to take me down.

"It used to be that one feared goliaths and generals, but now we have more to fear from a pimple-faced boy on his computer in the basement or a seventy-five-year-old man with a phone and an army of pimple-faced boys."

While this was said with a slap on the knee and self-effacing humor, he waved his phone like Juno's invisible wand, and I heard the threat. He looked to be about seventy-five.

"Did you know that in the time it takes you to write one chapter of your novel, with one of my programmers I could produce a novel with the DNA of Austen's and Dickens's full body of works?"

What a strange, perhaps wonderful, literary love child that would be. He had shifted gears and was becoming more belligerent and ruder, but at least he'd bothered to note I was a writer.

I was tired and scared to death, but not dead yet. "I'd like to see that. Whose style and voice would the child take after, or would it develop its own style?"

He ignored me and continued on with an inexhaustible supply of science fiction stories. My ability to focus and to follow him into the realms of spaceships and the warping of time and space in wormholes was compromised by a now irritable and overripe bladder. He spoke with a captivating cadence and a transitional refrain.

"And when we got *tired* of that technology . . ."

Here I was in the larger-than-life presence of the one who must be the Guru, and all I could think about was peeing. And like his tired old technology, I needed to sleep and reboot. *Now*. Realizing the extreme pressure and discomfort was no longer under control, and unable to mask my irritation, I stood abruptly and asked, "How much longer will this take, and am I free to go?"

In a patriotic gesture, he placed his right hand where his heart should be and said, "I'm sorry for going on and on regarding matters of national security. One always assumes one's own passions to be of interest to everyone. And of course you're free to go anytime. You must be so tired, but we need to discuss access to your phone and computer."

My panties in a twist, I asked plaintively, "May I go to the men's room first?"

Bill, my chaperone, said, "Sure. Follow me."

When I got to the door, something said *look back*, and as I did, I again saw the interrogator's eyes on my carry-on bag. I stepped back and picked up the bag. "Never go anywhere without it."

Bill followed me into the bathroom to join me in a pee, which made me uncomfortable. I took out my phone while he peed first.

"What are you doing?" he asked.

"Making a call. I assume I still get one, arrested or not?" I couldn't call the police to protect me from the FBI and CIA, but I wanted to speak to M, though I wasn't sure what I would say or she could do.

"Sure, go ahead. But it won't work here."

He was right; I had no reception.

I peed for a couple minutes. The bathroom break allowed fear and agitation to replace extreme discomfort and exhaustion, so each step back to my interrogation room, and *him*, brought on an increasing sense of doom.

The interview was concluded quickly when *he* asked, "May we keep your phone and laptop for the evening? You really shouldn't use them until they're swept. And we'd like to come by in the morning, after you get the good night's sleep you need, to look at your computer as well."

"I want to cooperate and have nothing to hide, but I am too tired to think. I'll keep my electronics for now, but please come by in the morning if you like." I lifted my bag to my shoulder. "You know where I live. I should be up and dressed by ten. I'll show you my phone and computers then."

My interrogator couldn't mask his displeasure, and his eyes blazed at me. "Professor, this is your government telling you your patriotic duty, and you're telling me to wait? I can see you're tired and confused. Bill and Bob, will you excuse us for one moment? Sean and I share a mutual friend, and I want to relay a private message. It'll take just a minute, and then we all can go home to bed."

As the door shut behind Bill and Bob, the still unidentified Guru smiled a wide, overly friendly, and thin grin. His gaze punctured mine, driving me backward into my seat. He was prepared to enjoy what he was about to say.

"You're exhausted, Professor. I understand. I just wanted you to know that the NYU dean and I are close, with him eager to please me regarding an ongoing top-secret research project. Did you know Dean Sitwell has political ambitions and is quite the ladies' man? He was amazed to learn how, in the age of the internet, none of his, your, or my information is private any longer. Well, that relates to our work together, and I should say no more about it. We want to protect your secrets and academic life and position too. We're on your side and need your full cooperation—for your country. I'm going to call Bill and Bob back in, and I suggest you agree to leave your electronics now." He folded his hands with a flourish. "We have a warrant on the way. Now, do try to get some sleep. You look so very tired."

I was too frozen by his words and his hypnotic refrain to respond.

He opened the door, where Bill and Bob stood sentry. "Please rejoin us. I think Sean will leave his phone and computer now."

"No," I said, shaking off his spell and standing up. "Sean wants his passport, and he wants to go."

"That doesn't sound right. Gentlemen, excuse us again and try to find his passport. Those things are always getting lost around here, and we can't let our friend into the country without it."

He reclosed the door so we stood alone, face-to-face. The Guru stepped too close, violating my personal space with his eyes and dark energy. He had old man breath that felt hot and metallic in my nostrils. We shared a moment in the thin air between us.

I felt as helpless as a twelve-year-old asylum seeker separated from his mother. Stripped of my passport, I stood naked and alone at the threshold of America, under the withering eyes that held my fate and barred my bed.

He enjoyed his power over me. "We have Emily," he said, wielding words without restraint.

"What do you mean you have Emily?"

"What do you think? I didn't say we have her; we have *located* her for you. For your career and country, for your safety, for Emily's safety . . . you must drop this matter. Let your friend's pipe dreams rest in peace."

"What are you talking about?" I didn't know what else to say. In my face was the CIA's Guru, a distorted horror-house mirror of humanity, a grim reaper with a cell phone. He knew everything, and he was standing two feet from me.

"You and I know what we're talking about, so I'll ask you directly, Professor—professor for now, that is—did you find the theory you were looking for, my theory of everything?"

I was no yogi and had taken no vow. "No."

He looked deep into my eyes, twisting his head, a human lie detector. I stepped back to try to diminish his power. He stepped forward so I'd have to be a coward to continue my retreat.

"I'll ask one last time, but before I do, please know I am no bluffer and the price of lying is always greatest for the would-be noble traitor who thinks he knows better than his government what is best for the people, only to later learn that power is truth and truth is power. So one more time, do you have the theory?"

I peered deep into the red vortex behind his laser eyes, and the surprising words shot through me. "No, it's lost. Unless you took it from Dylan's phone after you killed him."

He stepped back and smiled. "Ah. The price if you're lying . . . your career. The lengths we will go to in order to protect our intellectual property you well know. And you're being watched. We will know your every move. So go home and go to bed and close the blinds and lock the door, and we'll see you in the morning."

He watched to see that what he'd said had sunk in before he opened the door. "Gentlemen, we're done. Please find his passport. He's agreed to cooperate, and with warrant in hand, we'll collect all his electronics in the morning."

He spoke in a way that made it sound as though he had gotten exactly what he wanted.

The passport was quickly found.

"Good night, Professor. Bill and Bob will be by in the morning for all your electronics. I'm sorry I can't join them, and hope for your sake you told me the truth. If you did and we can get the Chinese out of your devices and see what they've been up to, we may be able to return them to you in a few short days. Remember to say nothing about this to anyone."

I meekly managed a barely audible *okay*. I was a bad child being forgiven by his father for talking back right before bedtime.

As Bill led me away down a corridor, an image of Hope dead in bed next to me appeared from the crypt of my mind to shatter me. That memory, grown darker and fouler over time, I had self-diagnosed as a post-traumatic stress reaction that paralyzed me under conditions of extreme stress. Rubbing my face was no antidote to PTSD.

I was escorted by my FBI chaperone, who I believed to be one of the Guru's henchmen, to a sign that said Baggage Claim. Bill shook my hand, looking sorry for me.

I wouldn't pull out my phone, afraid he might grab it, so I asked, "What time is it?"

He checked his watch. "Almost midnight." He marched away.

I found my lone bag by the side of the carousel where it had long ago gone around and around.

I needed to speak to M.

CHAPTER 65

A FEARFUL REALIZATION rushed over me—in Big Love, I wasn't separate from even the Guru. When we were alone together with his threats, our eyes had met, and we knew each other in that moment we shared his old breath and consciousness. Or was it just a trick of my tired mind that I was now possessed, compelled to read the Guru's mind—his motivations and next moves—drafting the fiction of a waking dream? I was overtired to the point where reality started to shift, allowing the subconscious to hold sway.

The Guru wanted all my electronic devices to determine if I was lying and had the theory. I wondered how long it would take to get a warrant using the Chinese Bitcoin story.

Why would Dean Roland Sitwell move to terminate me, a tenured professor? Did the Guru really have the leverage over the dean, or intent, to make good on his threat?

Worst of all, he had threatened M. I'd risk everything other than M.

My mind racing with unsettling thoughts and images, I decided to wait to call M until I was safe in the taxi and out of the airport, where the Guru might have some fancy high-tech surveillance ability. I handed my arrival form to the customs agent on the way out, lying when I said, "Nothing to declare."

I was a John le Carré courier carrying a top-secret theory, which the CIA had classified as governmental property, into the country with the intent to distribute. If this was the Guru's story, I was the traitor about to leak the DNA of the universe to the unready masses and to our mortal enemies. And I was about to lose my treasured tenure for my treason.

While waiting in the long taxi line at JFK, I became lost in thought about how to get out of the damn mouse trap threatening my career. The Guru all but admitted to causing Dylan's death, acting as if it was no big deal for him to take a life with impunity. When it was my turn, I caused a fuss by insisting on getting into the cab behind the one that was next; I guess I'd seen too many Bond movies when I was young. As we left the airport, I was watching to see if I was being followed but realized it didn't matter. They knew where I was going, so they could just meet me in Chelsea on my way to bed.

The driver was blasting rap. He had no interest in me or my espionage. I called M just before the Athens dawn. I told her of my detention and the Guru's threats and asked her what she thought we should do.

"What a wake-up call—I just got to sleep. Sean, I'm so sorry. You okay? I wish I was with you. He sounds like the Antichrist."

"He is. For being sleep deprived and threatened, I'm fine. Especially speaking to you. You're always with me." I wanted to bury my face in her chest for a good face rub. M and the drumming rap refrain of *bubba love, bubba love* were waking me up.

"Bubble love?" she asked, and I didn't correct her. "We can't let him stop us now. I've been up reviewing the theory, studying the ToE; it's truth, *the* Truth, in its beautiful super symmetry. I've got it now. What do you think our next move should be?"

"I'm thinking we should delete all references to and copies of the ToE from our computers and hide our hard copy, then plan to get it out into the world as soon as possible."

"I agree. Your plan sounds good, but the threat to your career—"

"Yes, and to our lives. But the career threat sounded more real and imminent. I guess we'll call his bluff. We can't cower in fear now that we found Big Love and the truth. We already survived an earthquake and shots fired in the night."

"Not to mention death threats and Gypsy fever dreams," she said, laughing softly. "But, Sean, this is your career you're risking. All the years you put in. Your reputation."

"You wouldn't hesitate." So how could I? "And anyway, that gamble has already been made. He said my career would be the price of lying, so let's erase the evidence and delay their knowing that I lied until the theory is out in the world."

Irritated by the incessant rap, I shifted left and then right, trying to find comfort on the lumpy seat that conspired with the rattling beat and gangster poetry to ensure my ride was excessively uncomfortable.

"What are you listening to?" she asked.

"The taxi driver's rap. My wailing wall of sound to prevent electronic eavesdropping."

"Oh, damn. I know it sounds crazy, but what if they're listening to us now?"

"That's a scary thought, but you're right. He said they are watching me—found you. Call me if anything happens to you. Keep your phone charged and on."

"Okay. We have a plan. Be safe, Sean. I love you."

"You too, M. Lock the door and don't go out till we speak again. Love you. Bye." I echoed the Guru's good night.

As the driver let me off, I had to bark, "Five back!" to get my change. As I waited, the female rapper's voice got heated: "Wake, yo mofofucker! / Sleep and I'll be gone / Before the bloody dawn."

Not something I could write, but I grudgingly admired its lyrical muscle.

New York City. I was back in Kansas from Kathmandu. I was home. I entered my Chelsea apartment ready to disappear into bed. I saw my old sanctuary with new eyes that looked on it compassionately—as one does a childhood home—recognizing all that had changed even while every book remained in its place.

I deleted the ToE and all digital references and emails related to it and then deleted those from my trash bin. I folded M's handwritten copy of the ToE with my introduction neatly into the volume of *Ulysses*. No one would notice only twenty more pages there. I then placed it among the books on my full-wall bookshelf, on the highest shelf next to Eric Ambler. It was now hidden among millions of pages and billions of words.

I collapsed into bed. I texted M. "Operation Creation on. Going to bed. Get some sleep too."

She immediately texted back a thumbs-up and a heart emoji. Better than poetry to me. I read M's email and wrote her mine. Both were steeped in Big Love and passionate innuendo.

I had just drifted off into that good night when my ears started buzzing. An insistent ring said someone wanted in and wouldn't likely go away. I got up, mumbling and stumbling, and tried to clear my head of dreams. Had the Guru or one of his Dicks come to kill me in my jockeys?

Next thing I knew, they were ringing my apartment door. They must have rung every buzzer until some neighbor let them in. I looked through the peephole, relieved that it was Bill and Bob. I didn't think they were my assassins. I told them to wait while I put my pants on. "Hurry," the unwelcomed guests rudely replied. I dragged on sweats and a T-shirt and checked that *Ulysses* was still hidden on the wall of literary fiction. I then let them in. Four in the morning.

Behind them were another seven men I hadn't seen, all with FBI jackets and IDs around their necks. I was the Pablo Escobar of literature. The neighbors would be talking.

"Here's a warrant to seize all electronics and any files or papers related to your time in Nepal and your contact with the Chinese," Bob said. They didn't seem happy to be working so late.

"I thought you were coming in the morning?"

"Technically, it is the morning, and we have reason to believe you weren't fully cooperating and may have lied to our colleague when we were out of the room. Sit down and tell us where your files and papers are."

"I don't know what you're talking about, but look around. It seems you have a right to." I skimmed the warrant; it looked legitimate, providing them access to everything. I wondered if it covered a cavity search but didn't want to read all the fine print.

They searched everywhere. Bill patted me down to see if I had anything up my sleeve or down my jockey. Bill and Bob took my electronics, which they proceeded to search, and sent files somewhere else; I heard several *swooshes* of emails being sent.

Shit. They had my novel draft, and though I hadn't yet found the ToE in my story—James was stuck in a Chinese prison cell for poisoning Juno—the Guru wouldn't like his depiction or the suggestion that he had Dylan killed, even in fiction. Though I *had* already accused him to his face. Probably not a wise move, Sherlock.

The other G-men were going through everything else: my desk, drawers, linens, closets. But one bright young FBI agent was of particular concern. I didn't like his clever eyes as he scanned my books like an avid reader. He removed from a case what looked like opera glasses but with a light switch, which he turned on—red-light goggles? I chided myself, recalling that the general and the Chinese had searched every book in Dylan's small room at the yogi's place. But I had a thousand times more books than Dylan, and this young reader with his magnifying laser-light glasses was scanning only the titles and not shaking every book.

Then he went right to it, climbing up to *Ulysses* on the top shelf. I felt like shouting, "No one really likes that book!" to the literary whiz kid, but too late. He was taking it to Bill and Bob, revealing the precious M-written copy of the ToE and my introduction. He said, "No dust on this big book." Damn. The curse of bad housekeeping and not watching enough crime-solving TV.

Bill and Bob took pictures of the ToE and sent them, I imagined, to the Guru. I was caught. They insulted me by all but ignoring my introduction, tossing it on the couch before filing it along with the ToE into an evidence bag. I would soon find out if the Guru was a bluffer; it was only a matter of time until he found out I had lied. I'd just wanted more time. M and Natalie still had the ToE, and we would release it into the world. Tired, sweaty, cranky, and zapped of all energy, I felt as if I were both watching a movie and playing a part; unfortunately, it was a Tarantino film, and I was on the wrong end of the gun.

Bob handed me my phone when it rang.

"Hello, Pro—" The Guru. So his discovery was a matter of no time.

"Sorry. I can't call you professor anymore. You'll hear from the dean shortly. Then we will understand each other, I trust. Think of me as a simple man. I live alone with my memorabilia and state-of-the-art technology for companionship. One drink before curling up in my recliner to rest. Oh, and I have a cat. Siamese. We are quite the dynamic duo. Cat's-eye takes care of the mice and roaches while I take care of bigger game. I'm a man whose sole mission and responsibility is America's mastery of scientific advance and technology—to control the world and keep it safe. You should have stuck to literature, something everyone may read. Scientific knowledge is power, and the theory of everything will unlock infinite power. Would you give that power to the Russians and your friends the Chinese?" He paused to dramatically clear his throat.

"I'm a simple man who will let no complications stand in his way. McQueen, are you ready to stop betraying your country? Anyway, there will be no further attempts from you or your girlfriend to deceive me or orchestrate a reemergence of the theory. Ask if your Emily's life is worth the price of fucking around. She's an incredible woman with a genius IQ, and we should both try to keep her safe. She will grasp the theory's sum and substance pointing to the source of energy and God-like power. I will ask her to work with me, the way she worked with Byrne on the theory, to harness that energy with quantum computers for American dominance in the race for artificial intelligence. I'm not sure she'll care for an unemployed traitor. Stop now."

The phone went dead. That mofofucker. It was as if he could read my mind, threatening the two things most dear to me—M and being a professor—in that order of priority. I'd gamble one but not the other.

Bill took the phone back. The FBI concluded their search, taking all my electronics and papers. Even took my dust-free *Ulysses*. They left with all my means of communication.

Needing to hide, I turned off all my lights. Like an amputee looking for his missing hand, I went to check my phone. But I was cut off. I had to protect M at all costs but needed a phone and her number to call her.

It was very black out.

Even blacker inside my formerly secure sanctuary. The darkness seeped into every part of me, poisoning my recently enlightened mind and body's ecstasy. To paraphrase Mick and Keith, maybe I'll just fade away, not have to face the facts. No colors anymore, as the Guru paints it black.

CHAPTER 66

I SHOULDN'T HAVE BEEN SURPRISED to lose my electronics, but I was, and I had no plan for how to communicate in their absence. I hadn't expected a raid at four in the morning, adding to my sleep deprivation. And I hadn't expected the Guru to be up so late making more threats, or to lose M's precious handwritten copy of the theory. Without a phone, I couldn't contact M; I didn't know her number. It was just *M* on my speed dial. And I didn't have a landline.

I paced my lightless living room with my thoughts tied up in knots, not wanting but needing to reach M. I stopped in front of the window, imagining her standing beside me in my reflection there. *What should I do?* One streetlight was all that opposed the darkness and isolation of my disconnected night. *How can I reach you?*

Her number was on my PTBT list at NYU.

And there was a phone in my office there.

I ran the twelve blocks to campus, a mile at half-miler speed. An Olympian torch bearer, street light to street light. Though exhausted and desperate for sleep, I was moving fast. I felt as if the Guru was chasing me, watching me, one step ahead of me, with his artificial intelligence and CIA army.

When I got to my office, the computer was in its place on my desk. My novel but not the ToE had been backed up to that computer. That must have been why the FBI hadn't seized it too. They didn't care for literature, just science and technology.

Sitting at my desk, I wrote a script for my call to M. It took me an hour and several drafts—not for artistry but to thread the needle of communicating to M while not telegraphing my next moves to a listening Guru. We needed to release the theory while we still had a copy.

When she was on the line, I started by quietly reminding her not to say anything in case we were being listened to. I then explained the FBI raid and my failure to successfully hide the ToE. And damn it, I was so sorry to lose our *only* remaining copy of the theory after all of our searching. I begged her forgiveness, summoning the emotion of the scene at the yogi's when we believed the ToE would remain lost, which made for a convincing performance, I thought.

M was understanding, which meant she understood the game. She too was crestfallen but didn't blame me. "We can't fight our own government and expect to win. They'll release the ToE once they see it's meant for all of humanity," she said.

"He wants to work with you and your genius IQ if you will agree to keep it secret. You didn't mention you were a genius, but I guess I knew. Maybe you can convince him? And that way, you'll get to see the ToE again. Let's not say yes or no now." I knew M, and there was no way she'd agree the theory should be hidden for his AI weaponization.

"You know me, always an open mind. How does he know my IQ?"

"Like a good writer, I imagine he does his research and has a lot of AI and computer support. It feels like playing Deep Blue, a computer grandmaster in chess. Like he knows my next move."

I told her again of the Guru's declaration that he was coming after my job now that he'd discovered my lie. Then, with true fear in my voice—I didn't have to act—I told her of the stark threat to her life if we continued our efforts, which, of course, theory-less, we no longer could. I mentioned he would have to kill me too, and he couldn't go around killing everyone with impunity. Although such a note was superfluous, I'd left it in the script for future reference. And to sound heroic.

Then I took a coded quantum leap, hoping M would make the jump and continue to follow the subtext. "You know I'm no yogi and took no vow, so you'll understand. Whether he goes after my career or not, we need to stand down. He has the ToE and we don't. He's won, M." I paused to let her catch up.

"But let's remember better times," I continued, "like getting stoned, with Dylan dead but looking down on us from the Nepal mountaintop. I want to go there again with wine and weed, to sing with you, celebrating our manifesto of Big Love freely for all to see." I imagined the Guru listening and hearing two latter-day hippies celebrating free love.

"Sean, that's embarrassing. What if someone's listening to your come-on, *flower* child?"

She was improvising, so I went off script too.

"I don't care. I'm just desperate to know I haven't lost your love with my failure. You know my heart."

"Have no fear. Big Love is nothing if not free. And I don't care if they're listening. I hate that they have the ToE and we don't. You do what you need to do. I trust the Guru was bluffing about your career. Ruining you serves no purpose now."

"We'll see. But now I'm going to get some sleep."

"Okay. I'll keep my phone on. Let's both get to bed though; it's near midday here. I've only slept an hour since we left Kathmandu, and you sound tired too. My curtains are drawn, so it's nice and dark here, and my Do Not Disturb sign is lit, but you can always call. Goodbye, love. *Love is the absence of fear.*" She reminded me of Juno's catchphrase, the true guru.

M was a brilliant Agent 99, and I was getting smarter as the Sherlock I always imagined myself to be.

The light was coming up; it was almost six. I leaned forward to shut down my computer just as an email from Dean Sitwell, a fair-weather colleague, popped up.

Re: Urgent—Important Meeting—Please come to my office at 9 a.m. today, and bring your lawyer if you can. Come in any event. Time is of the essence. No frills or pleasantries.

He must have known I was already in my office. I laid my head on my desk. How was everyone tracking me? I'd never get to sleep. I felt watched. Hunted.

Since I'd always thought of my agent as my lawyer, I called him and left a desperate message asking that he call me immediately. As I was leaving the voice message, the cursor on my computer moved almost imperceptibly, but it was not just my imagination. They were on my computer—looking for what? Wait . . . The computer was looking at *me*. That was why it hadn't been seized. I shut it down and covered its peephole.

What secrets of mine could they see? And could they and would they really destroy my career? I pushed out of my chair and paced around my office. I looked at the posters. At the books. What I saw was memories. I'd loved my career, but for too long it had been just a job. And now I was a writer first and a professor second, and no one could take away my ability to write. If they took my hands, I could use a voice-activated computer. If they took my voice, I could use the Hawking device and move one eye to create a new voice. They would have to kill me before I would bury the theory that meant so much to M and, therefore, to me.

My concern was for M. What secret would I not want her to see? That I used Rogaine on my thinning hair? That I'd exchanged some-what provocative and embarrassing emails and texts with my crush students over the years? I'd never sent compromising photos or solic-ited an affair. That I still liked Woody Allen films despite his becoming an alleged Humbert Humbert? M would forgive me all that. She would even forgive me all my adolescent sexual fantasies, some of which I'd written into fictional erotic scenes—never to be seen, of course, but to make them feel real. I'd learned a lot about myself over the past month and had grown up just a bit; I was able to be the man she loved, even though the remnants of my old self flickered not far behind me.

After I completed my mind's embarrassment scan, a Bob Dylan lyric came to me, the one about having no secrets to conceal. No secrets apparently made one invincible. Or was it invisible?

I truly would become invisible if I lost my identity as a professor. The old Sean, the one from a month ago, emerged in that moment of reflection, wanting to experience the full and utter devastation of a helpless victim crushed by a powerful authority.

As a tenured professor, I wondered what the pretext would be. Did the Guru have some secret I couldn't think of that would justify my termination? I'd been a professor of literature for almost twenty years. It was my life, my history and future they were taking. Only now did I realize the bastard was no bluffer. The devil would have his due.

The elf on my desk mocked me as I wallowed in clichés. The picture of Dylan and Hope still lay facedown on the desk. I set it upright, angled toward me, as I readied to face death. I had survived an earthquake, death threats, and bullets across my face. But more fundamentally, I'd gained the perspective of one who had been graced by Big Love and who was loved by his beloved. Dylan's words about our having many incarnations in one life came to mind. I knew without a doubt that losing my position wouldn't alter M's love. She would see me as even more the hero for my sacrifice in the service of science and Big Love.

Those thoughts eased my concerns about being forced out of NYU, but they also left a deep-seated fear of not having enough money to live in New York City for even a couple months on my savings. M was in New York City.

I was comforted with the words Juno had spoken about trust. She had no fear, because she trusted life to provide only the challenges needed for wakening to fulfill our life's purpose. The earthquake came, and she transformed her precious Xanadu into a refugee camp without a second thought.

Thinking about Juno and all I'd learned gave me the buoyancy of Big Love in the face of losing my identity as an NYU professor, a status that had been my entire life just a month ago. But all that was before.

Elliot returned my call. I was still playing spy and asked him to come to the office. "Yes, now! I'll explain when you get here."

CHAPTER 67

THOUGH I WANTED TO TELL M that Dean Day had arrived early, I decided to let her sleep. The Guru coming after me meant M was safe for now. But I was in his crosshairs.

Elliot met me in my office before eight. Because my office was crawling with bugs that made me itchy and jumpy like a dog on the way to the vet, I quickly ushered him outside to explain the game plan. Elliot liked the adventure I described for the novel and was pleased at being dragged into the real-world version of it, if only at the tail end, for his dramatic role.

He eagerly agreed to portray my legal eagle. He really was a good friend and a good man, and not only for his willingness to enter the fray.

I asked him to go home and dress down a bit, by which I meant less flamboyantly, to look more like a lawyer. I was already prepared. In lieu of sleep, I meditated on the peace and oneness of Big Love. It was still with me in my deep heart's core.

We met again in busy Washington Square Park at nine. Elliot didn't like his costume, though he had placed a colorful handkerchief in his suit's breast pocket. I approved of it as something an older senior litigator might wear to show a little peacock. He also wasn't without his favorite prop—his cane.

He quickly told me he had found time to scan a legal article on tenure rights and due causes of dismissal and that we had a strong case.

I showed him my prop, the fifty-page introduction to my novel about Hope that he had left behind in my office over a month ago. I would wave it around as the legal memo that he'd supposedly prepared for me on short notice.

To minimize the deception of his imaginary legal license—and with some difficulty—I convinced Elliot that his was a nonspeaking role. I assured him that even without lines he would steal the show as the only one truly playing a part. I wanted a witness, not an advocate.

As we headed into Dean Sitwell's town house office on Washington Square Park, Elliot told me with pride, "You know, I played Gregory Peck playing Spencer Tracy playing Clarence Darrow on stage in *Inherit the Wind.*"

I acted as if I knew, though I didn't; I hadn't met Elliot until fifteen years ago, when he'd already given up acting to become a literary agent.

"Yes, Gregory Peck is more you."

He nodded, liking my concurrence regarding his looks and stature.

I worried how good an actor he would be in the high-stakes, real-life drama that was about to unfold.

The dean's town house office, overlooking the park, took up most of an entire floor. Although square, it was furnished like the Oval Office. It was less the office of a teacher and more the domain of a successful and important political bureaucrat.

Elliot made a grand entrance for us both, acting like a counsel to a titled peer. At our entrance, the dean introduced the man across the room.

"Sam Fur—from HR legal. He attends these meetings just to be safe."

HR. The ironic misnomer used by large organizations for the department that treated humans like resources and didn't provide resources to humans. Sam IDidn'tCatchHisLastName looked to have never known a moment of joy in his life and didn't bother to get out of his corner chair. His pallor suggested he didn't like the sun any more than he liked joy. I immediately recognized his type and passed negative judgment upon this surly flimflam Sam.

"This is Elliot, my legal representation."

Sam, rudely not realizing that Elliot had a nonspeaking role, asked, "Do you have a business card?"

Elliot beamed under the spotlight, thrilled to be given lines so early in the show. "Yes, I have a business card. You have a business card. I'm sure we all have business cards, but let's get to business, shall we, and not play cards?"

My tall and lean solicitor moved to his mark, cane stabbed into the floor in front of him, to stand sternly erect over the seated Sam. Elliot was covering him like a basketball player determined not to let his opponent score. Elliot, however, was already on the board.

Dean Sitwell, following his perfunctory greeting and an invitation for me to be seated, had returned to the chair behind his desk, giving him reign over his square court. He had obviously been counseled to say as little as possible while attempting to appease me on my way out the door. He got started from his script.

"Sean, we've known each other a long time. It's obvious you know why you're here. I'm sorry it has come to this, but we've decided to change direction in your department and would like your resignation."

I too had a script prepared. I pulled my introduction from my bag and crossed in front of the dean's desk, reviewing it as if it were a legal memo. Holding the pages up like exhibit 1 for the defense, I said, "Thank you, Elliot. This was quick work, and I'll heed your advice." I turned to face the dean. "Why would I do that, resign?" I motioned with my hand to halt Elliot when he inhaled a deep breath in preparation to speak.

"To avoid the alternative and an ugly scandal," Sam said from beneath the shadow cast by my man.

"Please tell me what scandal. I can't imagine." I really did want to know.

Sam said, "Let's just say certain significant and embarrassing improprieties and more." I wondered if, after not finding what he needed on my computer, the Guru had just placed dastardly deeds or perverted pictures there.

Elliot raised his cane as if he might pop Sam on the head, but he merely tossed it from his right hand to the left, distracting Sam with his theatrics and potential threat.

"Which ones exactly, and what more?" I asked.

"Let's not get into specifics." The dean, playing the good guy, jumped back in. "We're willing to pay a generous two years of severance for you to leave amicably."

"But this is my life, my career. What will I do?" I asked plaintively, gilding the lily. Elliot's performance was stoking my own.

Elliot lifted his weapon and, unable to control himself, started speaking off script. "This is outrageous. I insist—"

My upraised hand asked him to cease and desist.

"Okay, Sean. But you know my views on this." He relaxed the cane tip to the floor with a *tap tap* à la Fred Astaire.

Dean Sitwell said, "We know you loved being a professor here and this is most unfortunate, but you'll find another position."

I laughed insincerely. "You know that will be difficult to do under a cloud of suspicion concerning the reason I left my post here."

"That's why we're willing to pay you two years' severance. Here's the paperwork."

Sam got up, chafing as if he wore burlap underwear, to hand the papers to the dean, who handed them to me, who handed them to Elliot, who pulled out his reading glasses and immediately frowned. The dean finished by saying, "A simple and gracious resignation and severance agreement."

Sam slunk back to his chair. "Or we can go another direction with this, one that would cost the university a lot less." He spoke with the forced assertion of a two-bit bully.

Elliot glared menacingly down at Sam over his reading glasses, angrily tapping his cane—Morse code for *shut up*. Sam got the message.

I had two years free and clear and was starting to relax and enjoy the parlay. I gestured at Elliot in homage and held up the now rolled-up introduction. "After he provided me this brief with only a couple hours' notice, I asked that he refrain from speaking today. But he has very strong views as to my tenure and my rights to fight this and win, and not just maintain my position but receive damages for the threat of termination and any slander you may come up with."

Elliot beamed like an attack dog that thought he was about to be unleashed. Sam was also champing at the bit, but Dean Sitwell waved him off too. The two *lawyers* both growled in their corner.

"Sean, as a friend and colleague, I can make it three years' severance under university bylaws. That's all I'm empowered to do." The dean laid down his final card. "Sam, would you make that change, and I'll initial it."

Elliot, still holding the papers, received my nod of consent to return them to Sam; he complied grudgingly, holding on to the papers longer than necessary. Sam waggled his outstretched hand impatiently, vying to show who was the bigger shyster dog.

Face pinched with displeasure, Sam made the simple change of number by hand on that copy and on a duplicate copy, as instructed. The dean initialed the change and signed the papers as if we were done, saying, "Sean, let's not say more, as I can tell tensions are high and this means a lot to you. I need the agreement signed today or the board will become involved and we will move to terminate you without severance."

Having nothing to lose or hide, I said, "I've been advised"—I looked at Elliot—"that I must know what scandal I may possibly be involved in." I nodded in Sam's direction. "Just to be safe, you understand. For, I'm sure, this is just some minor misunderstanding."

Sam answered, "We're not at liberty to say, and you can pay your lawyer here and lose three years of severance to find out, only to find shame for yourself along with your loss of position."

Elliot couldn't restrain himself, and I let him off the leash.

"Well, thank you. That sounds like excellent advice to me, and that's exactly what we'll do. Yet it will be you and the university that pay. Sean, I cannot allow you to sign this."

He came over to me, genuinely grinning, and snatched my rolled-up introduction—his brief—and waved it over his head. He lit up like a fire-and-brimstone preacher to declare, "We can get a lot more. And if we find the CIA is behind all this, what sensational and adverse publicity that will be. We'll file suit against them too. Sean, you'll be a whistleblower and get triple damages."

"That's not the way the law works," Sam said, his darting eyes watching Elliot's cane as Elliot marched back to his corner.

"Oh, now you're going to tell *me* how the law works. Sean, let's go.

We're wasting our time with this supposedly esteemed liberal college doing the bidding of illegal government overreach."

I hadn't thought it advisable to bring the CIA into the matter and didn't think to warn Elliot, since he wasn't supposed to open his mouth. However, those initials clearly spooked the dean. He too feared the Guru.

Sitwell stood up to pace behind his desk, staring out the second-story window as if he might be watched from the park below. "Wait. Just wait." He circled his desk, eyes on the pricey carpet under his feet, before slowly saying, "There's one last thing I can do, though it's a stretch, and I might be questioned later. But we can characterize this as a retirement package—twenty years of service—and not a resignation. We'll remove the normal restriction on future employment and provide you fifty percent of your current salary for life starting after the three years of the full severance, which is normally paid as a lump sum up front in the case of retirement."

Sam, quite animated, jumped up and moved away from Elliot, hurrying to the protection of the dean's desk to speak to his client. He half whispered but could still be heard to say, "I strongly advise against that, Dean Sitwell."

Elliot and cane stalked him across the room, and in a mockingly pleasant voice, he asked, "Any more good advice from you, Iago?"

"Let's not get personal," Sitwell said. "Yes, Sam, it's more perhaps than we should offer and is all I can do. Please sit here and make those changes—on my computer." He moved aside for Sam to take his seat. "We need this done today. Sean, we shouldn't let our lawyers mess this up."

Mess it up? Grace Byrne had nothing on my dear Elliot. He was a class act.

Sam started his work on the computer. Elliot, now fully in charge, said, "Sean, let's step outside a minute. I think you're being railroaded. There are a few compelling points that I lay out in my brief that make this a great case, points you may not have gotten a chance to review."

Fearing he might overplay his part, I was eager to step outside.

We walked down the hall and out of earshot of the dean's assistant. Elliot had to hold back giggles he was so happy to be acting again, and I too had to fight to maintain my poker face. "Let's just wait till they come out to get us," I said. "You don't know who may be watching or listening."

Though they couldn't hear us—unless the Guru was somehow listening—we were careful. Elliot spent the next ten minutes lecturing me on fictional employment tenure law and why I should fight this deal and never take it. If I didn't know better, I would have thought he was a lawyer.

The dean opened the door and asked us to come back in if we were ready. Inside, there were two new copies of the agreement printed for execution. Elliot stood reading one while I sat reading the other. I was reading the provision about receiving fifty percent of my current salary each year for the rest of my new life—I'd be free to write!—when Elliot slammed the papers down with a dramatic bang.

He glared at Sam. "What kind of sleazeballing trick is this? It still says two years—not three years—of severance." The initialed change on the prior draft had inadvertently—or intentionally—failed to make it into the final draft.

Slippery Sam snarled, "A mistake." He returned to the dean's desk and computer, where with painful sighs he punched keys, transforming two years into three. When he removed the updated pages from the printer, you'd have thought he was pulling the additional lump sum out of his own pocket.

Elliot was still shaking his head as he tapped his cane to the floor three times, his signal for *done*. I signed the two copies. The dean signed too and gave me one of the executed copies, saying, "You really got the best deal I could possibly offer, and the alternative would have been a disaster for us both." He pressed his lips together and quietly added, "And I think you probably knew that." We shook hands. "Good luck. There are people you'd be ill-advised to cross. Be more careful in the future."

I was tempted to repeat the warning for him, though it was probably too late; he was already caught in the Guru's web.

Elliot refused to shake Sam's hand, shaking the point of his cane at the shyster instead as his way of waving bye-bye. I managed, by making no effort, to avoid shaking Sam's hand too.

As we stepped outside and started to walk through the park, I had to consciously keep a shattered face and refrain from teaching Elliot the shake-off dance in case we were watched through the windows above or by a Dick skulking nearby. I was perhaps the happiest man ever after being fired from my lifelong position and the apex of my ambition since high school.

The Guru had taken his best shot, and it was best he was left thinking he'd won. I used Elliot's phone to call M. She didn't answer, but her voice message did. I asked her to call Elliot's phone as soon as possible. Her sleeping through my call was not supposed to happen.

I went back to my NYU office; they hadn't thought to ask for my key. There I still had a phone and a compromised computer. Elliot insisted on joining me, as he wanted to go over the details of his acting comeback again and again. I warned him to assume we were being listened to while in my office. I tried M again using Elliot's phone. She still didn't answer. I tried the office phone in case she was checking the number coming in. Still no answer. Something about the overseas ringtone made her feel terribly far away.

To finish my career, I composed my retirement letter—a short yet elegant release of a life—as required by the official-sounding Retirement and Severance Agreement dated that day. I wrote it for the Guru to satisfy his spite, to reveal the depths of despair he had flung me into. I concluded with "Thrust from my life as a teacher, I will attempt to write novels of dark mystery, searching for the lost light. May the muses find me in the darkness and whisper in my ear their secret way back into that light."

Elliot laughed as I let him read the flowery prose. I cautioned him with a glare.

I hoped the dean and the Guru wouldn't recognize the snark, but as a literature professor, I'd been trained by the best in how to wallow in deep despair. I was entitled to dive into that dark pool of romantic creativity. Plus, I had a couple of days' grace; the agreement required the letter to be sent by old-fashioned mail. I printed a copy and slid it into a stamped envelope and added the dean's address.

I was going home to post my resignation prose, eat something frozen from the fridge, shower, and finally go to bed. We were using acting and writing to battle the government and artificial intelligence. And the old school was winning its game of chess against Big Blue.

Elliot, despite some reluctance, agreed I could keep his phone until I could reach M. She must have been sound asleep not to hear that overseas distance call ringing, buzzing like the "murmuring of innumerable bees."

CHAPTER 68

AS SOON AS I GOT TO my apartment, I dropped the retirement letter down the old post slot of my prewar building. With a *swoosh*, that life was gone, gone, gone.

I wanted to tell M about my loss and liberation, but again there was no answer. Her voice mail was full of my increasingly desperate messages, with no room for another. And having forgotten the hotel's name, I had no way to reach her.

She must have been exhausted. I certainly was. After we both got some sleep, we'd agree on the best means to release the ToE. With Elliot's phone, perhaps we could speak more freely, and I could ensure she was on board for any further action, since the threat had now shifted to her.

Getting a foreign court to agree to a search and seizure would take time. The Guru had already shown his teeth and bite. I assumed he'd heard on our last phone call that we were without the ToE and standing down. M was safe for now.

I curled up in my bed like a mountain climber succumbing to sleep and certain death on a frozen Everest. I would wait to shower until I got up.

Hovering at Jackson Browne's dark and silent gate of sleep, I heard a woman's voice—Eastern European accent—say, "McQueen, stay awake!" I was back with the Gypsies in the queen's caravan, and she was unhappy with me, repeating those words, chastising me. All I wanted was some rest on the cushions by her feet, but she kept insisting until I shook off the death of sleep—literally shaking my head until the circling images of the queen and caravan disappeared like a merry-go-round lifting into the sky.

The wake-up call—Queen Mab's admonishment, a red alert—had me on edge. Something wasn't right. I rubbed my face, trying to think past my brain fog and alarm. I imagined myself a boxer that had gone ten rounds and had my bell rung and didn't know to which corner to head. I went to the bathroom and splashed cold water on my face. As I looked in the mirror, I heard Dylan speak to me from the other side: *I'm always in your corner, but this is your fight to keep you and Em alive.*

Two more rounds? I asked as he pulled the metaphorical chair out from under me and thrust me back into the ring.

M knew the stakes, *and* she'd said she'd leave her phone on. I got up—still dressed—grabbed my bag, and headed to the only place I could find the ToE. As I got into a taxi, I said, "West Village. I forget the name of the street, but I'll direct you."

Without any rap in the taxi and with M's life at stake, my heavy mind was full of counterweights—a call to action and a call to wait. The Guru's threat was dire, suggesting harm to M if I didn't quash the ToE and allow him alone to possess it. He had shown that he was no bluffer. Perhaps our phone call hadn't convinced him and he was even now taking a preemptive strike at M, looking to erase all copies of the ToE.

That line of thinking led to a singularly horrifying thought—M could rewrite the theory herself now. Maybe not word for word, but she knew the scientific concepts by heart. The Guru would have to erase M too!

I recognized that I was crazed, but in my mind that man was a psychopath. He might assume she could be silenced by threats to her life and mine, but he didn't know M. Or maybe he did. I rubbed my eyes and then my face again. I thought M had understood my coded lies signaling my intent to still release the theory, but I couldn't be sure.

How could I protect M, in Athens, from Manhattan? We'd already survived an earthquake, a death threat, and gunshots; could I honestly expect we'd be lucky any longer? Bad luck was due. Snake eyes were watching me everywhere. M might already be dangling from the Guru's web, which he now could spin from my phone as he unspooled my secrets there. I couldn't live if it meant M's death.

I phoned Natalie from the taxi, but she still looked surprised when

I showed up. I must have looked like an unemployed man who hadn't showered or slept for days. Still, her welcoming hug was warm. She was a ToE holder that the Guru couldn't trace. I had deleted that evidence from my phone.

I apologized for the intrusion and explained to Natalie the incredible events that had led me to her door—and that M still wasn't answering her phone, her texts, or her email.

"Sean, please sit down. You look exhausted and can't possibly be thinking straight. Glass of wine?"

"Thank you. No wine. Not yet." I sat in the same seat in the living room where I had sat so pleasantly high a month before. Dylan and Grace still stared down in joyful compassion from the fateful mountaintop.

"I have a plan and need your help," I said. "Once we hear from M, I believe for everyone's safety, including yours and Grace's"—I leaned forward to speak my treason—"we should release the ToE into the world."

An hour later, Schrödinger's box was built and his cat placed inside, ready for when we learned M was safe and that she agreed to the plan.

After Natalie wholeheartedly gave her consent, we'd called Hope's ELF, a woman who'd gone on to become a popular blogger. She called right back and agreed to post the ToE. She'd met Dylan at Hope's funeral and thought him a fascinating man. I rewrote the ToE's introduction from memory, as it was mercifully short, while Natalie typed up the ToE from the pictures of the handwritten pages I'd sent to her phone.

The ELF quickly made format changes and corrected my and Dylan's spelling, and we were ready to set the ToE free.

The ELF understood the urgency and would wait for my command to post the ToE and my introduction for the world to see. With the First Amendment on her side, the ELF wasn't afraid of the Guru. I was and grew more afraid as I laid out all the dangers to her.

Natalie poured us glasses of red wine, and we toasted Dylan and the ToE as we tried M again without success.

"How long has M been asleep now?" she asked.

"Around four hours. She must be exhausted—I know I am. I feel an amazing sense of relief about this all being over soon, yet I'm filled with a perhaps irrational dread about M." I drank down my wine. "I will be until we speak."

To my dread's relief, a call chimed in on Elliot's phone. M! I answered Elliot's phone to speak to my lost love, only to hear the Guru's voice. I jumped out of my seat and moved close to Natalie.

"Are you crazy? Have you not learned? You can't just double-click Delete and think an email is gone, you idiot." He was agitated, winded, and backed by street sounds.

"I don't understand," I said.

"Don't lie to me again! I need you to be a rational partner in our dance, or tragedy will ensue. There's already a woman missing in Athens. Such a loss of a brilliant young mind and body that would be. I'm a magician who can make people disappear. Do nothing but get some sleep with your dead friend's wife."

The phone screen went blank, either out of power or cut off. It was dead.

A missing woman . . . loss . . .

"The Guru . . . He knows I'm here."

Natalie grabbed my hand and squeezed. "Sean, it's—"

Her phone rang. She answered it on speaker.

"Natalie, we know Sean McQueen is with you and that you have a copy of your dead husband's theory. What your friend hasn't told you is we have reason to believe the Chinese abducted Professor Edens in Athens. I fear the same fate for you, maybe Grace if we're not careful. The Chinese need to be assured there are no drafts outstanding. We believe that McQueen may be in league with the Chinese. The FBI will be there soon with a warrant. Please be smart about this. I'd hate for other lives—your life, your daughter's—to be ruined by McQueen's lack of patriotism and inability to follow orders. This is a matter of national security."

Her phone went silent too, the screen blank. He was a high-tech magician.

The doorbell buzzed. I could see Bill and Bob and their SWAT team.

"Don't they sleep?" I turned to Natalie. "Is there another way out of here?"

"Yes, but I don't have a ladder. If you go out into the garden and can get over the high wall, you'll come out on the side street."

As I headed into the garden, I told her, "Do what they demand of you. Protect you and Grace. I'm going to release the ToE. Blame me." Less than a minute later, I was out the back and had scaled the eight-foot wall like a decathlete.

CHAPTER 69

MID-ESCAPE, MY FIRST, SECOND, AND THIRD thoughts were to get to my NYU office. There before they barged in, I would release the ToE and suffer the consequences.

Hyperventilating, I ran the ten blocks like Benjamin from *The Graduate* racing *Marathon Man* from the dentist to the church. My writer's bag swung wildly from my shoulder, rattling and whacking passersby, with me a demon mailman desperate to deliver his message. The sidewalks called after me, "Slow down, douchebag." The intersections honked. I thought someone was chasing me—perhaps Bill or Bob or a street cop—but they couldn't keep up with my surging adrenaline.

Arriving at my office drenched in sweat, I collapsed and wheezed while my thoughts raced on. I couldn't call the FBI or CIA, and the police seemed useless to me. I barred the door with one of the chairs and set all devices to the ready—to text, email, and speed dial the ELF telling her to release the theory as planned. At the first sign they were coming for me, I'd give the command.

However, the Guru might jam all my outgoing means of communication. I called the ELF and gave her very specific instructions to release the theory in exactly sixty minutes unless she heard from me. The ELF was always in hiding, ever since taking her liberal views on the freedom of education. She assured me no one, not even the CIA, could find her location in sixty minutes. I was not so sure.

I closed my curtains to avoid the unlikely event of sniper fire. I was dazed and confused and taking no chances. The Guru was mad as a hatter for whom time had stopped. He was moving faster than my thoughts. He must have read Dylan's theory about traveling at the speed of light and still thought it would in some crazy way illuminate his quantum computer or his brain-computer interface.

I caught my breath and googled *US citizen international abductions* and found it was the State Department's jurisdiction.

As I was looking up contact numbers for the State Department, the haunting image of Hope dead slammed into my head. Oh God, not again.

I phoned the State Department and got a runaround that basically said someone had to be missing for forty-eight hours and be reported by a relative. I said I was her husband and she went missing three days ago. They asked the name of the hotel where she'd been staying. They said they'd have to start there and would send me forms to fill out. I couldn't invoke any sense of urgency and was reluctant to say the CIA was behind it all. The woman said she could do no more and to call back after I had the hotel name and had filled out the forms, which required proof of relationship. They would then check phone records and the hotel to ensure she was missing the requisite time. I hung up.

I googled hotels in Athens, and under the *E*s I recognized the name M had told me in passing—Electra Metropolis. I phoned the hotel. Overseas ringing in Athens sounded like the *brrrr brrrr brrrr* of angry bees incited by the shattering of their hive. Finally someone picked up, and I asked for M.

"Yes, I speak English, but, sir, she is not here."

"Please ring her room for me."

"I might, but she left with the police a while ago."

"What? Why?"

"I don't . . . Maybe you should call them."

"Do you have the number?"

"They did not leave one. Maybe check information."

"Would you please help me get the police precinct phone number? I'm in New York and have no idea how."

"Please hold." Greek folk music played.

M, what do I do?

As I waited, the image of Hope dead in the hotel bed battered me. Desperate, I intoned *Mmmmm*—M's name as a mantra—and the image disappeared.

I hoped the clerk was helping me and not checking someone in or just leaving me hanging in my living, burning hell. After minutes of me alternating between slow breathing and *mmm*ing, he returned with a number for "the nearest police house." I gave him Elliot's number, asking him to please have Professor Edens call that number if she returned.

More of the foreign-sounding ringing followed at the police station, and it took three tries to reach someone—Darrien—with adequate enough English to understand who I was looking for.

"Em-ile E-dens?" He spoke English with a nervous lisp and stutter.

"Yes, Emily Edens," I repeated. "I need to speak to her. Her mother is dying, and she wants to say her final goodbye."

"Sorry. She may have been here."

"Please tell me, did anyone take her? It's a matter of life and death."

I heard two voices, Darrien speaking to someone in Greek and then another voice speaking to me.

"Sir, we don't know you. If you give me your information . . . But we cannot tell you more even for a matter of life and death."

I hung up and picked up the elf and banged the bronze down, bruising my wood desk. I put my hands to my face, rubbing, thinking, slowly losing my mind to the voice of the Guru and the buzzing bees.

M must be being interrogated in some black site. Tortured in a twisted job interview. *Extraordinary CV, and I love your genius mind. Come work for me or die.* If she wasn't being held, she would have called when my messages became increasingly emphatic. I'd told her to use Elliot's phone, but she also had my work number and email. Yes, they were being watched, but if she had to reach me . . .

If someone had M, she might be safer with the ToE released. M would want the ToE released.

Natalie, Grace, and Juno were now also at risk. I was rubbing my face with both hands so hard it hurt. M would want the ToE released.

But what if the Guru took his cruel revenge and in spiteful rage killed M?

M would want the ToE released.

I phoned the living ELF. "Release it now. Don't wait."

"Consider it done. So exciting!"

"I'll call you later to confirm. Thank you and . . . Thank you."

Mmmmm. Was that the right move? I was speaking to M, and that scared me even more. I sat—no, I stood and pulled back the curtains, staring out the window before I remembered the potential for sniper fire. Then I sat back at my desk, not knowing what to do next. I looked at my makeshift barricade to bar the Guru's goons entry to what was no longer my office. I looked down, at no longer my desk. He could take anything from me by the perversity of his power and authority.

My office phone rang. Thank God.

"M?"

"Em? How cute. She's with me. Sean, I told you not to mess around with this. Why didn't you wait for me? This would be easier face-to-face so you could see I'm deadly serious."

My body shook uncontrollably, rattling to *his* horrific voice.

"You're all over the place, son. We're all at Natalie's lovely apartment having coffee and looking at a draft blog post you two prepared. Traitor and Chinese spy are not good résumé builders. Boy, you better think twice before pushing that button to release your country's property. What a bloody mess that would be. Byrne's theory is my baby now. Helter-skelter, you're all over the place, not thinking straight. Do you want me to unleash the dogs of hell? You better get your act together. That blog post we found ready to go on Natalie's computer would, if released, drive the Chinese into a murderous rage. You know we believe you are working for them and killed my man there in Nepal. We hope to find evidence of that on your computer." I wasn't sure if he was lying or just prepared to manufacture his own reality.

"Where's Emily?" I demanded. It flashed across my mind to confess and beg he take my life, not hers—since I was the one who had released the theory into the world.

"I told you she's with me. We'll have to see. Maybe she's a patriot and will turn on you. In any event, she'll only be safe once you see sense and stand down. I hope that happens before it's too late for your Em." He laughed at my pet name. "Em is so lovely. She sleeps . . . What a beautiful picture I received. I think that's a teddy. Yes, a teddy . . . Maybe just the tip of a nip there . . . Sexy come-hither smile. As if she's taunting me. No, teasing me. She's been waiting for me. I wonder if she'll wake soon or ever. The Chinese are so adept in snatching people overseas and torture. I'll send it to you, the picture. Don't do anything stupid."

"What the hell? What picture? If you're going to kill anyone else, why not me?" *Should I confess?*

A click introduced dead air. I couldn't breathe. He would soon find out I'd already released *his baby* into the cruel world. And he'd know I lied to him again by my omission.

My email chimed. An image. I opened it. There was my love, sound asleep in her hotel bed, in her soft white-cotton muscle tee, not a teddy. So beautiful. So horrifying. The caption beneath the picture read, "She asks if you have a message for Dylan." As I stared at that picture of horror and beauty, it disappeared from the screen. He was controlling both ends of the message.

Had I killed M by releasing the ToE?

Thinking it might not be too late, I phoned the ELF. "Did it go out?"

"Yep, published. I admit I didn't know what to do after all those emails and texts."

"What emails and texts?"

"First they said not to post the blog, to erase everything and not to contact you, that it wasn't safe. But I knew they had your phone. Then more messages from Natalie's phone. I didn't know what to do, but it's too late now. And no sooner did it go live than we're fighting off a sophisticated hack attack. Luckily our international servers are keeping us lit."

Another call was ringing on my office line . . . "I have to go."

"McQueen, are you a complete idiot? We've seen your blog post— posted! Really stupid. You're not acting logically. Your girlfriend is now on life support. The Chinese are already dripping water on her forehead and sharpening the knives."

I searched in my bag for my missing letter opener to dive it deep into the university's desk or my chest. I wanted to speak, but no words came.

"You listening closely? If you want to see her again, you need to listen very carefully. There's not much time now, but let me make clear how easily these things are done. Did you know the Chinese contacted me about the theory? My team now tells me your notes indicate the Chinese abducted and tortured a yogi in their mad pursuit of the ToE. Perhaps you agreed to sell it to them. So unpatriotic, but who knows what else we'll find now that we have your hard drive and our own keyboard and time stamp?"

Still no words or knife. I picked up the poor elf and banged it down again, this time splintering the wood under its weight and my impotent rage.

"Bang, bang, bang—are you throwing things? I was hoping she'd be more a patriot than you and would work for the red, white, and blue team, but she too refused reason and her duty. So you see, M—as a scientist who had seen the theory—was an obstacle the Chinese had to remove. You understand, I'm sure. I'm moving fast, but I'll figure it out—a lot of high cliffs in Greece where hikers fall to their deaths all the time. The Athens Police would agree. And your former dean tells me you were a bit unstable following your first wife's death, and now losing Emily and your career for an unsavory cause . . . You'd go crazy with conspiracy theories regarding her disappearance, wouldn't you? Unbelievable theories . . . Then with the guilt of working with the Chinese and causing her death, maybe you'd take your own life. You listening?"

"Mmmmm." I couldn't say anything else.

"Have that blog pull down the ToE now and replace it with the updated version I'm sending you. You're lucky for my foresight and AI abilities. You have fifteen minutes. After that, your treason will be irreversible, and the correction will be of no value to me. Did you hear me? Do you understand? The attachment is on its way. Last chance, boy. Her life is in your hands. Such a waste."

Oh God. I couldn't breathe.

"Remember, reality is malleable to will and power. Do it!"

"Motherfucker, it may take more time. Release M now—" The demand was launched into dead air.

Ten seconds later, an email attachment came in.

I already had the ELF holding on the line.

"How long would it take you to substitute a new version of the ToE? It's critical we do it now."

"Why? Never mind. I can do it in five minutes when I have the new file."

"It should be there now. Stay on the line and let me know when you get it and are prepared to substitute it. We have only ten minutes."

"Got it!"

While I waited for the ELF to prepare the substitution, I opened the new file and started to read. It was a jumble of the ToE that sounded logical but uninspired. Artificial intelligence had kept the ToE cogent in sentences and meaning, though the bastard theory had each section's insight leading back to the big bang. Constant creation was just a matter of time and space marching away from the singularity of the big bang, which had set the clock in motion with a starter pistol's pop. Though it sounded like the chairman's voice behind the gibberish, this was the work of the Guru's AI machine called Apate. My love song of an introduction was also bastardized, removing all mention of my love and her true scientific endorsement. What remained were the confused ramblings of a Romantic poetry teacher describing the deep cosmos and the infinite from a shallow pool of limited knowledge.

As I pictured the Guru playing the chords of his AI organ to produce this tidy piece of misinformation, it hit me where I'd seen him before. He was the minister of death, the nattily dressed, white-faced choirmaster of the piper's battle song on the balcony at Dylan's wake.

The ELF said, "I'm ready. Should I hit the button?"

"Thank God!" We were still within the fifteen-minute window.

I rubbed my face violently and then winced from the agony of cartilage cracking in my nose, from the pain that shot into my head and caused a loud ringing in my ears and brought stars to my eyes. I thought I might pass out, but then everything rushed back into focus.

I inhaled for a Juno pause in that moment of truth. I saw the choice we had each moment of creation as the *I am* arises in us. *I am fucked, I have no choice, the Guru has all the power* or *I am Big Love and will act without fear as guided by my heart.*

I listened as a message of clarity cut through my tempest-tortured mind. The incongruity of the Guru's threats—my career but M's life? Why not my life?

He was bluffing.

He couldn't afford to take a woman's life to no end other than spite and then look to blame the Chinese.

He had acted rationally till now. Taking away my career was a punishment and a warning. Killing M would be trouble for him; he'd have to kill me too. With Dylan's death—with the ELF, Natalie, and Juno—the cover-up would be immense and far from airtight. And the real ToE would still be liberated for all to read.

My stormy mind sent back tsunamis of doubt and fear, shouting that I couldn't gamble with M's life. But either way, I was rolling the dice.

The Guru had figured out that M had learned the theory and that he could never control it while she was alive.

M, what should I do?

Her answer, free of doubt and fear, came.

To the ELF I said, "No! Do not replace it. Leave it exactly as is. Sorry, but I'll explain later. Bye."

As soon as I finished speaking, the image of Hope morphed into the Guru's picture of M.

Oh God, what had I done?

Nose burning and ears still ringing, I sat in prayer, not knowing what else to do. "From the heart," Juno said. My heart cried out as the Guru's fifteen-minute window slammed shut.

My God, what had I done? I'd incited the Guru's need for immediate revenge. Instant black karma. Now by simply typing a code word, he would make M permanently disappear. God save her! God save us.

Now I turned to God, the author of life, for it was in his hands and the Guru's cell phone.

After my crying prayer, I tried the State Department again, using my office phone so the Guru would hear. I wanted him to know he'd have to kill me too. I was explaining how time was of the essence in a life-and-death drama to a sympathetic ear, but when I mentioned the CIA, that sympathetic ear said, "Wait. If the CIA is involved, you need to speak to them. I'll transfer you." And with that *click click* and more damn ringing, I was being transferred. I hung up.

I next tried M's hotel again in Athens. It rang *brrrr brrrr brrrr*.

Eventually someone picked up; it was the same clerk as before. I had to speak to Professor Emily Edens, but before I could say "life or death," he said, "Sir, we don't have rooms available on that date." And then to someone in the hotel, he said something in Greek. The person responded harshly with what sounded like "*Sikoste to tilefono!*" which I interpreted as *Get off the phone*. The clerk said something else and then was back with me. "Sir, I'll call you back to see what might be arranged. There's a work detail here, and I need to get off the phone."

"I don't want—" *Click*. The Greek line was dead. Click, and all the people I loved were dead.

I wanted to shout in burning frustration and sleep-deprived madness and despair.

I rang back the Athens police station. More foreign ringing. More *brrrr brrrr brrrr*—the whole fucking swarm stinging me. *Brrrr brrrr* fucking *brrrr*ing bees.

Again someone answered, and again I couldn't understand.

"Please, do you speak English?" Please speak English. It took three tries, but finally they put on someone who spoke my language.

"Yes. Hello, this is the Athens Police."

"I'm calling from New York. I need to speak to Professor Emily Edens. She was taken there. I'm her lawyer and need to speak to her."

"Sir, whatever you are, I cannot confirm where she is or anything about her. You may come to the station house if you like, but she is not here. Never was . . ."

"Shit. I told you I'm in New York!"

"I don't like your tone or cursing."

Click. More deadly clicking.

With the Guru's poison net of threats and lies contracting around me, I couldn't breathe. There was always so much we could never know, but now the unknown might have led to the death of my love from an internet post. Each morbid thought arising from the Guru's voice forced me to see through his beady eyes. He'd have to kill M after abducting her. Blame the Chinese. Blame me. And I'd be crazy, ranting about theories and conspiracies unless he killed me too. An ex-professor barricaded in his old office after being removed from his post, resisting arrest. Perhaps my time had come too. I wondered if they would knock first.

I tried to breathe, focusing on the picture of Hope and Dylan on my desk, not knowing what to do. They told me to pray for the dead. My heart was stuck in my throat and choking there in unintelligible prayer.

I was considering calling the hotel back when it struck me that maybe the hotel clerk wasn't confused. Maybe the work detail wasn't a work detail. Maybe he was under duress too. My inability to communicate and connect was torture by technology. I had made a life-and-death decision for M under a dark cloud of confusion cast by the Guru. My only source of information was the devil himself.

I wished he would call so I could beg him to take my life, not M's, as his revenge. Any word was better than silence, better than all the foreign ringing and clicking into dead air without knowing.

That dawn when Hope had died, my heart knew before I turned over in our hotel room bed to see her eyes dead . . .

Mmmmm.

Mmmmm.

Mmm*mmmmmmm . . . What did I do?*

Stop! You know you only speak to the dead that way.

I was damned and didn't know whether it was Dylan's, M's, or my own voice that reminded me of my medium-like ability that now, in my head, was the kiss of death.

I bit my lip and pressed both hands to my heart. Closed my eyes. And I heard it. Felt it. The echo of a fearless heart that beat in tandem with mine. She couldn't be dead!

Elliot's phone rang in my pocket. The Guru now had his number too. My death sentence had arrived. My mind couldn't fathom the dark curtain falling around me, though I welcomed his call. Funny, the word I chose to greet the abyss.

"Hello?"

"Sean?"

M!

I broke down. All the way down. The shell not only cracked but exploded, and a blithering idiot held the phone on my end of the line.

"Sean, is that you? Are you there?"

"Tell me you're okay. Are you alive and free?"

"*I'm a free girl in Athens, and very much alive,*" she sang into my heart, "though a bit poorer and disconnected. Are you okay? I was detained for so long . . . until ten minutes ago. And with no way to reach you."

"Oh God, M. I'm okay, yes. And you're okay. You've been missing all this time. I'm a puddle now." I squeezed my eyes shut and then opened them to see sparkling diamonds floating through my vision. I felt their warmth roll down my joyful cheeks.

"You're a poodle? I always saw you more as a Labrador. You sound awful. Are you really okay?"

"I'm fine—hurt my nose—wonderful hearing your voice." God, her voice . . . "Where were you?"

It was a miracle. She was safe.

My heart did not lie.

CHAPTER 70

"HOLD ON—DON'T YOU GO ANYWHERE. I'll be right back. Stay on the line! Don't go anywhere!" We were reconnected, and I was back in the light and taking charge of my decisions.

I quickly wrote the ELF, Juno, Elliot, and Natalie a cryptic email message disclosing that the Guru at the CIA had threatened M's life and suggested he would frame the Chinese. I let them know we were now safe, and we intended to let the matter go unless he took further action against us. To be safe, I asked them to forward the message to a couple of people they trusted.

Vengeful Big Brother was still watching, but he couldn't go around killing everyone. The message was an insurance policy. The Guru was evil but rational, and we had called his bluff; the ToE was free.

M was still on the line, and I explained my side of the story to her— my race with the Guru, his raids on my apartment and Natalie's, his calls and threats—and concluded by confessing, "He made me believe you were dead if I released the ToE, and I made myself believe you were dead if I didn't. Then I convinced myself I had killed you by gambling your life." I released the breath I'd been holding for hours. "I felt you blow on the dice before I rolled them. Did I do right?"

"Oh, Sean . . . And I've been sitting around drinking strong, sweet Greek coffee. Well, if you'd done what he said and been his puppet, I'd have been very disappointed in you. But you didn't give way to fear. Sean Byron McQueen, do you see? You had a Big Love reaction to that egomaniac's attack! Thank you, my hero!"

M included my last name when chiding me, but adding the sexy *Byron* served as foreplay to a compliment or favor. I danced around the office like an Irishman to a fiddle after nine pints.

"Hurt your nose? Let me guess how. But if you did substitute the faux ToE—as you called it—and he killed me, he'd have to kill you and maybe the ELF and Natalie too, wouldn't he?"

I stopped dancing. "Maybe. I couldn't think of everything and maybe didn't think it all through. The ELF would need Natalie's approval to publish Dylan's real theory, and he was threatening Grace, and with you out of the way—who knows? There wasn't any time on the clock. The what-ifs . . . We'll never know. But thank God you're okay."

"Thanks to you. Sounds like you risked your life," she said, striking back up the fiddler's bow.

"Yes, once again. There's so much we'll never know, but . . . while we still don't have concrete evidence he had Dylan killed, I no longer doubt that the Guru was behind Dylan's death."

"You know or just suspect? That's so wrong. So, so horrible!" Her raised voice trailed off into a groan of frustration. And then lowering it, she added, "Sean, I don't have the words if that's true."

We had put the cause of Dylan's death on hold while we searched for his theory, and now I'd brought it back with a horrid accusation, opening a cold case and freezing the joy out of our moment of celebration.

"I'm sorry. Now's not the time. I'll tell you later all that he said that makes me think it's unfortunately true."

The whisper of soft deep breaths revealed her grappling with the pain of my indictment. I imagined her settling herself with prayer hands at her heart, and I lowered my head in solidarity.

A moment later that lovely voice was again light. "Sean, you did great! Your saying 'I'm no yogi' and mentioning Natalie's picture above the mantel were nice touches, by the way. Only I could have followed your clever clues, my flower child."

"You understood my code!" My heart was dancing again.

"I'm a quantum physicist. That makes one very adept at seeing things two ways at once. So the ToE is released on this ELF's popular blog—it's out in the world?"

"Like Schrödinger's cat."

"And it's alive! You're learning your quantum physics."

"Well, I noted you were schooling yourself in Romantic poetry."

"There's no way the Guru can stop it now, my double-oh-seven. Do you have a computer there? I want you to pull up the blog."

"Okay, M." Giggling like a schoolboy, I started to do just that. "Wait. First tell me your story. What happened to you?"

"Well, I was apparently quite tired after we hung up. I . . . you're not going to believe this, but I slept through a ransacking of my hotel room. I'm sure I wasn't drugged or anything, just exhausted. Probably best I slept through it. When I woke up, my papers, passport, wallet, phone, all gone."

"Your laptop too, I suppose?"

"That too. Don't laugh at me—you know I'm not romantic—but with no way to reach you, I kept shaking my dervish bracelet, ringing it for comfort anytime I was left alone by the police at the station."

"I'd forgotten all about that." I reached into my bag, pulled out my bracelet, and put it on. "There sure was a lot of ringing going on, though." I gave my bracelet a jingle into the speaker of my phone. She sent back her jangle. We were, had been—would always be—connected.

"Did they find your hard copy of the theory like they found mine?"

"Well, that's embarrassing too, but thankfully they didn't." Her laugh had me both smiling and wanting to cry. "I realized Dylan's written ToE was only valuable as a precious sentimental memento, because . . . well, because I now had that theory in my genius head. The theory was safe within me. I rolled up my hard copy and crawled into bed with it tucked into my shorts."

"So you were sleeping with my best friend."

"His masterpiece, anyway. You jealous?" she asked.

"Nope. It's big love."

She laughed and then said, "After I woke up, the hotel called the police, and I spent a couple hours at their station filling out a report. I omitted telling them about the Guru and the CIA—I wanted to speak to you first. After my report was filed, they asked me to stay in a holding room. There was a language barrier, but I don't think I was free to go. They said it was for my safety, that it wasn't yet safe for me to return to the hotel. The plainclothes men and the uniformed cops seemed to be at some odds as to what to do with me—debating jurisdiction and custody or something in Greek. The suits spoke better English, and I wondered if they were my thieves. Something about them I didn't like, but I guess, as you say, we may never know."

"Did you hear from the Guru? He said you had refused to work for him."

"No job offer, no. Damn, I would have jumped at the opening for mad scientist's assistant. No one mentioned his name, not even me."

"Why am I surprised he lied to me? So are you still wearing my best friend's theory?"

I'd never tire of her laughter. And not everybody likes my humor.

"No. After waking up to the mess of the room and before the police arrived, I hid it in a cushion they'd already searched. Good thing too, because to get into the police station, I was quite thoroughly searched. I had to slap their hands twice, but when I clenched my fist and they saw the next slap would be a punch to the face, they stopped."

Picturing M's introduction to the Athens Police Department, I said, "Men are such pigs. So we still have Dylan's original work of art!"

"We do."

Those pages to me were now more precious than Shelley's lost final pages of *The Triumph of Life*. "*Cardenio!*" I exclaimed.

"*Cardenio!* And Dylan led us to it. Well, if the ToE is right, Shakespeare's lost play is recorded in the infinite omniscience of creation."

"Just like your chairman's black hole event horizon." I did a little shake. "I can't wait for more of your pillow talk, but all you really need to do is tell me about Zeno. But back to now. After being groped and eating doughnuts and coffee, then what?"

"I couldn't call you, since you didn't have your phone and I didn't know your office number and the police said both were unlisted. When the suits refused to let me call Natalie, saying her number too was unlisted, I asked to use the phone to call *whomever*. I was going to call my friend the Athens professor and get him to find a way to reach you. They said, 'Sure, just a minute,' and that was when they locked the door of the holding room with no windows. Worst of all, the coffee had gone cold. Eventually they just let me leave—the police quite apologetic and the suits all gone.

"Whose number is this? The hotel gave it to me, and I'm on their phone. I'm not sure how much longer I can stay on the line. The clerk here is so nice." I could see her smiling at him. "Are you back in your office?"

I'd tell her another day about the sleeping-beauty picture the Guru had taken of her. "I'm in my NYU office, though I shouldn't be. But this is my agent's phone number I left for you. Good bet they're listening to us now. Been listening the whole time. I wonder if the police detained you for the Guru or to protect you from the Guru."

"I don't know; it was all Greek to me. They seemed to know a lot about the band of cat burglars that hit my room and insisted they were a continued threat. Should I amend my police complaint?" she asked.

"No. Not yet anyway. Assuming the Guru stands down, we will too. That was the email I was writing while I had you on hold. I sent copies to the ELF, my agent, Natalie, and Juno. I believe we both—all—are safe with the theory out. But I'm unemployed."

"Wait, what? You already heard from the dean? That's not right. I'm so sorry, Sean. But wait." I heard her charming the hotel clerk to stay on the phone. "Such a nice man. Go ahead, Sean, you heard from the dean?"

"I did. The Guru wasn't bluffing about that, but it's okay. I've been busy running around like a chicken with its head cut off, thinking the earthquake's race to get you was just a dry run, a dress rehearsal for your death caused by me. I'll have to go see Natalie to apologize for the raid on her home and assure myself she's all right. I also need to take her the yogi's hemp bag full of the urn's shards. She texted me that she and Grace wanted the urn for Dylan's ashes."

"That's awkward. But I'm sure Dylan couldn't care less. Maybe she'll feel better if you tell her I'll keep Dylan's original pages safe for her. They're a treasure to me, so I can only imagine what they'll mean to her. We'll get them to her first thing when I get back. Do you think Juno and the Deeksha might have been raided too? Oh . . . I forgot they might be listening."

"That's okay. We never gave Juno a copy of the ToE. We should still be careful, but I think she's safe."

"That's good, though I'd bet on Juno in a fight with the Guru."

"Me too. She's a powerful force of nature illuminated by Big Love. And he's a black widow spider trolling around the dark web of illusion."

"You're writing your novel in real time for me, my honey-tongued man."

"Sort of . . . yes." She wouldn't be able to see the heat in my cheeks. I wanted so much to be with her. "What are you going to do now?"

"I have to go to the Apple Store and to the embassy for a passport. Not sure I'll make the embassy today. Sean, that's horrible for you to lose your tenured professorship. Is there anything to do?"

"Not much, but it's been the least of my worries till now. I'll figure it out, so don't worry about me. He also said he would release all my deep, dark, and perverted secrets to you, so be prepared. No dick pics, I assure you."

"Too bad. Unless they're photoshopped, of course."

I laughed. "That's a scary thought."

"Sorry, I shouldn't joke. Can you still check your computer there?"

"Yes, why?"

"Pull up the blog site."

"Okay."

"I want to see how many hits and likes the ToE has."

I was excited to see that too. "I did get to include my introduction."

"Oh, you had time for that, did you?"

"Yeah, while I was waiting endlessly for your call. The introduction was dedicated to you and your collaboration with Dylan on the theory."

"That's a bit of a stretch and impossible to posthumously authorize."

"I discussed it with Dylan first, and he and Natalie approved of it before it went out. We were moving fast. I was sleepwalking and running. It was hell, but now that I look back, I see that I was guided through it all. At every critical moment, guidance came, or I knew what to do." I laughed. "Or maybe I just got lucky."

"Discussed it with Dylan? I thought you only did that with Gypsy queens in your dreams. You can be so weird." She laughed too.

I pulled up the screen and checked the ToE's stats. "Nine thousand and seventy-two views and eighty-nine likes. Is that good?"

"How long has it been posted?"

"A little over an hour."

"Not good, phenomenal."

"It's a popular international blog. I'm not sure how they all read and digested it so fast."

"Just because it says *view* doesn't mean they read it. Even with the *likes* you can't be sure."

"Here's a comment I like," I said. "'The introduction reads like a love poem to constant creation and Professor Emily Edens.'"

"Aww . . . I can't wait to read it. What's the link? I think the hotel has a computer I can use. They're being so kind to the poor victim of a robbery at their hotel. I don't want to wait, and I'm not sure I'll make it to the Apple Store before it closes."

"The ELF gave me my own link on her blog so we can manage responses to the theory and my brilliant introduction. The site is thelosttheory.com."

"But it's to be found there?"

"Yes, that's how I've thought of it for the last month, as the working title of my novel. And I thought maybe the Guru would be slower to find it under that name."

"Wow! You always have your reasons. Got it. I'm going to the lobby to see for myself!"

"That mean you're hanging up now?"

"We both have stuff to do, and I'm sure they'd like to use their phone here. You sure you're okay losing your position at NYU?"

"Yes, I'm a full-time writer now. I'll explain the meeting and terms later. For now, you be careful and check in with the hotel—I'll leave messages there. I need to get to the Apple Store too."

"Sean, you be careful too."

"I love you, M."

"Love you too, *buddy*."

Buddy had lost all its sting.

I called Natalie on her landline. She said she was having more than one glass of wine to calm down but was fine. We agreed it was best to speak in person, so she invited me over for coffee in the morning.

M and I both got our new smart phones, and with the *ting ting* of quantum touch, we were reconnected.

I finally got home and into bed and wrote my four-o'clock goodnight email to M. Smiling, I floated in the ocean of Big Love for twelve hours straight.

CHAPTER 71

I AWOKE TO MY EMAIL from M. All was quiet in Athens; M was enjoying herself with her friend from the university. The storm had passed. I was eager to hear about Natalie's encounter with the Guru the day before. Perhaps she would know more about what he might do now that the ToE had been released.

As I hiked to Natalie's with the hemp bag over my arm and bagels and cream cheese in hand, I didn't think I was followed. Still, I was unable to shake the sensation of being watched. We'd been victims of high-tech assaults and would need time to recover.

Natalie looked good but complained of a hangover as she led me to my seat facing Dylan and Grace on the Nepal mountain peak.

"I'm so sorry for the raid yesterday," I said. "Tell me everything about the Guru's intrusion into your lovely home."

"Guru. A perfectly ironic name for him. He was sitting right where you are."

I immediately moved to the couch next to Natalie.

She studied my face. "What happened to your nose? Did that happen during your escape yesterday?"

I stroked my tender nose. "Ow! I had almost forgotten that—the Guru bent it out of shape. It only hurts when I think about it or touch it. So tell me what happened."

"He was all charm masking rage. Not at me but at you, I'm sorry to say. He said he assumed our work together posting the blog was your idea, and he thought me an innocent accomplice who had not been warned and should steer clear of you—you who would be ruined for your 'crimes and lack of patriotism.' Something to that effect."

"Could you tell if he was only focused on my career or if he intended more revenge on me? On us? Anything else I should know?"

"No, sorry. They took my phone and computers. I was mostly with the FBI in the kitchen. They tried to convince me that you and the Chinese would harm Emily if the theory was released and that the Chinese were a threat to Grace too. He didn't say anything else of note and never moved from that seat, mostly letting his lingering eyes do his talking. He had red hair and—" She shivered and widened her eyes, finally exhaling with a half whistle. "He couldn't also have red eyes, but that's how I remember them."

"He does have red eyes, or light reddish-brown translucent eyes, yes," I said. It was the first time I consciously associated a color with those lasers.

"And skin so white, almost albino-like," Natalie added. "I didn't make anything of it, other than it being strange, until I googled red eyes and found albino's eyes may appear red."

"Well, he is a vampire who drove me near insane and, perhaps, to breaking my own nose. M and I agreed, after he scuttled my career, that it's best to let our battle with the Guru settle now that we've succeeded in releasing the theory. Trying to get back at the Guru or further push his crimes against us into the light would keep us all in danger. I can't prove it, but I believe he was behind Dylan's death." I paused to make an apology with my eyes for the dagger to her heart. I didn't continue until she lifted her eyes back to mine and was ready. "Do you agree we should let matters rest for now?"

"I agree, and I'm not sure what we could do in any event. So Dylan's murderer was in my home, sitting right over there." She again rubbed her arms as though she had the shivers, smiling sadly at the picture of Dylan and Grace. She turned toward me. "I'm so sorry about your career. What will you do?"

"Natalie, I don't think he pulled the trigger, if that makes a difference. But I'm pretty damn sure he was responsible." Again the heavy words were landing hard on Natalie where I wanted to be a comfort. To lighten the load, I added, "Unable are the loved to die, for love is immortality."

"Emily Dickinson." She remembered and smiled. "But what will you do about being fired?"

"Well, technically I retired my professorship . . . Losing my academic post would have been devastating to me a month ago, a loss of my life and identity. And there's one part of me that still feels that way. But like Grace, I returned from Kathmandu and the Deeksha with a new perspective.

"Now I want to focus on my novel and write—a healthy midlife crisis as opportunity. I'll finally be the struggling artist I always envisioned I'd be."

"You know Dylan would want us to help."

It took me a moment to grasp her meaning.

"Please, no. I hope it won't come to that, where I need a wealthy patron of my art. How Victorian would that be?"

"You were a brother to Dylan, and he left us well off."

"I couldn't possibly, and I don't want to gloat, but I did quite well in the severance negotiations thanks to my agent's legal representation."

"By the way, I received back—*again*—that letter I wrote you around the time of Dylan's service."

"Oh, sorry. I think I lost it in the cab home that night. I meant to tell you. May I see it now?"

"Of course. I also made a copy of Dylan's poems for you. I found a binder full of his poems in his desk drawer here, dedicated to me. He must have stopped here the day he died. I don't think they were there before. Hold on."

When she stepped out of the living room, I smiled at Dylan. *Well, the ToE is loose upon the world, and soon our novel collaboration will be too.*

Natalie returned, saying, "Here's that letter. Knowing that you like letters, I'd also included a copy of Dylan's last letter to me with it. And here are his poems. They mean so much to me. May I read you my favorite?"

"Please." I settled back.

"It's called 'The Gift.'"

I listened and smiled as Dylan's widow read the familiar words M and I had sung on a Nepal mountaintop, spinning like children full of abandon. The same mountain peak from which Dylan and Grace now smiled down on us from their perch above the fireplace.

Natalie's voice softened as she read with a distant gaze, as if she and Dylan were alone, intimate as lovers. There was grief and its release as she recited words she knew by heart. I closed my eyes.

"As you read my lips, they will drink your tears, until tongues eclipse and their union weaves . . ."

She moved to the fireplace and the picture above it, joining her family there. Natalie's voice rising like an aria for the last stanza opened my heart to hear.

> Enlightened innocence witnesses this:
> God's abundance to give that never ends—
> These moments of small miraculous bliss—
> And wills for time and space to make amends—
> Renouncing all distance between true friends—
> Sharing in the speed of light, one slow kiss.

After a long Juno moment of silence, I opened my eyes and said, "That's wonderful, Natalie. A Petrarchan sonnet! And hearing you recite it . . ."

Natalie was overwhelmed after reading his poem. That was when the idea—a brainstorm—came to me.

"Natalie, I've always viewed the novel I'm writing as a collaboration with Dylan. I know it sounds strange, but I consult with him and believe he guides me at crucial moments, even now with this inspiration. It was his idea to write the book—his theory, his family and friends, his poetry . . . Please approve my putting his name on the cover as a coauthor."

She started to cry happily, agreeing wholeheartedly by nodding and hugging me. "Now, please read these so I can collect myself."

I looked at the two lost letters, together now found. In the one Dylan wrote to Natalie, the conclusion read:

I sit at my desk here in remote Badhrahni, surrounded by my treasures: my friend the yogi meditating in the other room, my books, a picture of Grace with me on a mountain peak, a Buddha statue (a mirror image of the one I sent you), and an urn of bees humming on a hive of white porcelain. Ask Grace to tell you about the urn. It holds a rare significance for me. I'll say good night, love, and will see you soon—Sunday in the country. I'll get the early train that arrives at 10 a.m.

Love, Dylan

What a dope I was. Hindsight is so clear-eyed. Would I have connected the dots of "it holds a rare significance," or would it just have reinforced the synchronicity after I heard the "honey from the bees?" My grimace slowly eased into an uncomfortable smile as I excused myself for all my bungling, asking Dylan, *All's well that ends well?*

But now I had to explain my shattering of the family urn and Dylan's would-be burial pot.

"You may have been wondering about the fashion statement of this lovely hemp bag." I lifted it from the floor. "I've not gone full hippie; it's from Yogi Mangku. This is what's left of the urn of bees. It's where we found the ToE hidden. Please forgive me. I hadn't seen your text before I smashed it open."

She gazed for some time at the shards that I spread out on the table. My casual approach had clearly miscalculated the raw emotion of her seeing the urn so shortly after reading Dylan's sonnet.

"Thank you, Sean. Grace told me her father wanted her to have the urn he had shown her in Nepal *someday*, and then we discussed placing his ashes there. We were going to drill a small hole in the top and use a funnel for his ashes before resealing it and placing it there on the mantel with their picture."

She knelt on the floor and carefully moved the shattered porcelain remains of the bees and hive about the table, like pieces of a jigsaw puzzle, starkly illuminating the devastating beauty of the broken vessel. She started to cry. I cried too. I joined her on the floor.

"Forgive me for destroying his resting place, but he and Yeats led us to the urn and the ToE hidden there. M has the original draft of the theory in safekeeping for you."

She smiled.

In an act of forgiveness, she put her hand gently to my head. "You have a bit of sunburn just here," she said, gently stroking my right temple.

I had all but forgotten my battle scar and was glad it had remained. "My face has taken a beating. That's a good story. I'll tell you next time, but I should go now. There's no putting the genie back in the bottle."

She smiled again while I regretted the unintended double entendre and inadvertent one step. She fully let me off the hook, saying, "It's good. Better the ToE was found. So much better than it being covered in Dylan's ashes for eternity. And tell M we'll share Dylan's original ToE, as I know it means so much to her too. That way I'll know we'll all keep in touch."

We hugged goodbye at the door, agreeing to keep in close contact until the dust settled and we were sure all was safe and the Guru was back in his cave. As I started to descend the town house steps, she said, "Last I checked, there are over eight hundred thousand views."

"Our post's timing was perfect. Any delay and . . . Well, enough said. Well done," I said. As our eyes met in parting, I saw the Big Love there. And I saw Dylan there too.

I walked home with a full and light heart. Again I didn't think I was followed.

As soon as I got home, I called my love. M said, "There are almost as many hits on the ToE post as people in Kathmandu *before* the earthquake."

I pictured all those nines from the welcome sign.

"Most of the comments are questions posed to the writer of that wonderful introduction."

"Yes, well, you know that writer? He's not so very clever. A funny thing about that letter I left in the cab the night we met Natalie . . ."

She laughed very hard at my expense. It was the best of all possible reactions to my bungling of clues. I'd have to reread *The Adventures of Sherlock Holmes*.

"Sean, I'm starting to see from the perspective of constant creation that we are guided by some invisible hand or universal mind or maybe the very heart of Big Love itself," said my quantum beauty and genius lover.

"That hand must have picked my pocket in the cab that night to show me that I am flawed but life is still perfect," my own heart sang back to her. "From now on I'll be fully open to all of Big Love's messages, whether they come in the form of letters, a book, or words from you."

CHAPTER **72**

IT WAS TIME TO WRITE. I was still floating in the wake of multiple sea changes, and while they'd been dramatic, the experience hadn't been devastating but liberating. Crisis as opportunity, held in perspective by what I'd discovered inside me. The old Sean was dead and born anew each instant of constant creation.

Three years of severance in a lump sum would be more cash by a large measure than I'd ever had. What auspicious days were yesterday and today. Dylan was right that each day is auspicious as we awaken to the dawn, reborn a new incarnation.

A sabbatical to write was just what I needed. I would teach again when the true teacher in me returned. Unexpected satisfaction washed over me, and I realized that what would have appeared to my peers—and to me just a month ago—as the worst tragedy that could have befallen this Hamlet was instead a blessing, a transition into my dream of a writer's life.

I superstitiously looked at my books—to comfort them and let them know I hadn't entirely forgotten them. It was then I realized I hadn't read a book for over four months, not since receiving Dylan's letter. That was the longest reading hiatus since I'd learned to read *Curious George*. I was living my fiction now.

My books looked back at me as if I were a cheating husband who didn't bother to hide his affair. I asked for their forgiveness and for inspiration to write. Their harsh answer indicted and did not forgive. *All is not well. You bungling idiot, you've betrayed the most precious and cherished of confidences, and you sit here celebrating, triumphant in your ego.*

The FBI and the Guru and who knows who now had my novel notes and chapter drafts. I'd been relieved knowing they were safely backed up on my NYU computer, but I hadn't thought much about the fact that the seized computers contained my unedited fiction.

I had unconsciously violated Juno's trust and privacy. She was all reserve and cultivated solitude, and I had exposed her. I hadn't even bothered to change her name. I would have preferred the novel pages had been lost or destroyed. It was my creation in gestation, and it felt as if the government was reading my draft love letter. And though it was fiction, some of it was embarrassing to me; so much worse than that, some of the words would put Juno in danger.

I'd written the episodes of the attempted poisoning at the Deeksha and Juno's interview with the general regarding Dick's death much as they had occurred, except she drank the poison in my version. I'd written flights of fancy of Juno as a beautiful young spy and musician traveling around China as a Mata Hari for her uncle. I prayed my government wouldn't be as literal in their reading as the general had been.

Desperate for forgiveness and a way out of this new pit of disaster, I immediately wrote Juno an email confessing all. There was a fine line between being the celebrated hero and the guileless goat.

I thought I'd have to suffer a long time, as I never saw Juno carrying or checking her phone and she was still in the solitude of her sanctuary, but her reply came instantly.

Dear Sean,

No worries. But do be wary of stories of the past and imaginations of the future—they become our reality, while our ever-present heart can only cocreate more love.

As you know, I wrote my uncle afterward about the events that evening over tea, informing him of the general and An's wicked attacks, so all was disclosed through the proper channels. And who knows? Maybe I was a beautiful spy in another life (winking-face emoji). Be joyful and focus on Big Love with full certitude of belief. The family eagerly awaits your novel. We will read your mind soon. Truth is beauty.

Peace, love, and light, Juno

Her words of forgiveness and release lifted a lifetime of guilt experienced in fifteen minutes of hell. The lessons of Big Love that graced me on the mountain would take practice to live, but I was determined to always move toward that light and its full realization—day by day and moment by moment.

With Juno's blessing, I was back in heaven and ready to create a novel out of the adventure. That was the life of constant creation. Nothing good or bad endured, as all of life cycled quickly through our radiant loving awareness. And that might have been why Dylan said we were living many incarnations within one life now. I was no longer the professor or the Sean I was a month ago.

I sat down to start work on the novel. The first draft had stalled, leaving James on his way to a firing squad for the alleged blue-vial intended rape and red-vial attempted murder of Juno.

"Truth is beauty."

I started a new draft, with my hero returning to NYC to confront the Guru much the way it happened. Those pages of terror rang true. And that was when it struck me to write the adventure as it had occurred, sprinkling in pages of fiction to illuminate the events. That approach would require the sacrifice of a lot of pages of pulp fiction and my toothless Chinese cellmate with his charming vocabulary that I'd grown so fond of. I had the time and money to follow art and life wherever it led me. I would still use my fictional accounts where they impacted or shed light on what really happened.

I found myself in a heightened state that came from discovering my life's purpose—to create Dylan's and my novel out of the true-life adventure. Readers like Juno would love it, and the Guru would hate it. Good and bad weren't just the way people seemed to me but objective reality based on their actions and words. Juno's level of awakening allowed me to see only the Christ faces and Buddha hearts of my family and, in stark contrast, the darkness of those that looked to deny and snuff out that light.

The book I would write from memory and my notes would be my imagination looking into the rearview mirror. The past is never real.

Not really. The dreamlike events of the past two months were already hard to believe and had radically changed my concept of self. I had a much looser and more playful grip on my separate identity and my subjective reality. Ambivalence had been replaced by belief in Big Love. I now knew imagination and reality weren't opposites; the first preceded the latter, and both arose from, and fell into, the source of constant creation.

The ToE's source, Big Love, was the primordial sea we all swam in but rarely realized. From that collective consciousness, all life and art emerged. It was the author of life, and we were its characters, some playing their parts in wonderful alignment with the source, acting as directed, and some wandering far offstage, disconnected, into dark alleyways. The powerful plotting with their Calibans to attack Prosperos.

We all were constantly writing an epic first-person novel in our heads with the relentless drumbeat of I, I, I. Who were we telling that story to? I and I. Juno's promise that the family would soon read my mind magnified in me the haunting last fear an author must overcome: to believe that their mind will tap into something more than *I*—perhaps Queen Mab's universal mind. To listen within their deep heart's core. To hear the omniscient voice of true creation that moved Shakespeare's quill across the blank page in perfect iambic pentameter.

As the days passed and the blank pages filled, there was no indication that the Guru intended to inflict more revenge on us, and no scandalous stories had been released from my digital history. M agreed that naming the devil and his deeds in my fiction not only would be the right thing to do but must be done for truth's sake and to hold him to account. We debated, neither sure, whether the novel's publication would put us more or less at risk of further reprisal. Regardless, we weren't going "to limp away like a frog in frost."

My mind and body's longing to be with M was an expression of spirit that I projected onto the page as I wrote of our adventure and the discovery of Big Love and hidden truth.

If new beginnings *were* disguised as painful endings, as Dylan had quoted from Lao Tzu in his last letter, I wondered what glorious endings foretold.

I was eager to discover the answer with M as my partner and guide.

CHAPTER 73

SUMMER WAS ENDING, and my flight to Athens was leaving at seven that evening. In Big Love there was no time or space between M and me, but the mind and body didn't know that, and they were in a very excited state to be with M again. Zeno's bow was strung taut and the arrow set for flight.

After reading my morning email from M, I went to the jewelry store and bought a ring. Earlier the same day, M had awakened to find her email from me and went to the pharmacy and bought a kit.

As I admired the many-faceted ring on the way to the airport, I remembered Iya's bracelet and the ringing dervish bracelets that connected us each instant without regard to the laws of physics. I knew M and knew we'd be donating that expensive diamond ring to charity. Our shared free bracelets were a stronger—a perfect—symbol of our bond, one without bounds or limits. Ours was not the culmination of romantic love but of Big Love, where the vow is *to be* and not *I do*—to follow the calling of the true heart in love with love. I knew now that death would not do us part.

The big banging of Big Love was transforming me in quantum leaps. I was no longer just little me but also the source of constant creation. The ever present, once found, is never lost.

The challenge I made to my Huxley students and Hope eighteen years ago now came back to me. If there is truth and that truth is God and God is in us as the loving awareness of constant creation, how can my life not have that realization as its focus?

As I settled into my economy-plus seat on the runway to Athens, I was moved to write one last letter to my best friend.

Dear Dylan,

Auspicious is the day!

Our novel will be finished very soon. I know this honest account of the events may reopen our battle with the Guru. So be it.

My hope is that the light will keep the dark at bay. I have no fear. Big Love is the absence of fear. M and Juno have approved and assumed the risk with me.

Since your disappearance into silence and space following your 7 p.m. wake-up call at the Beekman, you've been constantly with me, opening a portal to love and creation. Thank you for M, the family at the Deeksha, the mystery, the adventure, Big Love, and the theory of everything . . .

THE END

EPILOGUE

ON MY FIRST DAY IN ATHENS, M and I developed a private practice that we continue to this day. Each night we meditate in our bed, in what M calls shavasana and I call the dead man's pose, until one of us starts to chant our favorite mantra, which we then chant together. And then my favorite part, we make love, joining in infinite consciousness with our malas on.

In the morning, our practice is reversed, as upon first light we make love and then move to meditate and chant. I reveal this singular and silly-sounding mating ritual knowing that it sounds over-the-top and New Age–ish, but so it is. I'm one with the incredibly brilliant and entirely beautiful M in those moments, and I don't mean to gloat, but I feel singularly blessed.

I only note this intimate practice because the first morning's meditation led to an incongruously dark vision. As I floated in bed after our dead-heat finish—in a blissful meditative state with M's awareness enveloping mine, our index fingertips touching—the future started unfurling in hazy images across my mind's eye in a near-death review of my life, but a review projecting forward.

The following is a frame-by-frame account of those dark images and my interpretation of their import. Each frame was separated by a wild spinning of my mind, like film reel spooling.

It started out benignly enough with an image of Dylan sitting with our novel at my desk, the book and the theory rising together, increasing in popularity and acceptance.

Spinning . . .

Into Detective Mulhearn's office with the novel sitting on his desk, him on one side and me on the other. He was angry that the novel had spun off conspiracy theories regarding Dylan's death that had forced him to reopen the case, and he was dangerously unhappy with his depiction. He was also eager to pin the murder on me.

Spinning . . .

Into an image even more disturbing, of Juno sitting in a government room in Beijing with the novel on a conference table beside a copy of Mao's little red book—maybe the one Juno's uncle had given her. She was being grilled by five angry-looking military men.

Spinning . . .

Into a darker film of the Guru rising like the creature from the black lagoon to loom over a cavernous high-tech facility dedicated to brain-computer interface. There he was sitting in an electric chair–like throne. Standing next to him was a striking Slavic woman and a man whose back was to me. From that seat, behind glass, he was directing lines of techno-slaves hunched over computers like rowers of a Viking ship. The image zoomed in ominously on the Guru's red eyes.

Spinning . . .

Spinning like dervishes as the vision leaped forward in time. I was at a desk in an office overlooking a flourishing vineyard and, farther in the distance, an ocean, writing a sequel to *The Lost Theory*, when an image of the Guru's face again rose alarmingly to blot out the incredible view. The horror villain who never dies. His old cruel face slowly faded to pitch black, then equally slowly became a movie poster with a clown-white face and two coal-red eyes on a dead-black background. The caption *The Devil's Calling* spewed from his enlarged clown lips in a blood-dripping font.

Spinning . . .

Into a dark forest illuminated only by a fire—hungrily chasing M and me—and by the lights from our third eyes that enabled us to see the dark winding path as we attempted to escape.

Spinning . . .

Spinning, spinning, the wildest spinning yet, spinning that I thought would never stop. Yet when it did stop, it ended on the darkest of images—an open casket. But I couldn't bring myself to look inside or even look around to identify the survivors. Afterward I regretted succumbing to that dreadful fear.

The vision faded to black and then lightened as M's chanting brought me back from the bardo to life and to her.

After our mantra was sung, I told her everything I'd seen and how it seemed a warning that even in the midst of constant creation, people still did evil. They would look to corrupt each apple of knowledge, and we might be forced into some dark chapters that we'd narrowly averted in pursuit of Dylan's theory of everything.

M smiled in her fearless, Big Love, we-will-see sort of way.

But I was thinking about Dickens.

And wondering if the visions were shadows of things that only might be or shadows of what must be.

ABOUT THE AUTHOR

MICHAEL KELLEY is a former lawyer who, prior to pursuing his passion for writing, built an international business on Wall Street before founding his own investment management firm. His love of literature and creative writing began during his years at the University of Pennsylvania.

Michael currently lives in New York with his wife and daughter. After years leading a busy life in the city, he now spends the majority of his time in the peaceful woods of Dutchess County where he enjoys meditation, yoga, wine, reading, and hiking, all of which inspire his writing.

His debut novel is *The Lost Theory*.